# REMIND ME

## A MYSTIC BEACH FANTASY ROCKSTAR ROMANCE

### AISLINN ARCHER

MYSTIC BEACH PRESS

# CONTENTS

# CONTENT WARNING

A content review for these books, and others in the series, is available on the author's website at AislinnArcher.com. Some of the contents of these stories may be disturbing to some readers. If you have any concerns about whether you might find the content of this work disturbing, please take a few moments to check the content review on the website and do not read if you think you might find any of the content disturbing. *But with this story, in particular, keep in mind that appearances can be deceiving and assumptions can change a life. Reading this story with an open mind and reserving judgment is encouraged.* The recommended reading age for this work is 18 or older.

For Dad.
I might not have handed you this to read,
but it wouldn't exist without you.
We miss you.

# PROLOGUE

## Declan

There's too many people here.

Normally, I like people. I mean, *people* like *me*. OK — people like to be *around* me, have their pictures taken with me, touch me, get me to autograph... things — parts and things. OK — they don't so much like *me* as they like what I mean to them, for a minute, or an hour.

But *these* people... I know most of them already. They're focused on each other. They don't want anything from me. After the better part of two years on the road, I don't know what to do with that anymore. There's Alex, our keyboard player. Kieran, our lead guitarist. Rhys, our drummer, who's been acting even weirder than usual lately. Dave, my brother and our bassist. Then there's Billy, our manager. Luke, Rhys' drum tech, who spends hours setting up that monstrosity of a kit whenever we have a regular gig — which this decidedly is not. Grant, the guitar tech who Kieran barely lets touch his Fenders once they leave the cases but who happily cares for Hunter's PRS Dragon, even if he's also not allowed to touch Hunt's green PRS most of the time. And Nick, the keyboard tech who Alex actually never lets touch his "ladies" — his keyboards, not actual girls — except for load-in and load-out or when they need a full breakdown and refit. So, most of our techs...

Looking out at the crowd made up mostly of Brighid's friends, I can just barely see Piper, the cute little sound engineer who

Dave thinks we don't all know he's got a thing for. Can't say that I blame him. She's too petite for my tastes, but Dave's a couple inches shorter than me, so they fit. Or they did. Something's happened that's put them at odds the last week or two. Not that Dave would confide in me. I was kind of a dick to her early on. It wasn't personal. With that long brown hair, she just reminded me of... Well, everything here in Mystic Beach has been reminding me of...

"Surprise!"

Lost in thought, I miss the moment when Brighid arrives, pulled along behind that big hairy beast of hers.

No, not Hunter, though our rhythm guitarist has gotten pretty damn big and hairy since we first met here in Mystic Beach when we were both 15. His dark blonde hair is almost as long as hers now, and he's sporting a short beard I never would have expected back then that he'd even be able to grow. We're a study in contrasts now, me and Hunt — I never let my hair get past my chin, and I don't go even a day without shaving, even when we're on vacation, just in case the paparazzi spot me on the street. But, no — the hairy beast leading Brighid in is her hound, Crógan, who's been hanging out with us in the studio lately, until Hunt was ready to give him to Brighid, which he did last night. Tonight...

Hunt steps up on the stage, holding his hand out to a confused Brighid, who only gets more confused as the private party he apparently told her we were playing here tonight at the Pirate's Cove turns into a surprise engagement party — that is, if that very smart woman of his will have the giant idiot as a husband after all he's put her through in the last fifteen years.

I'm just glad Hunter finally got his drama sorted out with Brighid. Now he can put a ring on it, and stop punching houses and falling drunk off fences. Because that sprained/broken/freakishly healed hand put a serious cramp in things for all the rest of us this last month or so. We're behind on the album we came here to record, though it seems like maybe our rhythm guitarist's dry spell for songwriting is finally coming to an end. Maybe all the craziness in that best-friend-to-girlfriend transition was worth it.

"And that truth is that we belong together," he tells her, looking deep in her eyes. "We have always belonged together. Best friends, childhood friends become a two-person family..."

I blot it all out of my mind, looking instead at the water lapping at the boat hulls off the dock. Too close to home, all of this sappy stuff. But then someone says something about lovers, and I jump on board with the rest of the guys, hooting at the pair of them. It's about damn time Hunt took the girl to bed.

"They say you should marry your best friend..."

My mouth goes dry. My heart races. My mind goes blank.

Everyone else laughs, and I have no idea why. I lean back on the bar stool behind me, grateful to find myself in the shadows for once.

"My beautiful, wonderful best friend... my soulmate... Will you marry me? Again?"

Sometimes you get a second chance. Sometimes... you're me, and you throw away the one chance at happiness that you ever had.

I'm fine with letting the guys and Brighid's friends offer their congratulations to the happy couple. I don't think anyone expects me to be all giddy and back-slapping. It's times like this when my carefully cultivated reputation as a dick comes in handy. No one notices I'm in an even shittier mood now than I had been, so no one asks any questions about why.

At least now, with the smarmy stuff over, we can do what we came to Delaware to do: get our songs down and test them out with audiences here at this little bayfront bar before we release our fourth album and, hopefully, land ourselves in the charts once again. Our stars have been on the rise since we were teenagers, and they show no signs of stopping now. But we've been in Telltale Signs' shadow for too long, and as much as I respect Mace, their lead singer, I'm ready to break out and surpass him, to become a legend among rock vocalists.

I'd rather be performing tonight in front of a sold-out crowd, even in this tiny venue in the beach town where my family used to come to vacation every summer. But the small group of our friends and family members here to celebrate Hunter and Brighid's engagement will have to do for an audience.

Finally, it's time to perform — something I've been looking forward to since Hunt first told us what he was planning. We've been able to perform exactly three of our own songs since we got here, and still we nearly outed ourselves during that one incognito performance, by sounding too much like ourselves, like aMUSEd. Tonight — no worries. Everyone here knows who we are, though a lot of them haven't had the chance to see us perform before, and none of them have ever seen us in a venue this small. Except Brighid, of course, who was there from the first. For the rest of them, this will be a rare treat.

Hunt starts off with the opening chords of "Fire in the Head," and I immerse myself in the headspace of his lyrics, a story of the creative spark and the muse who captivates you. I knew from the first moment he played this song for us that it was Brighid who had given it to him, who was his muse. It's taken him almost too long to see it himself, but I'd been there. I'd had a muse of my own. All too briefly, but I'd had her.

And it's with that feeling pushing the sounds from my throat that I start the vocals with my customary growl, which transforms itself into a wail as I think about that lost muse of mine, putting the emotion into the song, like I always do. No — even more so tonight, here, in this town where we met, where we fell in love, where we...

With only one of my in-ear monitors in, I can hear Piper adjusting the house mix in the first few moments of the song. But there's a clatter by the bar behind her. Wood on wood. A bar stool knocked over onto the wooden deck. We've done enough bar gigs over the years that something like that would never knock me off my game, but it's a small crowd and we don't have the mains up very loud, because we wanted to avoid drawing attention to this private party featuring a band with three platinum albums.

The clattering noise reverberates, and the audience turns as one to see what caused it. My bandmates keep going, as we've trained ourselves to do, but my eyes follow the sound and see something that's impossible. Simply impossible. I must be hallucinating on the fumes of all this lovey-dovey crap that Hunter set up for Brighid. This has to be a ghost from my past coming back to haunt me, because there's no way she's real.

But as the woman looks up to see all eyes trained on her, my heart stutters, because it's *her*. I know it's her. There's no doubt in my soul that it's her, even if my brain can't quite comprehend it. A bit above average height, with curves in all the right places and long mink-brown hair that just begs you to run your fingers through it. Her expression is harder than I remember, the softness and gentleness that my memory shows me now worn away. Her eyes, too, are hard, like steel instead of mist, but that could be just from her expression, which conveys terror with a dash of contempt. It's not a look I ever wanted to see on her face, and I know that its being there is my fault. And I need to fix that. After all these years, I need to fix that.

She takes off running.

"Callie!" I bellow into the mic, the younger me calling out with the pain of losing her once. I can't let her get away again. I drop the mic to the ground and start running after her, and I can see Piper cringe. *Sorry, sweetheart.*

I tear off between the tables full of friends, all of whom are blatantly clueless as to what's going on, but I've only got eyes for Callie, with all that luscious brown hair swept up into a high ponytail that bobs as she races for her car. She's got a head start and I've got a bunch of stunned bystanders to get through, and by the time I round the corner, she's already pulling out of the parking lot.

"Callie!" I scream after her, panting from the effort to reach her before she's gone from my life once again. My biggest regret, my greatest mistake, the best thing I ever had, all rolled into one.

I had once told myself that when I was rich I'd buy a time machine and go back to that moment when things went so horribly wrong and do them the right way. I'm richer now than I ever dreamed, but there's no time machine to fix a mess I created more than a decade ago. I'm going to have to work for this one. Because Callie is mine, and there's no way I'm letting her go again.

# CHAPTER 1

## I WILL FIND YOU

I ignore the open stares as I return back the way I came, though at a considerably slower pace, all my adrenaline from the surprise of seeing her... from the unsuccessful chase... drifting away like flotsam on the tide. With a careful, deliberate motion, I pick up her abandoned bar stool and set it to rights before sitting down atop the stool next to it, my eyes glued to the empty space above, as if I could will her to still be sitting there.

The bartender is giving me the hairy eyeball, but he's not alone in that. Most everyone is either openly staring or glancing surreptitiously back at me while trying (and largely failing) to keep their focus on the newly engaged Brighid and Hunter.

"Jameson. Neat. And make it a double."

Dave pulls out the barstool on my other side and sits, saying nothing, and simultaneously demanding answers, in his usual quietly intense way.

"How is she even still here?" I ask, of myself as much as my brother.

I slam back the whiskey the bartender has already placed on the bar in front of me and nod to him for another.

"I've got to find her."

The look Dave gives me is knowing. He knows as much about my history with Callie as anyone, except the people who were there that one day, when it all came together, like magic or something... and then that second day, a week later, when it all fell apart.

Dammit. I have to find her. There's no other option. Living in New York and spending so much time on the road, I haven't had a car in nearly that entire decade since I last saw her. But that doesn't stop my fingers from itching for keys that might get me chasing her down the highway, rather than sitting here, drowning my sorrows. I wonder if Brighid...

I look over at her now, by the stage, where she and Hunt are surrounded by her friends. She must feel my eyes on her, because she looks back, frowning at me.

Yeah... probably not a good time to ask to borrow her car. I wonder what Hunt said to her while I was off chasing Callie, who's clearly one of her friends here, since she was invited to their engagement party. Even if Hunt didn't put two and two together, seeing Callie run away from the mere sight of me... Yeah — Brighid's got my number. Probably more than anyone other than Dave. My eyes slide over to Piper, who's leaning up against the side of the restaurant, stealing glances at him. He's got no idea how lucky he is, even if they're on the outs right now. The girl's clearly got it for him, bad. My eyes connect with her, and I can feel the sympathy pouring off of her. I look away. Bad enough Davey's trying to be supportive. I don't think I can take another ounce of pity.

There's a touch at my knee. And for once it's not a girl looking to swoop in and snatch me up for an hour or a night. Brighid's dog lays his huge head in my hand, looking up at me with those deep brown eyes full of sympathy of his own. I can't take another bit of it, but neither can I resist the hound, giving him a scratch behind the ears before I start rubbing the space between them. I find it as soothing as he does, I think.

My brain finally shifts fully out of reaction mode, and I start to do the thing I do best: make plans to make reality match my vision of what I want.

I'm going to find her, no matter what it takes. I'm going to talk to her, tell her how I feel, explain what happened all those years ago, including the bits I didn't tell her, hoping to protect her from heartbreak worse than what I gave her that last day. I just need a car.

"Don't do anything stupid, OK?"

I glare at Dave.

"When have I ever..."

"Just about every night since things went haywire with Callie."

What the hell? Dave's got no right to judge me. He locks himself up in our tour bus every night, with his books and five seasons of his favorite TV show on repeat. He's never had a girlfriend, let alone... He's got no idea. And it's not like I've been a crazy player all these years, taking groupies back to my room on the bus every night...

OK. Yeah. It might seem that way to Dave, or to any of the other guys, but...

Nevermind. He's got a point, regardless of what he does or doesn't get about me.

He turns to look back at Piper, who's only got eyes for him now. He gets up and heads over to her, the air between them heavy with tension.

Yeah, maybe my big brother might finally understand what it's like to find the girl of your dreams and then lose her. I doubt it's his own stupidity that's created this rift between them, though. Me — I've got no one to blame but myself. Can't even blame the blonde. If I'd been a better man, even at 17, I'd have avoided all of this. Maybe I'd have managed to hold on to Callie. And even if I hadn't, maybe she'd at least be able to look at me without running away.

The Callie I knew wouldn't have run from anything. She was brave, bold, determined, ambitious, passionate. And I loved everything about her.

Truth be told, I still do. And maybe... just maybe... if I can find her and tell her that, I can fix at least some of what I broke all those years ago. Maybe I can make it up to her enough that she won't run away from me again. Maybe I can even get her running back to me...

But before I can do any of that, I've got to find her.

"Come on, Gryff! You can do this for me. I know you can. You've got your computer programs and your investigators, your inside people at the DMV or whatever. I just need an address. That's it!"

"No can do, Declan," our head of security says blandly, though I wonder if I'm not hearing a note of suppressed enjoyment in his tone. It's hard to tell over the phone. "If it's not a legit security concern, I'd be breaking the law — and the trust placed in me by the label — if I used our resources to find an old flame of yours. I mean, if I had to do that with every girl you've slept with over the last ten years, I'd need a two-man team on the case 24/7 for the next year."

Now I hear a definite note of amusement to his voice. Smug bastard. I mean, I haven't always made things easy for him, sometimes — OK, often — running off with a girl or two to a hotel room without telling him where I was headed, dodging his efforts to track me so I could go off the radar and indulge my... hobby. But he's close with Dave. Maybe he'll cut me a break once he realizes this is serious.

"I'm not asking you for every girl's address. Just the one, Gryff. I mean it — I need this."

"Have you tried Google?" he suggests, now openly chuckling at my expense. He hangs up before I can reply.

Fucking shit!

Fine.

I pull up my phone and start a search. Calliope Martino. Mystic Beach... Chef? Is she a chef by now? Maybe she ended up doing something else with her life. But, no — there's no way she'd have gone into anything except some kind of culinary job. That much I know. Search.

And... nada.

I stop myself from chucking my phone into the bay. I long ago stopped doing internet searches on myself and aMUSEd. We have a PR team that does that kind of stuff now. My Google-fu is so rusty it's more like Google-fucked. I contemplate using one of those online person-search services, but the moment I envision putting my information in to pay for the search I realize that's a non-starter. All I need is some geek on the back end recognizing my name and then blackmailing me with a threat to reveal the search subject to the media. We've already been there once this summer, with Hunt and his ex, Holly, who tried to blackmail him with Brighid and nearly torpedoed their brand-new relationship in the process. I've got no interest in doing a repeat, starring me and Callie this time.

No, I've got to do this carefully, work up a plan, be methodical in how I approach her once I find her. If I can find her. No, *once* I find her. So, Step One of Project Angel: Find Callie.

# CHAPTER 2

## STARLIGHT

## Callie

"Cal... You're back! I wasn't expecting you back tonight at all."

Drew looks up from the pan full of day-boat scallops he's searing, surprise clear on his face.

"Yeah. My plans changed."

Plans? Everything's changed. Nothing will ever be the same. Not now. Not after...

"Callie?"

"Hmm?"

"I asked if you wanted to take over. I mean — I've got everything in hand... But you don't usually..."

"Let you take charge if I'm within a five-mile radius?"

He nods, giving me a grin. He's right and he knows it. I don't give up control easily. Of anything. Ever. Especially not my kitchen. Tonight was a rare exception. I'd handed over the kitchen to make my appearance at Brighid's surprise engagement party — only the real surprise of the night wasn't the proposal, the engagement or the fact that I'd left someone else in charge. It was the appearance of my first love. My last love. The man who broke my heart and stomped it into ashes.

"Yeah. I'm back. Give me a second to wash up and I'll be right with you."

I grab a clean chef's coat, apron and bandana from my office before heading into the restroom to clean up. I pause to look at myself in the mirror, seeing the haunted expression still occupying my eyes.

"Pull it together, Callie. The past is past, and regardless of where he is, Declan Carter is in the past."

I garb up, scrub my hands and take my place at the center of my universe.

"OK, folks — let's finish this dinner service with style!"

"Yes, Chef!"

# *Fourteen years ago*

"Too hot, *cara mia.* Too much heat and you'll burn them before they caramelize." Nonna turns down the heat under the pan, taking the wooden spoon from me to give the sliced onions a stir. "Slow, steady — you have to give them time to yield their sweetness willingly. It's like love... It often takes a gentle hand to bring the best out of something — patience, persistence, letting them come into their best form in their own sweet time. Here," she says, handing me back the wooden spoon. "Keep stirring. Build the flavor over time. Sometimes, the most important ingredient is time."

I glance at the back door, tapping my feet with impatience.

"It is that boy, no? The singer?"

She looks at me with disapproval, but her warm smile breaks through.

"Go! Off with you!" She shoos me away from the stove, shaking her head. "Filling my food with impatience and thoughts of summer love! If you can't keep your focus on the food, it will all go wrong, and then I won't be able to serve it! I'll end up with diners wandering out onto the beach, looking for some pretty face to take home with them..."

She shakes her head as I hang my apron on a peg by the door and turn to give her a grateful wave.

"Come back and help with the dinner rush, *angelica*! It's summer, after all!"

I race down the employee access hallway and out the back door of the hotel, hitting the boardwalk at a full run.

He's been out here nearly every day this summer, just after lunch. I'd come out to get a break from the heat of the kitchen one day, and the sound of distant music had pulled me toward the boardwalk plaza, where I'd found a trio of buskers — two guitarists and a singer — with a crowd gathered around them. They were playing classic rock songs — a guy with brown hair with an acoustic guitar, a blonde with an electric and the most beautiful boy I'd ever seen, singing his heart out.

Nevermind that the acoustic player was clearly his brother, based on the close resemblance, nor that the other two produced beautiful harmonies of their own. No, this one, this singer... he glowed with an inner light, like no one I'd ever seen before, like his soul was shining out, illuminating the world through the lenses of his deep blue eyes, which fall on me in this moment and nearly drop me to my knees.

The sharpness of tomato, the warm earthiness of basil, the savory sweetness of the onion. My mind fills with the flavors of Nonna's gravy, even though I'd left the kitchen far out of reach of even my keen sense of smell. It tastes like... love.

He smiles at me, and the light in his eyes ramps up another notch, filling the air with warmth that puts even the summer sun to shame. That warmth flavors the music of the sweet ballad coming from his soft, sensual mouth, and I watch it work through the crowd like cream into the bright red as Nonna's legendary sauce comes to life. And just like Nonna's sauce, it fills each and every one of them with feelings of love. Couples turn to each other, gazing warmly, parents' eyes rove over children with a sense of being cherished, even the frozen custard and boardwalk fries get longing glances enhanced with the beauty of his song.

As the last notes fade away a minute later, it's as if the crowd is waking from a spell — not sleepy and drugged, but with the bright, crisp outlook of a new morning. They chatter eagerly and drop coins and bills into an open guitar case before moving off on their way down the boardwalk.

He stops to say something to his brother and their bandmate, giving them a nod before making a beeline for me.

"Callie..." he breathes, visibly savoring the syllables in his mouth, like they were sweet, smoky chocolate.

"Declan..." I reply, running my fingers through his hair — the exact color of that chocolate.

He leans in toward me, and now it's our mouths tasting each other...

"Chef? Callie? Callie? Callie!"

I shake my head free of thoughts I wish had been left in the past.

"Crap!"

Instinctively, I grab for the pan of now-burned cream sauce, but get my hand too close to the flame.

"Fuck!"

"I've got it, Callie," Drew says, taking the pan off the heat. "Go take care of that."

I don't miss the worried glance he gives me as I head straight into the walk-in, leaning my forehead against the cool wall next to the racks of refrigerated produce and placing my singed hand next to it.

"Fuck."

Drew finds me in my office, my head down on the desk in front of me.

"You want me to lock up?"

Is it that late? Damn. How long have I been sitting here, wallowing in the past?

"No. I've got it, Drew. Go ahead home, enjoy some time with that handsome hubby of yours before the baby gets here..."

"Thanks. It's getting close!"

"Make sure you take your full paternity leave, OK? No showing up on Saturday night to help out. Got it?"

"No arguments from me, boss. We've been taking the baby-care classes they offer all the expectant parents, and I know we've got some challenging weeks ahead of us."

"And thanks for stepping in tonight. The first time, and the second..."

I roll my eyes, pressing my forehead into the desk again.

"Not a problem. It's nice to run the kitchen for a change. But... if you don't mind my asking... You OK there, boss?"

I sit up and sigh.

"Yeah. Just a long night."

"Well, get some rest. We've got that brainstorming session tomorrow morning for the Taste the Culinary Coastline event."

I groan. This is why my past emerging from a decade of shadow right at this particular moment is the worst timing ever. We need to win the fan-favorite vote at Taste, in just over a month. The big cash prize will make all the difference between continuing to squeeze diners into this small space and taking over the lease from the bakery next door to nearly double our dining capacity. Suzie's mother-in-law has a larger space coming open in her building across the street and is cutting Suzie a deal to keep it all in the family. And Suzie knew I was looking to expand, since our dining room and the tables in the alley are full every night. She gave me the inside track on taking over the lease. But if I don't have the money in the bank to guarantee a full year's lease, the landlord will move on to the next prospect. A spot this close to the beach isn't cheap, but it's also in high demand. He won't have a problem finding another tenant. And with the unit already equipped for a food-based business, it would be my lousy luck to end up with another fine-dining restaurant moving in next door. I can't afford to let any of that happen.

"Thanks for the reminder, Drew. I've got some ideas I need to try out before the morning so we can get this dish narrowed down."

"You need some sleep, Callie," he chides. "First-in, last-out is a recipe for burnout. Or at least burned cream sauce."

"Ouch."

"You teed that one right up," he says, smirking. "How's the hand?" he adds, concern seeping into his voice.

"It's fine. Got singed worse pulling toast from the toaster this morning."

"A likely story."

"Better than an unlikely one."

I grin wryly back at him.

"Go — out! Go get laid before you've got a crying newborn interrupting every intimate moment."

"I'd give you the same advice — minus the baby — but we both know you won't take it."

"Out!"

I lever myself out from behind the desk, double-checking that the front doors in the dining room are locked and then locking the kitchen door out onto the alley courtyard.

I open the deep drawer in my desk and pull out a thick, heavy notebook marked with the stains and spatters of many years in a working kitchen. It's a cookbook. No — more accurately, a *chef's book.* In a home kitchen, it would be my grandmother's cookbook. Here, it's Nonna's chef's book — full of her secret recipes for her sauces, pasta, bread, desserts, uniquely Eastern Shore seafood dishes with her own special twists from the country of her birth. These are the recipes she cooked in the restaurant of a hotel that is no longer there — replaced years ago by condominiums. Hence why, when I came back to Mystic Beach, determined to start my own restaurant, I took this space down the street, rather than taking over a family legacy on the boardwalk, since that legacy no longer exists. I don't cook from Nonna's book here at Castalia. I take what she taught me and use it as inspiration.

That's what Castalia is all about — inspiration.

# *Twenty years ago*

"Come here, my sweet *angelica*," Nonna says, patting the space next to her on the bench in her garden.

"I'm not an angel, Nonna. Mama says I've got a devil on my shoulder, whispering in my ear. She says I don't listen, don't do what I'm told, and that I'll come to no good if I don't start following the rules."

"What? No! I don't think that's what she meant at all, *cara mia*. Everyone has an angel whispering in one ear and a devil in the other. But you need both to keep life in balance. Without the dark, there is no way to appreciate the light, no beautiful shadows and no dark sky for the stars to illuminate. It is like sweet and spicy — you need to balance both in your recipe for life, or you drown in sugar syrup, never knowing the joy of the bite of pepper on your tongue or the appreciating the acidity of the vinegar once the wine has fermented. Does that make sense?"

I nod fervently at her. I love Nonna's recipes — especially her special sauce — and I know she carefully tastes every batch to ensure it's got just the right amount of salt, spice and sweet.

"Now, *angelica*," she says. "Tonight, I want to tell you about the sacred fountain of the Muses. Do you know what a muse is?"

"Being funny?"

She gives a little laugh.

"Not quite, but it's closely related. A muse is like a special spirit, or a goddess, who brings inspiration to humans — artists and poets and musicians—"

"And chefs!"

Nonna blinks, her eyes opening wide in surprise before she gets a thoughtful look on her face.

"Well, I supposed chefs qualify, too. You're so clever," she says, giving me a squeeze and a kiss on the top of my head.

"But the story goes that each of the arts has its own muse —Calliope, Thalia and Erato, the muses of the different kinds of poetry; Clio, the muse of history; Euterpe, the muse of music; Melpomene, the muse of tragedy; Terpsichore, the muse of dance; Polyhymnia, the muse of hymns and sacred poetry; and Urania, the muse of astronomy."

"I thought astronomy was science, Nonna..."

"Well, we think of it in scientific ways now, but to the ancients, the sky was full of wonder, with tales to tell and knowledge of the future for those who were wise enough to read the stars. They looked up and saw gods and monsters, great animals from myth and the heroes and heroines of legendary tales."

"So stars have their own stories? Like the Big Dipper is a giant's sauce ladle?"

Nonna roars with laughter, tickling me until I'm roaring with her.

"Not exactly, *cara mia*," she says, smiling. "But the Big Dipper also has another name — Ursa Major, the Great Bear. I like that name better — it reminds me of the legend of King Arthur, whose symbol was also a big bear. He was a brilliant child, a tremendous destiny ahead of him, but as he got older and took the reins of his realm, he forgot some of the important lessons his mentor — the great wizard Merlin — had taught him, and his kingdom began to crumble."

"Oh, no!"

"A tragedy, indeed," she says. "But the legend says Arthur will return someday and bring a golden time of happiness and prosperity with him. I hope you'll see such a time in your lifetime, *cara mia*..."

"But what about the Muses, Nonna?"

"Ah, yes! Thank you! I wandered off the path. So... the legend goes that the god Apollo — who was the god of poetry, dance and music, among other things — fell in love with a naiad, a spirit of the water, and chased after her when she fled from him. Castalia — for that was her name — loved her freedom and wasn't ready to give up her freedom for a man, so she fled from Apollo, and when he continued to pursue her, she changed herself into a fountain to ensure he would never catch her."

"But then she'd be stuck as a fountain! That's no fun!"

"That's a very good point, Calliope."

I like it when Nonna calls me Calliope. I know it's a muse's name, but when she says it, it feels like I'm a musical instrument at the circus, and that sounds fun. Way more fun than being a fountain.

"But Castalia wasn't a fountain like you might imagine — she held the sacred waters of inspiration, and she offered that gift to all those who drank the waters or sat quietly to listen to the sound of the water whispering in the fountain. So she was much loved by poets and musicians, artists and dancers..."

"And astronomers!"

"Yes, and astronomers! And even the Muses themselves. In fact, Castalia was consecrated — made sacred — to the Muses. And they all came to visit Castalia, because her inspiration was a great treasure to them and a gift she gave them willingly."

"That sounds wonderful, Nonna — to give people inspiration so they can make beautiful music and art and... sauce!"

Nonna laughs heartily, then leans in to whisper in my ear.

"And now you know my secret, *angelica*! The inspiration for my dishes comes from the Muses, from Castalia herself. And as long as we honor her, that inspiration will bring people to our door, eager to feed their hearts and souls, as well as their stomachs!"

"That's what I want to do when I grow up, Nonna — feed people's hearts and souls."

"Then that is precisely what you will do, *cara mia*."

# CHAPTER 3

## STILL GOT THE BLUES

## Declan

"Declan, I'm sympathetic to whatever you're dealing with, but until I've talked to Callie and gotten her permission, there is no way I can give you her contact information."

After about twenty fruitless internet searches, I finally cornered Brighid, demanding answers. Maybe I should have been more circumspect or even just a little less aggressive, but having had Callie be so close and then losing her again... I'm wired tight right now.

"Come on, Bridge... I've been supportive of you and Hunt, despite all the ridiculous drama you've had going on for the last fifteen years... And here you are, with all this happily-ever-after shit. Can't you give me a break? Help me get another shot with Callie?"

"Supportive? I must have had a vision while we were having that conversation. I mostly recall jokes at my expense and a lot of eye-rolling."

Well, she's got me there.

"I apologized for the 'Sesame Street' thing."

"You did?"

Didn't I? I thought I did.

"Your brother did."

"I could have sworn…" I shake my head. "Well, I'm sorry. Truly. I thought I'd apologized years ago. If I'd realized I hadn't, I would have before now. So, I'm sorry. Now can I have Callie's number?"

Brighid rolls her eyes at me, takes a deep breath and sighs.

"I'm sympathetic, Declan. Truly. But I have no idea what your history is with her, and without her agreement, it would be a violation of our friendship if I were to give out her information. For all I know, she's been hiding from you with good reason. Or maybe she just doesn't want anything to do with you again. I can't do anything until I've talked to her, and I'm not going to bother her with it tonight when she's already clearly upset, just from seeing you here. She was nice enough to take a night off from the restaurant just to be here and bring us a cake. And now she doesn't even get to see everyone enjoying it. That's on you."

Now it's me sighing. Bridge won't budge, and I'm not going to delve into my past with Callie out here, with a bunch of unsympathetic strangers, restaurant employees and my bandmates around to overhear.

"If she's upset, you should check on her!" There — she'll call Callie, and I can memorize the number out of her contacts. If I can remember the lyrics to three albums' worth of songs, I can remember one phone number long enough to write it down.

"Siobhan went after her. They're close. She'll make sure Callie is fine."

Dammit. I could have appealed to this Siobhan to let me come with her.

"Which one is *she*?"

"The really tall one with the long white-blonde hair, tattoos, piercings, combat boots…"

I'd have remembered a girl who fit that description, if I'd seen her. But I was kind of in a fog for most of the night, my head filled with thoughts of Callie from the past, not even realizing my angel was sitting thirty feet from me. I wonder if that's why she was on my mind so heavily tonight, because she was right there… maybe thinking of me? We did always have that way of being on the same wavelength…

"And she'd have kicked your ass if she thought for a second you'd hurt Callie. Now or in the past. So you might want to steer clear, if Callie has good reason for avoiding you."

Yeah. This Siobhan would have plenty of reason to kick my ass. Brighid makes her sound like some kind of Amazon warrior.

Tattoos? Piercings? Combat boots? Probably best to avoid that confrontation if I can, at least until I can find Callie and ask her forgiveness.

Wait... Did Brighid say restaurant?

"She's working in a restaurant? Here? In Mystic Beach? Is she a pastry chef?"

Brighid rolls her eyes at me.

"I shouldn't have said even that much. And I'm not saying anything more until I've talked to Callie. I'll let her know you want to talk to her. That's the best I can do, Declan."

A little silver-haired lady commands Brighid's attention, and I look around me, wondering who else I might be able to ask who'd be more cooperative.

Maybe Billy can help.

"That was quite a scene there, Declan. Anything I should be aware of from a PR standpoint?" he asks before I can say a word.

"No. But I could use your help. Gryff said he couldn't make use of his resources, but I need to find her."

"If Gryffin said he can't, he can't, and I don't have any additional resources beyond him," Billy says.

I growl in frustration, and Billy shakes his head.

"Pull it together, Dec. We're all friends and family here tonight, but this whole scene was dramatic enough that people are going to talk. And I don't think you want to take Hunter's place as our tabloid headliner for the rest of the summer."

"Can I borrow your car?"

Billy scoffs.

"How much have you had to drink?"

"One or two."

"It's been twenty minutes, Dec. And you can't remember if it was one or two?"

"Maybe three. Doubles," I admit.

"Yeah... no."

"I need to get out of here, Billy."

"I can't leave yet. I've got to talk to Hunter about a few things first. You want me to call you a ride?"

I sigh, deflated.

"No. I'll just walk back to the studio. It's not far."

"You sure? I don't want you stumbling into traffic on the highway."

"I'm not *that* drunk."

"If you're sure…"

I nod solemnly and head off toward the studio.

Cars fly by me on the highway. I briefly contemplate stepping out in front of one. Yes, on purpose. No, not like that. I can't fix this mess with Callie if I'm dead. Besides, I mostly like my life. It's just the personal stuff that sucks.

No, I'm picturing a dramatic scene from my future bio-pic, where I step out in front of the oncoming car, arms raised, and it comes to a stop mere inches from my knees, whereupon I commandeer said transport and execute a perfect sliding parallel parking job in front of whatever restaurant Callie is working in, and she then throws herself into my arms, in awe of my sheer manliness and stuntman-worthy driving skills.

Did I mention that I haven't driven on a daily basis in like ten years?

So, no… Not doing that.

My daydream of testosterone-fueled romantic glory comes to a screeching halt. Literally.

A passing car honks its horn, then pulls over in a sudden deployment of squealing brakes and burning rubber. A girl pops out of the passenger-side window, leaning half out of the car, waving at me.

"Hey — are you Declan Carter?" she calls out as I approach.

Normally, this kind of thing is my bread and butter. Being recognized by fans, schmoozing with my adoring public, signing some curvy bits of a random woman. I carry a Sharpie with me for just this purpose. But this is the last thing I want to deal with right now.

"We can give you a ride! We're headed to O.C. for some fun! Come with us!"

Again, more of my usual thing, but tonight it sounds like sheer torture.

"Sorry — no," I finally respond, keeping my head down and my hair in front of my eyes. "I get told I look like him a lot, though. And I'm nearly home. Thanks, though."

"Oh. OK," she says, clearly disappointed. "You sure do look like him. You're still cute. Sure you don't want to go to Seacrets with us?"

She's leaning forward over the car door, taking advantage of the angle to show off some serious cleavage. But I've signed so many sets of cleavage at this point that I'm all but immune to it.

"No — I'm good. But thanks for the offer."

She pulls back inside the car.

"I could have sworn that was him," I hear her say to her friends.

"Can't have been," one replies. "That guy seems nice. Declan Carter's a dick."

"And a manwhore. No way he'd have passed up what you just flashed at him if it was really Declan Carter," another adds before the window slides firmly shut.

And now I know exactly the scope of work I've got cut out for me. Not only do I need to find Callie and somehow make it up to her that I dumped her a decade ago, I've got to make her believe that "Dicklan" Carter, manwhore, deserves a second chance.

"Hey. Dec... You OK?"

Dave sticks his head into my room, and I'm both touched that he cares enough to ask and irritated that he can't just leave me alone in my misery. He's interrupting me singing the blues. Literally and figuratively.

None of my internet searches have yielded any hint of where Callie might be. There aren't even any Martinos listed in Mystic Beach now, and her grandmother had lived here for decades. I'm guessing Nonna's gone now, passed away or in a nursing home. I hope it's the latter. I kind of liked the old lady, and I don't like picturing Callie alone here, with no family nearby. Maybe Callie's living farther inland, or in Ocean City. Maybe she's just got an unlisted number. I certainly do.

I rub my thumb against the soft fur of that plush grizzly bear Dave teased me about all those years ago. He doesn't know its history or the secret it hides. He just knows I keep it tucked in a drawer most of the time. Or in my suitcase when we're on the road. Actually, he probably doesn't know I take it with me when we're touring. I like to keep that shit private. Bad enough the guys know I have the thing, thanks to my brother...

"Dec?"

"Hmm?"

"I asked if you were OK."

"Yeah. Hunky-dory. Spiffy, even."

"Uh-huh…"

I finally look back up at him, finding him leaning against the door frame, looking skeptical.

"You come back just to cheer me up?"

"Nah. Things were winding down. Hunter and Brighid left a while ago, went back to her house."

"I guess I know what they're doing right now." I smirk at him. "Why aren't you off with your little engineer doing the same?"

"We're not like that."

"Not buying it."

"Doesn't change the fact that we're not together."

"Now. But you were."

"No comment."

"Come on, Davey — I've seen how you look at the girl. Short of a new Spector or a seal, I've never seen you so enraptured with anything."

He gives me a look I can't quite decipher. Something's up with him, and it isn't just the girl.

"What are you going to do about Callie?" he asks, not at all subtle in changing the subject back to my love-life, or lack thereof.

"Can't you get Gryffin to track her down for me?"

"If he said no, he meant no, Dec. You know him. He's always got to have a good reason to go digging."

"And my broken heart isn't enough of a reason?"

"Apparently not. You've been kind of a dick of him over the years, so you really shouldn't be surprised."

"I'm a dick to everyone."

"Yeah. You are. Why *is* that?"

He's asking me, but the tone of his voice says he's got his suspicions already, and if anything, he's suggesting I need to consider the question for myself.

No need. I know the answer. I was an arrogant, egotistical jerk even at 15. At 29, even I recognize that cocky teenager had no business thinking he was the shit. Hell, Declan Carter at 20 was an unmitigated asshole. I'd almost single-handedly torpedoed landing us one of the best lead guitarists on the planet. I know that. I don't need it pointed out to me.

"Go fuck yourself, Davey. Better yet, go fuck that cute little engineer."

I like to think I've mellowed. Yeah.

"Her name is Piper."

I know this. But it defeats the purpose if I tell him that.

"Whatever. Your dick is weeping for her, so go get her. Take a page from your little brother's book for once! She's begging for it. And if you don't help her out, maybe I will. Her name's Pepper, right? Sounds hot."

"Fuck you, Dec. You stay away from Piper."

He stomps down the hall and slams the door to his room, then the sliding glass door onto the deck. Back to his beloved beach, where he belongs, and out of my hair. No more know-it-all Davey and his armchair psychology.

The thing is he's right. He knows he's right. *I* know he's right. Before I even hit 18, I'd gotten so jaded and soured on life that it's a wonder we got signed at all. The timing wasn't coincidental. At 17, I'd fucked up, and I'd hurt the woman I loved, and after that, nothing I did, no one I met, ever filled the gaping hole in my heart. In fact, I'd spent years punishing myself for it, figuring that an asshole like me didn't deserve anything more than an hour or two of physical pleasure with a groupie whose name I'd never remember.

Don't get me wrong — the girls usually went away happy, having crossed Declan Carter of aMUSEd off their sexual checklist. Even if I didn't propose marriage and give them blue-eyed babies, it was a mutual win-win in nearly every case. For the most part, they knew the score. I was a true asshole to a few of them, no doubt, and I'd realized that before we got far into our second headlining tour. Shaped up my act, made sure all the girls knew the deal before I'd so much as touched them — one night only, no repeats, no numbers exchanged, no chance of anything more than a mutual orgasm, with condoms and an NDA being non-negotiable.

Eventually, even that got boring. No — not boring. It got painful. What's the point of getting off with some girl I'd never see again when all it did was make me think of the one I wanted but couldn't have? The bittersweet flavor of hot-and-cold-running blowjobs tipped decidedly toward the bitter. My attitude about everything soured.

The only thing I had left that I enjoyed was performing. So I put everything I had into that, into becoming the best. So what if my heart was a gaping wound? I'd use that. I'd split myself open on that stage every night and let every girl in the audience dream of how she could fix the broken rockstar, let the guys in the crowd dream of being that guy that every girl wanted to make whole again. They ate it up. And that was good enough.

Until it wasn't. I'm sure my bandmates thought I had my own special case of PMS with all the mood swings I put them through.

But then I got a brilliant idea — a new fix to keep my mind off what I'd lost. It took some doing, and that's half the reason Gryff is pissed at me. But it made things better. Not great, but better. But I'd kept the guys out of the loop, kept everyone out of the loop. So, as far as they all knew, everything was status quo. "Dicklan" was out on the prowl, a manwhore in all his glory, just a little less in-your-face about it. But that wasn't it at all. It was my secret. That, and this...

I poke the chest of the little stuffed grizzly bear, feeling for that rock-hard spot I know is...

There. Under the haphazard threads of the only sewing I've ever done.

My chest may have a gaping wound where my heart is, but this little guy — he carries my heart with him wherever we go.

And if I can just figure out where she is... if I can just find a way to make it up to her, what I did... Maybe I can finally take my heart back from a plush bear and give it once again to the woman I love.

# CHAPTER 4

# FOOD AND CREATIVE LOVE

## Callie

I flip through the pages of Nonna's book, seeking out some inspiration for the dish that will guarantee a win precious weeks from now. Nothing on our current menu speaks to me where the competition is concerned. I need something new, exciting, uniquely mine. Something that will knock the socks off the voters and knock the competition to their knees.

And then there's a knock on the kitchen door. I slip Nonna's book back into the drawer and open it to a familiar face cloaked in a mile of white-blonde hair, warm brown eyes full of concern I don't even want to acknowledge.

"So, you didn't burn down the restaurant?"

"Hi, Siobhan." I sigh. "Wouldn't I have done it by now if I was going to?"

I let her in and lock the door back up behind her. She follows me back to my office, taking the chair in front of it after she moves a stack of receipts back onto the desktop.

"I don't know, honestly. You came pretty close earlier."

I look up at her in surprise.

"How do you know about that?"

"I have my ways."

I frown, suspecting I know how she knows, and it's not one of her sometimes Brighid-like intuitive guesses.

"Drew squealed."

"He didn't have to. I was standing in the doorway when you did it. Wanted to check and make sure you were OK. Should have known you'd go right back to cooking…"

"I didn't see you."

"I'm not sure you were seeing much right then. Definitely not the color of that sauce as it shifted from cream to brown to black…"

"Yeah… First time I've burned a sauce since my first session of culinary school."

"And why was that?"

"Erik Feldman. He turned up the heat under the pan when I went to grab the basil, because he was jealous that I already had my own recipe developed and memorized."

"No — I mean tonight, which I think you know. Stop deflecting." The ring in her left eyebrow quirks up.

I sigh. Siobhan is nothing if not direct. It's one of the things I love about her. And one of the things I sometimes hate. She calls you on your shit, whether you're ready to deal with it or not.

"Got lost in some old, old memories."

"Of…?"

"An old boyfriend."

"Who, I have to assume from that scene tonight, was Declan Carter."

The look I give her is pleading.

"Out with it. You're just going to stew in it if you don't tell someone."

Stew! Maybe something like Nonna's fisherman's stew would win over the crowd at Taste!

I grab for the drawer and start to pull her chef's book out again.

"Callie!"

Siobhan frowns at me.

"I've got to get a dish selected for the competition next month! That's the important thing right now. If I'm going to get that space next door to expand, I've got to win it."

"And how are you going to do that when you're burning sauces and zoning out in your own kitchen?"

I sigh, deflated.

Declan fucking Carter. I haven't slept with him in more than a decade and still he's screwing me.

"It was nothing. A teenage summer romance. I barely even remember it."

"Bullshit."

Did I mention that Siobhan has a habit of calling people on their shit?

"Girl, you lit out of that place tonight like your hair was on fire. If I hadn't been determined to make sure you were OK, I would have decked Declan Carter purely on principle."

Now *that* makes me smile.

"You should have."

"I like to know why I'm giving people black eyes before I do it. It changes the dynamics of the punch," she adds with a grin as she smacks a fist into her palm. "Now — spill."

Before I say a word, I've already decided not to tell her the whole story. Just enough to get her off my back, so I can go back to Nonna's book and see if that stew recipe might be on the right track.

"I met Declan Carter the summer after I turned 15. Right on the boardwalk here in Mystic Beach... I came to visit my grandmother that summer, as usual. My parents took off for Italy. Mama wanted to study Italian art, in person, after all those years of studying it in college. Papa wanted to see the ancient ruins firsthand. I told you he was an archeology professor, right?"

She nods.

"He'd already been to Egypt, to Greece, and Italy was next on his list. So, they sent me off to Nonna's for the whole summer this time, instead of just a few weeks, saying I was old enough to help her in the restaurant and get used to working for my money, instead of getting an allowance. I didn't argue. I loved it here, living with Nonna, learning to cook her recipes, spending time on the beach, the amusement parks, the concerts... I *so* loved the bandstand concerts every week... All these different kinds of music, and these talented musicians making everyone so happy. Next to cooking, music was the thing I loved most. I spent all my allowance on music, and I was hoping to save up some money that summer for concert tickets so I could see some of my favorite bands, even if Mama and Papa didn't approve."

"And you met Declan Carter."

"I did. He and his brother and their bandmate—"

"Hunter Graves," Siobhan interjects.

"I honestly had no idea it was the same Hunter. When Brighid said her friend was coming to visit, and then all of that craziness ensued between them... I mean — Hunter's a pretty common name, right? Sounds like a rockstar name. And even if it was the same guy, how was I supposed to know that Declan was in his band?"

"You'd honestly never heard of aMUSEd? They're pretty famous."

"When I knew Declan, they were the Carter Brothers Band."

"That's a stupid name."

"I know, right?" I chuckle. "Declan said his bandmate kept pressuring them to change it to something else, but he wanted his name on the thing. He was hypersensitive about it, so I kept my mouth shut and never told him I thought it was stupid, too."

"I know you said you don't follow social media, but Declan's all over the place, has been for a long time. I think he's on a couple billboards in New York, even."

"I haven't been back to New York since I took the lease on this place, and before that I was working my ass off, trying to ensure I could even open my own restaurant. I barely slept, let alone looked around to see what billboards were up. And I've spent the last twelve years avoiding anything that had to do with music, or pop culture, or anything where..."

"Where Declan Carter might have shown his pretty face."

I sigh, this time wistfully.

"He is pretty, isn't he? That's not just me, right?"

"If I didn't already know he's a dick, I'd have done him."

I grimace. The image of Declan with Siobhan turns my stomach, and I'm not entirely sure why. They'd make a handsome couple, though she's too edgy for him. Most guys, she'd eat them for lunch. He might actually stand a chance with her, though.

No, there's that nauseated feeling again. I push away the image.

"He was nearly as pretty when he was 15. Even prettier than that when he was 17..."

"So, this wasn't a summer flirtation between a couple of teenagers."

"No. It was not," I admit, which is the closest I'm going to come to telling her the whole truth.

"I never met Declan's brother..."

"David. David Carter."

I file that away for later, not analyzing why I'd need to know the name of the brother of the man I hope to never see again.

"Or Hunter. Or Brighid, for that matter. Like Declan, and David, I was a summer kid, only they'd been coming here every summer since they were toddlers. I'd come for a couple weeks of vacation each summer with Mama and Papa, until that summer. This was the first time I'd been here long enough to actually meet some of the local kids. I'd met one girl who lived next door to Nonna, and we'd started becoming friends... But then one day I took a break from the kitchen, came out to get some air, and the rest is history."

"Your eyes met across a crowded room," Siobhan jokes.

"Not quite — I heard the music first. I followed it down to the spot on the boardwalk where the Carter Brothers Band was busking. I listened, enraptured, until it was past time to go back to work, and then they took a break... Their lead singer — he'd been watching me as intently as I had him. It wasn't that he was the most beautiful boy I'd ever seen, though he was. He just had something special about him, a spark that I couldn't ignore. When he walked up to me and smiled, I was done-for..."

## *Fourteen years ago*

"Did you enjoy the show?" the boy asks, smiling broadly at me, his deep blue eyes twinkling. I could dive into those eyes and drown...

"You're very good. The music was wonderful."

"Thanks. We've only been playing together for a couple weeks. We'll only get better. You should come out and see us tomorrow."

"You're out here every day?"

"Most days." He tilts his head, considering me. "I haven't seen you before. Did you just get here for vacation?"

"No. We usually come for a couple weeks in the summer, but Nonna — my grandmother — she lives here. She's the chef in the restaurant at the hotel," I tell him, pointing in that direction. "And I'm spending the whole summer with her this time, helping in the kitchen."

"So you cook?"

"A little. I'm learning. Nonna's food is amazing. I have a lot to learn."

"I've been known to eat."

"I've heard that about teenage boys," I reply with a laugh. The boys in the cafeteria at school inhale anything they get their hands on.

"Maybe I could try your food sometime... Uh..." he gestures at me.

"Callie. Calliope Martino. But Callie for short."

"Nice to meet you, Callie. I'm Declan. Declan Carter."

He holds his hand out to me, and I take it, shake it. Neither of us lets go. Our palms fit together like two puzzle pieces. Magnetic puzzle pieces that don't want to be separated. I look down at my hand, his hand, unable to explain why they're still acting like they're fused together. I glance up and find him looking, too, and my face heats up, my cheeks getting red. Until he looks up and our eyes meet, and it steals the breath from my lungs.

Has any human ever existed on this planet who is more perfect than Declan Carter?

A guitar chord rings out across the plaza, and Declan breaks our locked gazes to look over his shoulder. He doesn't release my hand, though.

"I think that's my signal to get back to work," he says, reluctance clear in his voice.

"I need to get back to the restaurant," I admit.

"See you back here tomorrow afternoon?" His smile nearly knocks my legs out from under me.

"Yes!" I blush again, knowing I'm showing too much enthusiasm for such a small invitation from someone I've only just met.

"I'll look forward to it, Calliope Martino. Maybe I'll sing a song just for you..."

His hand slides slowly free of mine, almost a caress as our skin finally breaks contact. He smiles at me again and steps back, watching me for another moment before he turns and jogs back to his bandmates.

I want to stay and watch, but... Watch! I glance down at my watch, already knowing I've been gone too long. Nonna will be unhappy. She keeps telling me that I need to take this job seriously. Just because it's her kitchen doesn't mean I can slack off. With a last glance at Declan Carter, I turn back the other way and run. Tomorrow. I can see Declan again tomorrow.

## *Present*

"So, love at first sight?" Siobhan asks.

"There's no such thing. We proved that."

"Why do you say that?"

"We were kids. It was a silly little crush. Over almost as soon as it began."

"Why do I suspect you're lying about that?"

"Too much time spent with Brighid?" I tease her.

"Brighid has extraordinarily keen insight, especially with people."

"And yet she still didn't see Hunter's dumbass rockstar nonsense coming in time to steer clear."

"They're happy. They're together. That's all that matters. And they'll have a story to tell their grandkids. A romantic, if slightly embarrassing, story. Kind of like the one you just told me."

"Hopefully, she gets her happily-ever-after. Mine's more like a tragic tale to warn young girls about falling for the first pretty face they see."

"What happened?"

"Long story short, we dated for the rest of that summer. And the next one. And the one after that. And then, right when I'd started to plan a future with him, he dumped me — to go off and become a rockstar."

"Ouch. No warning?"

"None. One day we were discussing how to mesh our careers, our families... and the next — boom. 'Sorry, this isn't going to work for me.' 'I'm a rockstar, groupies, hot-and-cold-running blowjobs...' 'Yada, yada...'"

"He actually said that? 'Hot-and-cold-running blowjobs'?" Her eyes are wide with disbelief. And Siobhan's seen — and done — things I can't even imagine.

I nod, then shake my head.

"That's my fairytale prince for you — more like a fairytale frog with warts on his ass."

"He's got that reputation."

"Oh?" I ask without thinking. "You know what — nevermind. I don't want to know. I didn't want to know for twelve years, and I don't want to know now."

"You sure? Seemed like maybe you two have some unfinished business, based on what happened tonight. Maybe clearing the air would do you both some good, get rid of the baggage you're clearly still carrying around."

"Baggage? I am baggage-free, girl. Just me, my restaurant and a soon-to-be expanded dining area."

That eyebrow ring rises up again.

"Right," she says, clearly unconvinced. "Well, on that note, I'm going to head home, now that I know you're OK." She looks skeptical about that, too, despite the fact that she's the one who just said it.

"Hey, Siobhan..." I call to her as she heads toward the door. She looks back, expectant. "Thanks. For checking on me, I mean. You didn't have to do that."

"Yeah, I did. That's what friends do. Even when their friends hold out on them with the full, juicy story."

I avoid making eye contact. She's letting me get away with it, for now, even if she's calling me out on doing it.

"Hey — why'd you wait to come talk to me about it?" I ask her, curious. "You must have left the party right after I did if you saw that cream sauce debacle."

"You needed your food to tell you that you weren't OK. You wouldn't have believed it if I'd corralled you before you burned it. You'd have pretended everything was fine and gone on about your night. Once the food told you that you needed to deal with your past, you had no choice. I knew you'd be ready to talk once everyone else had cleared out and left you alone here in your spiritual center. And that's when I came back. And since you're done talking — for now — I'll let you get back to your recipes. Good luck! Just remember — things come in their own sweet time. You can't hurry along what isn't yet ready to be."

And those are the words that stick in my head as she lets herself out and I lock the door once more behind her. It's Nonna's lesson of caramelization, in a different form.

A different form!

Maybe the fisherman's stew could be deconstructed... Hmm...

I pull out a heavy pan, a sweet onion and my favorite knife, and I start to hum to myself. It's time to caramelize.

# Chapter 5

# Kindred Spirit

## Callie
### *The next morning*

"So... what do you think?"

I can't take the suspense any longer.

Drew took his first bite a full minute ago, and his expression is impossible to read.

"Rick, Devon — opinions?" I demand when Drew remains stoic in the face of my impatience. My two main line cooks know food almost as well as Drew and I do. Almost. If they like it, I'm golden. If they don't...

"Come on, guys! Give me something here!"

Drew takes a deep breath and lets it back out slowly.

"It's awesome!" he says with a smile. Which then falters.

"But it's not a winner, is it?" My shoulders sag along with my spirits.

He shakes his head. Rick and Devon repeat the gesture.

"It'd make a great addition to the seasonal menu, Callie," Devon says.

"But it's not going to..." Rick begins.

"Knock their socks off," I finish.

"No. I don't think so," Drew says.

I sigh.

"Back to the drawing board. OK. Thanks, guys. Let's get going with the prep. We'll have the Sunday brunch crew lined up at the door before 11. I'd rather get ahead of things, since we're all here."

"Yes, Chef!" they chorus.

## *Three days later*

"Chef?"

It's a timid question from a new member of my staff. The rest of them know by now not to interrupt when I'm on the line, unless it's something urgent. If it was, they'd be comfortable interrupting, rather than this mousy intrusion that I'd find annoying if it was... OK — I *do* find it annoying, but I bury my irritation in this case, because this is Raquel.

"Yes, Raquel?"

"One of the customers is asking to speak with you."

Oh. Fun.

This is either going to be a delight or a disaster. Either way, it's a disruption I could do without. But that's not Raquel's fault.

"I prefer we call them patrons, or diners, Raquel. We're not handing them a package of mass-produced socks over a counter."

"Yes, Chef. Should I have told them you were busy?"

Raquel was hired out of the culinary program through the local food bank. She's from a disadvantage background, her mother homeless, battling addiction, but now that the family is in transitional housing, her mother in treatment, Raquel has blossomed. Straight-A student, with a passion for food. She's taking the late-night shift at the food bank as part of her culinary education so she can work here and attend school at the same time.

She'd never even been in a fine-dining restaurant until she stepped through Castalia's doors, but I've caught her thoughtfully sampling menu items as she shadows our waitstaff. She's absorbing more from what she puts in her mouth than the immediate flavors of sweet, salty, savory... She's had some keen observations on the nuanced balance of my flavor palate. She'll make a solid chef someday. Maybe an outstanding one.

"No. You were right to come get me right away. Don't be afraid to speak up when I'm needed. Did they say what they wanted? Were they unhappy with the meal?"

"No. He didn't seem like he wanted to complain. He ordered two entrées and three appetizers, just for himself, and he ate most of what he ordered."

"A restaurant critic?" Drew asks quietly from beside me.

"Maybe. Take over this risotto order — with the grilled shrimp."

"Got it."

I wipe my face and hands with a clean kitchen towel, rebutton my coat with the clean surface out and follow in Raquel's wake. She stops a few feet from a two-top occupied by just one man. A man who looks familiar.

He's not dressed like a food critic, that's for sure. Black graphic T-shirt, black jeans — way too hot for summer at the beach, though probably not horrible here in the air conditioning, especially with those strategic rips — inky hair down below his shoulders, ink decorating one arm to the elbow and black leather cuff bracelets on each wrist, just to keep within the theme. And rings galore. I haven't worn a ring since... Well, since before culinary school. Totally impractical for a chef, especially one who sometimes indulges in making her own desserts and breads. This guy — clearly not a chef. Unless he's one of those rebel types, cooking in steel barrels and trying to make muskrat the next big thing.

"Wow. Hi. Fancy meeting you here!" he says, as if he knows me — as if I should know him.

"I'm sorry... I don't..." I'm at a loss, wracking my brain for where I know him from.

"No — I'm sorry. I have the advantage, I guess. I was watching while you were... running. You probably didn't get a good look at me."

Oh, no... There's no way.

"Alex Winters," he says, standing up and holding out a ring-clad hand. "Keyboardist for aMUSEd." He keeps his voice down, clearly not wanting to draw attention to the celebrity he is.

I'm torn between mortification and righteous anger.

"Did he send you? Couldn't face me himself?" I demand, venom creeping into my voice, even though I try to keep the volume down to avoid making a scene myself.

"*He* has no idea I'm here," he says. "He's been looking for you since that night, without success. He's flummoxed and being an even bigger pain in the ass than he normally is. For that matter, *I* didn't know *you* were here. Brighid gave me a list of restaurants to try when we first got here, and with all the drama we've had, I'm only now getting to check them out. I was working my way down from the north."

Brighid. Of course.

"I'm sorry. I just assumed... when you told me who you are..."

"It's fine. It's to be expected under the circumstances. But why I'm here has nothing to do with Declan." I cringe at the name. "And why I asked to speak to the chef has nothing to do him, either. You just blew me away. Your flavor profiles are some of the best I've had in years, maybe ever, and I've been eating at some of the finest restaurants in the world — whenever I'm not stuck with tour catering and fast food on the road, that is."

"You're a foodie."

"And an amateur chef. Very amateur," he admits. "I cook for the guys sometimes, though I usually let Declan handle the steaks." I cringe again.

"Can you stop saying his name, please? I'd really appreciate it."

"Sure," he says with a shrug. "No more talk of the Nameless One. But I have a favor to ask in return."

My hackles shoot up.

"I'm not interested in meeting with him, talking to him... Dancing on his grave, maybe..."

"Ouch." Now he cringes. "Point taken. I give you my word that I won't tell him where you are. But, no — this would just be a favor for me personally. And feel free to say no. I know how busy a chef's life can be. I've got a few other friends who have their own restaurants..."

"What's the favor?"

"Give me some cooking lessons while I'm here this summer. I'll pay you for your time. I'll share your dishes on my social media accounts, if that appeals to you, though it looks like you have all the patrons you can handle."

"And then some," I admit. "I'm hoping to expand our dining area in the near future."

"That's expensive."

I nod.

"So a little extra revenue would be helpful, right? Would a thousand a lesson make it worth your while?"

I'm so startled at the amount he's so casually offering me that I choke, leaving Alex to pat me on the back until I get it under control.

"I'm sorry — that's just outrageously more than reasonable. Why does it mean so much to you?"

"I could've been a chef. Maybe someday I will," he says just as casually. "Can't live a rockstar life into my 90s. My 60s, probably. But after that..." He meets my eyes, the watercolor blue of his irises reminiscent of... the Nameless One's... but only in their general shade. That one — his eyes are deeper, darker — bottomless pools like a clear lake in the summer. Alex's are a wash of cerulean, translucent, like cabochon gems set precisely in a face that — while not as strikingly handsome as Declan at 29, as much as it kills me to admit that — is perhaps prettier, more delicate, like a vampire in a supernatural romance or some fae prince out of a storybook.

"So, what do you say? I promise not to steal your recipes. But I want to understand how you build your flavors. I want to learn the techniques I never picked up since I didn't go to culinary school. I want to get better at making food that will do more than feed people's stomachs — I want it to feed their souls, and their hearts, like yours does."

I'm stunned into silence. There's no way he could know that I said almost precisely those words to my grandmother nearly twenty years ago, nor that I've spent my life trying to do just that, just as Nonna predicted I would do.

Alex isn't just a foodie with cooking as a hobby. He's a kindred spirit. And that is a rare thing that deserves some consideration, regardless of who he works with. Maybe, if the Nameless One throws me off now that I've seen him again, working with the clean slate that is an untrained chef will be a palate cleanser that gets me back on my game. Maybe his passion for food will even help spark inspiration for a dish that will ensure the future of Castalia.

"Let's do it."

# CHAPTER 6

# CRAZY LITTLE THING CALLED LOVE

## Declan
### *Two days later*

"Out! Get out!"

"Bridge — just give me something to work with! Is she married? Did she change her name? I can't find her in the telephone listings! Is she a pastry chef? She made that amazing-looking cake... Granted, I didn't get to taste it, but I'm sure it was amazing. It *was* amazing, right?"

Brighid rolls her eyes at me. She's really good at it. I imagine she'd have to be, with all the practice Hunter has given her...

"Of course it was, Declan! Callie made it. But I'm still not telling you anything."

"Did she tell you not to? Did you talk to her about me? What did she say? Does she remember me? I mean, of course she remembers me — I'm unforgettable. But there was also that running away thing... Does she still have some lingering feelings? Other than fleeing, I mean? Is there something I can say to remind her of the good times?"

"Were there good times? It sure didn't sound like it to me..." she says, half growling at me.

"So you *did* talk to her about me! What'd she say? Has she missed me?"

Brighid closes her eyes and shakes her head, her jaw setting and her mouth transforming into a grimace.

"Dec — it's time to give it a rest," Hunter says from behind me, observing the shift in his girl's expression. "Against my better judgment—" he looks up when Brighid full-on growls, this time at him "— and against my wonderful, very, very forgiving fiancée's express wishes, I let you in to talk to her about this. But you promised you'd be reasonable, polite... And this... isn't. You need to go."

"But she hasn't told me anything! I've been looking for Callie for days! I've combed every corner of the internet, begged a town clerk to tell me whatever she knew — I owe her front-row seats for a show on our next tour, and she didn't even tell me anything other than Callie makes amazing food! Come on! I already knew that! I did find out her grandmother passed away years ago, thanks to that reporter friend of yours..."

"You pestered Rory into helping you with this?"

Brighid is outraged. Maybe I shouldn't have mentioned that. The obituary in the newspaper's archives didn't give me any information that would help in finding Callie. In fact, I was lucky I found it at all, because I didn't know Nonna's first name, and it turned out she'd re-married or something, because her last name wasn't Martino. It was lucky that I remembered the name of the old restaurant. The obituary just mentioned a granddaughter as a survivor, saying she lived in New York City.

Can you believe it? Callie was in New York! I've been living in New York for years, at least when we weren't on the road, and Callie was there, too, and yet it's in Mystic Beach that I finally run into her again. What are the odds? OK — they're probably better than they were in New York, but still...

"I just asked for access to the newspaper archives. That's it. Rory just happened to be the one who was there to let me into that room stacked with newspapers and these giant books..."

"The morgue."

"What? That's creepy, Brighid. I mean, Callie's grandmother is dead, but I wasn't going to have them dig her up just to..."

Brighid screams, and I recoil, pushing Hunter in front of me. He's pretty big. She'll have a good distance to travel before she can put her hands on me, which it looks like right now she'd really like to do. And not in a good way.

"The newspaper archives is called a morgue, Declan," she says through gritted teeth.

"That's still creepy, Bridge. And not much help. I can make this easy on you, on everyone — just tell me where she lives, where she works, something, anything!"

"Hunter, get him out of here, or so help me, I'll forget every single magical ethic I've ever had and hex him until his dick falls off!"

I shield my crotch with my hands, hoping that's enough to ward off whatever witchy whammy Hunter's girl might throw at me.

"After what she told me, he deserves it!" Brighid yells from behind Hunter, who looks nearly as alarmed as I feel, and it's not *his* manly bits that she's threatening.

"Time to go, Dec. Now! Before I have to give up the idea of ever having kids with this amazing, intelligent, beautiful, sexy, patient, merciful—"

"Hunter!" she screeches.

"— woman of mine," he concludes abruptly.

He pushes me toward the door, and at his size, I don't fight him on it. But before the door swings closed in my face, I make one last appeal.

"Just tell me one thing about her! Please! I'm begging you!"

"She thinks you're an asshole!" Brighid yells through the now firmly closed, and locked, door.

## *A few weeks later*

David pulls Piper into his arms from behind, placing his hands on her belly, even though she's nowhere near pregnant enough for either of them to feel a baby kicking or even for there to be a "baby bump." He smiles down at her, and she smiles back up at him, and I repress the urge to walk out of the room.

They're so stinkin' happy, so stinkin' cute, the two of them — their new matching tattoos, their brown hair just a few shades apart, though David's has those bits of blonde he always gets when he's been spending time on his surfboard or paddleboard. Will the baby get Piper's brown eyes, or David's pale blue ones, I wonder.

And just like that, the future of aMUSEd is called into question. Because I can't imagine David is going to willingly leave his pregnant girlfriend to tour the world for a year or more. Hunter was already talking about shorter tour legs, longer breaks in between, maybe buying a jet of our own, just to get home more quickly between legs — home being here in Mystic Beach, as far as he's concerned, and not in New York, where all six of us have lived for nearly a decade now. It feels almost symbolic that I'm now the only one of us who doesn't have a tattoo, and specifically the aMUSEd muse inked permanently into my skin. The irony there is that everything seems to be changing — except me.

Maybe Marina Matthews is happy to accommodate the changes, but she's a label CEO, not the one who's going to have crying babies on her tour bus, if Hunter gets his way and brings Brighid on the road with us. And Marina Matthews is not the one who's going to have to find a bass player in my brother's league who can tour with us if David decides to quit touring altogether. If we can even find one that good who's also willing to deal with... well, me.

Yeah, I'm a dick. I own it. Most of the time, anyway. But the guys are used to it. Trying to break in a new bass player? That's a problem I don't need. I've already got enough problems, and that was before we even got here to Mystic Beach. I thought it would be fine, coming back to the town Dave and I had vacationed in as kids. Sure, I've got some memories here that don't exactly make me smile, but it's a vacation, and a vacation where we get to record our music and play out when we feel like it. Best of both worlds. Right?

But as soon as we got here, as soon as I saw that same stretch of highway, the same little town with its boardwalk and cute little shops, the quaint little restaurants...

Yeah, my whole outlook soured. Half the time I'm pissed off that things aren't going my way, and the other half, I'm wallowing in self-pity that I have to be here, where the worst thing I ever did haunts me every single damn day.

And that's the bottom line. I fucked up. Twelve years ago, I fucked up so badly that it changed my entire life. And, yeah, not just my life. I'll own that, too. I fucked up hers, too. Badly enough that I never expected to find her here when we came back for the summer.

Calliope Angelica Martino. Callie. The love of my life. From the moment I first saw her until this moment, right here. That's never changed. As much as everything else has changed, that hasn't.

I gave her up once, thinking I was doing the right thing. For her, at least. But finding her here again... Why does it feel like fate wanted to bring us back together, to give us a second chance? All I know is I can't get her out of my head, now that I've seen her again. But then she's never really been out of my head. Or my heart. And it's past time I told her that. I just have to find her so I can do it. And I think I finally figured out how.

## *A few days later*

"How would you girls like an exclusive selfie... with me?"

The girls — a blonde and a brunette — have me sandwiched between them on the dance floor of this club in Ocean City, midriffs bare above short skirts, pressed to my hips on both sides, room left for not so much as a cocktail napkin between us. Exactly what I was looking for, especially when roaming hands skate over my abs and back to caress each other. Perfection. Oh, this is going to be great...

They nod eagerly, fingers tracing up each other's sides.

"I've got the penthouse suite in the hotel next door. Would you ladies like to join me up there?"

"Yes!" "Definitely!" they reply in a gush.

Five minutes later, cell phone cameras having been pointed at us by dozens of other club patrons as we swept out the door, we enter the luxurious suite, the brunette on my left arm and the blonde on the right.

"They're bringing up a bottle of champagne and some sweets, so why don't we go ahead and get our selfie while we wait, and then it'll be time to enjoy the amenities," I suggest.

"Ooh, Declan... you're so sexy. Just like I thought you'd be!" the blonde says.

"Even sexier," the brunette adds.

"Why, thank you, ladies! You are both very sexy yourselves. Let's get this photo, and you can post it to your social media pages and show off your catch for the evening!"

We gather in close, arms around each other, capturing a photo on each of their phones and another on mine. Just in time, as there's a knock on the door, and I open it to allow the hotel staff to bring in a room service cart full of goodies, tucking a modest tip into the guy's hand with the classic finger-to-lips gesture to ask for privacy. I won't get it. I never do, especially not without a tip like five times the size of the one I just gave him. He retreats out into the hallway, and I know he'll have spread word of my being here with these two lovely ladies to all of his friends within ten minutes. Perfect. Just perfect.

"OK — Chrissy, Jenny — you ladies are together, right? I mean — *together* together?"

Chrissy nods, running her hand up over Jenny's bellybutton and then back down, dipping into the waistband of her skirt. Jenny licks a trail up Chrissy's neck before biting her earlobe.

"Perfect."

I've got a sense about such things. I've had enough practice picking girls out of a crowd to know a good candidate when I see her.

I cross the room back to them and plant a kiss on Chrissy's lips before doing the same to Jenny. Lovely girls.

My phone pings at me. I frown but pull it out of my pocket, frowning deeper as I read the message on the screen.

"Ladies — I must apologize, but there's a matter I have to attend to, right this minute. I'm going to have to offer my regrets."

Such a lovely pout on both their faces now. I feel bad about getting their hopes up. I'll make it up to them as best I can.

"You're welcome to use the room tonight. The champagne and goodies are on me, and I'll leave a tip for housekeeping, too. Just enjoy yourselves!"

"Aww... Declan. Do you really have to go?" Jenny asks.

"I really do, I'm afraid. But I thank you both for a lovely, if brief, evening. I enjoyed our time together. Make sure to share those selfies, make all your friends jealous that we got to spend time together. You can even tell them we had a wild time here in the room. I won't tell anyone I had to leave early! Enjoy each other in my stead!"

"Thanks, Declan! Maybe we'll see you again sometime soon?" Chrissy says.

"We'll see. I've got a lot of nights yet to fill on my vacation."

I blow them both a kiss and head back out into the hallway, checking to make sure no one is watching. Down fifteen flights of stairs and out a side door, and I'm in my Lyft driver's car before anyone can spot me.

"This really where you're going? At this time of night?" the guy, who must be at least 65, asks.

"Yes. And if you pretend you never saw me, there's an extra fifty bucks in it for you."

"You got it."

Now, it's time for my evening to really get started.

# CHAPTER 7

## LADY ICE

## Declan
### *The next day*

I finally got the information I needed. I had to work for it, but I was overdue for some penance anyway. Putting in the time overnight may have cost me a night's sleep, but it's a price I'm willing to pay to get to where I am now. Today... Today is the day. Today is the first day of the rest of my life. Of *our* lives. I'm going to make it count. Even desperately in need of a haircut and a day overdue for a shave for the first time in my life, Charming Declan Carter is back and ready to sweep my angel off her feet. She just doesn't know it yet.

I walk between the little tables she has dotting the covered space in the alleyway. They're empty now, waiting for the diners who'll start clamoring for space before lunch and won't stop until the last dessert is served late tonight. I found that out when I found out the rest of what I needed to get me here today.

My girl — she's the successful chef I always knew she would be. It was half the reason I took myself out of her life. It's good to know that at least that much of what I intended came to pass. As for the rest...

For now, it's quiet here. And while it was a hardship getting up at O-dark-thirty — otherwise known as 8 a.m. — it's the only time I can be relatively sure of finding Callie alone, before her staff comes in for the day, before she's swamped with prep work and orders. (So my informant told me, at least. Hopefully, she was right.)

The kitchen door leading off the back of the alley is ajar behind the screen, and I can hear the sounds of chopping and sautéing before the scent reaches me. And then I hear voices — a woman and a man — and I'm hit with a wave of... jealousy? It's probably just her sous-chef, but that doesn't stop the green-eyed monster from instantly taking up residence behind these deep blues of mine. Am I really that far gone? For a woman I dumped more than a decade ago? Yeah. Maybe. Probably.

I pull the screen door open, walking into the kitchen like I own the place. And my plan instantly goes awry.

"What the fuck are you doing here?"

That's directed at Alex, who is standing alongside Callie at the prep table, wearing an apron, and apparently in the process of chopping something, judging by the knife in his hand.

"Good morning to you, too, Dicklan," he snarks. "I'm caramelizing. That's what I'm doing here."

"I need to talk to Callie."

"But does *Callie* need to talk to *you*?"

We both look at her expectantly as she stands next to Alex, her hand dropping to her side from where it had been hovering over a pile of pecans. She looked startled, alarmed, when I first walked in. Now she stares back at me, utterly impassive.

"O... K..." he drawls, clearly having noticed the tension in the room, which he'd need that knife to cut. "And on that note... I think I'll call it quits until tomorrow," he says, starting to untie his apron. "Unless you'd rather I stayed — make it a threesome?"

He looks cheekily back and forth between me and Callie.

"Get out, Alex," we both growl at him, not taking our eyes off each other for a second.

He chuckles and shrugs, dropping the folded apron on the table next to him and heading past me and out the door.

"Let me know if you change your mind!" he calls out from the alley. "I'm very flexible!"

I'm not sure I want to know how he meant that...

"Get out, Alex," we both yell back. His distant laugh floats back in through the door.

Aiming to break the ice — and, boy, is it some Antarctic-level cold — I look down at the pile next to the pecans, to what she and Alex had been working on.

"Well, you won't have to worry about vampires anytime soon."

"That's garlic, Declan. These are onions."

"Vampire repellent, Fruit of Satan — six of one, half a dozen of the other..." I observe with a shrug.

"You don't like onions?"

"I had a traumatizing experience involving an onion."

"Do I want to know?"

"Not unless you want me to act it out, in which case we should call Alex back in here and take him up on that threesome after all."

She snorts.

"Not happening. Not with Alex and not without him."

"Party-pooper."

She rolls her eyes at me.

"What do you want, Declan? I've got staff due in soon, and I need to clean up after Alex's little lesson before they get here."

"You're giving my keyboard player cooking lessons?"

She shrugs.

"He asked. Nicely."

"I'm not nice."

"I know that — better than most." Her expression is bitter, and I'm hit with a wave of guilt, reminding me of what I'm supposed to be doing here.

"I ask you again, Declan: What do you want?"

"To talk."

"About what? What could we possibly have to talk about? You made yourself very clear a decade ago, when you informed me that you'd realized you'd never actually loved me. Despite all prior statements to the contrary."

Rather than cleaning up the onion, she picks up her knife and starts finely dicing what Alex had roughly chopped. I could be wrong, but she seems agitated, based on how vigorously she's applying that sharp blade to that innocent onion (though "innocent onion" is an oxymoron). Kind of like she'd prefer to be using the knife on something, or someone, else. I unconsciously move my hand over my nuts. As opposed to the ones on the table. What is it with these Mystic Beach girls threatening my manly bits?

"Look, Callie — it's been twelve years, and that's all a lot of water under the bridge for me. I figured it would be for you by now, too."

She pauses with the knife, picking it up from the table and gesturing at me with the point in a manner that makes me decidedly uncomfortable.

"You didn't leave me with much choice on that, Declan. 'I need to be free. I can't be tied down at 17, 18, when I'm going to be touring, promoting the band, trying to sell us as sex symbols, hot-and-cold-running blowjobs...' yada yada..."

"I never said that." I pause. "I never said we'd be sex symbols."

She rolls her eyes at me.

"But the 'hot-and-cold-running blowjobs' part?"

"I may have said that..." I admit. "Turned out I was right on that count." I chuckle, trying to lighten the mood and failing entirely. "Seriously — Callie, I didn't want to hurt you."

"Well, you did a shit job of that."

"I was trying to protect you. I knew what was coming, where we were headed as a band. The chances of the two of us staying together were slim."

"And a lot closer to none when you dumped me."

"I knew I couldn't do it, Callie. I didn't trust myself to be a good partner. We were 17. We had so much left to do before we'd be ready to settle down and commit to one person. I thought you'd cry for a week or two and move on, find somebody who'd be better for you. I didn't think you'd carry a torch for me. I wasn't good enough for you, and I knew it, even if you didn't. Everything that happened after that... most of my life since then... It's just proven I was right."

I feel like I'm actually digging myself a deeper hole here, but just like the last time, I'm helpless to find a way out of it now that I've started. I'm trying to be honest with her while also trying to make amends, and those two thing aren't going together as well as I had thought they would. And the look she's giving me makes me think that I was also right when I decided not to give her the details twelve years ago. She's a smart girl. On some level, she knows exactly what I'd have to say if I gave her the details now, and I already feel like a scumbag... I have for a long time.

Manwhore — they've called me that for more than a decade, and it's a reputation I embraced. I'd already gone over to the dark side that night in O.C., and I knew there was no going back.

I'd cheated on my girl less than a week after I'd promised her *forever*.

"I had a wakeup call that week, Callie. It woke me up to the reality that what I'd asked of you wasn't fair, and what I'd asked of myself wasn't realistic. Not given the circumstances. We were on two different paths, and I couldn't see any way for us to walk those paths together, let alone happily. And I couldn't do that to us — to you.

"But I shouldn't have said I was never in love with you. It wasn't true. I broke things off *because* I loved you. But I was 17 and I was stupid. If I'd known it was going to hurt you so badly that you'd still be suffering all these years later, I would have found another way."

The silence is stunning. No chopping, no sizzling, not even the sound of her breathing. Everything has just stopped.

"You really don't get the scope of what you did to me, do you? Still. Twelve years later. You self-centered, narcissistic asshole! You really can't conceive of why I'd still hate you for what you did."

She pauses, clearly gathering up the energies of an oncoming storm — one I already know is going to be hurling lightning at my ass when it finally breaks...

# CHAPTER 8

## WHAT DO I HAVE TO DO

### Declan

I'm waiting for it, willing to take whatever she wants to throw at me.

"You destroyed me, Declan," she says quietly. Too quietly. "You took every dream I'd been building and crushed it in an instant. You took the foundation of all of it and yanked it right out from under me the moment you took back the one thing I counted on — that you loved me."

True to her words, she looks ready to crumble, and I start to raise my arms, ready to pull her into me and comfort her, hold her up until I can find a way to rebuild that foundation under her feet, since I'm the one who stole it from her.

Instead, she turns around and stomps toward the door to the dining room, once again running away from me, from us... But before she hits it, she freezes, like the door has been suddenly transformed into a wall.

I watch her still standing there, expectantly. Something has to break here. The tension in the room builds... my hair feels like it's starting to stand on end.

She looks around her and growls in frustration.

"This is my damn restaurant! I'm not the one who's leaving! Out!"

She points at the back door with her knife, which she clearly didn't even realize she still had in her hand.

"This is where you leave, Declan."

I stay where I am, determined not to let it end like this.

"I left once, Callie. I'm not doing it again."

The ice in her grey eyes melts for a second, then freezes solid in an instant.

"Why not? You're very good at it," she says bitterly.

"I left for a good reason, Callie. I had to let you move on with your life. Without me."

"Why, Declan? Why? All that bullshit you spouted at me never made any sense. We were good together, I thought. We were planning a life together. Then, suddenly... 'Gotta go, babe. No hard feelings, huh?'" she says, mimicking my deeper voice.

I know I didn't say that, regardless of what else I did say. But maybe it seemed like that to her.

"It was for the best, Callie. I'd had a wakeup call that night, at that hotel gig, and it made me realize how much my life was going to be changing, and how incompatible that life was with us being together. It wouldn't have been fair to you."

"Wasn't that my choice to make? I mean, what could have changed so much for you at 17 that the plans we'd made were doomed to failure? We'd had two years apart, with just the summers in between. We'd managed the long-distance thing already, proven we could handle it. Anything else, we could have worked it out... I knew we could. If we loved each other. And I certainly loved you..."

A tiny spark of hope kindles in that hole in my chest, then gutters out when I realize I have to explain it to her, realize *what* I have to make clear to her, after all these years.

"You know I have a reputation."

"No, I don't know. What's your reputation?"

She's serious. Not a hint of sarcasm in her.

And now I'm reluctant to say it. Fuck — it's *killing* me to say it. I honestly figured she'd know. It's not like I haven't been in the headlines of every gossip site on the internet for the last ten years. I assumed she'd have followed my career to some degree after what we'd meant to each other a decade ago. But you know what they say about making assumptions... And god knows I'm a well-established asshole. That's the other major part of my reputation, even.

Callie is looking at me expectantly, like she doesn't really want to know but since I brought it up, she needs me to tell her anyway.

"Manwhore."

She looks stunned. A little disgusted, perhaps. And out of her comfort zone.

"I guess I should have known you'd go all-in on groupies once you gave up on us," she says bitterly.

"I never gave up on *us*. I gave up on me being a good partner to you. And, yeah, afterward, I went all-in. If I couldn't keep it in my pants anyway, I might as well enjoy it."

"I shouldn't be surprised. When you left, you all but told me that's what you wanted from your career."

"It wasn't what I *wanted*. But it comes part and parcel with the job, and I'm good at my job, including attracting female fans. And since I was single, I enjoyed myself. Regularly. I refuse to be ashamed of that. And it's not like you locked yourself in a convent for the last twelve years."

She's looking at her feet, the table, the stove, the door... anywhere but at me.

My blood runs cold. There's no way...

"Callie... You have had other boyfriends since I left, haven't you? Other guys in your bed?"

Her eyes glance right back off me as they make a reluctant pass over my face. She's looking over my head now. She never could lie worth a damn.

"Callie... Tell me you've been with someone since me. Tell me you went to culinary school and got your brains fucked out by some hotshot pastry chef, or you hooked up with a regular rotation of waiters at one of your restaurant jobs..."

"I went to culinary school and got my brains fucked out by a hotshot pastry chef, and I hooked up with dozens of waiters at one of my restaurant jobs," she parrots back at me, repeating too closely what I told her I wanted to hear.

"Fucking shit!"

She quails at my sudden outburst. It's the first time I've ever seen her intimidated by anything — other than when she ran from me at Hunter and Brighid's engagement party. I'm running my fingers through my hair in pure consternation, leaving it spiked up in a reflection of my emotional state.

"You broke me, Declan," she says quietly. "I've tried to tell you. I've tried to explain exactly how badly broken I was when you left. Did you think I was exaggerating?"

"But why, Callie? You should have gone on with your life when I left. I set you free for a reason. I didn't want you tied to me like that when I couldn't promise that I'd be faithful. When I *knew* I couldn't be faithful. Why would you have done that?" There's a tortured tone to my voice that wakes me up to the fact that I'm actually feeling genuinely horrible about this. At what I've done to her life.

"I haven't trusted anyone enough to get close to them since the day you dumped me, Declan. I barely had friends, let alone a boyfriend. I put everything I had into the one dream I had left — my restaurant. I dedicated myself to it, and I made it happen." She gestures around us.

"You can't work to the exclusion of having a real life, Callie. It's a hollow existence. I at least have my bandmates and my momentary pleasures, traveling around the world..."

"Maybe it is a little hollow," she admits with a nod. "But I'm used to it."

*Holy fuck...*

I'm shaking my head, still not quite able to believe what I'm hearing.

"No one? Not one guy? Hell — not one girl?"

"No, Declan. No one. Why does that bother you so much? Being celibate hasn't been that horrible."

"It isn't who you were, who you *are*, Callie. It wasn't what I wanted for you. Not at all. I wanted you to move on with your life, find some nice guy who could be faithful to you, support your dreams — the things I couldn't do with the career I had ahead of me."

"Yeah, well... it seems neither of us got what we wanted."

She sounds like that satisfies her, that I didn't get what I wanted when I broke things off with her, even though what I wanted was for her to be happy and loved.

The bitter taste of this conversation is only getting stronger, like I need to drink something just to cleanse my palate. Salt and lime to chase this emotional equivalent of shitty tequila. Damn — now *I'm* thinking in food metaphors. This girl is right back in my head. Where she's been sitting for the last twelve years, if I'm honest...

"I need a drink."

"That makes two of us."

We look at each other, and we're in total agreement for the first time since I dumped her.

"The bar's through here." She gestures toward the dining room, and I follow.

"What do you even drink these days?" she asks. "We weren't even legal when I knew you before... or thought I did," she adds with a frown of disapproval.

"Whiskey. Jameson if you've got it. Hunter drank all of Kier's, so he's hiding it in his room now. Definitely not tequila."

She glances back at me with a raised eyebrow.

"I just don't want anything requiring salt and lime. Too close to home at this moment."

"I need a chaser to get the taste of this conversation out of my mouth," she replies.

I give her a look.

"What?"

"That's why I said no salt and lime."

"We're brain-sharing again, aren't we?"

I nod gravely.

"Fuck," she says, instantly looking exhausted.

She hands me a glass of Jameson before knocking back her own and immediately refilling her glass.

"I can't do this, Declan. I spent years ensuring I wouldn't even hear your name, let alone your voice, wouldn't see you online... I couldn't tell you the name of a single band that had a Top 40 song in more than a decade. That's how total my avoidance has been of anything that could possibly have anything to do with you. And in the space of one night, all of that was destroyed. What little peace of mind it gave me is gone. And I need that back. I need you gone from my life. Again. This is just too bitter a pill to swallow."

I down my Jameson and put the glass back on the bar, hoping she'll actually refill it. Because now I *really* need a drink. She'd dropped back into my life like a gift from heaven, and I'd sworn I wasn't going to let her go again. And she not only doesn't want me back — she wants me *gone*.

But I didn't come by my reputation as a selfish asshole by accident.

"Then let me give you a taste of something sweet instead," I tell her, grabbing the hand that's reaching for my empty glass and pulling her hard against me.

She's too stunned to push me away, and I take advantage of having disarmed her so thoroughly, diving straight for those luscious lips I've dreamed of for years and wrapping my hand around her neck to pull them against mine. The kiss is hard and heavy, almost punishing, and it's not just me. She's kissing me back with a ferocity that I both didn't expect from her now and knew from our life before that she had in her. Our teeth clash, our tongues tangle together, wrestling for control, for dominance in this whiskey-flavored kiss laced with unexpected passion.

I wrap my other hand around her waist and pull her sharply against me. I'm already hard, having longed to touch her again for so many years, and I know she can feel me through our clothes. Too many layers between us. I slide my hand up under the back of her shirt. Her skin is as soft and smooth as I remembered, especially with my fingers having lost most of their calluses in the years I've spent at the mic instead of behind a guitar.

She moans as my fingertips trace up her spine, grasping at my arms as if she wants to pull us closer, but we're already as close as we can get without shedding some of these clothes. Which sounds like a great idea. I reach for her hand and press it to the hard-earned six-pack underneath my T-shirt. She's panting hard between kisses. So am I. I want this girl — my girl — so badly. I'm not sure I'll make it until we can get all our clothes off.

"Callie! The back door was open. Are you out front?"

*Shit.*

Callie's eyes open, startled — panicked, even. She pushes me hard away from her, still breathing hard.

"Yeah — I'll be back there in a second!" she calls out toward the kitchen.

"Get out, Declan. Just get out," she growls at me.

"Callie — we need to talk about this, about us."

"I'm done talking, Declan. I was done talking to you, about you, twelve years ago. Please leave me alone. You did it once already, so I know you can do it again."

"I don't want—"

"I don't *care* what you want. You didn't care about what *I* wanted a dozen years ago. And I've come too far to let anyone do that to me ever again. Especially you. So just get out."

I sigh, knowing I'm not winning her over with her staff fifteen feet away. I raise my hands in surrender, walk to the front door to the restaurant and unlock it to let myself out. Despite the gesture, I'm not going to back away from this challenge, and she should know me better than to think I will.

"I'll be back, Callie. I'm not giving up on this, on us. I did it once, but I won't repeat that mistake, not now that I know you still love me."

"I don't love you, you egotistical asshole."

"That kiss told me otherwise. As did your too-long-empty bed. So, I'll be back. And I'm going to prove to you what you should already know, since we're brain-sharing again: We're meant to be together. I'm not going away until you admit it, and then I'm never letting you go again."

# Callie

I resist the temptation to hurl the whiskey glass at Declan's head. Barely. Which is a good thing, since there's a dozen eyes clustered to watch me through the open kitchen door.

Great. Just great.

There are very few gossip mills more efficient than a restaurant kitchen. Everyone who works for me will know about this in an hour. And their friends will all know by the end of the day. Especially since Mr. Rock God takes pride in everyone knowing his face. God, he looks sexy with that scruff and his hair grown out. *What the hell am I even thinking?* There's no way my staff will keep quiet about this. If I'm lucky, the paparazzi have all left town after Brighid's short-lived scandal with Hunter and his blackmailing ex.

Let's hope I *am* lucky. I've got enough to deal with already, between this gossip and the dick who is my own ex. I may not have seen or talked to him in the last twelve years, but if I know anything about Declan Carter, it's that he doesn't give up easily when he decides he's going to go for what he wants. And he'll bulldoze his way through anyone who stands in his way.

"What are you all standing there for? Get to work on the lunch prep! I can't do it all myself. Well, I could. But I won't. Move it!"

At least I know *they'll* do what I tell them.

Declan, unfortunately, can't be counted upon to do anything he doesn't already want to do. Including staying out of my life.

## CHAPTER 9

# NOBODY'S FAULT BUT MINE

## Declan

B y the time I get back to the studio house, pent up
excitement and determination have merged with my earlier
irritation over finding my bandmate so casually hanging out with
my missing girl. So when I find Alex standing in the kitchen,
doing his laidback Alex thing, leaning back on the counter
while something sizzles in a pan nearby, like nothing unusual
happened today, I lose it.

"What the fuck, Alex? How long have you known where
she was? And why the fuck didn't you tell me? You knew I
was looking for her! I've done everything but take hostages to
get that information, and here you were not only sitting on it
without saying a word to me — you're taking fucking *cooking
lessons* from her? How long has *that* been going on?"

Alex picks up a glass of wine from the counter and coolly sips
at it before gently putting it back in place.

"Which question do you want me to answer first?"

"All of them, asshole!" I yell back at him.

Rhys' head peeks in from around the corner, looking alarmed,
but is quickly withdrawn in what has to be the first sensible thing
our drummer has done since I've known him. Alex takes on a
look of surprise that has to match the one on my face, then sighs.

"I found her by accident, a couple weeks ago. I've been
checking out the restaurants Brighid had recommended when

we first got here. I liked the food, asked to talk to the chef. Who, it turned out, was Callie."

Hearing him speak her name makes me even more furious with him.

"When she *begged* me not to tell you where she was, I agreed."

And that hits me like a bucket of ice water dumped over my head.

He looks at me carefully, scrutinizing.

"What did you do to the girl, Dec? What did you do to her that she'd run away like that, that she'd beg me not to tell you I'd seen her? That you'd piss sweet Brighid off so much, just on her friend's behalf, that she'd actually threaten to drop a curse on you?"

I avoid meeting his gaze. I don't want to tell him the whole story. Not like this. Not now. It's humiliating, shameful. I don't even want to think about it now, when I finally have some hope I can fix it, let alone relive it. Dave knows. Hunter knows. They were there. They know what I did. And I can't undo that any more than I can undo the thing I did. Where is that time machine when I need it?

"I broke up with her. A decade ago."

"That's a long time for there still to be so much emotion attached to it, for both of you."

"No kidding."

I lean forward, elbows on the kitchen island, my face buried in my hands.

I've spent twelve years burying my feelings. First, in other women, in my career, and then in my penance... Callie clearly buried hers in her work.

But still... that kiss today. We're both still feeling it — her, the love and the pain, me the love and the guilt. If I can just get us both past the pain, past the guilt, and back to the love, I can fix all of this.

Alex waits in silence, clearly hoping to draw me out. When I say nothing, he flips over the contents of the pan, turns off the heat and then positions himself on the other side of the kitchen island, leaning in to me.

"Why are you *really* so bent out of shape about this girl? The day after the engagement party, you told me she was old news, an ex from way back in your past. Brighid said she doesn't date. Ever. What's the big deal?"

"She's my *wife*! Alright?"

Alex's jaw drops.

"What? Your wife? Since when are you married?"

"Not legally. We were just kids." I sigh. "Well, not kids. Teenagers. Under-age. It was the end of our third summer together, and David and I were heading home in a couple weeks. And she and I didn't want to be separated again... not without something tying us together until we could be together again. We wanted to get married, but you had to have parental consent if you were under 18, and the 'rents weren't on board with a couple of 17-year-olds getting serious and then maybe not going to college as planned."

And we know how that worked out, regardless. Mom and Dad are still holding my lack of a college degree against Hunter, ten years and three platinum albums later.

"So we did the next best thing — a religious ceremony. She had a friend who was 20, registered as a minister, legally able to perform a marriage. But it wasn't legal without a marriage license, and we were too young to get one.

"Honestly," I admit, looking Alex in the eye, "it didn't matter to either of us whether it was legal. We belonged together. We knew it. Her friend *told* us that... A second-generation Pagan priestess." He gives me a significant look. "No — Brighid was not the first witch I'd met." I sigh. "She said she *knew* we were destined to be together. 'I'm just cementing what was already meant to be,' she told us. I believed her. There was just something about her, a certainty, that made me believe her. It's a lot of woo, I know. But I knew in my bones, down to the marrow, that this was right. So we had a ceremony, and we promised ourselves to each other 'forever.'"

I laugh, but it's painful and wry.

"She — the friend — asked us how long we wanted the ceremony to bind us to each other. The tradition was a year and a day, she said, with the option to 're-up,' or we could pledge ourselves for a lifetime, or forever. And neither of us hesitated for a moment. 'Forever.' We said it at the same moment — that's how connected we were. 'Brain-sharing' we used to call it.

"'Are you sure?' the friend, the priestess, asked us. 'When I marry people, it sticks.'"

I look up at him, seeking mercy I know he can't grant.

"She warned us. Can't say she didn't warn us." I shake my head, marveling that I was such a hopeless romantic at 17 that that was exactly what I'd wanted.

"And now, more than a decade later, you still consider her your wife?" Alex asks.

"Yes. No... I don't know... It's complicated."

I run my fingers through my overgrown hair, trying to find something solid to grasp onto. The thing I latch onto is almost tangible — my own guilt, and the story I never wanted to tell.

"I fucked up, Alex. I cheated on her. Days after we got married. And I don't even remember doing it."

# Declan
## *Twelve years ago, six days after the wedding*

"Great work, boys! Just great!"

Phil loves us. Hell — everybody loves us. That's how he got a trio of gifted teenage musicians, plus one mediocre drummer, booked to play a bar in a hotel in Ocean City. We'd killed it, too. Had the entire crowd at the bar up and dancing, and kept them dancing — which is the key to future bookings, since dancing patrons drink and keep drinking. And some of these people had been drinking before we went on and were still drinking now that we'd left the stage.

"Head on up to the hospitality suite. I've got some clients and their friends coming by, and they want to meet you. Help yourself to the goodies!" Phil says, handing me a key card with the room number on it. With only a few doors on that floor of the hotel, you know the suite has to be huge, though when we get off the elevator it sounds like the party hasn't gotten started there yet. I wouldn't mind just chilling out and calling Callie to see how her interview went.

But that's not happening. The suite is pretty well sound-proofed, because the second I open the door, it's clear there's a raging party going on inside.

"Woohoo! The boys are here!"

Oh, man... It's that blonde from the bar. The one whose tits were barely staying inside her top and who wanted to make sure I knew it wouldn't take much for them to be unleashed. It's happened before. It'll happen again. Hopefully, for years to come, because that'll mean we're a success. She's definitely too old to be hitting on a 17-year-old, though, even if she's drunk. And she's *really* drunk now. Sloshed.

But, hey — we have to play nice with fans and with business contacts if we're going to keep that level of success and build on it. So when she puts a death grip on my arm and drags me over to one of the sofas, I go with her. Grudgingly, but willingly.

"You're so talented!" she practically shouts in my ear. "I bet you've got other talents, too — just more private ones than you show off on stage." The hand that isn't clamped to my arm lands on my thigh. I can't say I'm thrilled about that, and I tense up.

"Ooh — you're so wound up after being on stage! You need to relax... I think we can find you something to relax you," she says. "Marcie — bring this young hottie over here something to drink so he can relax and enjoy the fun!" she calls across the room.

A tall brunette, even older than she is and displaying only slightly less cleavage, brings me over a cup of I don't know what.

"Drink up, sweetie! It's time to celebrate!" the blonde insists. She shoves the cup into my hand, and when I don't immediately start drinking, she raises it to my lips herself. I've got no problems indulging in a little post-gig fun. My parents keep kind of a close eye on me and Dave when we're at home. Dave's happy to stay in, but I'm fond of a party — especially one where I'm the most popular person in the room. And this party may not be taking advantage of a classmate's parents being out of town, but I'm definitely the center of attention here.

Schmoozing with the fans. Schmoozing with Phil's clients. It's part of the job, especially when you're the frontman of the band. There's no better feeling than knowing you've entertained people so well that they're desperate to meet you, hang out with you. It's a feeling I've begun to crave, more than I'd ever thought I would.

Blondie's still got her hand on my thigh, but it's bugging me less now. Maybe I did just need to relax. Marcie and a couple other ladies are gathered around, telling me how great the show was, how amazing my voice is, how hot I am... They all agreed that the Carter Brothers Band is destined for greatness. And it's nice to hear that I'm not the only one who thinks so.

I lose track of time, of how many times the ladies have refilled my cup. I have a little weed to help take the post-performance edge off. But the party's gotten even wilder than it was when we arrived, with people spilling out into the hallway now and someone's got the music blaring. There's dancing happening. I'm not doing it, but there are several short skirts shaking their thing right in front of my face. Blondie's hand has made its way up to my crotch, and she's now stroking me through my jeans. Man, so many drinks... I should probably go pee. I start to get up. Unsuccessfully.

Blondie grabs my hand and stands up, but when she pulls me up, I wobble and bump into a couple of the dancers.

"Sorry, ladies! Looks like I need a hand!"

"I can give you a hand, honey. Come with me!" the blonde says. I'm not sure how she's going to help me get across the room when she's wobbling even worse than I am, but hey, maybe the two of us can manage to make it work together, like training wheels on a bike. Sounds like a plan.

I'm now holding myself up by leaning against the wall of the hallway inside the suite. And blondie, too, because she's draped on me like ragdoll, though she's still got a firm grip on her cup. Before I do anything else, I've got to get her somewhere she can lie down before she falls over and takes me with her.

"Let's go this way," I tell her, pulling her down the hallway with me. "You need to lie down."

"Yeah... lying down sounds like a great idea."

I manage to get us to one of the bedrooms in the suite and lay her across the bed.

"Shit!" I forgot about her drink. Which is now all over me. And there's no way I'll make it back down the hall to the bathroom. Blondie seems to be passed out now, and I'm not counting on making it more than a couple steps from where I stand, weaving back and forth. I push her over to the other side of the bed and sit, shucking off my soaked shirt and... what the hell — my damp jeans, too. She's too wasted to even know there's anyone else in the room. Just need to take a breather and get my bearings again.

## *Four hours later*

"Fucking shit!"

There is a naked blonde passed out in bed with me. And she's not the only one who's naked.

I jump straight up out of the bed, like it's on fire... Need to get out of this room, out of this hotel, back to my girl...

Oh. My. God. I'm a married man naked in bed with some fake-ass blonde, who is very much not my very beautiful, very brunette and very teenage wife.

Callie!

"Fuck! Fuck! Fuck! Fuck! Fuck! Fuckity fuck!"

I have to think of a way to fix this. There's got to be some way. Can we turn back time twelve hours and I go home to Mom like some normal teenager? Maybe just ten hours, and I don't take that cup. Need a damn time machine either way. Maybe when I'm 30 and rich I can buy one and then go back and undo this nightmare.

At this point, I'm frantically pacing back and forth in the living area of the suite, trying to think of anything I can do to make this better.

*"Sorry, angel! I didn't mean to cheat on you with a woman who's nearly twice my age, but she kept refilling my cup with something other than soda."*

*"Can't remember actually doing anything, therefore nothing actually happened! Right?"*

*"I know we just got married like six days ago, but I'm apparently a teenage manwhore and I had no idea that was going to be a problem until right this moment."*

"Dude — put some clothes on!" my brother says, only barely awake. "I haven't had to see that since we were kids. I have no desire to see it again now. Or ever."

Who gives a shit about him seeing my naked ass? It's blondie in there who shouldn't have seen that little mole on the bottom of my left cheek that Callie — *my wife* — loves so much.

Hunter grabs a blanket off the sofa and hurls it at me, and I go ahead and wrap it around me. Because Davey and his quaint sensibilities. How is he even going to survive the rock-and-roll lifestyle we've got coming our way? And why am I having to worry about that when I've got this giant shitstorm to deal with? I glare at him.

"What's up, Dec?" Hunter asks.

"There's a blonde in my bed."

"There's a brunette in mine. Wanna trade?"

Hunter's smiling at me as if this is amusing, and I want to just grab hold of his stupid Hunter face and tear it off, feed it to the seagulls. He can't possibly think this is funny. I settle for a glare.

"You cheated on her?" David asks solemnly.

And that's it right there. A naked woman in bed with naked me, and who's not my Callie, who was supposed to come to the gig last night so I could try to sneak her backstage and finally let her see us — me — perform in a real venue before the summer was over, and Dave and I head back to Virginia for our junior years. But Callie had a closing-time job interview at a local fine-dining restaurant, hoping to kickstart her career as a chef next summer, so she'd missed this gig, too.

And now this. Me, cheating on her with some stranger I don't even remember kissing, let alone fucking, because I was stupid and got wasted on booze and weed in the hospitality suite after our gig.

"Where the fuck is Phil?"

"Did I hear my name?"

Phil comes down the hall, wearing more than I am, but still not nearly enough. To add insult to injury, the universe has seen fit to send him my way wearing only boxers, an undershirt and dress socks.

"You sure as fuck did, Phil! What the hell was this scene here last night? You brought a bunch of minors back to a room full of liquor and groupies?"

"Hey, hold on a minute now," Phil says, immediately defensive. "The people who attended your post-performance party were clients and friends, not groupies. If some of them happened to be very big fans who wanted to wish you well as your career takes off under my tutelage and offered toasts involving alcoholic beverages, I can't be held responsible for that."

"You sure as fuck can, Phil," David points out, and I'm glad my brother, for once, will take a stand about something. "Providing alcohol to minors is a crime, in Maryland or Delaware."

"Oh, like you all have never gotten wasted at a party before..." Phil says.

"I haven't. I didn't last night," Dave says, and I'm tempted to punch in his goody-goody face, but Mom would kill me. "Slept alone, sober, and was doing just fine until my brother started screaming his head off. Naked."

*Get over it, man. We've all got the same parts, even if some of us were gifted with a more generous set of male anatomy.*

"So what's the big deal? You all aren't exactly teetotaling virgins here. You're objecting to booze and some pussy?"

"Declan's got a girl." Dave explains, and I'm glad he does, because right now I'm so pissed at Phil — and myself, really — that I'm not sure I could say anything coherent.

"Hey — not my fault you can't keep your dick in your pants after a few beers, man..."

I lunge for him, and the only thing that stops me from ripping *his* stupid face off is my brother's arm around my neck. Dave's shorter than me by an inch or two, but we've had enough fights over the years that he's learned I won't risk my vocal cords by fighting a choke hold.

Phil's showing a tiny amount of intelligence by backpedaling down the hallway.

"You're fired, Phil!" I tell him. This asshole, who makes light of boozing us up and letting me get so out of my mind that I fucking cheated on Callie. He's not making another dime off of us.

"And you all are done here! You won't book another gig on the peninsula once I get done with you!" he yells back. I'm ready to test that threat, because his weasely ass has a lot less to recommend itself than my voice.

"Dec — you realize Phil doesn't actually work for us, right? He's a promoter, not our manager."

"Oh. Yeah. Right."

Man, I can't even get firing this asshole right today. Can't do anything right. Oh, shit... Callie...

"I can't believe I fucking did that. I don't even remember touching that woman, other than her grabbing onto my arm when we got here. I was drunk, but I'd remember that, wouldn't I?"

"Depends, man," Hunter says. "I've had nights I got home from a party and didn't remember whether it had been two girls or three."

Hunter's changed a lot in the last year. He'd gone from hanging out with that girl who made puppy-dog eyes at him all the time and followed us around like a lost pet, to happily taking older women to bed and not even blinking.

"What?" he says. "I got very popular last year after the talent show at school. I've been busy making up for lost time."

Dave shakes his head.

"I want to tell you to just be honest with her, Dec," he finally says. "But I don't think that's going to cut it here. We're on the verge of breaking through, and you're going to have a lot more nights like this one from now on. If you can't be faithful to the girl now, what's it going to be like when we're on the road for four months at a time?"

And the worst part of this is I know Dave's right. Last night was the tip of the iceberg on the lifestyle I know we'll be living in a few years, which would be great, except for one thing: I love my wife! Granted, I haven't told anyone that we're married yet and it's not exactly legal, but I promised the girl forever, and I fucking meant it! Too bad my rockstar ass couldn't make it even a week without screwing around on her.

"Well, are we actually breaking through anywhere now that Phil's decided to ruin us?" Hunter asks.

I'm not sure my day could have gotten any worse, but that's a thought that chills me to the bone. To have gone through all this work to break out and now to almost certainly lose Callie over this stupid mistake, and the band could be over before we really began.

"He won't do a thing, Hunter," Dave assures him. "We're under-age, and he supplied alcohol to a party he encouraged us to attend, and which he attended, fully aware we were drinking. He's got nothing to leverage against us that won't end up with him in jail. And I'm going to remind him of that right now."

Dave heads down the hall.

"Well, at least we still have a career ahead of us," Hunter says.

"Yeah. That's going to have to happen, since the rest of my life just imploded."

He pats me on the back, and I know that support is all he's got for me in this shitty situation. Because there's no coming back from this with Callie, and I know that as surely as I know I'll never love anyone like this ever again.

# CHAPTER 10

# SHIP OF FOOLS

## *Present*

"So, you married her, and a week later, you got drunk after a gig and cheated on her with some cougar?"

Alex looks like he can't quite believe it. Welcome to the club. "Yeah..."

"So what did you tell her?"

"I dodged her for a day while I tried to figure out what to say. I mean — I couldn't just pretend nothing had happened, right? It was either confess what I'd done and beg her forgiveness, which I knew I didn't deserve, or accept that I was a scumbag cheater who didn't deserve *her* and let her go, so she could find some guy who *was* good enough for her."

I look up and catch Alex's gaze.

"She was an *amazing* girl, Alex. Way out of my league. Smart, sexy, incredibly talented in the kitchen, even then."

"She still is."

I grimace at the reminder that he's been taking cooking lessons from her for weeks now.

"I have no doubt. She had a way with food that was almost... magical. I wasn't a foodie or anything, not like you are. But I knew what I liked, and everything she cooked just left me in awe. It made you feel good, you know? Like a vacation for the senses. I knew she had a bright future ahead of her. I'd thought maybe we could have that and still be together. Until I fucked it all up in one night."

"So, what did you decide? You said you broke up with her, so I assume you didn't tell her you'd cheated."

"I told myself I was trying to make it easier on her, to hurt her less than I would if I told her what I'd done, but now... I think maybe I was just too much of a coward to admit it. I couldn't handle it, even the idea of how she'd see me if she knew. Even if she never spoke to me again, I couldn't deal with her thinking she hadn't been enough for me, when she was all I thought I'd ever need."

"So what'd you say?"

"I lied."

## *Twelve years ago*

"Did you at least manage to get some sleep? Working all day yesterday with the band, you had to be wiped out!"

Callie wraps her arms around me from behind, pressing a quick kiss to my neck.

"Not really. I was too wound up."

"Well, I'd love to help you work off all that tension," she says, rubbing my shoulders, her beautiful brown hair sweeping across my collarbone, "but Nonna's expecting me at the restaurant in like half an hour."

"You're sweet. You have no idea how much I appreciate that."

"It's just me, loving you."

I freeze. This is the point where I have to say it. I can't let her words stand, unreplied to.

The silence hangs between us, growing uncomfortable.

"I can't do this, Callie."

"Well, like I said, I have to go soon anyway. We can enjoy some more time together tomorrow, before I go to work."

"No, Callie." I turn around to face her, pulling her hands from my shoulders. "I mean I can't do *this* — us." I gesture between us.

"What?"

"The last couple days... I realized that this band thing — it's for real. I mean, I've always thought we had it in us, but performing in a hotel bar, all the fans, all the... groupies..." I cringe as the word hits her, her eyes going wide. "We're going to be big, Callie. Like national — maybe even international — tours big. We're going to be on the road constantly, surrounded by... people."

And by "people" she knows I mean groupies. Again.

"I don't think us trying to keep this long-distance thing going is going to work," I say, knowing we'd already proven it was possible. She's not going to buy it just because I say it. "It's not fair to either of us to commit to one person when we're this young, with all we've got ahead of us. You're going to be going to culinary school, in New York probably, and I'm going to be in D.C., in college, working with the band, until we get signed anyway, and then I'll be on the road all the time."

"With people."

She says it slowly, carefully, like she's still absorbing what the words mean.

"I think we've been a little naive, thinking about college, culinary school," I say. "I don't know how we would ever have made it work, living in different cities, getting our first adult experiences in life, but separately. It's a recipe for a break-up."

"So, you want to break up now, before any of that even happens."

I nod.

"Even though we got married a week ago."

"It wasn't legal, Callie. You know that. And I think it's better that way. If we kept this going another year, or even a few months, then we might have gone ahead and made it legal, and then we'd have a big, costly mess to fix."

"A mess. To fix. Our marriage. You look at me, your wife of seven days, and you see a mess that will have to be fixed."

"That's not exactly what I meant. I'm explaining this badly." I shake my head, knowing that part, at least is true. "But the bottom line is I think we have to do this — break up. It's the best thing for both of us."

"And you've decided this. In the last two days. You don't even want to see how the last couple weeks of the summer go?"

She's giving me a chance to change my mind here. She's begging me to. And I can't let her hope. I can't let her put her hope in me, the dick who cheated on her with someone he can't even remember being with.

"I need to be free," I finally say. "I can't be tied down with a wife at 17, 18, when we're going to be touring soon, and I'm going to be putting all my energy into promoting the band, trying to sell us to fans."

"And people."

She suspects what I'm trying to tell her, or rather what I'm trying to avoid telling her. And I can't let her think that she wasn't enough for me. She's everything. Even if I have to give her up, I can't let her think she wasn't enough.

"Callie... I didn't decide this lightly. I've been thinking really hard about it these last couple of days... And I just realized... I realized... I mean — I'm only 17. You're only 17. What do we know about love at 17, let alone marriage?"

"I know I love you."

"Well... I don't," I say in desperation. "I don't know that I love you. Not like I should. I mean, I must not, since I'm breaking up with you."

She looks hurt. Beyond hurt. So hurt I can't think straight. This was what I was trying to avoid. And the words... they just fell out of my mouth. And I can't take it back. Not now. I've got to see this through, make it my fault. Because it sure isn't hers.

"You don't love me."

"I don't think I ever really did." That's better. That makes it an "It's not you — it's me" thing. It's still not true. At least it's better. But she looks at the floor, won't meet my eyes. "It was a crush, Callie. Puppy-love, maybe. We're 17. There's a reason our parents flipped out when we started talking about getting married. They knew we were too young to know what love's really like."

"I knew. I know. I love you, Declan!"

She's looking at me now, but the tears are flowing down her cheeks, and I can't handle it. I turn away from her, trying to think of anything that will make this a clean break, that will ensure she isn't pining after me, hoping I'll change my mind. Maybe what it'll take is having her hate me. Maybe then she'll be able to move on, go off to culinary school next fall and find some nice New York banker or something who'll treat her like she deserves.

"I just can't do this, Callie. The life ahead of me is the life of a rockstar. This week proved that to me. And all the things that come with that... Touring, promotions, having a label trying to sell us to female fans. I mean — backstage at these shows — it's all sex, drugs and rock-and-roll. That's not something you want to be around."

"And you do?"

"It's just part of the life, Callie. Drinking, a little pot... hot-and-cold-running blowjobs..."

I don't know what made me say that. I mean, it's true. Maybe that night in the hotel suite is too fresh in my head. I've been trying to picture what happened, the bits I can't remember, and that seems like the sort of thing that might have happened. So maybe it got stuck in my subconscious. But I've said it now. Can't take it back any more than I can take back what happened that night, or telling Callie I never loved her. I've truly and royally fucked this up. All of it. Every word I say is just making it worse.

"Callie?"

She's been quiet for a while now.

"You stupid shallow, arrogant, immature bastard!" She shouts, rounding on me.

Whoa!

"You stand on the boardwalk, begging for change, for attention, for a couple of summers, and you decide you're the world's gift to music and women. Not enough of you to go around, I guess? Is this what you planned all this time? Have you been sleeping with the girls at school, too, and I'm just a convenient lay for the summer?"

"What? No! I just... I..." I'm at a loss for what to say now. If I'd wanted her to hate me, it seems I succeeded.

And suddenly, the idea of her hating me is almost more than I can bear. I consider, for just a moment, coming clean with her, telling her I slipped, once, and I don't even remember it, but that I'll love her until my dying breath, beg her to forgive me, make her understand that all of this has been a lie I thought would make it easier for her... if only she can forgive me...

"Get out! Get out of here right now, Declan Carter! I never want to see you again! Forget I exist, because I surely will be forgetting you ever did. Lesson learned. Never again!"

What does she mean by that?

She shoves me toward the door of her room, and I'm so taken aback by the ferocity of it that I just let her push me right out the front door of the house. She yanks on the chain around her neck, throws it at me. Instinctively, I duck. She slams the door in my face. There's a sound of something sliding against the door, and I think maybe she's put a chair in front of the door as a blockade against me. But then I hear it. Sobbing, down by the base of the door. I raise my hand, ready to knock, to beg her to let me back in, let me take it all back.

But I can't do that. I made this bed, and now I've got to lie in it. She's better off without me. Truly. This just proved it. A cheating bastard. Just like she said, even though she was wrong about when and who. Let her hate that guy. He deserves it. Fucking asshole rockstar. Can't keep his dick in his pants.

And that's the only future I have now. Any future I might have had with her has been obliterated. He fucked her over. Fucked us both over. Declan Carter, husband, is dead. Declan Carter, rockstar — he doesn't have time for love. He's going to be a legend.

## *Present*

"You know... Back in the day, I told Hunter he was either the stupidest smart person I'd ever seen or the smartest stupid person," Alex says, sounding reflective. "And he was. He still is, as the last couple months have proven. You," he continues, pointing at me, "are just plain stupid."

He shakes his head.

"What is it with the two of you? Why is your automatic response to hurting the women you love to then tell them that you don't love them? As if that is somehow going to make things better?"

"In my defense, I was 17. Most 17-year-old boys are stupid. I freely admit it. I was stupid. All the more reason to spare Callie having to deal with my stupidity. It made sense at the time."

"I'm not sure you shouldn't spare her your stupidity now."

"Hey! I'm trying to fix this!"

"And exactly how do you propose to do that? She hates your guts! She was talking about dancing on your grave!"

"Ow."

"Yeah."

"But she doesn't hate me — not really!" I argue. "She's still in love with me!"

"Why do you think that?"

"She kissed me!" I smile brightly at him, reveling in the memory. "Well, technically, *I* kissed *her*. But she kissed me back!"

"Did she *tell you* she loves you?" He's looking skeptical, and I can see why, but I won't take anyone raining on my parade today. Not after Callie kissed me.

"No. But it was right there, between the lines."

"I see..."

"Besides, the opposite of love isn't hate — it's ambivalence! And she is *so far* from ambivalent toward me that it's obvious she still has feelings for me."

"I think they call that feeling hatred, Declan."

"Nope. That's not it. If she'd stopped loving me, she'd have gone off to culinary school and moved on with some investment banker or pastry chef or something. But she didn't! She never got over me. I can see that now. She hates me because she hates the fact that she still loves me. After twelve years! That's the best news I've had all week! All year! Hell, in the last twelve years!"

"Better news than getting signed to a record deal?"

I have to think about that, and the fact that I have to think about it gives me the answer.

"Yup! Even better than that!"

Alex tilts his head and scratches his eyebrow.

"Alrighty then..." he says. "So, what's your plan for fixing this?"

"The way to a man's heart is through his stomach. The way to a chef's heart is through her cooking!"

# CHAPTER 11

## FOREVER YOUNG

## Declan
### *Thirteen years ago*

I peek around the half-open door, breathing in the scents of sauce, pasta, seafood and fresh produce. The aromas overwhelm anything else, including the sea air outside. But I can still smell my favorite fragrance in the world: Calliope Martino — a subtle floral scent, warm, with just a hint of spice, and a delicious light herbal layer over it all, from whatever she most recently added to a pot of pure yum.

OK. Being able to detect Callie's scent across a busy restaurant kitchen may just be in my imagination, but these days I know that scent better than my own shampoo, and I'm about as eager to dive face-first into it as I am to taste her Nonna's cooking, which is what I'm here for today. Callie invited me to come have lunch with her in her Nonna's restaurant! After more than a year, I'm finally worthy of entering the sacred space that is the kitchen!

"Arturo! Welcome!"

I've been spotted by the silver-haired woman wielding a wooden spoon, and her bright smile reminds me strongly of Callie. The resemblance between them is clear — slightly taller than average height, prominent shoulders and lots of curves (even more ample in Nonna's case), capped by eyes nearly the same shade as her hair. I instantly loved her.

But Arturo? Maybe Nonna is starting to have memory problems?

"Mrs. Martino! It's Declan — thank you for having me!"

"Nonna, call him by his name, please! No more of this 'Arturo' nonsense!" Callie calls from across the kitchen.

"I'll call him Arturo if I please, darling granddaughter — this is my kitchen!"

"Nonna has declared that you are 'Arturo' to her, Declan," Callie explains, wiping her hands on her apron as she approaches and grabs my hand. "She says you remind her of King Arthur, the Great Bear."

"Oh. Well, I won't complain about being compared to a king, or being called 'Great.'"

"See — I told you, Angelica — 'Arturo' fits him!"

Angelica? That must be Callie's middle name. It hasn't come up. But then we're apparently focused on names today, so why not now?

"Come sit over here, Declan — we get the chef's table!"

Callie gives me a wink as she shows me to a tiny table in the corner of the kitchen that's set for two. I hold a chair out for her, but she shakes her head.

"Nonna's letting me cook the appetizer by myself!"

She reaches for a bottle of wine from a rack nearby.

"Angelica!" her grandmother calls, her back still turned to us. "Put that back where you found it! You're going to get me in trouble! This is a restaurant, not our kitchen at home."

"Nonna! Just one glass!"

"When you cook Arturo a meal in our home, you may serve wine. Not here, Calliope!"

Callie looks at me and frowns, giving a little pout. I crook a finger at her, and she leans into me. I give her a peck on the lips and whisper, "It's fine. I'd much rather taste you than even the finest wine."

The hungry smile she gives me shoots straight to my heart. Then the feeling immediately dips south. I grab one of the cloth napkins from the table and seat myself, napkin in my lap, so no one can see. Callie's smile shifts from enticing to knowing. She's got my number, that's for sure. God, this girl is hot.

She sets a plate in the middle of the table.

"Focaccia col Formagio, just to whet your appetite," she says, drawling those last few words and making my napkin situation even worse.

She prances away, giving me a flirty glance over her shoulder, while I busy my hands and mouth with the crisp, flaky, cheesy bread.

I watch her move confidently around the kitchen, pulling together the ingredients for her dish — a pot of rice, cheese, herbs, breadcrumbs... What is she making?

"So, Arturo, how is your band doing? My Angelica tells me you are quite good and getting quite a following locally..." her grandmother says.

"We are, ma'am. We've gotten some bookings in some restaurants and small clubs that have live music."

"Call me Nonna, Arturo," she corrects. "You're nearly part of the family..." she adds with a knowing tone.

"Nonna!" Callie objects, a blush creeping across her cheeks and cleavage.

I look away, not wanting her to see the redness creeping into my own cheeks. I mean, I can't say I haven't had a few daydreams about what life might be with Callie when we're 20 or 25. The girl is everything I've ever dreamed of, and more, and I've only fallen deeper in love with her since we've been together this summer. But I haven't even said those three terrifying words to Callie herself, so having her grandmother talking about us getting married like it's a done deal is a lot of pressure.

"What? You make a handsome couple! And you'll make sure Arturo eats well, even while he's busy entertaining people. It's perfect!"

Callie just shakes her head, focusing on her food. She starts humming to herself while she works. It's not a melody I've heard before, but it feels like a love song. My lyricist's brain latches onto it, trying words on for size, starting to pull together a string of notes with a syllable here and there, making changes, shaping...

"Arancini, made with fresh mozzarella, and arrabbiata sauce!" Callie says, snapping me out of my headspace and placing a small plate containing three golden-brown balls atop a bright red sauce in front of me and a second one at the place setting next to me.

"Sit down, Angelica — eat! I'll bring you your entrées shortly," Nonna urges her.

I stand up, napkin issues having retreated while I was focused on the music in my mind, and hold Callie's chair out for her before I push it in behind her.

"It looks delicious," I tell her, taking her hand and kissing the back of it.

"Such manners, Arturo! Your mother taught you well!"

"She tried, Nonna," I say. "She and Dad host a lot of parties for their clients, and my brother and I have often been asked to attend, on our best behavior." We mostly managed it, even as kids. God forbid we embarrass them. I once got grounded for a week for taking too many pieces of cheddar cheese from a cheese tray, when the rest of what was on it was stinky goat cheese. Yuck!

But Callie's appetizers look and smell delicious.

"Arancini?" I ask.

"Balls of rice and cheese, coated in breadcrumbs and fried," she explains. "And the mozzarella — I made it myself!" she adds, looking down, almost like she's embarrassed. "And the arrabbiata sauce is a slightly spicy tomato sauce, designed to contrast with the creaminess of the arancini."

I dig in with fork and knife, dipping a bite in the sauce and then raising it to my mouth. It smells amazing! And with that first taste, I'm in heaven. This has to be one of the best things I've ever tasted!

"Wow, Callie. That's... Just wow."

"It's Nonna's recipe, but I added a few little touches to make it my own," she says, tasting her own portion. She nods in approval, a satisfied smile creeping across her face.

"A bite for your Nonna, Callie?" Her grandmother moves across the kitchen, fork in hand, and snatches a piece off Callie's plate, inhaling the scent before she slides it in her mouth, chewing thoughtfully.

"You used fish stock for the risotto?" she asks Callie, eyebrow raised.

"It seemed the best way to go when you were cooking seafood for the entrée," Callie says.

"Quite right," Nonna replies. "Vegetable stock is often the best choice when you're cooking in the restaurant, since not everyone will order seafood for their entrée and some of them may be allergic or vegetarians. But when you know what the entrée will be... It was a thoughtful choice, *cara mia.*"

Callie smiles proudly.

"And you added herbs to the breadcrumbs, I see."

Callie nods, looking a little nervous.

"You have to be extra-careful when you fry the arancini, so the herbs don't burn before the breadcrumbs brown."

"I know, Nonna. I was careful."

"Yes, you were..." she says, looking thoughtful, then stabbing another piece of rice ball from Callie's plate and swiping in the sauce. "Yes..."

"Something wrong, Nonna?" Callie asks.

Nonna doesn't immediately respond, continuing to chew thoughtfully.

"Nonna?"

"Hmm? No — nothing wrong at all, Angelica. In fact, the opposite..."

She looks over at me, scrutinizing, her gaze resting on me just long enough that it starts to make me uncomfortable. Then she smiles widely.

"What do you think, Arturo? Has our Callie proven her skills as a chef today?"

"Definitely, ma'am—uh... Nonna," I correct myself when her expression shifts briefly to disapproval. "Her food is wonderful!"

"Good... You children finish up your arancini, and I will finish up your entrée."

She returns to the stove and her cooking.

I take Callie's hand in mine and latch our fingers together, hands resting on my leg, while we continue to eat with our free hands.

Nonna glances back at us and smiles approvingly.

I'm not sure I've ever felt so welcomed into someone else's family before. I'm not sure I feel this welcome in my own family sometimes, really. Dave is... Well, he's Dave. A little weird, and he mostly keeps to himself. Mom and Dad... Well, like I said, they're focused on their careers, and it seems impossible sometimes to find something that really makes them proud of me.

I'd kind of hoped our musical success would do it, but lately they've been harping on my grades, saying I should spend more time and energy on schoolwork than music. But everyone who hears us loves the Carter Brothers Band — and they're paying to hear us these days. It's starting to feel like this might be the thing I do with my life. Everything else is feeling like a distraction from what's important.

Except Callie. Callie's important. And I really want to take her on this ride to the stars with me.

I squeeze her hand, giving her a smile as I finish off the last bite of arancini. She smiles back at me, and that warm feeling spreads through me again.

"Frutti di Mare Fra Diavolo," Nonna says as she places a plate of pasta and seafood in front of me, and a second in front of Callie.

"Nonna uses her arrabbiata sauce for her frutti di mare, but she gives it some extra spice," Callie warns.

"Thank you," I tell her, growing a little concerned about exactly how spicy this sauce might be. But I dig in.

The first bite is delicious — a sweet scallop with the most amazing spaghetti I've ever tasted. I get a hit of tomato and spice as the sauce hits my tongue, and I hum in enjoyment. I spear a mussel and drag it through the sauce, immediately regretting it as the spice hits twice as hard. I swallow but sputter as my mouth heats up uncomfortably.

Callie pats me on the back, looking concerned, but Nonna sweeps in with a glass of milk, which I take gratefully.

"Too spicy, Arturo?" Nonna asks, looking a little amused at my expense.

"A little," I say. "I got too much sauce on the second bite."

"Ah," Nonna says, holding out her hand. "Give me just one moment."

I hand her my plate, feeling bad that she's having to remake my food because my mouth isn't up to that much spice. But she's back a minute later, handing me what looks like the same plate.

"What did you do, Nonna?" Callie asks, clearly curious.

"I replaced my arrabbiata sauce with yours, Angelica. What was left from your arancini. Same pasta and seafood, but the spice from the little bit of my sauce clinging to them is cut with the milder flavor of yours. Try now, Arturo," she says, gesturing at me to eat.

I take a deep breath and try again, pushing myself to drag a piece of shrimp through the sauce. The flavor is similar — not quite the same as it was on the arancini earlier, and yet not as spicy as what Nonna initially served me — but somehow, it's even better. Just enough spice to set off the sweetness of the seafood and the acidity of the tomato, the texture of the pasta complementing that of the protein.

"Wow."

"Better now, yes?" Nonna says.

Callie's been holding her breath, but she releases it when I nod and smile happily.

"Of course it is," Nonna says sagely. "What Callie put into her sauce is just what you needed."

She seems to be talking about more than just how spicy the sauce is, and Callie gives her a look, as if she senses that as well.

"Eat, you two... Mangia!"

She smiles at us both and goes back to the stove, leaving Callie and me to eat quietly, sharing glances between us. I reach out and grab Callie's hand again, and she smiles back at me.

"You're amazing. You know that? You really are just what I needed."

Callie blushes, and it's far more than the spice in her grandmother's sauce that's causing it.

"You, too, Declan. You, too."

## Callie
### *Three weeks later*

"Mama, I am not at all happy with how you've handled this situation. We trusted you to be the responsible parental figure when Callie was here for all this time, and we get back from Japan to find that you've been letting her spend all of this time with a boy we don't know at all — a boy whose life dream is becoming a rockstar!"

Mama is half-pacing around the kitchen, gesturing wildly with her hands, as she does when she's agitated. Nonna is sitting calmly at the kitchen table, watching her.

"Your concern is misplaced, Mina," Nonna says, shaking her head. "Arturo — Declan — is a very nice boy. Excellent manners. And he worships your daughter." She gives me a smile where I'm standing in the doorway to the kitchen, my nerves on edge as I listen to Mama's tirade.

"And you thought it was appropriate to allow them to spend time alone, at night? Do you want Callie to ruin her life, become a teenage mother with some boy who'll disappear the moment she tells him she's pregnant?"

I look over at Nonna, knowing what she's going to say next, and knowing it's not going to go over well with my mother, with either of my parents.

"Callie is on birth control."

"What?"

Mama looks over at me, her eyes wide.

"I took her to Planned Parenthood the first week she was here this summer. She's a responsible girl. She's been taking her pills as prescribed."

"Mama! I cannot believe you! You thought this was OK? No — you encouraged it?"

She's focused on Nonna now, and I'm only a little relieved. Nonna's having to deal with Mama's outrage, but I'm the focus of the argument.

"I encouraged nothing," Nonna says. "They're 16 years old. The responsible thing was to ensure there would be no unplanned babies. Callie has a bright future ahead of her as a chef. It's not an easy profession, and a baby would be a complication she doesn't need until she's settled in a kitchen of her own. So, yes, I did the responsible thing and ensured that wouldn't happen."

"Callie is going to go to college, which should be reason enough for her not to be in the position where she even has to consider worrying about getting pregnant!" Mama's wrong about that. About the college part. The last two summers in Nonna's restaurant have confirmed for me what I want to do with my life. College isn't it. "I... I just don't know what to say to you, Mama. This was something you should have consulted with us about before you did it."

Except Nonna and I both knew Mama would react like this. I don't even want to think about how Papa's going to respond.

"You gave me legal responsibility for Calliope's healthcare while she was with me for the summer," Nonna reminds her. "I had every right to make this decision. You and Phillip were so occupied with your travels that you barely took the time to call your own daughter all summer." I look down at my feet. Nonna and I haven't talked about this at all. I expected it. Nonna should have. She knows how Mama and Papa are. But I can't say I haven't been a little hurt by the lack of interest in my life. At least until now.

"The fact that you show up now," Nonna says, her irritation becoming more and more clear, "after she's done well here for a second summer, working a full-time job, in a committed relationship with a nice boy — that doesn't give you the right to judge my decision, nor your daughter, nor young Declan. You should get to know him before you make judgments."

I don't think that will help, but it won't be Declan's fault. My parents aren't going to like any boy they know I'm spending time with.

"I don't want to know him!" That I can believe, but it still makes me furious. "He's not the right kind of boy for Callie. A musician? A rock musician? Mama — what were you even thinking?"

"I was thinking that he's a nice boy, and they're in love."

Nonna's not blind, and she's been hinting all summer that she took Declan's and my relationship seriously. Maybe even more seriously than he and I did. I appreciate the respect, and I feel like her confidence in us is something we have to live up to. So there was no question that I was going to take my birth-control pills exactly on schedule every day.

"They're 16. What do they know of love?" Mama says. "It's a crush, a teenage infatuation. It'll be over by the time school starts, when they haven't seen each other for a few weeks."

Now I'm getting really angry, and I take a step into the kitchen, ready to confront Mama, make her understand how Declan and I are together.

"They've been dating for more than a year," Nonna says simply.

"What? How could they be? I thought this boy lived in Virginia!"

"He does. But they've kept in touch all this past year. This isn't just puppy love, Mina. It's a true match. Fate put them together. You cannot tear them apart."

Fate? What makes Nonna say that? What does she mean?

"Fate..." Mama shakes her head and sighs. "Mama — you and your romantic notions. This is a matter of practicalities. They're teenagers. They live hours away from each other. And the boy dreams of being a rockstar! It's a pipe-dream, and one he'll have to wake up from not long from now. It's better that Callie recognizes that and focuses on her education. She's got to be focused on school, applying to colleges, not some teenage boy parading around in leather pants so he can have girls scream at him! Or worse..."

And that's all I can take.

"Mama, that's unfair, and I refuse to stand around listening to you badmouth Declan — who is a wonderful person and an incredibly talented musician and performer. He's going to be a star someday not too far in the future. You'll see. And he does love me! And I love him! We've been careful, responsible. And I really think he's the one. I want you to meet him, get to know him. You and Papa have two weeks here before we go home. You've got time. You should come see his band tomorrow on the boardwalk."

"They've got a concert booked?"

"No... Not tomorrow. Tomorrow, they're just busking."

"Begging for money thrown in a guitar case? That's not a concert, Callie. And if they were as good as you claim, they'd know it was beneath them to do it."

"They've had other shows this summer — in restaurants, the pool bar at the hotel!"

"Teenagers, performing in a bar? That sounds illegal, Callie. Why on earth would we want you spending time with a boy whose career involves something illegal?"

"It's not illegal, Mama! They're allowed to be in the pool area while they perform. They just can't go near the actual bar! Honestly!"

"I still don't like any of this. Your grandmother's judgment here was flawed. This whole situation is out of control. And it's past time you had someone reining you back in. In fact, I don't want you here a moment longer than necessary, with that boy around. I'm calling your father, and we'll head home tomorrow."

"No! I've got two weeks left! In the restaurant, and with Nonna. And, yes, with Declan! You need to meet him before you dismiss him like this."

"I'm the adult here, Callie, and I decide what I do, and what you do. And we're going back to Philadelphia tomorrow. End of discussion!"

She walks out of the room, heading off to call Papa, no doubt. I know there's no point in arguing. Once she's made up her mind, there's no changing it.

"Oh, *cara mia*," Nonna says, gathering me up in a hug. "My angelica... I'm so sorry. I thought I had raised your mother with more empathy than that, with more appreciation of the ways of love and fate. I named her Mina, after all!"

Mama hates her name, but I'd never tell Nonna that. She says everyone thinks of "Dracula" when they see it, not of love or protection, as Nonna intended.

"I can't leave without seeing Declan, Nonna. He'll think my parents didn't want to meet him. And even if that's true, I don't want to hurt him like that. And I got him a gift, to remind him to think of me until we see each other again — I can't leave without giving it to him!"

"Go see him now, Calliope. I'll tell your mother I sent you off to run an errand for me. But be quick. It's late and it's getting dark. You need to be back before bedtime!"

"Thank you, Nonna!"

I grab Declan's gift and run out the door, headed for my boyfriend like a homing pigeon for its nest.

# Declan

"Declan, there's someone here to see you."

Mom sounds curious, and a little irritated, and I'm kind of curious myself. It's nearly dark out, and Callie was expecting her parents this evening after their flight in from Tokyo, planning to spend the evening catching up with them. I wasn't expecting to see her until at least tomorrow. And I don't know anyone else here in Mystic Beach, aside from Hunter and that blonde girl he still hangs out with sometimes. Could a fan have tracked me down? The idea is both flattering and a little creepy.

I head for the front door to the beach house and find Callie waiting for me out on the deck, pacing back and forth with a bag in her hands.

"You could have come in."

"I didn't know if your mother would want us alone in your room..."

Yeah... She might have been right about that. Mom's been a little weird about the fact that I have a girlfriend. That's why I hadn't introduced them yet. I was hoping maybe later this weekend, when Dad was down, now that Callie's parents are here, too...

"Oh. That's OK. We can talk out here." I gesture to one of the chaises, and Callie takes a seat. I sit next to her and press a kiss to her cheek when she doesn't say anything. Even if Mom looks out the window right now, we're beyond reproach, but Callie seems nervous, and I hope the kiss will reassure her.

"Here," she says, thrusting the bag at me. "I got this for you."

I take it from her, noticing that it's pretty light. It's not food, which is what I expect Callie to give me these days. I've been taste-testing all her recipes for her, each one better than the last. I'm not sure she couldn't take a job as a chef right now. She's that good.

"Go ahead and open it," she adds, still seeming nervous.

What is she giving me that's making her so nervous? We've gotten pretty serious this summer, but I'm not expecting her to beat me to the punch on proposing. Maybe someday... But we're only 16.

I dig into the fancy tissue paper until I hit something solid. Soft. Fuzzy.

"It's a bear!"

"Yeah. A grizzly bear. It reminded me of you. And I wanted it to remind you of me... after you went back home."

"Arturo! The Great Bear. Like your Nonna talked about."

"Yeah." She's quiet again. "Do you like it?"

"I love it, angel!" I tell her, genuinely touched. I mean, it's a stuffed animal, but it's a cool, semi-realistic grizzly-bear stuffed animal. And it'll definitely remind me of her until we're back together again next summer. I grab her in a hug, pulling her hard against me, nuzzling into her neck, under her beautiful hair, whose color reminds me of the bear's fur. "Thank you so much!"

I push back from her so I can look in her eyes when I explain.

"I don't have anything for you. I thought I had another couple weeks." I cringe, knowing I'm coming up lacking here, but she's jumped ahead of me and my plans for a remember-me gift.

"Yeah..." she says, slowly. "About that..."

Something's wrong. It wasn't giving me the bear that made her anxious.

"What is it, Callie? What's going on? I didn't think I'd see you tonight, with your parents getting in, and you're acting all nervous..."

"We're leaving tomorrow."

"What? Your parents were supposed to be staying two weeks before you all went back to Philly! Did something happen? Are they OK?"

"They're fine," she says. "It's just..."

She looks away from me, and I can't let that stand. I grab her chin and turn her back to me, looking into her eyes and seeing tears forming.

"What is it, angel? What's wrong? What's going on?"

"I told Mama I wanted her and Papa to meet you, see you perform. But I guess they hadn't realized we'd stayed in touch since last summer, didn't understand that we're in a relationship, and all that goes along with it..."

"She realized we've been sleeping together."

"Yeah."

"And she's not happy about that."

"She's really not. And Papa is going to be even less pleased that I'm no longer his virginal little girl."

"Ouch. And that's on me."

"Well, no. It's on me, too. We both made that decision. But Mama's blaming Nonna for getting me on the pill, letting us spend time together alone. She doesn't want me staying here another day. So they're going back home tomorrow, and I have to go with them."

No! I had two weeks left with Callie. And I'm not going to see her again until June! It was hard enough last year, when we'd just started really getting to know each other before we were separated. Now, we've spent at least a little time together almost every day this summer. We've been exploring our feelings... and other things... for months. She's my best friend, and... dammit — I love her! I was thinking of telling her before we left. And now she's leaving tomorrow?

I grab her hard against me.

"I don't want you to go."

"I don't want to go. But I don't have any choice. There's no way my mother is changing her mind. I couldn't even get her to come see you all play tomorrow, so she could see how good you are!"

"She objected to you dating a musician?"

"She wasn't thrilled about it."

I sigh.

"I'm sorry, Callie. I kind of hoped to have met your parents under better circumstances. Now, it seems like I've got my work cut out for me whenever we *do* meet."

"You'll meet them. Maybe next summer. They're talking about going to India and Nepal this time, but they'll be coming back to get me at the end of the summer. I'll make sure you meet them then. I'll be 18 not long after that. They'll have to listen to me then."

Another thought hits me.

"You're going to miss my birthday... I wanted to introduce you to my parents before then, maybe this weekend."

"I was going to cook you a special birthday dinner, and a celebration cake... Now..."

"It's OK, Callie," I say, pulling her back into me and rubbing her back to console her. "We'll do it in June, when we're both back here. We'll celebrate both of our birthdays in June, even with mine in August and yours in December. It'll be special that way. We'll pick a day and make that our joint birthday celebration!"

She sniffles, and I pull her face between my hands, kissing her gently on the lips. When I let her go again, she smiles, and I know she's trying hard to keep a positive attitude, even though this is hard on both of us.

"That'll be nice. That's a good idea, Declan. It'll be special — just for us."

I wrap my arm around her, tucking her into my side, and she leans her head against my shoulder. We sit there quietly for a while, watching the sky get dark, the only sounds the crashing of the waves on the beach nearby and the occasional squeal of excitement from young kids playing on the sand.

"I have to go, Declan... Nonna's running interference for me so I could come see you. And it's getting late."

"And I won't see you tomorrow." It's a statement, not a question. I know I won't.

She shakes her head anyway.

"I'm sorry."

"Don't be sorry, angel. It's not your fault. It's just how things are right now. But we've done this once already, been apart for a while. We made it through, kept in touch, and we were even closer when we came back together again. We can do this." I hug her hard, hoping she'll believe me, take heart in what we've already come through.

"I love you, Callie." I kiss her on the top of her head.

She looks up at me, eyes pooling with tears again, though this time I hope they're happy ones.

"I love you, too, Declan," she says, kissing me hard on the lips before the kiss becomes one of open mouths, tangling tongues and passion, mixed with tears.

I kiss those tears away, tasting the salt on my lips, savoring it, knowing she's becoming part of me, body and soul. It's only fair. She already owns my heart. And I watch her walk away with it, hoping that, between the two of us and the love we share, we can keep each other's hearts safe for the next nine months, no matter the time and distance in between. If we can do that, we can do anything. When we're together, we can do anything.

# CHAPTER 12

# MUSKRAT LOVE

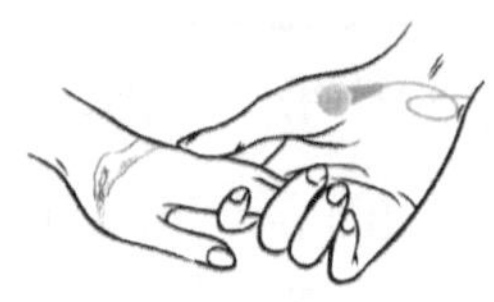

## Callie
### *Present — The next night*

"How's it going out there, Raquel?" I ask, sliding a plate of short ribs atop a bed of sun-dried tomato polenta and asparagus her way as she plays food runner for the first time.

"Good, Chef!"

"Excellent! Remember — keep your fingers off the surface of the plates, and check if the patrons need a refill on drinks before you leave the table."

"Got it, Chef!"

I smile as she grabs that plate and one of day-boat scallops with a risotto set that Drew has placed next to it. She's sharp. She's going to make a career in this business, regardless of exactly what she chooses to do.

I've settled back into my kitchen after yesterday's surprise visit from my past. Despite his promises, Declan Carter hasn't darkened my doorstep. No flowers. No apology letters slipped under the door. Not so much as a "Let's get drunk and fool around" bottle of wine. I shudder at the thought. I can't believe I let him kiss me. Because I did. I let him. OK. I kissed him back. A little. Briefly. Probably less briefly than I should have. Because it shouldn't have happened at all.

Fuck him and his pretty rockstar face! And especially the extra few inches of hair he's grown in the last few weeks, falling into his eyes just so, the sexy scruff on his jaw as he brushed his lips against mine, the pierced ear he'd always talked about getting but hadn't dared while he was still living with his parents. Fuck all of that!

Yeah. Fuck him.

Oh, god... I *so* want to fuck him.

What is *wrong* with me?

I told Alex I wanted to dance on Declan's grave. And I do. But part of me wants to fuck him first.

That's it! Fuck him and then dance on his grave when I'm done.

No. Not happening. Can't let any of that happen. He's been gone for twelve years, leaving decimation in his wake. I should be over him by now. I should have been over him the moment he started talking about groupies and backstage... people.

"Chef?"

Raquel's standing in front of me, waiting, as I stand there like a fool, a finished plate in my hand, hovering in the air between us.

I place it on the pass-through and give her a forced smile. She adds it to her load and returns to the dining room.

I can feel Drew looking at me without even turning my head.

"What?"

"Nothing, Chef."

I can feel his smile, too, as if he knows I'm off-kilter again, and exactly why.

I haven't heard any of the staff talking about the incident with Declan yesterday, but I know they all know about it. I've been getting odd looks from people all day, little smiles, whispering when they think I'm not watching. But this is my kitchen. I see all. I know all.

"Chef?"

"Yes, Raquel?"

"There's a patron who would like to speak with you."

I roll my eyes. It hadn't better be Alex again. He was just in here this morning, helping me caramelize a batch of onions for the soup of the day. He's tasted everything on the menu at this point, I think, though he's still learning to cook most of it.

"He hasn't ordered yet, so I don't think it's a complaint," Raquel adds.

"Thank you, Raquel. I'll be right there."

Drew takes the tongs from my hand and slides in behind the searing filet.

"Standard set, Drew. Medium-rare by request."

"Yes, Chef!" He smiles at me again, and I'm tempted to clock him over the head with that pan, but I decide to pretend he's smiling happy daddy-to-be thoughts and cut him a break. This time.

Raquel is standing next to a two-top in a far corner of the dining room. She's talking to the diner, and I can't see behind her to see if it *is* Alex again, so I walk up with no idea who it is or what they want. Maybe it *is* a restaurant critic this time?

"What can I do for you... sir—"

Fuck me. Just fuck me.

No — I take that back. Don't fuck me. Nope. Not happening.

"I'm sorry to pull you away from the kitchen, Chef, but I was hoping you might have some recommendations for my dinner tonight. I'm in the mood for something... special."

Declan smiles brightly at me, giving Raquel a wink.

"That will be all, Raquel. I've got this."

She does what looks suspiciously like half a curtsy — to me or to Declan, I'm not sure — and quickly retreats back to the kitchen, where, thankfully, she won't be witness to the fiasco that is taking place at this table in my restaurant.

In my restaurant. With a room full of diners.

Fuck you, Declan Carter!

Ack! No.

I've got to find a better form of profanity to use where he's concerned.

"What do you want, Declan? Really?"

"Dinner."

"Right. Sure. You came in here, spur of the moment, just because you were hungry."

"No. I made a reservation, because I wanted to enjoy a special meal, and I heard you were the best chef in town."

"We don't take reservations."

"Yes, you do. I had my manager check into it. You're part of the private reservation system they use for VIPs."

Oh. Yeah. Drew keeps an eye on that. I'd forgotten we'd signed up for it, with all the senators and actors and such who've been buying vacation homes in coastal Delaware.

Apparently, rockstars use it, too.

Joy.

"So... You asked for the chef. What can I do for you?"

"Well, I saw your specials menu, but there were so many things on there and the regular menu that sounded wonderful that I couldn't pick just one dish. I was hoping you might have something extra-special to recommend, maybe something off-menu?"

He says those last two words slowly, sensually, with just enough extra emphasis that I wonder if he isn't asking for an off-menu item that would be more appropriate to a bordello than my restaurant. And he's asking that of me.

I frown at him but decide to take him up on the challenge. If it's off-menu he wants, it's off-menu he'll get.

"Do you have any food allergies?"

"No. None that I know of."

"Any preferences? Requests?"

"I trust you. Surprise me."

His smile is inviting, warm. Rockstar charisma reduced down to its most concentrated and potent form.

Heat pools in my core.

You want surprises, Declan Carter? You'll get them. And we'll see if you regret trusting me as much as I came to regret trusting you.

"Uh... Callie?" Drew whispers in my ear. "What exactly are you doing?"

"There was a special request. I'm fulfilling that request."

"For extra — raw — onion in your perfectly balanced French onion soup, that you spent hours this morning caramelizing onions for?"

"He asked me to surprise him."

"I see..." He glances through the door into the dining room. "Dare I ask who 'he' is?"

The look I give him in reply is half knowing and half smirk.

"Oh, boy... Should I get the lawyer on stand-by? Or the paramedics?"

"Nope. Won't be needed. He's going to get exactly what he asked for. Exactly what he deserves."

Drew swallows his reply.

Raquel comes back in the kitchen and holds her hand out for the hefty soup bowl I've prepared, having topped it with a particularly goaty goat cheese and crispy toasts topped with extra garlic.

"No — I'll deliver this one myself, Raquel. It is a special order, after all."

Declan is sitting quietly at his table, a glass of red wine half-full in front of him. If I didn't know him better than that, I might think he was nervous. But when he sees me coming toward him, he smiles, and my steps falter. I remember that smile. Not the rockstar schmoozing smile from before. It's the one he hit me with when we were wrapped up in each other's arms after the first time we slept together. Sweet and loving and utterly earnest.

I shake myself free of the memory, forcing myself to keep moving toward him, setting the bowl down in front of him.

"Your first course, sir: French onion soup, specially made for your discerning tastes."

He looks up at me, and I see his smile falter for just a moment.

"Is there a problem? You said you didn't have any food allergies, right?"

"Right. No allergies. And I did ask you to surprise me."

"I hope I've met your expectations. Bon appetit!"

I give him a nod and retreat to the kitchen — but only far enough to peek around the doorway to see what he does. I may have just solved my own problem. Because if this spoiled, onion-hating rockstar doesn't put his spoon back down and walk out the door at the first taste, I'll eat my apron.

I watch as he picks up his spoon, dipping it carefully into the soup, through the melty cheese, and coming back up with the deep, dark broth filling the bowl of the spoon, and a neat pile of stark white raw onion in the center. He takes a deep breath and sighs, clearly leery of what he's seeing, before it's even made it into his mouth. I smile in triumph.

And I watch as he raises the spoon to his mouth, sips at the broth, nods and eats the entire contents in one bite. He chews pleasantly, even though I can hear the crisp, uncooked onion being mashed between his teeth. He swallows. And he smiles.

The bastard smiles! Like that was the best thing he'd ever tasted! And then he goes back for another spoonful.

I frown, defeat snatched from the jaws of victory. It's going to take worse than extra-oniony onion soup to rid me of Declan Carter. I can see that now.

I turn, heading back to my spot at the stove, and I see Drew smirking at me again.

"What?"

"Nothing." More smirking.

"Do we any of the escargot left from that experiment I tried over the weekend?"

"The one none of us liked? Including you?"

"Nonna had to have left an ingredient out or something... She'd marked that recipe with a star! I was certain it would be a winner!"

"Maybe she put a star on it so she'd remember never to cook it again?"

"Maybe."

"It's in the freezer."

"Go get it."

"Anything else?"

"Do you think the Country Café would sell us some muskrat at this hour?"

## *Three hours later*

"How's he doing?" Drew asks from behind me.

"Fine. He's fucking fine. He's eaten every bite I've put in front of him, no matter how strange or off-putting."

I can't believe it. It's taken him a while, and he's the last diner left in the restaurant at this late hour. But nothing I've served

Declan has phased him in the least. He finished every bite of soup and even tipped the bowl to get to the last of the broth. The escargot dish even I couldn't stomach disappeared like it was a bowl of chocolate ice cream and not snails. Smothered Muskrat & Onions required sending Drew down the street for a cleaned and brined muskrat, much to our fellow restaurateur's amusement. It didn't smell half-bad. I'll say that much. But I had to adjust the seasonings by feel, because I couldn't bring myself to taste it and couldn't get any takers from among my staff. They're utterly loyal to me, but not that loyal.

Declan... I'm not sure what he thinks he's trying to prove, but if he thinks eating everything I throw at him will make up for ruining my life all those years ago, he's got another thing coming.

The dessert I've prepared is chocolate mousse. But it's made with unsweetened chocolate and flavored heavily with chilies. Its roots are in the earliest recipes using cocoa, but it defies expectations of a modern dessert. Not to mention the hint of ghost pepper I layered on top.

After all he's been through tonight, I have Raquel on standby with a glass of milk and a bowl of vanilla soft-serve from the custard place down the street. I wouldn't admit in a million years to be softening toward him, but I don't want to actually damage him, as tempting as that might be.

I set the bowl down in front of him, and this time I stay at the table to see his response.

"Chocolate Mousse Azteca."

"Azteca?"

"The ancient Aztecs were known for their use of chocolate in some very unique ways."

"Oh?"

"Yes. Enjoy."

He looks up at me, trepidation clear on his face. I resist the temptation to grab the dish back from him before he tastes it.

He dips his spoon in, scooping up a small amount. He takes a deep breath and puts the spoon in his mouth. His expression puckers as the bitter chocolate hits his tongue, then his eyes bulge as the chilies make their presence known. Now he's panting, his mouth overwhelmed by the heat.

And he looks up at me and smiles.

"Very... unique," he says, breathlessly. "Thank you."

What the fuck? He's thanking me? I can't take this anymore.

My head drops. My shoulders sag. And I trudge back into the kitchen, past a crowd of cooks, waitstaff, bussers and runners that's accumulated in the doorway, watching this scene like it was the final in a grand-slam tennis tourney. They look a little frightened, to be honest. Which is kind of how I'm feeling right now.

"Go put him out of his misery, Raquel."

She rushes out to the table, handing Declan the glass of milk and setting the frozen custard in front of him.

He smiles at her in thanks, taking a long, slow sip from the glass.

He takes the spoon she offers and sets it down next to the custard. And picks up the other spoon and continues eating the mousse.

Drew looks at me and frowns.

I take off my apron and hand it to him.

"Get him out of here. Tell him it's closing time and the staff has to leave. Thank him for his patronage. Tell him his dinner's on the house, that the tip is covered. But get him out of here."

"Where are you going?"

"I need some air."

"Want me to lock up?"

"Yeah. Thanks."

And I walk out the back door, down the alley and straight down to the beach.

Maybe the ocean, being ancient, has some answers to the questions raised by what happened tonight. I just know I don't. Not a one.

# CHAPTER 13

## FATE

## Callie

"Rough night?"

Siobhan plops down on the sand next to me with a small smile.

"What did you hear?"

"Just lots of excited chit-chat from restaurant employees headed home after watching some kind of reality-TV-caliber live celebrity food-torture special."

Ugh.

Siobhan bumps my shoulder with hers.

"Do you feel better now?"

"No."

"Do you think he does?"

"Physically or otherwise?"

"Either."

"I was too careful for him to end up in the hospital, if that's what you're implying."

"I didn't think you'd injure him. I wasn't *entirely* sure about that, but I didn't think you would."

"Thanks for the vote of confidence."

"You're welcome," she replies with a smirk.

"Why is he doing this?"

"He's in love."

"The man who told me he'd never really loved me in the first place?"

"He did what?" She's incredulous. "Tell me he didn't actually say that."

"I wish I could."

"Now I wish I *had* decked him. Who actually says something like that? Who ret-cons an entire long-term relationship by retroactively nullifying a core emotion? On what planet is that ever OK?"

"He seemed to think it was important for me to know, to explain why he was breaking up with me after more than two years."

"That sucks. He sucks."

"But he's in love with me..."

"Yeah. I think so." She shrugs.

"That makes no sense."

"No, it does not. But it also does. Guy-logic. They're stupid. Especially as teenagers."

"So it's OK that I tortured him tonight?"

"Definitely."

"Is it also OK that I wanted to jump his bones?"

"Do people still say 'jump his bones'?"

"I don't know. It's been so long since I've done it that my vocabulary is a decade old."

"You're kidding me!"

She looks a little freaked out.

"Seriously — you're kidding, right?"

"I kind of wish I was."

"Wow."

"That's more or less how Declan responded."

"You told him you hadn't gotten laid in a decade?"

"I told him I hadn't gotten laid since the last time he and I slept together."

"Fuuucckkk..."

"Yeah. That."

"He really did a number on you, didn't he?"

"Yup."

"No one? Not once?"

"You sound like Declan now."

"I should stop that."

"Yeah."

We're quiet for a while.

"Not even a little oral?"

"Siobhan..."

"Sorry. It's just... I'd have lost my fucking mind."

"What's the longest you've gone?"

"Three years."

"Bad breakup?"

"You could say that. It wouldn't begin to touch it, but you could say it."

"Sorry."

"Yeah. It was a long time ago. I put it behind me."

"Wish I'd been able to do that with Declan."

"I imagine it would have changed a lot of things for you."

"Probably."

"Would you be here now? Would you have your restaurant?"

"I don't know. Maybe not. When I lost him, I put everything I had into my career. If I hadn't, I might still be working in someone else's kitchen, in New York, probably."

"Then things are as they were supposed to be."

I look at her, puzzled.

"How can you say that?"

"Easy. If you were still in New York, Declan would be here, with no idea where you were or what happened to you. Him breaking up with you eventually led to you being here, now, where you became friends with Brighid, and me, and had me wheedle you into going to Brighid's engagement party, where you just happened to run into Declan, who fate made the bandmate of Brighid's fiancé."

"That's nuts."

"It's also the way fate works."

"Fate is nuts."

"Yup. But it's still fate. And that's why I know he's in love with you."

"Even after I tortured him?"

"Almost certainly."

"What would make it certain?"

"If he comes back."

"I'm not sure I want him to."

"Are you sure you *don't* want him to?"

I think about that for a minute.

"No."

"Then he will. It's fate."

# Callie
## *The next morning*

There's a frantic knocking at the kitchen door onto the alley courtyard. I pause for a moment before I get up from Nonna's book and my desk to answer it, praying it's not Declan. Regardless of Siobhan's assertion, I don't trust that he's not motivated here by something other than lingering feelings for me. If anything, maybe he's just missing the attention he's used to getting from girls backstage and he's looking for an ego boost from persuading an ex to get back in bed with him, even if it's just once. That sounds like the Declan Carter, rockstar, who left me cold a week after our wedding.

The knocking continues and I answer it, warily. It's early yet and Alex isn't coming for a lesson today, since the band is busy in the studio, working on one of Hunter's songs. Hopefully, that guarantees this isn't Declan showing up, unwanted and unannounced, again.

"Oh, my gods! I am *so* sorry, Callie! The kids have been going stir-crazy all summer, and this is the first time I could get Rory to babysit so I could get over here to talk to you, alone and in person!"

Lyric brushes past me, grabbing my hand and dragging me behind her into the dining room, where she falls bonelessly into a chair, like taking another step is asking far too much. She looks exhausted, older than her 32 years. Brighid's talk of sending Lyric off for a spa day is starting to sound like a vital rescue mission. So why is she here, and why does she seem so wound up?

"Sit!" she insists, and I do, after glancing at the clock and confirming I've got a good half-hour before anyone else shows up.

"Why didn't you tell me *your* Declan became *that* Declan?"

"I didn't know there *was* a *'that* Declan.'"

"He's like the first result when you put 'Declan' into a search engine! How did you not know that?"

"I don't do social media, or any media, really. I don't listen to music. You're the music teacher — I thought you knew that."

She takes a deep breath and sighs.

"Maybe I did... I don't know. My brain is whirlwind. I'm working on lesson plans, organizing the fundraiser for the music department, dealing with the kids twenty-four/seven, scheduling summer enrichment for Aria and therapy for Tommy, trying to get this submission ready for the fellowship... This is only the second time I've let myself ask Rory to watch the kids for me this summer. She's been so busy with work, and things..."

Lyric's head dips down, her blonde hair falling into her eyes, and she's carefully avoiding meeting mine.

I don't know Rory very well, and I have no idea what she's been dealing with, though Lyric has hinted that something big happened that seriously changed her life in the last year — including Lyric moving out of Rory's house and back into her old family home. I haven't pried. I tend to keep my head down and focused on the restaurant.

Honestly, I don't have a lot of time for friends, period. Lyric and I have only spent a little bit of time together since I got back here from New York a few years ago, and that mostly because she was in the process of moving out of her house at the same time I was selling Nonna's house so I could afford to open my restaurant. I didn't want to do it, but with a loft apartment above the restaurant space that was plenty of space for me alone, I needed the capital more than the memories — especially when some of those memories were not so happy.

But Lyric... despite the role she had played in the drama that ensued that last summer, she'd been a good friend to me, before and after. And I'd missed her. When I saw her next door, looking a little lost as she boxed up the pieces of her life, of her kids' lives, to move in with Rory... We both knew loss, and we were both dealing with challenging new phases in our lives. We bonded over that, reaffirmed an old friendship I think we'd both thought had faded into time. So, even if we don't have a lot of time to just hang out, our friendship has become important to us both. And I know I'd have seen her after Brighid's engagement party if she'd had any free time at all.

"It's fine, Lyric. I know how busy you are. You've got to put the kids first. And maybe you need to be putting yourself first sometimes, too. Maybe?"

The look she gives me is sheepish. She knows she's running herself into the ground. And judging from her unwillingness to admit it, it may take an intervention to get her to take care of herself for a change. I'll find the time and talk to Brighid about it. Maybe we can all find a few hours, give her some respite with the kids once a week or something. I can find some time to make a batch of cookies with them or something, surely.

"So... Declan..." she says, changing the subject firmly back in my direction.

"He's back."

"And..."

"Siobhan says he's in love with me."

Lyric starts to say something, then seems to think wiser of it, shaking her head. Then she takes a deep breath and plunges ahead.

"I told you — told you both — when I marry people, it sticks."

"Yeah. You warned us. We didn't listen. Or, he didn't, I guess..." It was what I thought I wanted at the time. It was what I'd thought *he'd* wanted.

"Did you... Did you keep the handfasting ribbons? I could try... again..."

"They're in a box somewhere. But — no offense — I never really believed in all that magic stuff. Even Nonna's talk about fate, and the power of food... And now Siobhan, talking about fate again." I shake my head. "I don't believe in fate, Lyric. Not anymore. Maybe back then. But I was a kid. I had no idea what life was really like — what love, relationships were really like. I don't even really believe in love anymore."

Lyric frowns at me, like I've said something blasphemous.

"Declan said he loved me! He said it over and over again, and I believed him. And then he tells me he was wrong about that, that he'd never really loved me at all. It was like the whole concept of love evaporated in that one moment. It wasn't real. It never had been. And it's not now, no matter what he says, no matter what Siobhan says..."

I stand up, hoping she'll take the hint and leave me in peace.

"Siobhan is wise. Sometimes, I think she's got that same claircognizance that Brighid has," she adds with a shrug. "And I'd trust what she was telling me if she was telling me something important — something involving love and fate, Callie. Because there's nothing more important in this world than love, and when fate hands it to you..."

She looks at her feet, but I can see the tears forming in her eyes.

"You have to grab hold of love when it's given to you. You never know how long you'll have it, or who'll bring it. But it's a precious gift. And getting that gift a second time... That's fate, Callie. Most of us don't get that second chance. And if fate offers it..." She grabs my hand, pulling on it to get my attention. "Don't throw it away just because you got hurt the first time. Sometimes the timing is what's wrong, and if fate truly wants to bring you two together, when the time is right, it'll do that. There's no fighting fate."

It certainly feels like I've been fighting something, but I think that something is an egotistical rockstar and his refusal to accept that he can't have everything he wants just because he wants it. It's past time he learned that lesson. Goodness knows I learned it twelve years ago.

"Thanks for stopping by, Lyric. I appreciate the support. I'll stop by sometime in the next week or so, cook some dinner for you and the kids."

"You don't have to do that, Callie. We're fine. I'm fine."

I don't believe that any more than she seemed to believe me about my long-dead feelings for my teenage crush, but I'm pretty sure it's Lyric who's denying reality and not me. The only reality I care about is the one in which I find a winning recipe. And I can't let Declan Carter throw me off my game.

# Chapter 14

## All In

**Declan**
*Later that day*

My wife tried to kill me.

OK, maybe she wasn't actually trying to fatally poison me with her food. She's a good enough cook that if she wanted to slip poison into my soup without anyone the wiser, she could have done it. But instead she took my little slip about hating onions and used it against me in the worst way. And then she added insult to injury by feeding me snails, and some kind of semi-aquatic rodent — I mean, it even has "rat" right in the name! And then — then she digs up some archaeological nonsense about the Mayans or whatever, as some excuse to feed me chocolate blended with lava!

I lick at the roof of my mouth, checking to see if some of my tastebuds have grown back in the last 12 hours. The survivors are still complaining. But maybe that's for the best. Who knows what she'll serve up tonight when she realizes I've come back for more?

I can do this. I have to do this. How else am I going to prove to her that I'm sincere about wanting her back? How else am I going to prove to her that I really love her and always have, regardless of what I said?

"Uhh... Dec?"

Alex's disembodied voice rings in my ears. Mostly because he's speaking into the talkback mic that's feeding sound directly into my headphones in the iso booth.

"Yeah? What?"

"You're supposed to be singing."

"Right. What am I singing again?"

"The lead vocal to 'Comin' Out on Top.' You know — the song we're recording."

"And why is that?"

"Because you're our lead singer. Unless you've changed your mind and have decided to let Dave sing lead on this album."

"No!"

I may be a royal mess right now, at least inside my head (OK — I'm kind of a mess on the outside, too, though I got the impression Callie liked the longer hair and the scruff, so I'm keeping it, for now). But I'm not so fucked up about Callie that I'm giving up my soon-to-be-legendary status so my brother can steal my parts!

"Start the playback over again. I'll get it this time."

I give myself a shake and focus on the space between my ears. Which immediately fills with the image of Callie's soft, sensual lips... which I desperately wish were right in front of me at this moment...

"Cut!"

Fuck!

"Take 10 everybody. Especially you, Declan!"

Now I'm in trouble. Malcolm Fisher has been here for a sum total of three days. He's a perfectionist. And, normally, that's fine. So am I. But my life is so utterly imperfect right now, and that's obvious to everyone, including our producer.

I drop my headphones on the hook by the door and walk quickly through the live room, and the control room, and the hallway, out the back door, between some trees, over a sand dune and straight into the ocean. Nevermind that I'm wearing jeans and a T-shirt, and my favorite Converse high-tops.

"Declan! What the fuck?"

The sound rings out over the water as soon as I re-emerge, shaking saltwater and my hair out of my eyes.

Dave's standing at the edge of the water, staring at me. Unlike me, he's dressed for a swim. But then he usually is. Especially these days, since he and Piper patched things up and started making little bass-playing sound engineers. I have no idea why those things all go together, but apparently they do.

I wish Callie and I fit together as naturally as they do, as we used to...

And there it is again — the thing that's fucking up my recording time. *Our* recording time. It's a good thing Dave owns part of the studio now and our label CEO owns most of the rest. Even then, Malcolm's taken over the elements of the studio operations that Dave and Piper didn't, and he's only going to cut us so much slack... OK — only going to cut *me* so much slack. Since I'm the one who needs it at this point.

"What's going on with you, Dec?" Dave asks as I trudge back onto the beach, dragging shoes full of water and sand with me and hampered by soggy jeans. "This isn't like you at all. You're usually the one demanding more takes so you can get your vocals exactly right. I've never seen you just space-out in the iso booth."

"How's it feel to have the woman you love love you back? How's it feel to fall asleep with her in your arms and wake up knowing she'll still be there?"

Dave does a double-take.

"Uh... Awesome. Unbelievable, really, considering how long it took me to find her."

"And if she decided she didn't want to be with you anymore? If you pissed her off and you weren't sure you could ever get her back?"

"I'd never do that."

I roll my eyes at him. He's right, of course. Mr. Perfect Husband...

Fuck. They're not even married. They're not even engaged. And still he's the perfect husband. And I'm... not.

"Let's say you and I swapped bodies for a day, and I did what I do and pissed Piper off. When we switched back, how would you fix it? How would you get her back?"

"That's not how love works, Declan," he says, shaking his head at me. "Love isn't about getting what you want, or doing X so you can get Y result. It's about putting the person you love first, taking care of them because they're the most important thing in your life. It's about accepting them for who they are and them accepting you for who you are, and working together through the hard parts, knowing neither of you is perfect but that together you can do anything. Even the impossible."

How has Dave gotten so wise in such a short time? I mean, the guy hadn't ever had a girlfriend until like two months ago. And now he's handing me sage advice on relationships.

*Together, you can do anything.*

Why does that sound so familiar?

I throw myself down on the sand, leaning back on my arms and closing my eyes. But I can hear Dave sit down next to me.

"Dec? What's going on with you and Callie? Really? Better yet — what exactly happened with you and Callie that summer? Because it seems like there's more going on here than just you having lingering feelings for an old girlfriend. It seems like there's been more going on than that... well, since that night. I thought I knew everything that happened back then. But this... this is something else. What don't I know?"

I sigh. And I decide, for once, to get real. No more player covering up for the 17-year-old who was so stupid he broke his own heart, on top of breaking hers. Besides... Dave's kind of earned it.

"We got married. That summer. Like a week before everything blew up. She's my wife."

"What? How? When? I mean — Mom and Dad, they refused to sign the paperwork when you dropped that bomb on them. I remember that much. They were afraid you'd skip college in favor of married life."

"A lot of good that did..." I chuckle, expecting Dave to join me, since both of us blew off college anyway.

"I'm actually nearly finished with my degree," he says, looking a little sheepish when he says it.

"What? How? When?"

Now we both laugh. It seems we both have some secrets we've been keeping.

"I've been taking classes online for years. All those nights you went out and I stayed on the tour bus?"

"You had your nose stuck in a book."

"And a few episodes of 'Leverage.'"

A horrifying thought occurs to me.

"You bought part of the studio. And you've got a girlfriend and a baby on the way. And now you tell me you're nearly a college graduate. Anything else you want to tell me before the rumor mill informs me I need to find a new bass player?"

"It's not like that. Not exactly, anyway."

"So how *is* it, then?"

"I need a break from touring. That's true. But Marina Matthews said she'd work things out with us so we could take a break, then break the tour up into shorter legs once the album is released, come home more. Between me and Hunter..."

"And you becoming a dad..."

"Worst case, I might want aMUSEd to find a touring bassist," he admits.

My head sags back between my shoulders. This is not good news.

"But I'm not quitting the band. And I'm going to do my best to making touring work. Piper and I will have some things to work out. But I'm going to try."

I nod. It's not like I have any choice but to accept whatever Dave is willing to give. We'll just have to figure it out.

"Now... about this marriage thing..." he prompts.

"It's not legal. Mom and Dad wouldn't sign the papers, and Callie's parents hated me, so that was a non-starter."

"So what is it then?"

"A friend of Callie's was an ordained minister. She could have performed a legal ceremony — if we'd been able to get our parents to sign the forms for the marriage license."

"But they wouldn't."

"No. So we had a religious ceremony."

"Religious? You?" Dave starts laughing uncontrollably.

"The ceremony. Not me. But I gave my solemn promise. Which I intended to keep."

"Until you got smashed and slept with a woman you didn't know."

I cringe.

"Yeah."

"So you didn't just cheat on your girlfriend..."

"No. I cheated on my wife."

"Ouch." His brows knit. "Wait — I remember suggesting you'd be better off breaking things off with her, since we had this career as musicians ahead of us and that wasn't exactly..."

"Compatible with having a committed relationship?"

"Yeah."

"Care to reconsider that conclusion with hindsight, *Dad*?"

"I'm not 17 anymore."

"Neither am I."

"You still act like it sometimes... all the groupies..."

Yeah. I spilled the beans about the wedding. I'm not talking to him about my reputation as a ladies' man.

"Mean nothing to me. Callie... Callie is everything."

"Wow. You really *are* still in love with her..." He shakes his head. "For what it's worth, if I'd known you'd gotten married, I probably wouldn't have said anything about it being better to break things off. I'm sorry if I had any part in—"

"You didn't say anything I wasn't already thinking myself. It was on me to make the best choice under the circumstances, especially since I was the only one who knew all of them. But, Dave — I promised her forever. And then I messed up. This was my fault, so I'm going to fix it. The universe gave me another chance, and I'm going to fix this."

"Like I said — you can't do X expecting to get Y as a result. It's a relationship, not a math equation. You have to be in it together — both of you."

"So, how do I get her 'in it'?"

"A good first step might be to show her that *you're* in it."

Well, that won't be hard. Because I'm in. All in.

## *That night*

"Right this way, sir. We reserved you a table out of the way, as you requested."

"Thank you."

I glance nervously toward the kitchen, partly worried about Callie's reaction to my return and partly in fear of what she'll put me through tonight when last night's torture wasn't enough to deter me from coming back. Will she throw me out instead of feeding me? Will she make a scene? Or will she just subject me to more culinary suffering?

It doesn't matter. I told her I wasn't leaving her again. And I'm not going to. No matter what she does to me. I think.

I take my seat, angling my chair toward the kitchen this time so I can see it if Callie tries to peek in.

"Water?" the young girl asks as she approaches the table.

"Yes, please, Raquel."

She pours a glass of ice water from the pitcher and then fills the one at the other place setting without being asked. Smart girl.

"Should I ask for a glass of milk, too?" I ask, quirking a smile at her.

"Might be wise. She's not in a good mood."

"Alright then. Jameson, neat. And a tall glass of milk. And ask the chef if she has a moment to consult on my menu selections, please."

"Let the games begin," she mutters as she clears the second place setting, minus the second glass of water. She gives me a guilty look. "I'm not sure I should have…"

I put a finger to my lips and give her a shake of my head.

That's one secret I need to keep up my sleeve, for now.

I give the menu a cursory perusal, just to further absorb the kind of food Callie has put on the menu in her own restaurant. It's classic fine-dining fare, but with a twist that's perfectly Callie — leaning toward Italian but not overtly so, a focus on fresh local produce and seafood, with some unique ingredients I haven't seen on the menus at the other restaurants I frequent. While I doubt muskrat is part of her regular repertoire, she's no stranger to cooking well outside the box, it seems.

Truth be told, I'm eager to taste her food just as she would present it to any other diner in her restaurant. I remember how wonderful the dishes were that she cooked at 16, 17. I'm doubtful I'll be able to do that anytime soon. She's got a decade worth of anger and resentment to vent at me, and she's clearly going to use her food to do it. That's fine. I'll take whatever she dishes out — literally. I earned it.

"You asked to speak to the chef?"

I look up at her and smile my most sincere smile. I'm truly glad to lay eyes on her again. In fact, I don't think I could ever get enough of looking at her, even if her expression is sour when she looks at me. For now. Only for now. I'll win her over yet.

"I was intrigued with your choices last night, and I wanted to explore your palate a little more. I hope you don't mind if I give you free rein two nights in a row."

"You sure you want to do that?"

I nod sharply.

"Absolutely. I trust you."

I trust her to make me pay for what I did to her. I also trust her to give me the best meal of my life once she clears all that venom from her system. Let's see if last night took the edge off.

"I hope you don't come to regret that."

"Never. I have a lot of regrets where you're concerned, but only the things that *I* did that I wish I could undo. Never anything that you did or were to me. You're perfect."

She looks at me, jaw slack, clearly stunned.

"Far from it," she says when she pulls herself back together. "But I'm a decent cook."

"You're extraordinary. And I don't just mean your food. But I'm hoping to experience that, too."

She swallows and gives me a nod before turning on her heel and heading back into the kitchen.

Maybe, just maybe, I made a little headway with her. I can only hope.

"I call this the 'aMUSEd Bouche' — an amuse-bouche of sweetbreads, served with Madeira sauce, flavored with culantro and calendula."

I don't remember what sweetbreads are, but they've got a negative association in my brain, along the lines of "beware."

I look up at Callie, and I know part of my expression has to be begging for mercy, but I quickly bury it beneath a smile.

"Looks delicious!"

She gives me half a smirk before she nods and returns to the kitchen.

Raquel sweeps by the table, ostensibly offering to order me another whiskey. I may need it, so it's not an offer I'm going to reject.

"It's veal pancreas," she whispers as she heads to the bar.

I kind of wish she hadn't told me.

But Callie's not only made this for me, she's named it after me... after a fashion. So I plunge ahead, taking a small piece of the breaded and fried meat and swiping it through the sauce.

Hmm...

Mmm...

Not bad at all. In fact, I quite like it, the sauce especially, which has some interesting herbal notes.

I eagerly dig in to the rest of the tiny serving, a little disappointed when it's gone.

I glance over at the kitchen, finding Callie frowning at me. I smile and give her a nod of approval. She can't fault me for that.

Raquel returns with my second Jameson, which I remind myself to enjoy slowly. The first one was enough to bolster me for whatever Callie had in store for me. And I don't want to get drunk tonight. I want to notice all the details, both of the food and of Callie's expression.

"Century egg in duck broth with Roman nettles."

The wide soup bowl contains a clear dark-brown broth with dark green vegetation floating in it and a sliced... egg? arrayed in the shape of a flower with pickled ginger in the center.

I know she hopes to stymie me with this one, but I've had a century egg before. We were served century eggs during a tour stop in Taiwan, and I know they're usually more like a hundred days old than a hundred years, despite the sulfuric smell and dark green yolk surrounded by the "white," gone firmly gelatinous and dark amber.

It's actually a beautiful dish, with the deep browns and greens offset by the pink ginger. Her plating is flawless.

"Beautiful!" I comment enthusiastically as I scoop up a bit of egg and broth in the large spoon.

Callie's eyes widen as she watches me eagerly put the spoon in my mouth and hum appreciatively. A sharp exhale of frustration, and she returns to the kitchen once more.

I savor the dish, taking my time with it while she prepares whatever she's decided to serve as my entrée. I'm actually pretty pleased with how this is going. Not only is she not trying to torture me with spicy foods, I'm starting to get a feel for how much she's grown as a chef. She's using unusual ingredients that aren't even on her regular menu — though that has me wondering if she prepared for my possible return by stocking up on things she thought I'd hate — and, from what she's said, some unusual herbs and vegetables to serve them with. It's innovative, and I find myself appreciating what she does when she goes outside the box of her usual cuisine.

There's a bit of a commotion behind me, and I turn to see an older couple arguing.

"You know I stopped eating meat a month ago! Why would you order for me while I was in the ladies' room and order lamb?" she says, irritation apparent.

"I forgot, OK? The month before, you were doing that keto thing, and it was all meat all the time!" he replies, not making much of an effort to keep his voice down, and I'm not the only one trying not to stare at the spectacle.

"I was doing keto because you keep watching other women, like you don't have your wife sitting right next to you!"

He rolls his eyes, his head sinking back.

"There! I saw that! I saw you looking at her!"

"Saw what? I'm not looking at anyone!"

"That floozy over there, with her tits hanging out!" the woman says, pointing at the table across the way.

The second woman gasps, and her dining companion objects, loudly.

"Now see here! You have no right!"

I'm expecting a fist-fight to break out at any moment, and I get ready to stand up and try to break it up when I'm hit in the face with a splash of wine.

"You swine!" the first woman yells, an empty glass still clutched in her hand. I may have gotten splashed, but her husband is soaked with the bulk of what was a nearly full glass. "I tell you I saw you look, and you take the chance to look even longer!"

"I'm not looking at anyone, except you making a fool out of yourself!" he says, throwing his wine-soaked napkin across the table at her.

She shrieks and hurls a roll at his head, which he deftly catches... after it bounces off his nose.

I consider that crossing a line and stand up, turning to break up the argument just as Callie emerges from the kitchen and makes a beeline for the rowdy diners.

"Sir, ma'am — I'm afraid you're disturbing the other diners. We'll have to ask you to leave if you can't maintain some decorum!" she says.

"Decorum! With this jackass! He's an utter failure as a husband!" the angry woman declares, grabbing her purse and stalking out the front door of the restaurant.

While not directed at me, her words are an arrow to my heart, and judging by her expression, they've hit Callie just as hard. She swallows and glances at me before she recovers herself.

"Can I box up your meals to go, sir?" she asks the man, clearly more concerned about resolving the problem and getting the couple out of the restaurant than whether their bill gets paid.

"Not necessary," he says gruffly. "I've lost my appetite."

Nonetheless, he digs into his wallet and drops a couple bills on the table. I breathe a sigh of relief as he clears the doorway and I notice they're both hundred-dollar bills.

"How odd," I say to Callie, who still looks shaken by the incident.

"Yeah," she says quietly.

Several staff members converge on the table, cleaning up the mess of wine and the abandoned food.

"You OK?" I ask her.

"Yeah..." she replies absently. She shakes her head and looks at me, as if she's only just realized who asked the question. "Yeah. I'm fine."

"I apologize for the interruption to your meals, everyone," she announces to the room. "Please enjoy dessert on us tonight!"

"Do I want to know what I'm getting for dessert?" I ask her with a smirk.

She frowns at me, but the question has the desired effect — she tugs her chef's coat down, visibly regaining focus.

"You'll see when it gets here. Meanwhile, I'll have your entrée out in just a moment."

I settle back into my seat to wait, observing the people around me. For the most part, they've returned to their meals, seemingly unbothered by the scene they just witnessed, but a few seem to have also lost their appetites, and one couple drops cash onto their table with their salads half-eaten and leaves. It's not good news for Callie or her staff.

What on earth got into that couple?

Callie appears suddenly and deposits a plate of tacos in front of me. Tacos? I wasn't expecting tacos. I actually love tacos. Maybe Callie is taking it easy on me after what just happened.

"Huitlacoche blue-corn tacos with papalo and epazote."

"Huitlacoche?"

"Corn fungus," she explains, straining to constrain a smile. "It's a Mexican delicacy."

I peek between the layers of blue corn tortilla and find a combination of cheese, something that looks a bit like spinach and some tiny mushrooms? Corn fungus... Interesting. Maybe she's trying to poison me after all...

I pick up a taco and take a bite...

"Wow." My mouth lights up with the flavors. The fungus... It has a vaguely sweet, corn-like flavor, blended with a savory taste reminiscent of mushrooms. Then the creamy Mexican cheese with just a hint of sharpness, the spinach-like vegetable a bit peppery, with hints of citrus and mint. It's a perfect balance to offset the creamy and savory components, and the nutty flavor of the blue-corn tortilla.

"This may be my new favorite thing I've ever eaten," I tell her.

A smile lights up her face, and it's instantly one of the best things I've ever seen. Beats a stadium full of cheering fans by a mile.

And then it falls, as if she's remembered who it is she's talking to and the fact that she's still angry with me about our past.

"Enjoy," she says. But her voice is flat, itself joyless, and she retreats to the kitchen.

For a moment, I consider leaving, giving her a break. I hate the fact that my mere presence here turned her pleasure at the compliment on her cooking into a failure and a thing to be endured.

But Dave's advice comes back to me — about getting through hard times together, proving to her that I'm all-in on us and won't pick up and leave again...

I have to stick this out, prove myself to her. I enjoy the rest of my entrée, but it's with my heart a little heavier, knowing the opposition I'm still facing if I want to get her back.

"Durian crepe cake."

I can't disguise my disappointment when it's Raquel who brings my dessert.

"Durian?"

"She took the fruit home to prepare, so she didn't stink up the kitchen," Raquel says, glancing behind her to make sure Callie isn't watching. "But the fruit tastes amazing if you can get past the scent," she adds.

Well, if it's as stinky as she suggests, Callie's preparation is disguising it. All I'm seeing is a stack of small crepes with layers of cream and custard in between. Raquel stands by the table, clearly curious about what the dessert tastes like.

"Feeling brave?" I ask her.

"I'll try pretty much anything once," she says, shrugging.

"Did you try any of last night's dinner?" I ask.

She shakes her head fervently.

"But she seems to be cutting you a break after all of that. This is unusual, but it's also more like what she usually prepares."

"I'll take that as a sign of progress."

I hand her the dessert spoon, while I pick up the teaspoon from my place setting. We both dig in at the same time, Raquel peeking behind her before leaning over the table to avoid making a mess.

The layers of creamy flavor hit my tongue, begging further exploration. I can taste the custard, the cream, the delicate crepe... but there's something else... It's fruity, yet also creamy. And pretty darn delicious. Well, huh. Durian. Now I know.

"Is it as good as I think it is?" I ask Raquel, just in case my recently tortured tastebuds are misleading me.

She nods enthusiastically, looking to me for approval before scooping up a second bite.

"There's a second piece back in the kitchen for you, Raquel," Callie says from behind her. "Let Declan enjoy the rest of his on his own."

"Or you could share it with me," I tell her as Raquel retreats, looking a little chastened. I point to the other chair at the table and wait with bated breath to see if she'll take me up on the offer. She appears to consider it for a second, then pulls the chair out and sits.

"Long day?" I ask as she sighs.

"A challenging one," she replies, looking at me meaningfully.

"Sorry about that."

"Not your fault. Not entirely, anyway," she says.

She looks down, clearly expecting to find a set of silverware, but Raquel had cleared it away when I first got here.

"Here," I say, scooping up a big bite of dessert and holding my spoon out for her. She considers it for a moment, recognizing the intimacy of the gesture, of eating from the same spoon. I hold my breath. And she opens her mouth, letting me slide it onto her tongue. All the blood in my body rushes straight to my crotch as she moans in enjoyment. Once again, I'm hiding behind napkins.

"Most people won't eat durian if they know what it is or have a chance to smell it first," she says.

"I think the preparation made a difference," I admit. "But I've eaten in places all around the world. I've had a lot of foods I didn't know existed when I was 17. I've enjoyed most of them."

"Of course," she says, growing solemn at the reminder of both our time together and our time apart.

I scoop up another mouthful for myself and then offer her a second one.

"I can get myself a spoon," she says.

"Why? We used to share all the time."

"That was a long time ago."

"It was," I acknowledge. "Some things change. Some remain the same."

She accepts the bite I offer her, her eyes full of questions, things left unsaid. Until they're not.

"Why, Declan? Why are you doing this?"

"I already told you. We're meant to be together."

"More of this fate nonsense..." she says bitterly.

"I didn't say 'fate,'" I point out, curious.

"Six of one, half a dozen of the other," she replies, recalling my comment on duplicitous onions.

"Seriously — you seem put-out by that word, 'fate.'"

"I've had a few people mention it to me lately. It's nonsense," she adds firmly.

"And why were they talking to you about fate?"

I suspect I know why, especially when I know she's friends with Brighid, but it doesn't sound like she's on the same wavelength as Hunter's witchy fiancée, nor her friend who married us back in the day.

She looks me directly in the eyes, and I can see the confirmation in them.

"They think we're fated to be together," both of us say at the same time.

She groans, irritated by this new incident of brain-sharing between us.

"Is that so unlikely?" I ask, "given the odds of us coming back together like this? With our friends getting married, in the town where we once did the same?"

"It wasn't legal, Declan. You said exactly that to me when you broke up with me."

"And your friend said when she marries people, it sticks. And we promised each other forever. Forever hasn't elapsed, last I checked."

"I didn't take you for someone who'd go in for this woo-woo stuff, Mr. Rockstar," she says derisively.

"I let a witch marry us the first time," I remind her. "And I've seen a few things since then... not the least of which is Hunter's freaky hand-healing thing."

"That break did heal up awfully fast, didn't it?"

I nod fervently.

"Brighid does that kind of stuff at her shop," she says.

"You spend a lot of time in her shop?"

"No — don't lump me in with her 'circle,'" she cautions. "But she sources some of my rarer culinary herbs."

"Like *papalo* and *epa*—"

"Epazote. Yeah. Among others."

"Where'd you learn to cook like that? That wasn't the stuff Nonna cooked, if I remember correctly."

"No. She was pretty much traditionally Italian-influenced. But she used some herbs that I still have to get through Brighid. Just not the Mexican ones. Those I learned about in New York."

"That still sounds unlikely. I mean — I live in New York. I know there are some amazing ethnic restaurants there, cuisines from all over the world, but rare herbs? Durian crepes?"

"After culinary school, I took jobs in every kind of restaurant I could find. Didn't matter if it was fine-dining or working from a food truck. I wanted to learn, and I wanted to do it without having to travel."

"Why was that? Why no traveling?"

The expression on her face is instantly unreadable. This is a sore subject for her, for some reason. If I'd known that I wouldn't have even asked. But now...

I reach across the table and put my hand over hers, giving it a squeeze.

She stares at our joined hands for a moment and then springs up from her chair.

"I've got to get back. I've been out here too long, with you," she says. "Goodnight," she adds with a nod before she walks briskly back into the kitchen.

There's more here than just a wounded girl hurt by a teenage boyfriend who couldn't find a good way to protect her from his own failures. There's more here than a successful chef and entrepreneur. More than a fiercely independent, but ultimately lonely, woman who's resisting my overtures. I don't know what it is, but whatever it is, whenever she ready to deal with it, I'm going to be there for her. Wild horses couldn't drag me away now.

CHAPTER 15

# LOVE POTION, NO. 9

### *The next night*

"Crispy brussels with balsamic reduction."

OK. Callie may be taking things too far now. I know I upset her when I asked last night about why she didn't travel. But brussels sprouts?

'You could take a page from Raquel's book and try everything at least once," she suggests with a grin. Maybe she's not too mad at me after all...

"Mom cooked brussels sprouts when we were kids. I was not a fan. Dave wasn't a fan. In fact, I don't know *anyone* who was a fan. I resolved never to eat another brussels sprout once I moved out and went to New York."

"With the band?"

She sits down at the chair across from me. I have to make an effort to keep from smiling.

"Yeah... We did really well in Virginia... the whole D.C. metro area, really. We added Rhys and Alex on drums and keyboards, and we got tapped to fill in for Telltale Signs' opening act on one leg of their tour."

"You opened for Telltale Signs?"

She sounds a little bit in awe. I know she said she's avoided music ever since we broke up, but Telltale Signs was already big by then, so she knows the name.

"We did. Twice. Mace is actually pretty cool, though he was a sensitive subject for Hunter for a while there..."

"Why?"

"Mace had a thing for Brighid. Or at least Hunter thought he did. He was a little fixated on the idea that Mace might have done more than just talk to Brighid the night they met..."

"Oh. Brighid hasn't mentioned Mace to me, so I don't know anything about that." She gestures to the plate in front of me. "Eat those, before they get cold."

I spear one of the little half globes, their edges dark brown, almost burnt-looking.

"Try it. Just once," she encourages.

I pop it in my mouth and chew, expecting the same sulfury, mushy, boiled-cabbage flavor and texture of Mom's brussels sprouts. But that's not it at all. It's like popcorn and vegetables had a baby. The savory-sweet acid flavor of the vinegar highlights the salty, nutty flavor of the crispy edges of the sprouts, which are just tender, rather than mushy.

"OK. You've made a convert," I tell her, spearing another sprout on my fork.

"See — try everything at least once," she says, a smile of satisfaction stealing across her face. "So, Brighid and Mace?"

"It was a long time ago. And Brighid's always been head-over-heels for Hunter. He'd just decided he wasn't good enough for her," I explain, suddenly noticing the parallel.

*I* broke up with *Callie* because I wasn't good enough for *her*. What makes me think I'm good enough for her now? Hunter wasn't even responsible for a chunk of who he became when we first started the band. I know that now. He knows that now. And he's also changed these last few years, cleaned up his act, even though he still made a mess of things with Brighid before they finally got together. But me — have I done enough yet to make up for my mistakes, to clear my karma? Have I managed to finally become worthy of Callie? Could I ever be truly worthy of my angel? I can only hope so.

"He just needed to believe in himself as much as she believed in him," I observe.

I've never before considered that I might be lacking in self-worth. If anything, I've been kind of an arrogant jerk at times. But the way I've dealt with women in the past... Does it all come back to me deciding I wasn't good enough to deserve a real relationship, let alone a relationship with the only woman I've ever actually loved?

Callie looks thoughtful, too, before she suddenly springs up and heads back into the kitchen.

I sure as hell hope I can do a better job of proving to Callie that we can be together again than Hunter did finally claiming Brighid as his own. That was an epic disaster, even if it all worked out in the end. Looking at it that way, I'm kind of glad that Dave and Piper didn't have that kind of relationship drama when they got together. But then my brother's nothing if not low-key. I got all the drama genes in the family, I think.

"Declan! What are you doing here?"

I look up from the last few brussels sprouts on my plate to find Brighid standing by the table across the aisle, Hunter behind her, with his hands on her hips, almost like he's restraining her, and Alex behind him, smirking.

Great.

"I'm eating dinner."

"In Callie's restaurant..." She sounds skeptical, and not a little hostile.

"Wait — this is Callie's restaurant? All this time I've been searching for her, and I was eating dinner nightly in her restaurant? What are the chances of that!" I add with a wink. "The food's really good, I have to admit."

"She knows you're here."

I nod at her, a little smug.

"And she's OK with that?" Again with the skepticism. Come on, Bridge, cut a guy a break!

"She hasn't tried to poison me yet. Tonight," I add.

"Mother of twelve gods... Of all the things I thought I'd see today..."

"Do you want to join us, Declan?" Alex asks. "Since you're here. We've got a four-top."

Really, I don't. I want to leave a seat open at my table for two, in hopes Callie will sit down and talk to me again, but I don't want to seem rude to Brighid, and I'd kind of like her to see that Callie's fine with me being here. At least she seems like it, even if she served me brussels sprouts as another one of her little tests.

Speak of the devil...

"Insalata di Mare," Callie announces before realizing that my attention is focused on the table across the way. "Brighid! Alex!"

"Wait... you know Alex, too?" Brighid seems pretty confused at the turn of events tonight.

"Of course I do," Callie says, setting my plate down in front of me. "You sent him to me, didn't you?"

"That was a while ago," Brighid hedges. "And I didn't realize he'd actually come in here, let alone met you."

"She's been giving me cooking lessons for a little while now," Alex says.

"Wow. OK. I get engaged and I fall totally out of the loop..."

"We've been a little busy lately, Bridge," Hunter tells her, looking down on her with an expression that is simultaneously adoring and lustful. I don't want to know.

"Yeah," she says, blushing. "Callie, this is Hunter, just so you've officially met." They nod politely at each other, and all of us ignore the fact that she'd have met Hunter already if she hadn't fled from me at their engagement party.

"So, Dec — are you joining us?" Alex invites again.

Callie raises an eyebrow at me in question, and since it seems the logical thing to do, "Sure," I say.

She places the plate at one of the settings at the larger table, and I move over myself and my drink, letting Brighid, Hunter and Alex settle into the other seats.

"That looks... interesting," Hunter says, tipping his chin at my plate, clearly a little dubious.

"As I was just saying — Insalata di Mare with cuttlefish, anchovy, squid, oysters and a touch of shiso."

I chuckle.

"No octopus?" I ask Callie.

"They're too intelligent. I won't serve them."

"I wouldn't either. Octopi never wear shirts, and eight is more shoes than I've ever seen on one."

They all look at me, puzzled. Then Callie bursts into laughter.

"No shoes, no shirt, no service," she explains, smiling at my joke.

The rest of them laugh mildly, and that's OK. Callie thought it was funny. That's all that matters to me.

"Octopuses," Brighid corrects. "Octopi if we were speaking Latin. Octopodes if it was Greek. But octopus is English, so octopuses."

"And now I've learned two things today," I observe. "One: I like brussels sprouts, and, two, the proper plural of octopus is octopuses."

Brighid, Hunter and Alex all stare at me in disbelief.

"What? Why is everyone looking at me?"

"You're acting very... un-Declan-like," Brighid says. "Cracking jokes..."

"Taking a correction without getting bent out of shape," Hunter adds, finishing her thought in a way that feels incredibly familiar.

Is this what the two of them are like now that they're together, on the same page? Are they brain-sharing, too? Do all couples do this? Or is it just the ones that fate brings together?

"Smiling," Alex adds, his expression curious.

"I'll send your waitress over," Callie says, again seeming thoughtful. "Enjoy," she adds, looking at me.

"You're really going to eat that?" Alex asks. "I mean, I'd happily eat anything Callie prepared, but you... You wouldn't eat pork chops the last time I made them."

"Pigs are highly intelligent. I stopped eating pork a year ago. Except bacon."

The three of them exchange a look. I shrug and start tasting all the varieties of seafood Callie has added to this cold salad. Wow. Again. Amazingly fresh and sweet. It reminds me of the seafood in her Nonna's spicy pasta dish all those years ago. There's no question where Callie gets the chef genes, even though she's expanded far beyond Nonna's recipes, it seems.

Alex reaches over and spears an oyster off my plate.

"Hey! This is mine. Made specially for me. Get your own food!"

"Oysters are an aphrodisiac," Brighid observes, frowning slightly.

"So you two have been indulging for a while now, I take it? In oysters, I mean," I add with just a touch of snark.

"Cute," Hunter says, nonetheless grabbing Brighid's hand and entwining their fingers in the small space between them.

The waitress arrives and takes their orders for drinks and appetizers, standing closer to Alex than she needs to.

"Chef Callie is handling my meal personally," I remind her when she gets to me.

"What would you recommend?" Alex asks, and she leans over his menu to point out a dish or two.

He smirks at Hunter and me, knowing we've both seen this happen a hundred times over the years. Alex never flirts back, let alone takes the girls up on it. That's Rhys' and Kieran's thing, or it was until recently. Kieran's off his game where girls go, for some unknown reason. It's not like he's trying to win back his ex-girlfriend of a decade ago. But something's up there.

"The arancini are amazing," she says, picking up his hand to point to the appetizer on the menu and letting her hand slide across his skin when she releases him. I half expect him to shake her off, but he doesn't. Interesting...

Wait... arancini?

"Could I have an order of those, too? Tell Callie I asked."

I don't know why I'm feeling territorial about what is a pretty standard Italian dish, but I am.

I busy myself with my own appetizer.

"OK, Dec — what's going on here?" Hunter asks.

"I'm eating dinner."

"With the woman who literally ran away from you at our engagement party?"

"Well, not at the moment. I'm eating with you at the moment."

"Obviously." He and Brighid exchange a look. Alex is too busy watching the waitress as she leans over to refill water glasses at the next table, causing her short skirt to ride up.

What the heck is going on with him? This is just weird. Was Brighid right about oysters being an aphrodisiac?

"Whole fried lionfish with bagna cauda over fresh linguine with a lionfish sauce," Callie announces as she returns with my entrée, smiling again when she sees I've eaten every morsel of the seafood salad. Except that one oyster that Alex stole. But I won't rat him out to her.

"Whoa..." Hunter says, his eyes going wide as he takes in the spectacle in front of me, the fish arrayed on its belly, looking like it just swam through some breading and onto my plate.

"Is that...?" Brighid asks.

"Yes, a lionfish, like those pretty ones you see in saltwater aquariums sometimes," Callie replies. "Some irresponsible aquarium owners released them into the wild years ago, and with no natural predators in domestic waters, they've been reproducing to the point they've become an invasive species and are destroying reefs, especially in Florida. I've been trying to get some in to help encourage the fishery, see if we can get them eradicated where they're invasive, or at least under control. They're actually really good eating," she adds.

"But aren't they poisonous?" Brighid asks.

I give Callie a look. Maybe I've overestimated how well tonight was going...

"Venomous. And it's just the spines," Callie assures us, "which I've carefully trimmed. We don't want any unfortunate accidents," she adds, smirking at me. I'm not quite sure how to take that. "Cooking neutralizes the venom. I also made some cuts so it's easy to remove the fillets from the sides, as well as to let the bagna cauda flavor the flesh of the fish. And there's an extra plate underneath to remove the bones to."

"That's..." Hunter starts, seeming at a loss for words.

"Amazing," I finish for him. "What an eye-catching presentation! Brava!"

"Do you have any more lionfish back there, or is that one special for Declan?" Alex asks, his tone teasing.

"I have a few more..." Callie replies, seeming a little reluctant to share my special dish with the others.

"I'd actually love to try that myself," Alex says.

"Count me in. I want to at least be able to say I've tried it," Brighid says, giving Hunter a look.

"Make it three," he finally says, caving in to peer pressure.

"Your appetizers should be out shortly," Callie says. "Including your arancini, Declan." She smiles shyly at me, and I about fall out of my chair. She remembered. It's been thirteen years, and she still remembers the first thing she cooked for me. And it made her smile... Maybe I actually stand a chance with her after all.

Nearly an hour later, we've all finished our entrées, though I'm the only one who didn't leave anything except the fish bones and skin. I'm going to have to double my gym time this week.

"Box, please," Hunter tells the waitress, who brushes against Alex's shoulder as she clears away our plates.

The smile Alex gives her is... well... lascivious. He had two glasses of wine with dinner, and he doesn't even seem tipsy, but he's acting so unusually flirty for Alex that I have to double-check my beverage count. I look over at Hunter, who surely would have noticed this strange behavior as well, but he's inched over closer to Brighid during dinner, and, if I'm not mistaken, is now running their joined hands along her thigh. And they didn't have any oysters. Well, they're also newly engaged, so maybe that's all this is.

"Dessert?" Callie asks, turning up at my elbow.

"You aren't going to just bring me something?" I ask, having gotten used to letting her take charge of my menu for the night.

"Well, I wasn't going to bring you something without at least asking the others what they wanted," she explains.

"What do you recommend?" Brighid asks.

"Better yet — what are you making for Declan?" Alex asks.

"I was going to serve him a strawberry cream cake."

"That sounds amazing!" Brighid enthuses.

"One for me, too," Alex says.

Hunter, who I know for a fact loves chocolate almost as much as he loves Brighid, once again caves to the peer pressure. Or maybe it's curiosity at this point, since these are Callie's special dishes for me. Whatever it is, soon we each have a piece of layered golden cake, custard and strawberries in front of us, topped with whipped cream and more strawberries.

"Wow, that looks good," the man at the next table comments. "I didn't see that on the dessert menu..."

"It's an off-menu special," Callie says.

"Could we...?" he asks.

"Sure," she says, nonetheless seeming a little reluctant again.

We all dig in to our desserts, the other couple not far behind us and catching up fast.

"Oh, yum," the woman says. "This is incredible."

"You've got whipped cream on your nose," Brighid tells Hunter, tapping the end of his nose with her finger and depositing the whipped cream she'd claimed was already there but wasn't. I start to envision another near food-fight, but instead, she kisses the whipped cream off his nose.

"Whoops!" the waitress says, stumbling as she goes to refill Alex's water glass. He reaches out to stop her fall and ends up with her sitting in his lap, neither of them seeming unhappy about that.

What is happening here?

The couple at the next table has finished their desserts before I'm even half done with mine, and they're scooched up next to each other, making out in a way that makes even me a little uncomfortable. And that's before I glance back over at Brighid and Hunter, who's eating with his left hand, even though he's not left-handed. Because his right hand is in Brighid's lap, moving methodically under the tablecloth, though I'm the only one seated at an angle where it's possible to notice it.

I look judiciously away. As many times as I've seen one of the guys being intimate with a groupie, or even one of their girlfriends, this is a bit much, being as it's in Callie's restaurant and not in a semi-private dressing room or hotel hospitality suite. My eyes land on the other couple, whose roaming hands aren't even hidden by a tablecloth, though they've still got a layer of clothing between their skin.

I look away, my eyes going to the kitchen door, hoping Callie will emerge so I can at least confirm I'm not losing my mind in some kind of libidinous fever-dream, and maybe get everyone back under control again. No such luck. I look around for a hostess, another waiter — someone, *anyone* who might restore sanity to the room...

A group at a table for six closer to the door is also acting strangely, a couple of them patting the others on the back. When I look more closely, I realize they're all crying. Over slices of a peach tart, from the looks of it.

"Nonna's was just like this," a man says, sniffling.

"I know! Do you remember all those times we went peach-picking when we were here during the summer? It's been too long! We need to go do that while we're here!" a woman replies, wiping tears from her face.

"I wasn't even here then, but you all make it sound so wonderful!" a second man says, beaming a smile under glassy eyes while his female companion rubs his back.

I look around and see emotional reactions at every table. Couples making out, a father gazing lovingly at his toddler, waiters happily chatting up a girls' night group...

Did Callie poison me after all, and I'm now hallucinating?

There's a moan next to me, and I glance over to find Hunter with his nose in Brighid's cleavage, her face suffused with arousal. He looks up at her, beaming proudly, then giving her an open-mouthed kiss.

"Better now, Bridge?" he asks seductively.

Her smile is shy, satisfied. Then her eyes open, and she looks around, startled.

"Oh, my gods!" she exclaims, catching my curious glance. She looks back down at the table and pushes Hunter away. "Hunt... I..."

She looks over at Alex, who has joined the free-roaming-hands contingent with the waitress on his lap, and her expression goes from mortified to alarmed.

"You, stay right here," she orders Hunter. "Do not move. Don't eat or drink anything. You hear me?"

"Sure, babe," he says, smiling up at her, obviously smitten.

"You," she says to Alex, leaning around the waitress, who is now kissing him. Brighid growls and grabs her water glass, dumping ice water into Alex's lap.

"Whoa!" he says, standing up, startled, dumping the waitress unceremoniously to the floor. "What was that for?"

"And you," she says, turning back to me. "You don't move an inch! This is all your fault!"

"What did *I* do?"

"You exist!" she hisses at me as she passes by, headed directly to the kitchen.

She turns on her heel as she hits the doorway, moving to the thermostat on the wall and sliding the switch way to the left. She rolls her eyes and grumbles before heading through the doorway for real this time.

I'm tempted to follow, but since she's already threatened to end my rock singing career by turning me into a castrato with her witchy ways, I decide to follow her orders.

# CHAPTER 16

## I PUT A SPELL ON YOU

## Callie

"Calliope Aoede Martin!"

First off, no one in my kitchen calls me Calliope. Second, no one marches into my kitchen and calls me by my full name. Until now, apparently.

In fact, no one alive today knows my middle name, except Lyric and...

Brighid.

Everyone in the kitchen is looking alarmed, knowing that no one would dare burst into my kitchen uninvited while dinner service is ongoing, even if it's nearing closing time.

"Come with me," she says, her tone brooking no argument and her hand on my arm offering no hope of escape without a struggle.

She drags me through the back door and into the alley courtyard, where I notice a few couples kissing as we fly past the tables and out through the back. She pulls me around the back of the building and up the stairs, holding her hand out impatiently when we reach the door. I dig my key out of my pocket and hand it to her. She unlocks the door and pulls me inside, shutting the door firmly behind us.

"What is going on, Brighid?"

"That's what I want to know, Callie," she says, frowning at me. "Hunter just... he just... Well, he just..." She looks embarrassed, and I'm trying to figure out what has got her so flustered.

"He just gave me an orgasm — with his hand, under the table, thank the gods! — in the middle of your restaurant!"

"What? Uh, Brighid — I think you know I can't have that kind of thing happening in the dining room... I mean, I would have given you my key if you couldn't wait long enough to walk a couple blocks to get home... Next time—"

"There will be no next time, Callie! Because neither of us planned for there to be a first time! Neither of us was... ourselves... in there just now. And we weren't the only ones. Alex was making out with one of your waitresses. The couple at the next table looked ready to strip each other naked. The group by the door was crying over old times and a peach tart!"

"What? Why didn't somebody come get me?"

"If I had to guess, I'd say it was because they were all under your spell!"

"Spell? *My* spell? What are you talking about? I know you, Lyric, Siobhan — you're all witchy types, but I don't even really believe in all that stuff. I wouldn't know how to cast a spell if I had a spellbook and an instructional video!"

"The food, Callie! The magic is in the food! Did you not know this already? Did you not know you could influence people, their emotions, with your food?"

Suddenly, I remember Nonna's warning about what would happen if she let me cook while I was counting the minutes until I could see Declan again.

*"Filling my food with impatience and thoughts of summer love! If you can't keep your focus on the food, it will all go wrong, and then I won't be able to serve it! I'll end up with diners wandering out onto the beach, looking for some pretty face to take home with them..."*

Is this what she meant? Could Brighid possibly be right about this? I mean, I saw the couples in the courtyard as we raced past them, but... I'd have to see this with my own eyes to believe it. I turn and head for the door.

"Ah-ah-ah!" Brighid says, dragging me back to the sofa in my little studio. "Not so fast, missy! You've got some explaining to do, and we've got to do something about this so it doesn't happen again! In fact, you can't cook again until we've taken steps to address it."

Not cook? Has she lost her mind? I've got a restaurant to run, and a contest to prepare for!

"Can't you put a spell on me, or something, make it so I can't do it again?" I ask, desperate enough to credit that maybe there is something to what she's saying. If so, she's the only one I know who could fix it, make it go away.

Brighid takes a deep breath and sighs.

"I could maybe put a binding spell on you," she says, sounding reluctant. "But, honestly, I don't know that it would work. Maybe if I got the entire circle to work together on it... It's not my specialty but... Lyric, Amber, Siobhan, even — they've got more experience with this kind of thing. Maybe Amber could make you an amulet or something..."

"How long would that take?"

"I don't know. At least a few days, I would think. That's assuming she could even do it."

"And the binding spell?"

"At least a couple of days. Lyric would need a babysitter, and Siobhan would have to find a night she doesn't have clients scheduled late..."

"And in the meantime?"

"You really should not be in the kitchen. And you really, really shouldn't be cooking for Declan."

"What's Declan got to do with this? I'm the one who's cooking!"

"You really don't see it, do you?"

"See what?"

"He's in love with you, Callie. He was frantic, trying to find you after the engagement party. I had to threaten to make his dick magically fall off, just to get him out of my house!"

"You did what?"

"I wouldn't. I couldn't. I have no idea how I'd even begin to follow through on that threat. But it seemed like something that would get his attention and get him to leave me alone. I mean — I'd promised you I wouldn't tell him where you were, but he was so persistent..." She sighs. "And now I start to see why... True love stops at nothing."

"What's that got to with what happened tonight? It's *my* restaurant, my food!"

"You were cooking for Declan, Callie! However you were thinking about him, feeling about him a day ago, a week ago, a month ago — clearly, you've got some unresolved feelings that aren't exactly hostile. And, frankly, I'd be kind of afraid what would happen if you were actively angry with him when you were cooking."

"I was angry with him when I cooked for him that first night," I admit. "I wanted him to go away. I... Siobhan didn't mention anything about that?"

"Uh... no. What did you do?"

"I may have cooked foods I knew he would hate — way too much onion, super-spicy... there may have been a muskrat involved..."

"A muskrat? Like a beaver, but with a ratty tail? That muskrat?"

"Yeah. They're native to the area. Old-timey Sussex County delicacy."

"I know. But you have them in your restaurant?"

"Well, no. I sent someone to one of the restaurants that serves them and they let me have one."

Brighid chuckles. "Remind me never to make you mad at me."

And now I'm remembering the couple from last night, the ones who got into a fight before I even got their entrées served... Could that have been me, too?

Brighid's expression is pensive.

"How did Declan react to what you served him?" she finally says.

"He ate it. All of it. Everything I served him, no matter how unpalatable."

"With no ill effects?"

"I mean, his eyes watered a lot when the ghost peppers kicked in..."

"Ghost peppers? Was that with the muskrat?"

"No, that was the chocolate dessert."

"You spiked his dessert with ghost peppers?"

"Yup."

I'm not proud of it. OK, yes, I was proud of it. Briefly.

"You're dangerous even without putting magic into the food!" She shakes her head at me. "But Declan didn't have any kind of unusual reaction? Like vomiting, or hallucinations, or crying inconsolably?"

"Not that I know of."

"Tell me again exactly how you two got married."

"Lyric did it. A handfasting, she called it. She said it could be for a year and a day, or a lifetime—"

"Or forever," Brighid finishes. "And you picked...?"

"Forever. We both said it at the same moment, no hesitation. We were really deeply in love. Or so I thought," I add. "We were just kids. We didn't know better."

"You said it at the same moment? Using the same words?"

"Well, yeah. We did that a lot. We called it brain-sharing..." I hesitate.

"What? What aren't you saying?"

"We've done it a couple times since he came back."

She closes her eyes and exhales sharply.

"What is it with these Carter boys and being lifebonded?" she says, sounding a little frustrated, but also marveling...

"What's that mean?"

"Nothing... Not my business to talk about. Sorry. But you two... you and Declan... Did you do anything to nullify the handfasting when you broke up?"

"I didn't see Declan after that. Lyric offered to try, asked for the ribbons back. But since I didn't really believe in that stuff, I didn't take her up on it. She offered again the other day, and I declined again, especially when she said she didn't think it was likely to work. Whatever that meant."

"It means you two made a sacred contract with each other when you were... what? 16?"

"We were 17. Just months shy of being able to marry legally."

"I'd say you got off lightly with no lawyers being needed, but you really didn't," Brighid says. "Lyric was right. When she marries people, it sticks."

"How'd you know she said that?"

"Who do you think is performing Hunter's and my handfasting?"

"Oh. You sure you want to do that, after all of this?"

"Yes!" She sighs. "It's not the same with us. We've had our problems and we've put them behind us. And we're already married in all the ways that count, except legally. This is more like a vow renewal. Well, a second one."

"Is that what he meant when he asked you to marry him 'again'?"

She nods.

"I know this is all foreign to you, but you dove in deep when you made the promises you did as teenagers. Hunter and I... We've been married before — in at least one past life."

I frown, unable to hide my skepticism.

"Doubt me if you must," she says. "But I had my first vision when I was just 15, and what I saw was Hunter and me, man and wife, living in Ireland about two hundred years ago."

"And you believe that was real?"

"I know it was. I've been back there, to that same spot. I've seen it with my own eyes. And I never told Hunter the details of what I'd seen, in reality or in my visions. But he knew — because after we finally got together, he had a vision of his own, and he saw what I'd seen."

I don't want to be disrespectful of Brighid or her relationship with Hunter, but none of this is real to me. And the only proof I have of what she's saying about my cooking is a few couples kissing, another fighting and Nonna's warning, which I didn't even understand at the time, assuming that was even what Nonna meant when she said it.

"I know. You don't believe any of this. That's fine. Except you need to understand what you're dealing with, in regards to you, your cooking and Declan. You two are bonded," she says definitively. "He's not affected by your kitchen magic the same way everyone else is, because you two are already tied together, almost like a single being. But your feelings for him are ramping up the power of your food, to a whole new level. And you've got to get that under control, or you're going to keep creating scenes like what happened tonight."

"I still don't know what happened in the dining room! All I saw was a few couples kissing when you dragged me up here!"

"Do you have security cameras in the dining room?"

"Well, yeah. Just in case there's a break-in overnight, or in case someone trips and files a lawsuit or something."

"How do you see the video?"

"There's a monitor down in my office."

She grabs my hand again.

"Let's go. You can see it for yourself!"

Ignoring the stares from my staff as Brighid and I parade back to my office, I cue up the security video from tonight's dinner service, starting when Declan first came in.

I'm startled to see how many times I smile at him as I serve his meal. Maybe Brighid is right about my unresolved feelings for Declan. And maybe he was right. As much as I hate him for what he did to me, the 17-year-old me who promised to love him forever meant that. And maybe undoing that isn't as easy as taking back the words or destroying some magical ribbons. The question now is whether I even want to. The woman in this video certainly seems like maybe she might still mean the things she promised all those years ago.

"See — there!" Brighid says, pointing to Alex's image on the screen as he snatches an oyster off of Declan's plate. "I told Declan oysters were an aphrodisiac!"

"They're just fresh local oysters — they're doing aquaculture in the Inland Bays now."

"All oysters are aphrodisiacs, Callie. You're a chef. You know that."

"I don't really think about them that way. I mean, it's not like I'm serving up a big plate of them in someone's honeymoon suite."

"Right... But watch..."

I follow along as Alex gets progressively flirtier with Vivienne.

"Ugh." Brighid groans, cringing and then closing her eyes so she doesn't have to watch as Hunter starts sucking on the side of her neck. If I'm honest, it's actually pretty arousing to watch. They could make a mint doing real-relationship porn, between that and that first kiss they had during Hunter's reality dating show — the one that went viral. Siobhan showed me. Really! I finally hit the fast-forward button, keeping my eyes on Alex and the other diners so I don't see way more than I should of my friend and her fiancé.

Throughout all of this, Declan is looking around him, visibly growing increasingly concerned about what he's seeing. And what he's seeing is exactly what Brighid described — the couples making out, groping each other (or more, in Brighid and Hunter's case), the larger group getting maudlin over my peach tart, which was based on Nonna's old recipe from the days when she sent me to pick peaches by hand, to ensure each one was perfect.

Vivienne might normally be one of my flirtier waitstaff, but sitting in a patron's lap? I don't care that Alex is a rockstar. That's just not something she would do, let alone the things that happen between them — until Brighid wakes from what I have to admit looks like a fairytale spell (if a very sexy one) and dumps ice water into Alex's lap.

Wow.

I've got to go deal with this. Right now. Whatever happened, however it happened, whoever is responsible — this is my restaurant and my mess to clean up.

It's very quiet in the kitchen. Everyone seems to have shifted into closing mode. I check the clock, surprised to discover that it's at least a half-hour earlier than usual for that.

I quirk an eyebrow at Drew, to whom I owe an explanation at least as much as he owes me one, but I can deal with my explanation later.

"The dining room got uncomfortably chilly, and people were in a hurry to get home," he says, shrugging.

I head through the door to the dining room, stopping at the thermostat on the wall. It's at the normal setting, leaving me with one more mystery.

"I turned it all the way down before I came to get you. I figured it was the closest thing to dumping ice water over everyone's heads," Brighid explains.

"Quick thinking. Thanks," I add, realizing that I owe her a lot for her help tonight. Like free-dinners-for-life levels of a lot.

The only people left in the dining room are a handful of bussers and waitstaff, plus Hunter, Alex and... Declan.

Hunter looks decidedly uncomfortable, refusing to meet my eyes.

"It's fine. Not your fault," I tell him.

"I mean, I know my fiancée is the sexiest woman on the planet, but I would never... not in public," he says. "Not after..."

Suddenly I remember Hunter and Brighid's mini-scandal, getting caught on camera while engaged in a little foreplay in her shop, and having that go viral, too. She flushes even more than she did when she was trying to explain to me what had happened.

"I'm so, so sorry," I tell them both.

"Erase that video and we'll just pretend it never happened," she says.

"Done. The moment I get the rest of this sorted out. At least for tonight."

"Alex, I think I owe you an apology, too."

"I'm not entirely sure why. Just like I'm not entirely sure what happened here," he says.

"Magic," Hunter says, wiggling his left hand in what looks half like he's casting a spell and half like he's showing off that his hand is no longer broken. Maybe both. He shrugs at Alex. "You'd be surprised how many impossible things you come to believe when you're marrying a witch."

"I am not a witch, Hunter!" Brighid objects. I'm not sure even she believes that, but she's very adamant about preferring to be called a priestess.

"Half a witch, then." He smirks at her. She smacks him playfully on the shoulder. I can't help but smile. The two of them are so cute together, now that they're finally together. Even the love skeptic spawned by that brokenhearted 17-year-old inside me has to admit that. I'm happy for her, even if I'm still a little irked about what he put her through.

"So, Callie's a witch, too?"

"Callie is something unique," Brighid says. "But mostly a chef. And I warned you, Alex — oysters are an aphrodisiac! Next time, listen."

"I can confirm that it's always best to listen to Brighid when she tells you something," Hunter adds, seeming very certain of that.

And I'm forced to take that advice into consideration myself, because Brighid has told me some things tonight that I'd desperately like to pretend were just the result of an overactive imagination. But having watched that video, I really can't. It wasn't just Alex and a single oyster.

"I think it would be best if we all stuck with that explanation for what happened tonight and pretend that none of it actually happened," Brighid suggests.

"Fine by me," Alex says, looking sheepishly at Vivienne where she stands on the other side of the dining room, doing fresh table settings on the cleared tables.

"I'll have a talk with her, Alex," I volunteer. "I'll just tell her we're all overlooking any behavior that was over the line tonight. She'll be glad of that."

"Thanks, Callie. Tell her I'm sorry... I don't know what came over me."

"The same thing that came over her," Hunter says with a chuckle. "And me..." He kisses Brighid on the top of her head. "Sorry about that, babe."

"You can make it up to me later... Or, rather, I'll make it up to you, since only one of us got to fully enjoy that," she says, smirking at him. "Gods, that was mortifying, though," she adds.

"You're beautiful when you come..." he murmurs, just loudly enough for all of us at the table to hear.

"And on that note..." Declan says, drawing my attention to him — the one person I haven't yet looked in the eye after this debacle.

"Dinner's on the house, guys. I'll cover the tips myself."

"That's not necessary!" Brighid objects.

"The food was excellent, regardless of whatever else happened," Alex says, pulling his wallet out.

"Nope! Not a penny from any of you. I owe you a lot already for tonight. So, please, go, enjoy your evening and try to pretend none of this happened."

"Except for me," Brighid says. "I'm going to pull together some resources, and we'll get back to you."

By "resources," I assume she means her circle, or Amber, or both.

"Thanks again," I tell her, unsure how I can ever really make up for what happened tonight.

I lock the door behind the three of them, noting that Declan hasn't moved.

"Everyone, go home. Anything you haven't done can be done in the morning."

"That was weird, with the heat and the air conditioning, Callie," Vivienne says, making an excuse for the odd end to the night that I think they're all glad to accept. I'll leave it at that.

"I'll have someone come in first thing tomorrow and look at it," I tell her, knowing I'll be doing no such thing. "You'll all get an extra fifty percent on top of your tips for tonight to make up for closing so abruptly."

"Thanks, Callie!" they chorus, filtering out through the kitchen.

I do a quick walk-through of the dining room, looking for checks and tips that might have been left behind, or any possessions the fleeing diners might have missed.

"Callie, I..." Declan starts as I get back to his table.

"Not now, Declan," I tell him, signaling him to wait.

I head back into the kitchen, finding it deserted except for Drew, who's doing a final wipe-down on the prep surfaces.

"I sent everyone else home. They'll come in a half-hour early tomorrow to get ready for service."

"Thanks."

I sigh.

"I don't know what to say," I finally tell him.

"Nothing needs saying," he says. "HVAC malfunction. Weird. People do strange things when they're overheated. Good thing someone turned the thermostat down when they did."

"Yeah."

I have no idea whether he's pretending nothing inexplicable happened tonight or whether he truly believes that sketchy excuse. Maybe he didn't see any of what happened in the dining room. I guess I can hope.

"I'll lock up on my way out. Get some rest," he urges me.

"I'll try."

I take a deep breath, not quite ready to face what I know awaits me in the dining room. Once Drew is outside, a locked door between him and the two people responsible for this disaster, I force myself to go out there.

Declan is sitting back at the two-top he'd occupied earlier tonight, a full glass of whiskey in front of him and a second one on the other side of the table.

"Sit," he says, gesturing to the other chair.

I don't have it in me to argue, or to have this conversation standing up, so I do as he suggests. I pick up the glass and take a hefty swig.

"So..." he says after a minute.

"So..." I repeat.

"That was... odd..."

"Yeah."

"And I gather from what Brighid and Hunter said that it wasn't something that could be explained by a malfunction of the heating system, nor by the chemical makeup of the food everyone was eating... especially since a lot of those people didn't have the same dishes the four of us had."

"Apparently," I agree, nodding solemnly.

"So... Hunter's hand..."

"Yeah."

"And now this reaction to your food..."

"Yup."

"It's a little odd that I was the only one who didn't seem to be affected."

"It is."

"Are you going to use more than a word or two at a time during this conversation, or am I going to have to start asking yes/no questions?"

I sigh.

"Nonna once told me to get out of her kitchen."

"That doesn't sound like her, from what I remember," he says.

"I don't mean it like that... She sent me out to take my break early, because I was antsy. I couldn't wait to go see you. It was that first summer, not long after we met. And I was so eager to see you again that I was rushing the food. Caramelizing onions, in fact."

He chuckles, shaking his head.

"Anyway — she set me free and finished the job herself, saying that she couldn't let me cook when I was feeling like that, because I'd ruin the food."

"Burn the onions?"

"No. Not like that." I look down at the glass in my hands, swirling the amber liquid around as I try to think how to say this and not sound insane. "She said if she let me cook when I was like that, the diners would end up wandering out on the beach, looking for a pretty face to take home. Because of my food."

"She thought you…"

"She said if I wasn't focused on the food, something like this might happen."

"And you weren't focused tonight?"

"Not like I usually am."

"And why was that?"

"I think you know."

"Because of me."

I nod.

"Do you want me to go? Do you want me to stay away?"

"I…" I genuinely don't know what to tell him. Part of me still wants him to suffer for what he did to me all those years ago. And another part of me wants to… wants us to be doing to each other what Brighid and Hunter, Alex and Vivienne, and some of my other diners were doing in this very room tonight.

The feeling shoots straight to my core. I haven't erased that video yet, but I don't need to be looking at it to remember the raw sensuality of it. In spite of his joking offer of a threesome, I haven't had a moment in all the time I've spent working with Alex in the kitchen where I felt an attraction between us. But watching him with Vivienne, even with all their clothes on… And Hunter's tongue sliding down Brighid's neck, into her cleavage, and even though it was hidden beneath the tablecloth, his hand between her thighs, the look on her face…

I glance up at Declan, only to discover that he's no longer sitting opposite me. Instead, he's standing next to me, holding out his hand. Without thinking, I put my hand in his, and he pulls me up and hard against him.

"I don't think you want me to leave," he whispers roughly. "I don't think you want me to stay away."

I shake my head fervently.

"I really, really don't."

I'm speaking into his chest, unable to look him in the eye, but I can feel his lips just above mine. So close… So…

He tips my chin up, and our lips meet, like waves crashing onto the beach. Inevitable, natural and utterly primal.

He grabs the back of my head, sinking his fingers into my hair where it's gathered up and pulling the bandana free, loosening it all to fall down my back.

"Regardless of the precedent set earlier tonight, I have no desire to have this be the place I make love to my wife for the first time in twelve years," he says.

I want to object to his calling me his wife. I'm not his wife. I haven't been his wife since the moment he reminded me that our marriage was never legal and then ended... well... us. I want to object, but I don't, lost in his touch as his fingers creep up underneath my shirt again, brushing against the base of my spine.

I grab his hand, not to keep it off my skin, but to pull him along behind me, in a much different way than Brighid dragged me up to my apartment earlier. I follow the same path, turning off the lights and locking the door to the kitchen behind us this time, tugging at his hand when he hesitates, not knowing where I'm taking him as we get to the stairs up to the loft.

I unlock the door again, pulling him inside and locking it once again, the two of us finally alone, in a space that not only isn't my place of work but that actually has a surface suitable for the things we both, clearly, want to do to each other.

"You live up here?" he asks, seeming confused. "What about Nonna's house? I mean, I looked there after I saw you the first time and found out very quickly that someone else lived there now, but..."

"I sold it after she died. It's how I got the money to open the restaurant. Property values really went way up after she and Nonno bought it. It was enough to get the lease, the equipment, tables, chairs, linens, signage, food, advertising... Opening a restaurant is expensive."

"I know, but..."

"It's fine. It's what she would have wanted. She would have loved Castalia so much. We talked about that old mythology so often in that last year before I left for culinary school, sitting by the fountain in her garden..."

"Year? You didn't go back to Philly with your parents after I left?"

I shake my head, not wanting to talk about it, about our breakup, about what happened after that... I just want to forget all the bad stuff and feel something good. It's been so long since I felt like this... Declan's fingers tracing along my jaw. I remember exactly how that felt, how his lips felt on my neck, sucking my nipples, my clit, into his mouth... I remember all of it. Like it was yesterday. I wonder if he remembers it, too, or have those memories been lost to all of the women he's had since?

I shake my head again, not willing to give up feeling like this, no matter what's happened since, for either of us.

I pull his shirt up, and he raises his arms over his head, letting me strip him down to the skin. This is one thing that has changed... his body is no longer that of a teenage boy. He's not musclebound, but he clearly spends some time in the gym. My fingers trace across the ripples of his abs, the planes of his pecs, the gentle hills and valleys of his shoulders and biceps.

"God, I missed this, angel. I missed you so much... I'm so sorry... I..."

I shush him, putting my fingers over his lips.

"Not now. Not tonight," I tell him firmly. He nods, moving to strip me just as naked as he is. I chuckle as he struggles with the fastenings on the chef's coat, taking charge of that while he watches, licking his lips in anticipation... or is it nervousness? Could the rockstar, the ladies' man, actually be nervous about being with me? A woman who hasn't ever slept with another man?

He shudders as I pull my shirt over my head. My body's a little more ample than it was at 17. My breasts a little bigger, more curve to my hips, my thighs. Cooking six days a week is physically demanding, but I didn't get into food as my career without also loving to eat. Siobhan's weekly self-defense refresher is the only real exercise I get. So, I can't help but wonder what Declan thinks of this adult body of mine, no longer quite as lithe as it once was.

He steps forward, running his thumb across the satiny fabric of my bra cup, along the straps, taking me in...

"How is it possible that you're even more beautiful than you were at 17?" he says, his other hand moving to my hip.

# CHAPTER 17

## SWEET SURRENDER

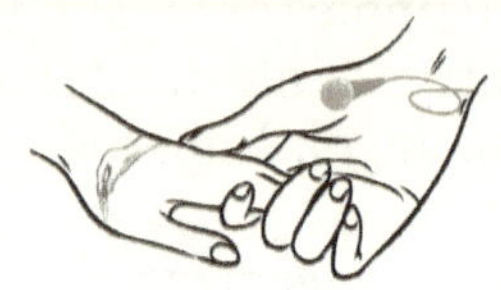

### Declan

I don't know... Maybe it sounds like a line to her, but I've lied to Callie exactly once in my life. I'm never doing it again. Especially not tonight, when she's finally giving me a chance to show her how I really feel about her, how I've always felt about her.

I don't look exactly like I did at 17. I'd like to think I've improved with age, or certainly with the time I spend in the gym. Our most recent tour included a mobile gym in the front part of our equipment trailer, though Rhys complained constantly that there was no climbing wall. Every time we were on a bill for a festival that had one, he spent half his downtime climbing the damn thing. But, hey, it takes the edge off for him, and with Rhys, that's always a good thing. Me, I probably spend more time in the gym than any of the other guys. I'm not shallow or anything. Really. Seriously. Stop laughing, OK? I just know what sells with our fans, and me taking my shirt off sells. But that's work. This is... so not work. Having Callie's hands on me again — it's like a dream come to life.

And she's a dream herself. She's not like I remembered. She's better. She's ripened, like a fine wine or a lush rose blossom. A woman, not a girl. In my head, she's still *my* girl, but she's a woman now — strong, independent, beautiful. I want to break down this wall, though — the things that are still between us after all these years. But not tonight. She says not tonight, and I can't deny her that — this chance to lose ourselves in each other, for just one night. It's a crack in that armor around her heart, and if I can get her to let me in just that much, I know I can find my way inside, back into her heart again.

"You always did have that silver tongue," she says, deflecting the compliment.

"All the better to taste you with, angel."

Her eyes fall closed, and she moans, and I'm rock hard for her again. I never needed anything more — just a look, a sound from Callie, and I wanted her. That hasn't changed, either.

But I do want to taste her... need to. I arrived in her restaurant already starving for her, twelve years going without, and the taste of her I got that day just whetted my appetite.

I pull her face between my hands, cradling her jaw, tracing my thumbs over her cheekbones, and I just barely touch my lips to hers, coaxing her to meet me halfway. She does more than that, pulling me hard against her. Skin against skin, but not nearly enough. I learned how to unhook a bra with this girl, and it's been a while, but I haven't forgotten how to make the experience a sensual one for her. I slide the straps down her shoulders, slowly, first one and then the other. I nuzzle into her neck, taking in the scent of her, pressing kisses down the side of her neck, and then I unhook the back of her bra. She throws her head back, and I dive into her cleavage, pressing kisses there, too.

Callie drops her arms, and the bra begins to slide downwards, ever so slowly, and I follow it, my arms wrapping around her, and my mouth traveling down to capture her nipple as soon as the bra falls free. She pants as I suck on it, reaching between us to pinch the other one lightly.

"Too long," she breathes, and I'm in total agreement. It's been too long since I've touched her like this.

She grabs for my waist, undoing my belt like it's been hours, and not years, since she last did this. And then my jeans, which I kick to the side the moment they hit my ankles.

And then it's my turn again. I may have had trouble with her chef's coat, but the pants are no problem, coming off easily as I caress her hips and then her thighs, bringing them down until she steps out of them. Again, those full hips, her thighs strong and shapely. I grab her ankle before she can put it back down to stand, pressing a kiss there, too — I'd kiss every inch of her given the time to do it properly. Now, though, I trail my tongue back up the inside of her calf, her thigh, until I'm facing what I'd really wanted for dessert for days, and pretty much every day before that for the better part of fifteen years.

I pull her pussy against my mouth, kissing her there, too, atop the satiny barrier between my tongue and that promised land.

"You were very good with that tongue down there, too, if I remember correctly," she says, still breathing heavily in anticipation.

"I'm a little out of practice," I admit. More so than she'd probably believe. But she said no talking about that stuff tonight, and I'll leave it at that. For now.

"I'd bet," she says, scoffing. "Lots of women would be happy to take care of the rockstar first..."

Hey, now! No fair! What can I say to that? *Sorry, babe — I'm not nearly the narcissistic jackass you think I am. I take care of my partners, one way or another!* That's not going to win me any points with her.

"Well, this rockstar is putting *you* first." Tonight, and from this point forward. And we *will* talk about that later. In the meantime...

## Callie

I'll believe that when I...

Oh, god...

That tongue of his... licking me through the satin.

Silver-tongued devil, indeed.

It *has* been too long. There's a very good chance I'll come at the first touch of his tongue to my clit. Or just another swipe through the damp satin.

I pant as he does it again, just barely holding it together.

He grabs the sides of my panties and slides them down over my hips, dropping them at my feet, and he pulls me hard against his mouth, nosing into my slit.

"I've dreamed of this so many times," he says. A likely story. It's not like he's had any shortage of available pussy over the last decade and change. But he's making an effort to seduce me, even now that he's got me stripped naked in front of him. I'll give him that much. I'd never admit it, but I've dreamed a lot of scenes like this myself over the years. That's half the reason it was so hard to resist tonight. And that's the point — indulge tonight, give him his walking papers in an hour or six, and then put this all behind me for good.

Oh, good god...

His tongue laps at me, and it's like I'm transported back in time. Could he have been telling the truth? Because either I'm perfectly responsive to his standard technique or he actually remembers exactly how I like to be touched. I don't let myself hold onto that thought, grabbing onto his hair and pressing him against me just as his hands caress my ass and pull me even harder against his face.

Oh, that's new — the brush of scruff against my pussy. It adds a new layer of sensation to what I remembered so well from before. Does he have any idea what that feels like? I moan, and I can feel him smile against me. Well, if he didn't know before, he does now. He brushes against me again, purposely this time. Then another caress from his tongue.

I'm already so close... And he knows that, too. He dives in with his lips and tongue, working me hard, fast, while I tangle my fingers into that grown-out hair of his, holding on for dear life. He slides a finger inside me, pressing against that one little spot, trapping me between sensations, and that's it. I explode, coming all over his tongue while his hand pressing me against him from behind is the only thing keeping me upright.

And then it's not, as my knees go weak and start to buckle under me. He stands, his hand cradling me, offering support from between my thighs while the waves continue to roll through me.

"You're so sexy when you come, angel," he whispers in my ear. "Let's see you do it again..."

He pulls me to the bed, pressing me down against the mattress before my spasms have even stopped from the first time.

He's proving a point. He's got to be. But it's not like I'm going to stop him.

He slides two fingers inside me, reminding me how long it's been since anyone's been in there, with fingers or otherwise. It's tight, but it feels so good, being filled up like this. He works me with the one hand, while the other spreads my lower lips apart for his perusal and then access for lips that feel like they want to suck me inside out. He's suctioned to my clit, pulling hard, and it feels incredible. This is new. New for us. And like nothing I've ever experienced before. So close to that first orgasm, it's too intense and perfect, all at the same time. And I'm on a rising tide again in an instant.

"Come for me, angel... I want to see you do it again."

I force my eyes open and look down at him, positioned as he is between my thighs. And it is — it's a dream come true. Those deep blue eyes, looking up at me, anticipating, almost... worshiping. And when he sees me looking back at him, he sucks me back into his mouth, thrusting his fingers inside me, never blinking as he watches... watches me...

"Aaahhhh!"

My eyes roll up as the sound rushes from my mouth, uncontrolled and probably loud enough to wake any neighbors who turned in early. And catch the attention of any who haven't.

Declan keeps working me with fingers and mouth until the last wave subsides, then he looks up at me, an expression of satisfaction on his face, that cocky smile barely budging as he swipes away traces of my arousal from his luscious lips and then from his fingers. It's pride, not arrogance, that I see on his face as he stands at the end of the bed. He knows what he did, breaking me free from any restraints I had on myself, and I can't for a moment regret it.

I sit up, knowing this has to be reciprocal, and reach for his boxer-briefs, sliding them down and taking him in for the first time like this, naked from head to toe.

The years have been kind to Declan Carter. He was glorious at 17. At 29, he's astounding. That teenager inside me wants to weep, looking at him like this — my eyes and mouth presented with some astoundingly beautiful manhood. It's not like I've had a lot for comparison, but I know what I like when I see it, and I can't help but see this nor keep myself from wanting it.

I pull his hips closer to the bed, remembering how he liked to be touched, with hands and mouth, and trying to sink into that memory. But he pushes me away.

"Not right now, angel," he says. "I'd like to say tonight's just about you, because it really should be. But I want you so bad right now that I won't last long if you put your mouth on me. Been wanting you too long," he says, reaching down to caress my jaw again. "And I need to bury myself in you, right now..." The look he gives me is... vulnerable? Could it be that Declan Carter is unsure of himself? Even after I just tried to go down on him? "It's been too long. I need inside you, Callie. Please."

His pleading tone confounds me, but he pulls my hand back to his cock, showing me how hard he is in a way that I can't deny. I nod absently, losing myself as soon as those blue eyes of his catch my own.

Declan reaches for his jeans, pulling out his wallet and then a short strip of condoms.

My expression is questioning. For someone who seemed unsure of himself a moment ago, he certainly came prepared.

"Expecting a sudden outbreak of orgies?" I ask him, at least a trace of hostility making it into my voice.

"Hardly," he says with a smirk and a shrug. "I just wanted to be prepared, should you take pity on me. Because, like I said — it's been too long. I won't last long the first time, not with you. And I want a chance for us both to enjoy it again, more slowly, the second time. And the third..."

"It's a bit presumptuous, thinking that I'd want more than a quick fuck." That's all bravado on my part. Can't have him thinking I'm easy. Even if I tortured him a little before we even got to this point.

"I've never thought of you as a quick fuck, Callie," he says, crawling onto the bed. "It may be quick, at least this first time, but there's no way it's just a fuck. Not between the two of us."

And that's when it hits me. He's serious. This isn't just a casual one-night thing for him. Whatever brought him here, to me, he's got something more in mind than just wham-bam-thank-you-ma'am. Just what that is, I'm not sure. And I don't trust for a moment that he's talking about any kind of commitment. Soon enough, he'll be headed back to New York or out on the road, back to his groupies. But whatever he's looking for tonight, it means something to him, even if that thing is just scratching an itch with an ex.

Realizing that, I'm no longer sure I trust myself to do this. It's a wordless invitation to get invested in Declan, in us, again. And I learned the hard way how much of a mistake that could be.

With both of us now on our knees hear the head of the bed, he runs his hand along my left hip, up to my breast, cupping it gently in his hand before brushing the hard tip of my nipple with his thumb. He pulls me against him, pressing his erect cock between us exactly where we both want it to go. Because I do. Whatever he's got in mind, no matter the things I will no longer consider on the table with him, this is what we both want right now, and I'm of a mind that we'll have that. At least this once.

# Declan

I pull her hand to me again, relishing the feel of her fingers as they wrap around me. Part of me never dared dream this could be real, not again. But there's no denying that it is real as she pumps my cock lightly, grazing her thumb over the tip of me, where I'm literally weeping for her.

The only reason I'm not coming all over her hand, over both of us, right now is that the condom conversation threw me. I don't want her thinking about me being with anyone else, let alone like that. The few condoms I brought were all intended for her. Yeah, I had high hopes after things started to improve between us the last couple nights. But it was just that — a hope. Now, it's real, and the reality of that is... well, it's going straight to my dick.

"Do you remember how to do this?" I ask her, hoping she'll put the condom on me herself. I used to love that, watching her do it, practicing, in the first weeks we were together, before she was on the pill long enough to ensure they were working. The condom was probably the only thing that kept me from coming in an instant that first time we were together. But watching her do it... feeling her doing it — that was indescribably arousing.

"I think I can manage," she says, giving me a teasing smile that almost makes me come right then and there. I remember that girl — unsure, but eager to learn, eager to explore, the two of us eager to explore together. Passionate — for food, and, for a while there, for me.

She separates a condom from the strip and tears into the wrapper, quickly pinching the end and rolling it onto me with a gentle hand. I hold my breath, trying not to watch her fingers work over me. No, this first time won't last long, even with the condom.

She looks up at me, seeming a little more sure of herself now that she's got that done.

"I need to be inside you, Callie. Need it like words cannot express. But I'm not going to leave you hanging. You'll get a third orgasm from me before I'm done. I promise."

I've already sworn to myself to keep all my promises to Callie, if belatedly in some cases. And it may take incredible self-control, but I'm going to keep this one, too.

I slide my hand up between her lower lips, rubbing her lightly. She leans into me, closing her eyes, and I take the chance to kiss her again, nudging her mouth open, and then she collapses into me, moaning, her tongue tangling with mine, her arms around my neck. I pull her hips against mine, rolling against her so she can feel how much I want her. She moans again, and I can't wait any longer. I line myself up with her opening and push inside, slowly, achingly slow, until I'm fully sheathed inside her.

I stop to take in her expression, which is relaxed, with her eyes closed, her head thrown back slightly, mouth open, cheeks flushed, just like her cleavage is. I've had dreams like this, but they were never this astonishingly beautiful. She looks like her namesake angel, fallen from the heavens and into my arms. And if I were to go blind in this moment, I'd be OK with that, since this is the last thing I'd ever see. Yeah. Totally OK with that.

I start moving against her, withdrawing and then surging back inside. Honestly, I'd forgotten how good this feels, being inside Callie. It's like she was made to fit me, and I don't just mean how we fit together physically. It's how we make each other feel when we're like this, and even when we're not. It's like coming home after too long on the road, like sliding into bed after a long day and just reveling in it. And it wasn't until right now that I realized how much I'd ached for this, for her.

And still I pull out of her. Because there's something else I want right now.

"Ride me, Callie... Take me into you and make yourself come all over me," I tell her, lying back on the bed and sliding my legs between hers.

She hesitates for a moment. Has she forgotten this part? Has she forgotten doing this with me? Does she not remember how hot it was for both of us?

But, no, she smiles again, that eager expression telling me she remembers this just as well as I do. And she sidles up over me, positioning herself over my hips, aiming my cock right at her center, and slides down slowly. Watching my cock disappear inside her is one of the most erotic things I've ever experienced, and I'm restraining myself, trying not to come just watching it happen.

And then she's sealed flat against me, enveloping me entirely. It's a different kind of ecstasy, being one with her like this. It's that feeling of home, but cranked up to eleven, like home was on the top of a mountain, looking down over a stretch of verdant valley leading to the sea. And then she moves. Her shoulders twist as she rises up, her hips following, and then back down again as she works herself on my cock. I reach up, cupping her breasts in my hands, tweaking the nipples, and her breath catches, a slow exhale coming from her as she settles down again.

"That's it, angel, I want to see you come again. That's all I want..."

She relaxes into her movements, chasing her climax. I move one hand to her hip, reaching my thumb for her clit, and letting her seek out the stimulation she needs, from my cock inside her and from my hand. Hottest thing any man has ever seen, and if I'm extraordinarily lucky, I'm the only one who ever will — first and last for her, despite all of what's come in between.

She speeds up, brushing against my thumb, and I'm holding myself back again, praying she gets there soon. I'll wait. However long I need to, I'll wait. But it's torture, watching this erotic show while feeling her pull at my dick with her pussy clamping down on me. That's a thing she'd only just figured out the last time we were together, but she remembers that, too, it seems. My breath is coming in staggered pants now as I'm on the edge.

"Come, baby... come for me. I'm waiting for you. Let go for me... Come on my cock, you beautiful angel, you..."

"Close," she says between pants, twisting her hips and pressing her clit against my thumb.

And then, her muscles grab me, release and grab again.

"God! Declan! Oh, god!" She's shouting, but she doesn't seem to care, and I revel in it, shooting inside her as I pull her hips hard down against me, then lift her up and slam her down again, the two of us joined together in a dance to a song only the two of us can hear, over and over again, until she collapses on top of me, her head nuzzled into my neck.

We lie there, panting, unable to move. Well, *I* can't move. Not yet. And if *she* can move, she's opting not to. But judging by the look on her face, she's been rendered just as immobile as I've been.

A smile breaks out across my face. At least I think it's a smile. It's been a while since I smiled like this. I'm not sure I'd recognize the expression, even if I saw it in the mirror. But I know how I'm feeling, and this is happy. No — ecstatic. So, yeah, that should be a smile I'm wearing. A smile and nothing else... Which makes me smile even harder. Except the condom. Still wearing the condom. Which I need to take off and dispose of, which makes me smile a little less. Because I'll have to pull out of Callie, and I'm quite happy inside of her right now. And probably forever, too. But eventually, we'll both have to move. So I should probably get on that condom thing.

But I kiss her first, making eye contact with her, hoping she's as happy about this as I am.

She's not quite smiling, but she looks satisfied, and I'll take that victory. For now. Two condoms from now, if I haven't made her smile, I may have to turn in my guy card. But, for now, I'll take satisfied and a deep, open-mouthed kiss. That much, at least, I get.

When I return from her bathroom, the condom disposed of and visual verification that *I*, at least, am smiling, she's tucked herself under the covers of her bed, and I slide into them with her, spooning up against her bare back, wrapping my arms around her and tucking her head into the crook of my neck.

"I missed this, Callie. Missed it a lot. Thank you so much for giving it back to me again, angel."

"It was good," she says, sounding preoccupied. I imagine this is a lot for her, especially as fast as it happened.

"Only good?" I ask her, teasing. I've seen her come before. I know it was better than good. And her third orgasm of the evening, too.

"Fine. It was amazing. If your ego needs that much stroking," she says derisively.

"My ego's fine. But give me a few minutes, and we can talk about stroking other parts of my anatomy."

She scoffs, but she pulls my arms tighter around her and settles in, seeming sleepy. And, for the first time in many years, I fall asleep feeling absolutely at peace.

# Chapter 18

## Girls on Film

## Callie

I wake up before dawn, unused to sleeping with someone else in my bed. In fact, I've *never* had someone else sleep in my bed. Declan and I never had that chance when we were younger. Both of us had beds we were expected to be in, especially me, and neither of us had the leeway to sleep over in the other's bed. Ever.

The full moon shines in through the little dormer window, casting a glow over Declan where he sleeps soundly on his back next to me. He was overdue for it, since he woke me up probably an hour after we'd drifted off the first time, his hand already between my legs. He'd lived up to his promise to make the second time last longer, and then, not long after, the third. Three condoms, six orgasms for me and three for him, and he's earned the right to sleep, even if I can't, even after all of that amazingly satisfying, exhausting sex. Because apparently I can't sleep when I'm not alone in my bed. Declan's fast asleep, of course, but then I'm sure he's had plenty of experience with sleeping not-alone.

And just like that, my determination not to revisit our past falters. This was spontaneous. I didn't think it through. I gave in to a craving, indulged in some physical pleasure. And now that I'm letting myself think, my brain is a jumble of reasons why this was a terrible idea.

For one, Declan is a rockstar. A rockstar who spends most of the year touring. And when he's not touring, he's living in New York, far from my home and business.

Secondly, Declan is a rockstar. A rockstar who's slept with who knows how many women in the last twelve years. He said it himself — his reputation is that of a player, a "manwhore." It's a vague classification that I not only can't quantify, it holds no sense of being past, present or future, instead suggesting an inherent state of being. That guy... he's not going to go for months without sex, just to keep faithful to the old girlfriend he already dumped once.

And that's another thing — Declan already dumped me once. What's to keep him from doing it again? And that's even assuming he's being honest with me — and himself — about wanting another shot at us.

And even if he honestly does want to try again, what are the chances of us making this work long-term? Maybe he was actually right all those years ago, even if he broke my heart in the process.

Maybe it's better if we keep this casual now. He's good at casual, from what he's said. And while I can't deny that last night scratched a long-running itch, who says I have to be looking for a commitment just because I slept with someone for the first time in a long, long, long while? A normal 29-year-old woman could handle a one-night stand. Why not keep it casual?

And then I remember that casual generally means non-exclusive, especially for someone with Declan's history. Am I OK with him seeing — by which I mean having sex with — other women? Even picturing him with Siobhan was like a gut-punch. What if that was random strangers? Groupies?

Declan turns over onto his side, grabbing me around the waist and pulling me against him. I think he's still asleep, and I don't want to wake him. Not because I'm worried about him getting enough sleep, but because if he wakes up now, we're going to have to talk about us, and that's a conversation I don't think either of us will enjoy.

"Callie," he murmurs, making me question my assumption that he's still unconscious. He snuggles into my neck and falls back asleep, silent and unmoving.

I lie next to him, wide awake. Maybe I'm just meant to be alone. Surely if I was built to be someone's bed partner...

someone's wife... I'd be able to sleep soundly with someone else in my bed. Maybe I'd even sleep better that way. This isn't... It isn't comfortable. It's actually quite uncomfortable, both physically and emotionally. I can't do this.

I carefully extract myself from Declan's grasp, grabbing a clean set of comfortable clothes from the basket of laundry I hadn't yet gotten a chance to put away. I dress quickly and quietly, and I grab my key, closing and locking the door behind me before heading down the stairs. The kitchen is quiet... Silent, in fact. And I inhale that peace like oxygen. This is where I'm truly at home.

I sit down at my desk, my hand hovering over the drawer with Nonna's book. But I resist the temptation to dive back into the search for a winning recipe. I've got one important task to handle before anyone else comes in. I pull up the security video from last night, watching it one last time to confirm in my mind that what seemed to have happened had, in fact, happened. There's no obvious explanation in the footage, and I'm left with Brighid's take on what happened. What I allowed to happen. No — what I *caused* to happen.

All because Declan turned back up in Mystic Beach and says he wants me back.

I watch him on the video, eating my food with enthusiasm, smiling when I'm talking to him, joking around like the Declan I remember, the Declan I loved. The one I thought loved me. Did he ever, really? And what does any of it mean now?

I sigh and click the delete button next to the footage. No one needs to relive that. And I certainly don't want to be responsible for Brighid and Hunter going viral again. Now, I don't have a single social media account of my own. Drew runs the one for Castalia, posting amazing photos and videos of our food, our specials, our drinks, and I know his posts are pretty popular. But I have an idea exactly how problematic social media can be, thanks to Brighid. And I've never even visited any of the sites myself.

Brighid doesn't even use social media herself anymore, now that she's famous. That's strange to say about the normally quiet, shy Brighid I know. But it's her reality now. On her own, she would never have stirred up social media like that. It's her connection to Hunter that amplified public interest in her and in their relationship. And, no offense to Hunter, but he's aMUSEd's rhythm guitarist. Declan is their lead singer, the primary face and voice of the band. How much more interest is there in Declan's love-life? What would happen if he had a girlfriend? What would happen if the news broke that he'd had a secret wife since he was 17?

My hand hovers over the computer mouse, and for the first time ever, I'm truly tempted to do an internet search on Declan. What does his social media look like? Is he followed by legions of fans? Is there an aMUSEd fan club that follows his every move? Is he fodder for the tabloids? Do the gossip websites send paparazzi to follow him around? Do they pay the women he's slept with for intimate details and any hint of scandal?

Before I can chicken out, I open up Instagram, where Drew most often posts for Castalia. I'm not sure where to start, but the search button seems like a natural place to begin. I type in the band's name first. An official account comes up. There are photos of the band on stage, candid photos of them hanging out on their tour bus, their album art, arrivals at awards shows, photos of the band members with fans. I click on the word "Tagged" and find so many more photos, mostly posted by fans of the band. Some of them are photos with the band members, but there is also artwork depicting each of the guys, even some tattoos.

One of the tattoos appears to be of Declan's name... his autograph. In some girl's cleavage.

I shrug it off. I'm sure that kind of thing happens all the time to famous people.

I click on one of the links in the tattoo photo — a tag with Declan's name this time.

I don't know if Declan handles his own social media or if the band, or the label, has someone who does that for him. The majority of the photos posted to his account are from the band's concerts, and particularly from their most recent tour. He looks incredible there, in his element, the dramatic frontman catering to an eager crowd. There are some publicity stills, too, and some that look like they're from everyday life — a few photos of food from restaurants, tour catering, some scenic images from around the world.

The images he's tagged in are more haphazard, much like with the band account. Fan photos, selfies of them outside concert venues, some of them with him backstage, a few photos from the incognito gigs they had before Brighid's and Hunter's engagement party. They apparently weren't as successful at retaining their anonymity as they'd hoped, especially after Hunter and Brighid went viral.

One photo catches my attention. It's a selfie of Declan with two beautiful young women, both dressed for clubbing, the three of them looking very... friendly. I recognize the view behind them — the penthouse suite at an Ocean City hotel, where I'd once catered a party as a special favor to a regular customer. If I had any questions about whether the photo was recent, the date of the post resolves them — the night before Declan first turned up at Castalia, claiming he was there to make amends and try to reclaim our relationship.

The tags on the photo include #DeclanSoSexy, #PenthousePlaymates and #UsedByaMUSEd.

I find myself glad that it's still too early in the morning for me to have eaten.

I close the Instagram page and turn off the monitor. Probably best that I've left our social media to Drew. Just a few minutes online, and my already chaotic life of late has been turned entirely upside-down. Declan sleeps soundly directly over my head, in my bed. Twelve years apart, and we came back together like it had been twelve days instead. But then what should I have expected from a notorious playboy and self-described "manwhore"? He's had plenty of practice so he could perfect his technique — both for seduction and for sex.

And, in the end, all it took was him showing up in my restaurant to eat a few meals, two of which I'd comped because of the circumstances.

Apparently, I'm not just easy — I'm also a cheap date.

Somehow, that seems a perfect way to look at what I've done to myself here. I've cheapened myself in service of a trip down memory lane and a night of — admittedly amazing — sex. And I've put my business at risk by letting my ex get under my skin. My mistake. One I won't make again now that I know he's been a busy boy since he arrived back in Mystic Beach.

I can't say he didn't warn me. I just wish I'd known that the warning was about his present and future behavior, as well as his past.

But the past is where Declan Carter belongs, really. And if I'm going to put him back there, I'm going to have to make sure he knows he can't treat me like one of his groupies — meaningless sex, selfies and hashtags being mainstays of his rockstar life, it seems. It's time the shoe was solidly on the other foot.

# Chapter 19

## Bleed to Love Her

## Declan

I stretch, my body waking slowly, comfortable and fully rested for the first time in I can't remember how long. I could attribute it to Callie's very nice mattress, but more likely it's Callie herself who's responsible.

When I asked Dave what it was like to fall asleep with the love of your life in your arms, I had no idea what doing so would do for the quality of my sleep. If only I'd awakened with her still there. Or even just in the apartment with me. The idea of wondering where she is doesn't even get fully formed in my head before I realize I know exactly where she'll be — downstairs, in her restaurant.

I throw yesterday's clothes back on and run my fingers through my hair as I look in her bathroom mirror. I could get used to the length. I could even get used to shaving every couple of days instead of daily. Especially if Callie likes me that way.

And who is that smiling, satisfied man in the mirror? I haven't seen him in a long, long time. He wasn't even really a man the last time he smiled like this.

The smiles I give the fans, the press, aren't the same. Maybe they can't tell the difference, but I can.

This smile — it's genuine and bone-deep. And I let that warm feeling suffuse every bit of my being as I flip the lock on Callie's apartment door and head down to find her.

"You sure about this?" one of her staff asks her as I walk through the unlocked door to the kitchen.

"Very sure," she replies, smiling back at him.

I'm instantly jealous. I want her smiles to be for me. I can't begrudge her a friendly moment with a co-worker, though.

"Good morning," I say to the room at large, but I'm focused on Callie — who, unexpectedly, isn't dressed in her chef gear for once.

I get some nods and lots of curious looks from the half-dozen or so people arrayed around the kitchen, getting things ready for the day.

"So, you're all set?" Callie asks the first guy, who I assume is her assistant.

"Yes, Chef," he says. "Especially since you had the place sorted before I even got here."

"Insomnia," she tells him, giving me a glance.

That would explain why she was missing from my arms this morning, even if I got a full night's sleep. I frown, concerned.

"You want to go back to bed?" I ask her, not happy at the idea that I might have deprived her of needed rest.

There's some giggling from a few of the staff, and I realize that question could be interpreted in multiple ways. I was genuinely concerned she might need more sleep, but now that they've suggested it, I wouldn't mind spending all day in bed with Callie, sleeping and not.

"No. I'm wide awake now," she says. "And I've decided to take the day off. On Brighid's advice," she adds.

Ah, yes — the bizarre events of last night's dinner. It's probably a wise decision. Let's give Callie a day off, let her regain her balance, settle in to our renewed relationship status. Hopefully, that will be enough to avoid future incidents like last night's.

"You want to come see the studio?" I suggest.

This is a part of my life she's never seen, and I'm eager to bring her into it. It's a good first step into integrating her life here with my life in the studio and on tour. We'll have some details to figure out, just as if we'd been together all along. But I like the idea of having my girl — my wife — in my work environment, with my brother, my band, my music. The idea of showing her off to the guys leaves me nearly giddy.

Everything I've ever wanted is suddenly within my grasp.

"Let's go have a picnic first," she says, gathering up a bag full of take-out boxes and leading me out the door into the alley. "I made brunch for us."

"You were very busy this morning while I was still asleep," I tell her. "Setting up everything for your staff, making us brunch."

"Once I'm awake, I'm awake, and I had a sudden burst of energy this morning. I'd deep-cleaned the entire kitchen before I realized it. Then I just had a few things I needed to talk to Drew about so I could take the day off."

"Drew's your assistant?"

"My sous-chef," she corrects.

"Ah. So, he's in charge when you're not working?"

"Doesn't happen often, but yes."

"Well, I'm glad you've got someone who can take over and give you a break. You deserve a break. You work really hard."

I run my hand over her back, knowing that her job is physically strenuous, as well as a pressure-cooker of stress. That's the only thing I don't like about this calling of hers. But she practically grew up in a restaurant kitchen, and it's the only life she's ever really known. It probably seems very normal to her. I just hope she can find time for herself. And for us.

## Callie

I have to admit it. Declan's picked a perfect spot for a picnic brunch. We're set up on a beach blanket just above the high-tide mark on a section of private beach, right in front of this massive beach house that also houses the studio the band's recording in.

We skated right through the kitchen, Declan grabbing the blanket, glasses and a bottle of champagne that goes perfectly with the carafe of orange juice I packed for this outing. Once we'd gotten everything set up, Declan excused himself briefly to change into clean clothes, muttering something about making sure we weren't disturbed.

"So what's for brunch?" he asks eagerly.

"Fresh croissants with local blueberry preserves, and a breakfast torte with tomatoes and greens."

"More of your exotic greens?"

"I put a few things in there with the spinach."

"Looks amazing!" he enthuses. "I love blueberries."

"More farm-fresh Delaware produce, along with the peaches, and strawberries, though strawberry season is long over now. They have you-pick farms all over the place."

"I remember picking strawberries when we were young kids. Mom always wanted to lie out on the deck at the beach house during the day, or under an umbrella on the beach if we pestered her into taking us out there. She only left the house to take Dave surfing and when strawberries were in season. We'd go out early in the morning and spend a couple hours."

"My parents never brought me here early enough in the season to pick strawberries when I was little. But Nonna took me to pick peaches for the restaurant when I was older."

He grows somber.

"You miss her a lot. I can tell."

And then *I* grow somber, though talking about Nonna always makes me feel warm inside, too.

"She was an amazing woman, an amazing chef, and a really amazing grandmother. She went so far above and beyond for me. Really, she was everything I wanted to be when I grew up."

"You've followed in her footsteps and succeeded admirably."

"In some things. Professionally, for sure. Though I'm in a frustrating phase with the restaurant."

"How so?"

"We're nearly full from the moment we open until we close."

"I noticed. That's why I made reservations. Didn't want to miss a night of your amazing food..."

He seems sincere in his praise, and my conscience nags at me. I put him through a lot, just trying to deter him from coming back to Castalia. Maybe he truly wanted to experience my food and not just to wear me down so he could seduce me...

"Well, you're not the only one, and at this point, I could use another fifteen or twenty tables to handle the overflow."

"Can you find a larger space, or is it too expensive to consider moving?"

"It would be tremendously expensive to move. And I don't want to move outside walking distance from the beach. I have too many good memories of Nonna serving people who were here on vacation. I want to keep that tradition, even though I can't cook in the same space."

"What happened there?"

"Property values, mostly. It got too expensive to keep up a small hotel with its own restaurant when the other option was to redevelop the property as condominiums. The owners got a rich payout, and Nonna retired."

"It must have been a big change for her, after so many years cooking for people."

"It was. I try not to be bitter about it, but I think losing the restaurant aged her. Work — doing something you love — keeps you young, I think. She'd probably have continued cooking in the restaurant into her 90s, if they'd let her." I chuckle, thinking of feisty Nonna ordering around sous-chefs and waiters at that age.

"I found her obituary when I was trying to locate you," Declan says, giving me a sad smile. "I'm really sorry she isn't still here. I liked the old girl."

"And she liked you... *Arturo*," I joke. He smirks back at me, clearly enjoying the reminder of those early years, when we were together and Nonna was our biggest cheerleader.

"So what's your plan for the restaurant? Just save up until a bigger space comes open?"

"Actually, I may be able to expand in the not too distant future. The bakery next door is moving, and I've got the inside track on getting the space, if I can show the landlord I have enough reserve capital to pay for the full year's rent and do the renovations we'd need to both spaces to add a second dining room."

"Wow! That sounds perfect. Just open a door between the two spaces and add tables, and you're good to go!"

"It's not quite that simple. And I have a big financial hurdle if I'm going to make it happen."

"I'll front you the cash."

I choke on a sip of mimosa and spend the next minute or two coughing, with Declan patting my back.

"I can't let you do that," I tell him after I catch my breath. Especially now that I know what he's been up to while he's been here. How awkward would that be? My twice ex-boyfriend as an investor in my restaurant? Besides, once Declan gets bored with me, with this town, he'll move on to some other fleeting interest, and I can't afford to have him back out midway into an expansion.

"Why not?"

"I need to do this on my own. I need Castalia to support its expansion, prove it's viable to expand."

"And is a full dining room every night enough to do that?"

I sigh.

"Probably not. At least not in time to secure the space next door. That's why I have to win People's Choice at the Taste of the Culinary Coastline event next month."

"What's that?"

"It's a local food festival. All the restaurants in the area get together and offer one dish each, and people pay for a ticket that entitles them to come sample all the food, and they can buy more sample tickets for extras and to vote. They split the proceeds between the food bank and the restaurant that gets the most votes at the event. That cash infusion would put me safely over on having enough for the expansion."

"You really won't let me invest? Or it can just be a loan, if you prefer."

"No, Declan. I can't. I really can't. I've got to do this myself."

"Well, do you think you can win? I mean — your food is some of the best I've ever had. I just don't know what the competition is like or what the voters go for."

"The competition is fierce. I'm going to be competing against some of the best chefs in the area, some of them trained at the finest restaurants in Europe or with long histories as sous-chefs at starred restaurants around the country."

"So, what's the winning recipe going to be?" he asks, his tone teasing but warm.

"I don't know."

"Isn't the competition next month?"

"Yeah. Just over a month away. I just haven't been able to come up with a dish that seems like it could be the one. It feels like I'll know it when I've got it. And so far, nothing has felt like that."

"I'm sure any of the dishes on your menu could do it. I loved your tacos. What about those?"

Declan seems to know where my soft spots are, and the reminder of the dish I made for him so recently threatens to knock my legs out from under me and everything I planned for today.

"If it's going to win, the dish has to be something truly special, Declan. It has to be unique but still have wide appeal. Tacos isn't going to do that, not even with twists."

He seems sympathetic, but it's not like he can really understand the kind of pressure I'm under here. After Alex's offer to pay ridiculous amounts for cooking lessons, I know Declan's got to be sitting on enough money that offering to invest in my restaurant is like a drop in a bucket to him. Having to watch overhead and carefully schedule my staff so I don't send us into the red is a day-to-day reality for me. And it's a reality I don't think he can comprehend from his place in the financial stratosphere.

"I'm sure you'll come up with the perfect thing. You've definitely proven that you're creative and capable of cooking outside the box," he adds with a wry chuckle.

I don't know what to say to him. I want to take his support at face value, but I also know that I'm dealing with a suave player who has an established history of caring more about scoring with anonymous women than building a real relationship, even if he's used that pretense to get into my bed.

"So, what's it like being a rockstar?" I ask, changing the subject without even a hint of segue.

He blinks but recovers himself quickly.

"A lot of fun, most of the time. And a lot of hard work. Long hours, always on the road, no privacy, dealing with critics and promoters and labels, though Billy does most of that part for us these days. He's our manager," he explains. "But it's me who has to do the interviews, schmooze with the fans..."

"And lots and lots and lots of women screaming your name, trying to get backstage to get their hands on you..."

He blinks in surprise again.

"Yeah," he says, recovering himself. "We do some paid VIP meets, and sometimes we'll pull fans out of the audience for a meet-and-greet. It keeps the spontaneity, instead of things being all about having a few hundred or a few thousand dollars to get access to the band."

"I bet there's not much some of those female fans wouldn't do to get your attention."

He frowns.

"We've had some crazy moments," he admits. "I mean, we do get panties thrown on stage sometimes, girls lifting their shirts like it's Mardi Gras every night... Sometimes they get someone to sneak them into the dressing room..."

"Sounds like rockstar paradise..."

"Callie... It's not—"

"It's totally normal for someone in your line of work, I know. It's like cocktail parties for a lawyer or courtside seats at a basketball game for a financial whiz. Comes with the territory."

"Yeah, but—"

"Brighid mentioned walking in on Hunter once... with a groupie."

Brighid confided that to me when I told her about my history with Declan. Even though that incident happened before she and Hunter were a couple, she wanted me to feel better about the fact that Declan had dumped me, so she told me he'd been right about the lifestyle they'd be living — a lifestyle that's not exactly compatible with being a 17-year-old newlywed. I don't worry about breaking her confidence, though, because she told me Declan was there when it happened.

"Twice. In one night," Declan clarifies. I kind of wish he hadn't, because Brighid's story was painful enough to hear as she told it. That it was even worse than that bothers me, makes me question her decision to give Hunter another chance.

"Wow. That sounds really wild."

"And that was before we got signed or headlined our own tour. In Hunter's defense, he and Brighid were just friends back then, even if we all knew she had a crush on him. He was careless that night. He'd never have let it happen if he'd thought it through, and he's regretted it ever since. He's really changed in the last few years, put those days far behind him, and now he's utterly devoted to Brighid."

"More for you and the others then, I guess..."

"Well, yeah, I suppose, but Dave's settling down now, too." He chuckles. "Get this — he's got a baby on the way." Wow. OK, I was not expecting that. "Brand new girlfriend, and the two of them are thrilled about this. I still can't believe it. I don't think he's even had a girlfriend before. And he's instant husband material."

Declan catches himself, but it's too late, another gut punch for me, the reminder that he married me and then acted like it had never been real.

"Tell them congratulations for me," I finally say.

"You can do that yourself. He'll be in later this afternoon to lay down some harmonies on the song we've been working on. Piper will be with him, since she's also our sound engineer while we're here. He's been staying with her in her apartment, and that's pretty close to the studio, apparently. I haven't been to see it yet. Been kind of busy, between writing songs and chasing down runaway wives," he adds with a chuckle.

The joke leaves me cold, but I plaster a smile on my face.

"That must be strange for you — having to chase a woman, instead of being chased by them."

"Well, yeah... But it's not exactly the same thing, you and me. Not at all the same, really."

He looks confused, and I'm hit with another wave of guilt, which I push down, knowing he didn't feel so guilty when he broke my heart at 17 that he didn't move right on with his groupies, and he won't feel guilty when he finds the next girl, or two, to entertain himself in a few days or a few weeks. But we should both be guilt-free here. No promises made this time, no forevers, or even a tomorrow.

"Well, you certainly seem to have perfected your skills in the bedroom... Though I'd guess it's *not* in an actual bedroom a lot more often than it *is* in one."

I say it lightly, hoping he'll think I'm taking all of this in stride. But I guess that brain-sharing thing comes with a side of expert-level reading of my body language.

"Callie, I'm not sure what's got you bent out of shape, but—"

"I'm not bent out of shape!" I interrupt, my tone bright, plunging ahead with the farce. "It's just the reality of your life, I know. You told me that the other day. It's fine. You gave me a heads-up. I didn't go into last night blind. I know the score."

"I'm not sure you do. You and me—"

"It's fine, Declan. We're on the same page. It's a little casual fun while you're here in Mystic Beach." Again, he looks confused. But I plunge onward. "It's not like I have time for a real relationship anyway. Castalia is my sole focus, like I said. Especially with this competition coming up. But it's nice to have a little stress relief. You were right about that part — I've been depriving myself unnecessarily. Actually, that's probably what caused that little problem last night..."

"*Little* problem?"

"Yeah. It's all sorted out now — no more video, and now that I know it happened, I can make sure it doesn't happen again. In fact, since it was probably having gone too long without having sex that caused it, it's probably best if I make sure I don't go too long without it again..." My tone is suggestive, seductive... or at least I hope it is.

"Oh? Well, that I can definitely help you with." See how easily he's distracted with even the suggestion of sex on offer? This is not a man who's going to turn down a groupie. Not when he's on the road, and not — as I now know — when he's here in Mystic Beach. Even if he pays lip service to wanting me back. #UsedByaMUSEd can go both ways, playboy...

"Somehow, I was sure you would offer to help me out with that." There — I'm getting better at this flirting thing already!

"You want a tour of the studio? Starting with the bedrooms? Or one of them, at least?" He's smirking at me again, seeming very pleased with this turn of events, confident. He's exactly where I want him. Or he will be, soon enough.

"Lead the way."

# CHAPTER 20

## NAKED

## Callie

We gather up the remains of our picnic and head back up the steps to the deck and into the house, which is huge. Way bigger than the normal McMansion people build here now, expecting to host an extended family.

"Alex's and Kieran's rooms are down here, along with the kitchen and the living area, and the gym. The studio's downstairs, and it's just Rhys and me upstairs now, along with our producer, Malcolm, since Hunter's living with Brighid at her house and Dave is with Piper."

"And where are Rhys and Malcolm right now?" I ask pointedly.

"Down in the studio, working on drum parts, last I checked."

"So there's no one upstairs?"

"I like how you think," Declan says, waggling his eyebrows at me.

He grabs my hand and pulls me along behind him, up the stairs and to a door at the end of the hallway.

"Since Dave moved out, I called dibs on the room with the view," he says, opening the door to a room with sliding glass doors that lead onto that upper deck I saw earlier.

The sunshine filters through sheer curtains. It's a gorgeous room, a gorgeous view, out across the dune to the ocean. Given the choice, I'd still rather have Nonna's garden as the view from my bedroom window, but I'd traded that for my restaurant, my dream, and I'd do it again, every time.

"Dave's talking about expanding from one house to a complex, so families could come stay here with the musicians when they're recording. I think building a family of his own has inspired him."

He says it with humor, but I catch a note of longing in his voice, too. He'd always described his parents as kind of detached, not entirely unlike my own, and I wonder if seeing his brother, and Hunter, settling down has him re-evaluating his life, what he wants. Is it actually possible that he could be sincere about wanting to try again with me? Or is he really just looking for a good time?

Declan brushes up behind me, hand on my hip, nuzzling into my neck. I lean back into him, enjoying the sensation, trying to shut down the part of my brain that's calling so many things into question right now. Can I really do this? My mind flashes back to the image of him cozied up with the two minimally-clad women in a hotel room in Ocean City. The night before he came to find me. Who does that? A player does that. A guy who can't be trusted to be satisfied with one woman. Even just one at a time. But I won't let him to do that to me. I won't let him fool me again. I learned my lesson. Now it's time for him to learn his.

I turn around to face him, pulling his lips to mine. I channel every bit of passion I ever felt for Declan into this kiss. I give myself permission to lose myself in this one kiss, this moment. It won't last, and the end result will be bitter, no doubt, even if the revenge is sweet. But, for now, I savor the taste of him, the feel of his mouth against mine, his breath across my cheek, his hand trailing up my neck, cradling it.

"You've got condoms, right?" I murmur in his ear.

"Of course..."

"Of course you do, rockstar." I chuckle knowingly. Of course he does.

"Gotta be safe. Don't want to be careless, get in trouble..." he says, smoothly, pressing kisses against my jaw, down my neck, into my cleavage.

"No, don't want to do that..." I drawl.

"Got enough problems already..." he says vaguely, his tongue licking up one side of my neck. I shudder. I can't help myself. It feels so good. I went so long without having anyone touch me like that. I didn't realize how much I missed it until Declan touched me again that morning... The morning after he'd been with those two women. I shake my head, reminding myself of what I'm here to do.

"You OK, babe?" He pulls back, looking a little concerned.

"Yeah... Just wondering — I mean, I went a long time without being with anyone. I've had a lot of years to think about things I'd like to try. New things," I tell him, the words and the shyness I'm feeling utterly genuine in this moment. How do I even...?

"Oh?" Again with the knowing tone.

I'd bet there's nothing sexual Declan hasn't done in the last twelve years. There's no way he wouldn't get bored with me very fast, as inexperienced as I am, as vanilla as what little I've done has been. That's why I have to push forward with this — it'll be just kinky enough to interest him as we renew our acquaintance, but not so extreme that he'll question the sincerity of my request.

"We never experimented with anything on the kinkier side of things when we were younger."

Yeah, that's a look of interest on his face.

"What did you have in mind? I don't have a lot of toys here with me. In my apartment in New York, yeah, but we basically came here straight off the road."

"I just so happened to have come prepared." I'm aiming for a seductive smile, hoping I don't slide over the edge into cat-ate-the-canary territory. I don't want to make him suspicious.

His expression is expectant as I put a little distance between us and grab my bag, digging deep inside and withdrawing a set of sturdy handcuffs. Not cop cuffs — the adult toy variety. One for each wrist, lightly padded, with a sturdy attachment for a headboard. Which Declan's bed here conveniently has. They're not mine, but they're brand new. I had a feeling Drew might have a spare pair...

"Oooh... Who's getting tied up? You or me?" he asks, not seeming terribly bothered about which option I'll pick.

"I think you, this time... I'd like to have free rein with you, since this is only the second time we've been together as adults. I've got some lost time to make up for. Is that OK?"

"Definitely, babe! I kind of owe you for that, still, and if you want to take charge, I'm totally good with that. Have your way with me, Callie!" he says enthusiastically, before throwing himself backward on the bed, spread-eagle. The look on his face is... delight? Eager anticipation? I nearly falter, but...

"You've done this before, right? I mean, I just assumed..." Again, my shyness is genuine. I'm not used to talking about sex, let alone initiating it, and definitely not like this.

"It's been a while," he says. "But I've been on both ends of the cuffs before."

"Which do you prefer? Being restrained or doing the restraining?"

"I'm good either way. As long as everyone's having fun, I'm open to pretty much anything."

"Sounds like a long to-do list in the making..."

"I hope so," he says, raising up on his elbows and giving me a smile that seems far more seductive than I suspect mine is. "How do you want me?"

"Naked as the day you were born."

"You going to help?" There's that smirk again. It seems like maybe it's his default expression, when he's not scowling or looking predatory. But it's me who's predatory right now. Just not in the way he's expecting.

"Shirt off," I order him.

"Yes, ma'am," he says, stripping his T-shirt off over his head in a single motion and tossing it at me. Again, that expectant look. His eyes drift from my face down to my cleavage and then lower. After he drinks his fill, his glance continues the motion until it reaches his own belt. He raises an eyebrow at me suggestively.

I set the cuffs atop the dresser near the bed and crawl across him, settling between his thighs. I can already tell he's happy about this arrangement. And I haven't even touched him... I reach down and unbuckle his belt. This, I've done before. It'd just been a while before last night. And it was also Declan back then. So, no big deal, right?

I draw it slowly through the loops, watching his anticipation grow. I drop it off the side of the bed and reach for the button on his jeans. He pushes up against my hand, and there's no question — he's hard. No napkins hiding things here. Not that there's a napkin big enough to hide this hard-on. He's not 17 anymore... But neither am I. And this grown-ass woman is going to pull up her big-girl panties and handle her big-girl problems. By taking off his pants.

I unbutton and unzip him quickly, moving things forward so I can get this over with. I slide back down the bed, grabbing the bottoms of his jeans and pulling downward as he presses up to let them slide over his hips. I toss them far behind me, with his shirt.

He's lying there, looking up at me, only a pair of boxer briefs covering those beautifully-formed bits of his... I close my eyes, trying to banish the impulse to strip him and then fall on him mouth-first. Yeah — that I've done before, taking him into my mouth, giving him pleasure with tongue and lips and hands... It's been so long, though...

"It works better if you're looking at me, Callie," he says, teasing. "Though I wouldn't mind a little blind exploration..."

I grab for the waistband of his boxer briefs and pull them straight down and off his legs. I stand there for a moment, the import of what I'm about to do hitting me.

There's a trilling beep behind me. A phone notification from the phone that's apparently still in his jeans.

"Ignore it," he says, pulling my eyes back to him. All six feet of him, totally naked on the bed in front of me, waiting for me to...

I grab the cuffs, pulling his hand into my lap as I sit beside him on the bed.

"Not going to touch the goods before you lock me down?" he jokes.

"No. Behave," I order him as his other hand drifts toward my hip. I tighten the cuff around his wrist. "Is that comfortable?"

*"That* is," he says. *"This*, not so much," he adds, palming his cock with his other hand.

"No touching!" I order, and he frowns just a little, sliding his hand away with obvious reluctance.

"You're going to have to restrain me if you don't want me touching myself, or you. God, you're sexy, Callie. You were exquisite at 17. You're so beautiful now, I'm having a really *hard* time holding back. This grown-up, successful, independent you... You're perfect. I feel incredibly lucky to have you here with me."

I'll just bet he does. Another notch for his bedpost. Well, not his, since he doesn't own this house, but close enough.

"Well, you're not getting lucky today, buddy — not if you keep touching things you aren't supposed to!"

"Ooh! Bossy Callie. In-charge Callie. I definitely like that."

He offers me his other wrist, and I tighten the cuff around it. "Still comfortable?"

"The cuffs are fine..." he says, his implication clear.

I pull his hand to the corner post on the headboard and attach it firmly, making sure he can't wiggle free, and snapping shut one of the little locks Drew gave me with them.

"Get comfortable, before I do the other one."

He squirms around a little, settling his head against the pillows and testing the stretch of his arms and shoulders across the headboard.

"Do your worst," he says, unknowingly challenging me to follow through with my revenge.

I attach his other wrist to the headboard, confirming it's secure and snapping shut the second lock.

"You good? You're going to be like that for a while."

"I'm fine, Callie. I trust you."

Those words nearly undo me. And then I remember that *I* trusted *him* once. And I'd trusted him again this time, trusted his intentions were honestly stated, that he'd shown up at my restaurant that morning, honestly intending to work to have something long-term with me, having learned his lessons from our break-up, having matured, having gotten the groupies out of his system for good.

His phone beeps again, and I look back over my shoulder toward the pile of discarded clothing, my decision made.

"Just ignore it. People tag me all the time. You've got me where you want me..."

Ignoring him, I fish his phone out of his jeans, finding an Instagram notification on the screen. It's an image of some woman's cleavage. No tattoo this time, but a lipstick impression in bright red, clearly pressed there by a second woman, unless this one is impossibly flexible. I recognize the user name, though, since it was the same one that had tagged him in the photo with the two woman in the hotel.

"Join us at Fager's," the message invites him. "Our bodies felt so good moving against each other the other night!"

My stomach turns, my temper flares.

"What is it, Callie?" Declan asks, noticing the change in my posture.

"Was it satisfying for you, Declan? Did you feel like you'd redeemed yourself once you got your ex-girlfriend back in bed again, despite how utterly you'd destroyed me? Or was I just a challenge to mark off your list before you went back to your groupies?"

My voice is low, dangerous. But I know he heard me when his expression goes from curious to concerned.

"What are you talking about, Callie?"

"You told me yourself, Declan, that first day you showed up at Castalia. 'Manwhore,' you said. 'I have a reputation,' you said. Did you think I was too stupid to figure out the evidence of your nature would be all over the internet? Did you think the fact that I'd avoided running across you — even accidentally — in all those years, meant I wouldn't check, even if it was *after* I'd been weak enough to let you into my bed again?"

"Callie — I'm not sure what you found, but I can promise, it's not the whole story, whatever it is. That stuff is all in the past for me now. It was even before I found you."

"Oh, really?" I demand, outraged at the lie. "This doesn't look like the past!"

I bring the phone close to his face, so he can see the photo up close and personal.

"I'd tell them you're free for more fun times in the penthouse suite — for some more 'moves' with both of them — but you're kind of *tied up* right now. Should I send them your regrets?"

The phone has unlocked now that it's been in proximity to his face. I tap on the notification.

"Or should I do it Instagram style and send them visual proof of exactly what's keeping you from revisiting your little threesome?"

"Callie — no! It's not what it looks like. Not at all! I swear!"

"That first photo was taken the night before you showed up at Castalia, aiming to seduce me, Declan. Did you seriously seek me out, kiss me, aim for more, just hours after you'd been with not one, but two other women?"

"That's not what happened, Callie. I'm trying to explain. Just let me loose so I can explain!"

"I've had enough of your explanations and your manipulations to last me a lifetime, Declan Carter! I should have learned my lesson the first time, when I was 17. But, like you said — I'm a grown-up, independent woman now. Twice is enough. You won't get a third chance to fool me with your player ways. And now everyone's going to know exactly what kind of man you are!"

I turn the phone camera on him and snap a photo before he can react.

"Good luck getting some innocent girl to fall for your shit ever again! I know my eyes are open to the reality now. I got an eyeful of the real Declan Carter. Now the entire internet will, too."

I text the photo to myself, satisfied when I can hear it ping in my bag.

"Callie! No — you've got this all wrong! Let me explain! Please! It wasn't at all what you're thinking!"

"I'm done with your explanations, Declan. So done. I should have been done the moment you explained you were dumping me a week after our wedding because you'd realized you'd never really loved me."

"I didn't mean it! It wasn't true, Callie! Come on — give me a minute to tell you everything!"

"You've stolen too many minutes of my life, Declan. You're not getting any more."

I toss the phone on the floor by his feet, very conspicuously tuck the key to the cuff locks into my bra, grab my bag, and slide open the door onto the deck.

"Callie! Come back!" he yells as I stride across the deck.

I ignore him, running down the steps to the ground and making the fastest three-point turn I can manage out of the studio's driveway.

# CHAPTER 21

## I WANT TO BREAK FREE

## Declan

"Callie!" I yell. "Callie — come back here and let me loose so we can talk about this!"

But I can see even through the sheer curtains that she's already off the upper deck and yet again running as quickly away from me as she can.

"Callie!" I yell again, knowing she's not only unlikely to change her mind, she's probably already too far away to hear me.

Now what am I going to do?

I mean about fixing this whole mess, but with my arms stretched out over my head and my dick waving in the breeze from the open door, I'm wondering what I'm going to do to get myself out of this physical predicament. Without humiliating myself even further than I already have today.

Oh, god... She didn't send that photo of me out on social media, did she?

I mean, I don't care all that much about the nudity. My fans will eat it up. But the vulnerable position I was — am still — in... People are going to make assumptions about me. Best case, our PR team plays this off as a case of revenge porn. Best case for the band, that is. If they play it like that, Callie's in huge trouble. Assuming she did actually publicly post that photo.

This is the reason NDAs have been mandatory for anyone spending time alone with me, ever since we hit it big. Female,

male, non-binary person, young, old — doesn't matter. Even if I didn't touch them, we needed to be sure they couldn't claim I had when I hadn't. If there weren't witnesses, they signed an NDA, period. Even after things changed. Couldn't be too careful.

And then I wasn't. Because I trusted Callie. I still do. But she's furious with me, hurt, by something she doesn't even understand, and I'm afraid she's going to justify doing something very unwise based on that misunderstanding. I've got to get to her, explain, stop her from doing something she'll regret.

I've done a lot of things I regret. Most of them, directly or indirectly, involving Callie. And now that I finally started making up for them, started repairing the mess I made, I'm caught in a web of my own making, and I may end up taking Callie down with me.

"Help!" I yell, choosing stopping this trainwreck over my own dignity. "Rhys! Dave! Kier! Alex! I need some help up here! Now! Hurry!"

It's an infuriating thirty seconds of silence. Rhys and Malcolm were in the studio, last I checked, and if the control room door is shut, they'll never hear me. I'm not even sure Alex and Kieran are home right now. If they are, they could well be in the studio, too. Chances are Dave is either on his way over or already in the studio with Piper.

Oh, god... Please let it not be Piper who comes running to my rescue right now. I'd rather wait here another hour for one of the guys — even Malcolm — than have to face my brother's pregnant girlfriend when I'm lying here naked and chained to my own bed.

"Alex! Kieran! Rhys! David!" I bellow again, using all my lead-singer's vocal techniques and lung capacity to maximize my decibel levels. "Help! I need some help up here! ASAP! Big problem! Hello? Is anyone there? I need some help!"

It's quiet again, and now I'm worrying that my voice will carry better through the open deck door than it is down the stairs to where the guys will hear me. All I need is for some stranger to rush to my rescue from the state beach to the north and get an eyeful of the rockstar in the sex restraints.

I wiggle in the bed, pulling against the headboard. Maybe I can break it. Better to have to replace a bed than any number of possible outcomes of this situation. But this is high-end furniture, built solid. It's almost like they expected a bunch of rockstars to be staying here and wanted to make sure the beds could take a beating. I sigh, picturing myself calling mildly for the guys for the next several hours, until someone finally comes upstairs to shower or make some food.

Food! Callie! Oh, god. She's got to be incredibly wounded by this. What was I thinking, suggesting the girls post that photo on social media? I mean — I know what I was thinking. I was thinking I was continuing the same sort of alibi creation I'd been using since I started my penance, keeping up appearances that I was the same libidinous dick — no pun intended — I'd been early in our career, using women and tossing them away hours later. It kept Gryffin off my back when I slipped my security detail. He worried less the more I did it, until it wasn't a big enough deal that he lectured me every time I did it. It worked.

But now... It had backfired in spectacular form, and it isn't just me paying the price. Callie is. And it will only get worse if I can't stop her from posting that photo. Assuming I'm not already too late.

"Dave! Rhys! Kieran! Alex! Come on, guys! I'm in major trouble here! I need help!"

No sooner does that last word clear my lips than I hear a rumble, what I presume is someone running up the stairs.

"Fucking finally! What the fuck took so long?" I ask, not able to see who's coming down the hall, since the bedroom door is still shut. Please let it not be Piper.

The door bursts open, and no, it's not Piper.

Well, it's not *just* Piper. It's Dave, who's seen all this before (aside from the cuffs), and it's Alex and Kieran. All four of them. Joy.

Piper gets an eyeful and turns around, ducking under Dave's arm on the doorknob and walking straight back down the hallway.

"Whoa." Kieran blinks a couple times and doubles over in laughter.

"Uh... Dec... Do you want to explain exactly what's going on here?" Alex asks.

"Not particularly."

"OK — I think I deserve an explanation, since you just flashed my girlfriend something she can't ever unsee," Dave says, clearly irritated.

"Afraid you'll suffer by comparison?" I snark back at him.

"Honestly — no," he says, barely containing a smirk. "Especially not with the cool breeze coming in off the beach."

"Fuck you. Just fuck you, Dave. This is not the time."

"Just pointing out that the door onto the deck is wide open."

"Mother of twelve gods! What the hell is going on in here?" Hunter yells, standing in that wide-open doorway.

Awesome.

"I think Declan's chained up to his bed. Naked," Rhys offers helpfully from over his shoulder.

"Thanks, Rhys. I'm sure they'd never have figured that out on their own."

"You're welcome, Declan," he says brightly.

"Any more comments from the peanut gallery, or is someone going to actually fucking release me?"

"More like 'penis gallery,' I'd think," Rhys says, smirking at me. "You sure you don't want me to memorialize this for posterity?"

"Callie already did that," I reply before I think better of it.

Dave shakes his head, rolls his eyes and walks off after Piper.

"Callie did this?" Alex asks. "What the hell did you do to piss her off bad enough to do this to you?"

"And threaten to post the photos online?" Yes, this is the depth of my fuck-up...

"She didn't!" He's genuinely surprised.

"Oh, she sure did."

"You've got to stop her. I mean, I'm trying really hard not to laugh here. And I have to assume you earned it. But I still don't want her getting into trouble over naked photos of your dumb ass."

Nice to know where his loyalties lie, after a decade living in each other's pockets.

"It's not his arse that's the problem, I suspect," Kieran comments, snickering some more.

"OK, guys — I realize this is very entertaining from your perspective, but I've seriously got to get to Callie to explain what actually happened. I didn't do what she thinks I did, but she's very upset and thinking I did do it. And, like you said, she's in a huge amount of trouble if she actually posts that photo, with the revenge-porn laws these days."

"Is a naked photo of you and your deflated dick really porn, though?" Hunter asks.

"I'd have to be desperate before I'd pay to see it," Alex says, garnering a raised eyebrow from me. Always yanking my chain... "Luckily, I don't have to. Nor do I really want to, since I've got to live and work with you."

"I'd need Callie to be in bed with you before I'd pull out my credit card," Rhys says.

"Rhys!" I yell, more upset at the idea of him watching Callie porn than I am anything else.

"Not cool, Rhys," Alex says.

"Hey — Hunter asked about the quality of this porn. I just answered. And you're too far away to smack me this time!" he adds jubilantly.

I take a deep breath and let out a very deep sigh.

"I realize you're all enjoying the entertainment portion of your afternoon, but I really do need to have someone set me loose so I can go fix this before Callie does something she'll regret."

"Don't you have the keys to these, Dec?" Hunter asks as he steps into the room from the deck.

"Callie took them with her. Stuffed them in her bra and left me here like this."

"I'll go get my keys," Alex and Kieran both volunteer at the same time.

They each take a step back and look at each other, curious.

"I'll go get my keys," Kieran says again.

"You must have seriously pissed her off, Dec," Alex says, stepping into the room from the hallway.

"If he doesn't have the keys, how are we going to get the locks open?" Rhys asks.

"Some locks designed for adult toys have a universal key, just in case you lose one while they're in use," Alex explains. "Makes for less embarrassment, since you don't have to call a locksmith."

"Yeah, this is very minimally embarrassing," I comment wryly.

"Be glad we had a spare in the house," he says.

"Two, apparently," I point out as Kieran returns with a key. "You two want to fill us in on why you both have keys handy?"

"None of your business," Alex says.

"Kneeling on a rug, fuck-all," Kieran mutters as he unlocks the first lock and tosses Hunter the key to unlock the second. OK, that's probably not what he actually said, but I don't understand Irish, and that sounded almost pertinent.

There's a clicking sound, and I look up to find Rhys taking a snapshot with his phone.

"Rhys!" everyone yells.

"What? I figured we really should preserve this moment for posterity."

"Delete that. Now," I tell him, rubbing my wrists, which aren't really all that uncomfortable. Callie made sure the cuffs were comfortable. Ironic.

"You sure? Years from now, you might— ow!"

"Rhys, one of these days, you're going to say or do something without thinking about it, and it's going to cause a real problem, for you or somebody else," Alex says. "You've got to stop and think! And, next time, make sure you're out of reach before you do something stupid."

"Fine," Rhys replies, clearly disappointed. "Hey — is that a teddy bear?"

"No," I reply, shoving the bear back under my pillow, glad that Callie, at least, didn't see it. She might have taken it back.

Hunter throws my clothes at me, shaking his head.

"Do I want to know how you fucked this up again?" he asks. "Brighid's going to follow through on that threat against your dick if you've hurt Callie again, and I'm not stepping in between you this time," he adds. "I really do want to have kids with my woman."

"It's a misunderstanding. I seriously did not do what she thinks I did. But it's my fault that she thinks I did, so I'm going to go fix this and hope she wasn't so hotheaded about it that she's already posted the photo *she* took."

I give Rhys a meaningful look.

"I deleted it! I swear!" he says, holding his hands up to proclaim his innocence.

"Everybody out!" Alex proclaims, holding the door open for them as they all file out, one by one.

I pull my boxer briefs back on, and then my jeans, taking note of the fact that Alex hasn't left the room himself. He closes the door and sits down on the corner of the bed.

"You want to tell me what's going on?"

"Not particularly." I pull my shirt on, searching the floor for my belt.

"I can try to talk to her, if you want me to."

"I need to take care of this myself."

"If she's as angry as you say, I'm not sure she's going to be willing to listen to you. I'm not sure she's going to be willing to be in the same room with you. I'm not sure she's going to be willing to be in the same room with *me*."

"I'll deal with that when it happens. I have to try."

He crosses his arms and leans back, observing me.

"What?"

"This is a good look on you, Dec," he says.

"What? Naked and tied up? Or now that I have my clothes back on?"

"Being determined to work things out with her, talk through a problem, sticking with the woman you love when times get rough. And it's just as obvious that she's in love with you," he continues.

Now he's got my attention.

"You sure about that? I thought so, but she's oddly unwilling to listen to me for a woman who's in love with me."

"I wouldn't have ended up making out the other night with a waitress whose name I barely knew if Callie wasn't in love with you."

"I thought we were pretending that never happened. Or that it was the HVAC."

Alex scoffs.

"I've been around Brighid enough to know that some things can't be easily explained. But that doesn't mean there's no explanation. You just have to be willing to open your eyes and believe what's in front of you."

"Callie has a special gift with food." That's as much as I'm going to say. Let him decide how to take that.

"One she clearly has no idea how to keep under control."

Yeah, he's on board with the magic stuff. I'm even kind of surprised that *I* am, actually. But at least I'm not stuck with trying to persuade him that what happened the other night didn't actually happen.

"She's been a little emotional since that night at Hunter and Brighid's engagement party."

"Gee... I wonder why." He rolls his eyes at me. "She's an amazing chef, Dec. But, moreover, she's a pretty amazing woman, too. I've spent enough time with her to know that. And you'd be lucky to have her..." He looks up at the ceiling, reflective. "Now, why does that sound so familiar? Oh! I know — I said it to Brighid before Hunter got his head out of his ass."

He frowns at me.

"Don't be Hunter-level stupid, Dec. Don't fuck this up any further. Either give the girl her forever or leave her in peace."

He lets himself out without further comment, and I'm left to sit with the knowledge that my promises don't mean squat to Callie anymore. Why should she trust me? I fucked it up once already. Does this count as twice? Well, it doesn't matter. It's a promise I'm going to fulfill, even if it kills me.

# Chapter 22

## REVENGE

## Callie

I did it! I followed through on my plan to make Declan pay for screwing with me and teach him a lesson he won't forget. And I have the evidence, the leverage to make that happen, right on my phone. All I have to do is upload it to Instagram or something, and this whole thing will be done. Over. Past. Behind me. Just like Declan will be. Right where I want him.

Right?

Right.

I shut and lock the apartment door, leaning back against it, glad to have the world outside and me, safe, in here, by myself. No one to bother me. No one to betray me. No one to leave me. Not anymore. Never again.

Let's get this over with. Just a quick upload.

OK. Not so quick. I don't have the app on my phone. Scheduling app, finance app, recipes — I've got all of that. No social media. Do I post this to Instagram? Twitter? Facebook? TikTok? MySpace? Alright, I'm not *that* old. But I have no clue what to do. Post to all of them? Stick to Instagram because that's where I found the photo of Declan and his groupies?

I download the Instagram app, just to start somewhere.

Username? Password?

Do I use the Castalia account?

Wait. No. I can't. Even if I had the login info, this can't come from Castalia. This can't be connected to my business in any way.

New account?

OK. Email.

Wait. If I use my personal email, they'll be able to trace it back to me, and that's the next thing to posting it from the Castalia account.

Ugh. I need help. Somebody who knows more about this social media stuff than I do.

I look at the door, remembering that sense of safety when I locked it behind me, and for the first time I'm dreading going into my own kitchen. The one up here isn't my real kitchen. The one downstairs is. And I don't want to risk running into Declan, who is undoubtedly going to come after me after what I did. Even if he gives up on trying to wiggle his way out of this, he's still going to push me not to post the photo. I don't have a moment to waste, then.

I run down the stairs and into the kitchen.

"Drew — I need to borrow you for a second."

I head into my office, knowing he'll follow me as soon as he can. A minute later, he's standing in the doorway.

"What's up, Callie? How'd things go?"

"Great. I've got a photo I need to post to social media. But it can't come from me. How do I do that?"

"What's in this photo, and why can't you post it yourself?"

"Well, A — still no account. I'd have to set one up. Could kind of use your help there... And, B — I don't want to associate me or the business with this..."

"I'll ask again — what's in the photo?"

"Declan."

"Declan and what?"

"Those cuffs I borrowed."

"Callie — what did you do?" Drew's tone is both knowing and concerned.

"I may have stripped him naked and tied him up to the bed."
"You did what?"

"Stripped him naked and tied him up."

"So, what's in this photo is..."

"A naked and bound Declan Carter."

"Oh, geez..." He smacks himself on the forehead, then lets his hand slide slowly down his face until he's left scratching his chin through his short goatee. "That was not how I imagined you using those when you asked for them."

"He earned it, Drew! He came over here to seduce me less than twelve hours after he was in a hotel room with not one, but two, women — groupies. And they sent him a cleavage photo while I had him tied up!"

"One cleavage or two?" he asks. "Not that I care, since cleavage isn't exactly a turn-on for me."

"Just one. But there was a lipstick kiss on it."

"Wow. OK. Serious heterosexual-male kink-bait."

"Apparently."

"How'd Declan like the cuffs?"

I glare at him.

"What? I'm curious."

"He was... into it."

"Hard as a rock, huh?"

I purse my lips, refraining from comment.

"Is that what's in the photo?"

"It might be. Probably a little less impressive after I started reading him the riot act about pulling the wool over my eyes."

"You really think he was with these girls right before he came looking for you?"

"Photos don't lie."

"Well, they do these days. But you wouldn't know that, since you don't do social media."

"But I need to now."

"Yeah. About that, Callie... Umm, I hate to break it to you, but they've been cracking down on people posting naked images of their exes. They call it 'revenge porn.' The law's been catching up with it, too. You might be able to get away with it if Declan doesn't object. But I expect he's got lawyers, PR people and a label that will, even if he doesn't."

"So, I'll set up a fake email account to do it."

"Yeah... That's unlikely to work. You'd need an anonymizer, a VPN, maybe even a sock-puppet account or two to share it."

"I have no idea what any of that is."

"Then I'm going to suggest you don't do this."

"Come on, Drew! It's a photo of a naked rockstar! There have to be thousands of those out there."

"Probably. But most of them are of Tommy Lee. He posted one himself not too long ago."

"He posted a naked photo. Of himself. On social media? Do they even allow that?"

"Why are you skeptical that they'd allow celebrities to post naked photos of themselves, but you're chomping at the bit to post one of your ex? You have no idea how social media works, do you?"

"Not really."

"Again, I'll suggest you not do this. It's a bad idea."

"I need to do this, Drew. I need to show him he can't use me like this and get away with it. I need to warn all the other women he might seduce and use like he did me, so they don't fall for it!"

"What did he say when you called him on the photo with the groupies?"

"He said it wasn't what it looked like and that he could explain."

"And did you let him explain?"

"Of course not! What is there to explain? It's a photo of him sandwiched between two scantily clad women in a penthouse suite in the wee hours of the morning."

"Were they naked?"

"Well, no... But you don't put that amount of bare flesh against someone you don't know, or don't plan on getting to know... very intimately."

"I think you'd be surprised what people do when they're in the same room with a celebrity, let alone a rockstar as hot as your boyfriend."

"He's not my boyfriend!"

"Well, not if you post that photo, he's not. That's not something you do to someone you care about."

All the air goes out of my sails in an instant.

"You *do* care about him, don't you..." he says.

It's a statement, not a question. I spend five or six days a week working shoulder-to-shoulder with Drew. I know more about him than I do about anyone other than Lyric, Siobhan and... Declan. If I can say I truly know Declan anymore.

"If this was some other ex of his threatening to post an embarrassing photo of him on social media, how would that make you feel? How would you have felt about it yesterday? Or when you were 17?"

"At 17, I'd have ripped her arms off. Yesterday, I'd have been annoyed. Or I might have gone to look at them. Maybe. Today? I'd probably help her."

"No, you wouldn't."

"Why not? He's a dick!"

"He's a dick you have some very strong feelings for, both positive and negative, and definitely unresolved, which is why you were supposed to be taking the day off today, remember?"

"My feelings aren't unresolved! I hate him!"

"And you love him, or you wouldn't hate him enough to go to these lengths to punish him. You want him to do better, because you know he can be better, and he owes that to both of you."

There's a feedback loop setting up in my brain, and I can't even think straight anymore. There's no way I'm going to be able to deal with anonymous accounts and VIPNs and whatever else Drew was talking about.

"Listen — if getting revenge on him like this will make you feel better, will let you get back to normal, where you can cook without burning sauces and... doing other things," Drew says, "then I will one hundred percent support you. But when torturing him with food only took the edge off, leaving you confused and conflicted, I'm not sure what posting that photo is going to do to improve your life. And that's the key thing here — you need to do what you can for you. Letting him continue to live rent-free in your head hasn't done you a lot of good."

If nothing else, Declan turning up in my life again has proven that he *has* been taking up a giant chunk of real estate in my head, and my heart, for more than a decade. Drew's right there. Again. He grabs me by the arms, getting my full attention.

"So, rather than making him extra-famous — and *you*, because they will eventually track that photo back to you — and getting a few moments of satisfaction by humiliating him, I'd ask what you can do that will help you finally start to heal, to let go of the pain he's caused you, and that you've continued to cause yourself by cutting yourself off from any sort of romantic relationship. You've held that pain close, like a security blanket, but the only thing it's done is isolate you from a life you might be able to enjoy, if you could just let the past go."

His words hit me so hard that I can't think of anything to say in response. His expression is compassionate, but Drew's a tough-love kind of guy. And maybe that's what I needed right now. Maybe. Right now, I know I need to think about this some more before I do anything I can't take back.

"When did you get so wise?" I ask him.

"When I got serious about a man who's much smarter than me and realized he loved me anyway. After that, it's all osmosis."

I chuckle, because we both know that's not true.

"How's the baby doing?"

"He's amazing! Getting huge. Maria's so uncomfortable right now. We sent her for a mani-pedi and a facial, since she's too far along for a massage. It won't be long now."

"Did I tell you to take all your paternity leave?"

"You did. That's why we need to get this situation with Declan sorted out, because you really, really, should not be cooking when you're like this."

I roll my eyes at him.

"Don't you roll your eyes at me! You and I both know something weird happened the other night. And that couple fighting the night before?"

"Oh. I thought I was the only one wondering about that."

"You were the one who called me wise..."

"Never happened."

"We both know it did."

"Maybe. But it'll be fine. I know what happened, and I can keep it from happening again."

"How?"

"I've got it all under control."

"Is that what this was? Trying to figure out how to post a naked photo of your boyfriend on social media, in the middle of your day off, by dragging me off the line to install Instagram on your phone?"

"Put that way, it sounds a little less under control. But I've got it now. I won't post the photo. Yet, anyway."

"Just think about what I said, OK? You've got to do the best thing for you. I can't be the only one taking care of you."

OK, now I feel bad.

"Especially when you're almost a dad and you've got a husband to look after."

"I've got enough to spare for you, my dear."

"But you shouldn't have to. I'm a grown, independent woman. I can take care of myself."

"You can. The question is whether you'll actually do it. Because I haven't seen you do much of that at all. Especially lately."

Ouch. My words to Lyric come back to me. I don't have two kids, a teaching job and a poetry career to worry about. But I do have a restaurant full of diners, a kitchen full of staff and, I have to admit, some lingering wounds from a relationship I had thought was twelve years in the past.

"You have the day off. For once," he gives me a stern look. "Go take a hot bubble bath, watch a Hallmark movie and drink an adult beverage. I'll even send Raquel up with dinner and a cocktail once she gets in."

"I'm not sure I'm opening the door tonight."

"You afraid he's going to show up?"

I nod.

"I'll have her use the special knock. You go do what you need to do, for you and for us. OK?"

"Yeah. Alright."

"Get out of my kitchen," he jokes.

"Fine. OK. I'm leaving." Despite my words, he senses my reluctance.

"You want me to send a scout to make sure the coast is clear?"

"Would you?"

"Yeah. Be ready to make a break for it."

I nod again, heading for the back door.

"Drew?" I ask as he heads back to the line and sends one of the runners up to my apartment.

"Yeah?"

"Thanks."

"Yes, Chef!"

# CHAPTER 23

# I'LL BE WAITING

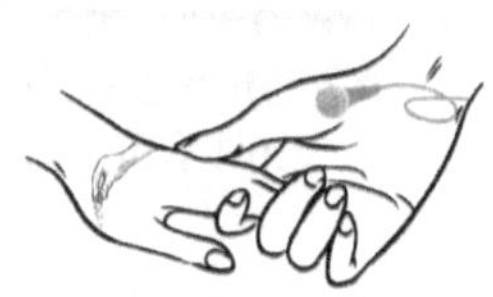

## Declan

"She won't answer the door."

I look behind me, and standing three steps below me is Raquel, holding a take-out box and a tall cup full of a bright green frozen drink with a lime wedge on the side.

"Why not?"

"I think you know why not."

"Uhh... I think I know why I think she won't. What I don't know is if *you* know why I think she won't."

"She's pissed at you."

"Well, that's not inaccurate," I admit. "Do you know *why* she's pissed at me?"

"No. But if I had to guess, I'd guess it's because you were a fucking dick to her again."

"Does your mother know you talk like that?"

"I'm 18, Declan, and Mom's in rehab again. So the better question is whether my nana knows I talk like that. And, yes, she does. She figures I've earned it."

"You're probably right about that. Sorry to hear about your mom."

"No — it's good news. She checked herself in this time, before it got bad."

"Oh. Well, that's better, then. Anything I can do to help?"

"Stop pissing Callie off?"

Hmm...

"I'm not very good at that. Yet. I'm working on it. That's why I'm here."

"She's still not going to open the door for you."

"Why are you so sure about that?"

"Drew told me to use the special knock when I brought her dinner."

"Special knock?"

"Yup."

"And that would be...?"

"None of your business."

Rats.

"I really didn't do what she thinks I did that got her pissed at me this time! That's why I'm here, to tell her that, to explain."

"I'm pretty sure she doesn't want to hear it. Not right now, anyway."

"Well... I— I need to make sure she's not so mad about the thing I didn't actually do that she actually does something that'll get us both in trouble."

"I think Drew talked her down. That's why she's not in the kitchen and why I'm delivering her dinner — and her adult beverage."

"Oh. That's good, I guess. But I still need to explain it to her."

"Give her a couple days to cool down. She's got a temper."

"No kidding!" I roll my eyes. "That temper she's got on her is hotter than a salamander."

"Don't you mean a fire-breathing dragon?"

"No. You don't know about salamanders yet? You're working in a restaurant."

"I'm doing front-of-house and running food until I finish this session of my training."

"How long do you have left?"

"Just a few weeks. The next session starts when school starts after Labor Day."

"You don't start school until after Labor Day?"

"It's the beach, Declan. A lot of kids work in their families' businesses or as lifeguards. The whole place starts to fall apart when the college kids go back to school as it is."

"Oh. Well, the last time I was here, I was still in high school, and we left right after my birthday, in August, to go back to school."

"And that was when you and Callie broke up? Didn't try to do the long-distance thing?"

"Well, no — we did that for a couple of summers."

"Ah-ha! I knew it!"

"What?"

"You and Callie were more than a summer fling. That's why she's so pissed at you."

"That and some other things."

"You two... I swear. If you weren't a rockstar and she wasn't my boss, I'd just bonk your heads together until you figured your shit out. This is getting really tiresome for everyone."

"Why do you say that?"

"Callie hasn't taken a full day off since I've known her. And she's been burning sauces and shit ever since you got here. You're messing up her cooking, Declan. And that just pisses her off even more."

"She said she has it under control."

Raquel's expression is both skeptical and condemning.

I mean, I know this is my fault. That's why I want to fix it. But I can't do that until she lets me talk to her and explain.

"Leave her alone until she's cooled down, Declan. I'll tell her you stopped by and listened when I asked you to give her a break. She'll like that. It makes you seem more mature."

"More mature? I'm almost 30."

"And yet you act like you're 15, and you don't get that she needs some space."

"Oh. Well... to be honest... I haven't had a girlfriend since I was 17. I don't really know how this stuff is supposed to work. Not as an adult."

"You haven't had a girlfriend in twelve years, and you're a rockstar?"

"Having girls throwing their panties on stage is not the same thing as having a girlfriend."

"At least you know that much," she says derisively. "You've been a slut-muffin since you were 17, huh?"

"What? You think I'm a stud-muffin?"

"I said *slut*-muffin,' not 'stud-muffin.' You're too old for me to be thinking about whether you're studly or not."

"Ouch."

"I mean, you're not old enough to be my dad or anything. Which is good, because I have no idea who he is, and that means you're not him."

"No. *That* I'm pretty sure of. I'm careful about that shit."

"Good. If you're going to be a slut-muffin, you need to be careful. Wrap it up, keep it clean. Don't be giving Callie anything. Including a baby."

"Uh... No. And I'm *not* slutty!" She gives me another skeptical look. "Really! I'm not like that... anymore."

"A reformed slut-muffin, then?"

"Exactly!"

"Then what's with all those girls taking selfies with you on Insta?"

"They're fans."

"Fans with lots of skin they want you to be looking at and touching."

"Well, yeah. That's the way it works."

"Part of the job?"

"Yeah."

"You need to fix that. If you want Callie back. And you do want her back, right?"

"Fuck yes! That's why I'm here!"

"She's not going to believe you if you've got girls posting selfies with you all the time."

"I know that. Now."

"Ah! So that's what you did to piss her off!"

"Well, yeah. But it wasn't what it looked like."

"You know every guy who gets caught hanging out with another girl tells his bae that, right?"

"Bay?"

"Wow. You *are* old."

"Thanks. Again."

"Bae, B-A-E — babe, baby, girlfriend, regular hook-up... That bae."

"Oh. Well, like I said, I haven't had one since I was 17. And I'm not sure Callie and I have made it back to bae—man, I feel ridiculous saying that! I'm not sure we're back at girlfriend/boyfriend status yet. And if we were, we're probably not now. Not until I fix this."

"Yeah. No. You still need to give her some time. Show her you respect her wishes, and that you trust her to think this through and be reasonable once she's calmed down. Then explain it to her."

"You don't think she'll do something stupid before then? I mean, she's pretty pissed, and there's this photo..."

"Are you naked in this photo?"

"I'm not talking to you about this. You're 18."

"So that's a yes."

"No comment."

"So, you're more than naked in this photo. You're going to want to practice that 'No comment' thing."

"You think she'll put it online?"

"Nah. I'll talk to her about the revenge-porn thing. Luckily, you're both over 18, or somebody'd be going to jail tonight."

"I don't want my lawyers and PR people going after her. There's only so much I can do to control them, with the band and the label involved and everything."

"That's nice of you, to think of her first."

"I don't care about the photo. Not much anyway. But I don't want her to get in trouble."

"You old softie, you," she says. "I'd chuck you on the arm, but I've got my hands full. And these are getting heavy."

"Oops. Sorry! I'll let you take it to her. And I'm not *old*!"

"You are. And you need to leave. No sticking around to hear the secret knock!" she says. "Be an adult and give her some space."

"Yes, Mom."

She rolls her eyes at me.

"You're too old for me to be your mother. That means you need to grow up, Declan. Go home. Chill. I'll talk to her. Come back when she's ready to see you."

"I'm not sure when that will be."

"She'll let you know. Don't be a spoiled brat about it. You don't always get what you want when you want it."

"You a Stones fan?"

"No. Why?"

"Man, I *am* old..."

"There! You've got the idea. Now, leave, before I sic Drew on you. And you don't want that. I hear he has handcuffs..."

"Waitaminute..."

"What?"

"Um... nevermind."

I move to the side to let her pass. She turns around when she reaches the landing, balancing the cup atop the box, and stares at me, giving me a look that says, "Scram."

"Fine."

I descend the stairs and walk around the corner. But just until I'm out of sight.

I hear a series of eight taps. I'm a musician. I should be able to memorize this pattern instantly.

Uh... nope.

Lucky for me, Callie doesn't answer the first knock.

Eight more taps.

Where have I heard that rhythm before? It sounds so familiar.

Oh, fuck me... It's the chorus from "Rolling in the Deep."

It's the angry girl telling her ex he fucked up and it's his loss.

Just old enough that Callie might have heard it before she stopped listening to music.

Just old enough that it would have been a song an angry Callie would have blasted when she was pissed off at me.

She may have been dodging every possible thing that would have reminded her of me, but this is a thing she held on to. Her anger, her disdain, her righteous indignation over what I did to her.

It's so obvious now — she's wrapped herself up in a blanket of anger and pain, and she's used it to keep the world at bay. Until I managed to pry my way back inside last night. And now... The only way I'm getting back inside is if I prove to her it's truly safe to let me back into her life.

And to do that, first I have to follow the sage advice given to me my an 18-year-old. I have to give Callie time and space.

Raquel was right. I'm a spoiled brat. Because I don't want to do that. I don't want to wait. I want this — us — fixed. Right now. And that's why I'm standing here, listening for that special knock. And now that I know what it is... the one thing I can't do is use it.

Fuck.

"So, you going to behave yourself and give the girl some space?"

Fuck!

I about jump out of my skin.

"Raquel took too long coming back. I figured something delayed her."

"Hi. Drew, is it?"

"Yeah. And I can't be gone from the kitchen for long, so let me make this short: Give her some time. You hurt her badly."

"I know I did. But I didn't... I didn't do what she thinks I did. Not this time."

"I figured as much. I talked her down out of the tree. She won't post the photo."

"She told you about that?"

"Where do you think she got the cuffs?" he says with a smirk. "They were unused — just so you know. And I don't want them back now that you're out of them. Maybe you can use them on her next time."

"Thanks. I think."

He cracks up.

"Just tell me one thing, so I can go on with a clear conscience, knowing you heard the knock: Do you love her?"

I start to answer, but he stops me with a raised finger.

"I don't mean, do you want her back in your bed while you're here? I don't mean, do you want to try dating until you go back on tour? I mean, do you plan on making her your top priority in life, even above your career? Because if you don't — I'm begging you — just leave her in peace. She comes off all ball-bustin' and independent, but you wrecked the girl way back when. And I want to see her whole. You're the only one who can fix that, I think. So, are you going to do it? Do you love her enough to do that?"

"I always have. I just didn't think I was good enough for her."

"You weren't," he says, not tempering that assessment in the least. "But I think you might be now. Don't disappoint me."

I give him a nod, and he walks away, back to the kitchen.

I peek back around the corner, looking up at the door at the top of the steps, wanting nothing more than to bust it down, take my girl in my arms and fix all the wounds I've ever given her.

And that's the one thing I can't do right now. Not if I want to fix things for good.

I turn around and head back to the studio.

# CHAPTER 24

## ROSE GARDEN

## Callie

“He says he didn't do it.”

“What?”

“Declan says he didn't do it. Whatever it was you think he did,” Raquel explains, setting my dinner and drink down on the kitchen island.

“Yeah. I heard that part when I was leaving. Doesn't mean I believe him.”

“I told him I'd tell you he was here, wanting to explain.”

“Oh?” I look at her, feeling slightly confused. “He let you come in to warm me up? Make sure I wasn't going to go after him with a meat cleaver or something?”

“You wouldn't use a knife for anything other than food. Knives are your life.”

“Heh. I was ready to do more than chop pecans the other day when he showed up in my kitchen.”

“Which day was that?”

“The morning before he showed up for dinner that first night.”

“Oh.”

“Yeah. The morning *after* he was out dancing and doing whatever he was doing in the penthouse suite with a couple of girls.”

“Is that why you're upset with him? Because he was with someone else before he came to see you?”

"Isn't that enough? I mean, I know it's very stereotypical for a rockstar, going from one girl to the next, days or even hours later."

"For what it's worth, I don't think that's what he was doing."

"Why? Because he told you that?" She looks down at her feet. "I've got news for you, Raquel — men lie. Especially when it means they can get you into bed."

"I don't think that's what's going on with him."

"You're swayed by that rockstar charisma. Don't be. Anyone with that much charisma knows exactly how to use it to get what they want."

"Well, I sent him away. Told him to give you some time and space."

"So, he's waiting at the bottom of the stairs, right?"

I open the door and peek down, ready to slam it shut in his face. But he's not there.

"Oh." I close the door again.

"You sound disappointed."

"No. Just... surprised, I guess. He's got a habit of not letting anything stop him when he really wants something."

"Maybe he's matured since you knew him before."

"Why do you think I knew him before?"

"You said he showed up in the kitchen before he'd even come in for dinner. It's pretty clear he knows you. I mean, you're awesome and everything, but no guy stalks a chef before he's eaten her food or at least met her. And since he hadn't been in for dinner before, and since you went out of your way to torture him..."

"I did, didn't I?" I'm still feeling both guilty about and proud of that.

"Yeah. I don't know many guys who would have made it past raw onion, let alone muskrat. And he was still going at ghost-pepper chocolate mousse."

OK. Now it's mostly guilty.

"So... you mind telling me what your history is?"

"I don't want to get into it. It isn't something I want to relive."

"So, all bad, then?"

If I'm honest, it wasn't all bad. That's why it's so hard.

"I really don't want to get into it. I need to clear my head, get him out of my head, focus on the dish for Taste, get back to work tomorrow."

"Sorry. I'll let you get back to that, then."

"It's fine. It's just..."

"It makes you emotional, dealing with him. Good and bad."

"I just need to toss all this baggage into the ocean, never have to deal with it again."

"Seems like that would be easier if you unpackaged the baggage first, lightened the load..."

"Maybe," I admit. "He really went away just because you told him to give me space?"

"Yeah." She shrugs.

I'm disappointed. And I don't like it.

"Let Drew know if you need anything else. I'm happy to run it up. Oh — and don't post naked photos on the internet, just in case Drew didn't already say that. I mean, they teach us that in health class now... You should know better."

"Drew already told me. Thanks, Raquel."

When I shut and lock the door this time, it's not with the same sense of relief at shutting out the world. It actually feels a little lonely in here.

I sit down with my dinner — Drew's short ribs over grits, which he knows I love but prefer to have him cook. The man has a way with meat that I've never really had. My specialties lean toward Nonna's Italian dishes, but also to the seafood that was the star in her restaurant kitchen. I have my own twists, though. If only I could figure out one dish that will stand out from the crowd but still be uniquely my own. I finish eating, but I'm still too emotional to focus.

Drew suggested a bath to help me relax. I can mull over what I remember Nonna making while I do that, maybe come up with something.

But I'm out of practice with this relaxing stuff. I run hot water into the tub and while it's filling, I dig into the box of bath stuff in the linen closet. Some of this was at Nonna's house, and I just never went through it. There's an ancient bottle of strawberry bubble bath that's probably from when I was a kid. I sniff it for nostalgia's sake and then drop the bottle straight in the trash. Artificial strawberry scent has not improved with age.

Some of Nonna's gardenia soap... That might be an option. And a sachet of... I squeeze it lightly. Mmm... smells like Nonna's garden, with hints of rose and... rosemary? It smells like the breeze across Nonna's kitchen window in the summer. I drop the packet into the bath and give it a minute to start giving up its essence to the hot water before I slide in with it. Now, to put Declan out of mind and come up with some culinary genius...

## *Five years ago*

"*Angelica?* Is that you?" Nonna calls from across the house.

"Yes, Nonna! I'm back from the store!"

"Come see me once you've put the groceries away, *cara mia*. You've been gone too long. We need to catch up!"

"Yes, Nonna."

She's right. It's been five years since I left to start culinary school, and I've only been back for a week or two at a time, mostly around Christmas. It was easy to justify — I had so much to do when I was in school, and the jobs I've been taking in kitchens and food trucks all around the city don't exactly offer paid vacation, nor have I wanted to leave people short-staffed once they've offered me a place in their kitchens.

But Nonna's had a rough time lately. First, it was a bout with the flu, then a fall when she was still recovering. We got lucky — she's always been incredibly healthy, incredibly active, even after the hotel was redeveloped as condos. She narrowly avoided serious injury in that fall. The doctor warned that if she'd fallen at a slightly different angle, she might have broken a hip. As it was, she was bruised from knee to ribs, with a small bump on her head to boot.

I'd just wrapped up a few months in a Peruvian restaurant, and I have a month or so yet before some friends with a food truck selling authentic Oaxaqueño dishes expect to need a new cook. So it only made sense to come stay with Nonna for a bit, help her recover, make sure the house was still safe for her.

"Here you go, Nonna." I hand her a mug, eager to see her reaction.

"Chocolate?" she asks after taking a deep breath of the liquid inside.

"It's a recipe I worked up when I was winding up my time at the Peruvian restaurant, as kind of an experiment. I figured since my next job is focusing on Mexican cuisine, it might be fun to see what I could come up with. It's not like American hot chocolate, though. So you've been warned," I add, chuckling.

Nonna takes a careful sip. She looks perplexed at first. Then she takes another sip, nodding.

"Cinnamon. Cardamom. Something sweet with some fruity notes..."

"Dates."

"And... rose?"

"I should have known you'd know that one," I tell her, pleased that she could puzzle out the elements of my recipe. "And the cacao, of course."

"It's nicely done, *angelica*," she says. "More of a tonic than a dessert, like tea."

"Yes, Nonna."

"Well, thank you, dear. For your care and for sharing your recipe with me. I think you may have picked up where I left off, exploring all these other cultures and their traditions, beyond our own."

"It's fascinating, Nonna. I've really enjoyed finding new herbs, new flavors from around the world."

She looks at me, her gaze intent.

"Is there a reason you get them second-hand in New York, rather than traveling to find them in their homes?" she asks.

"Nonna..." I sigh, weary of this conversation before it's begun. It's not the first time she's hinted that I've limited myself, my life. She's never said I've disappointed her in that, but I feel a bit... small. Like I haven't stretched my wings like I could have, maybe should have.

"Ah, my *angelica*... Of all the things that your parents took from you, intentionally or otherwise, your sense of adventure is perhaps the second-greatest loss."

Second-greatest?

"You and I have had more losses than any two people should need to bear, but watching you withdraw inside yourself has been so terribly hard. I wish I knew a way to help you open your heart again, to find the courage to trust — yourself and others."

"I'm fine, Nonna. I trust myself, my skill in the kitchen, being smart enough to keep to things I can control. New York isn't a place to be trusting strangers anyway. I've got too much to learn, and I'm doing that without having to even leave the city."

"Imagine how much more you could experience and learn if you were willing to take a risk, *cara mia*. Life is so... small... when you refuse to venture beyond the confines of what you already know, the people you already trust."

"I did that once, Nonna. And I regretted it."

Nonna sighs.

"I do not know what happened between you and Arturo, granddaughter. But my instincts are never wrong, and I know in my heart he was a nice boy who cared deeply about you."

"He disagreed, Nonna."

"Did he say that?"

"Yes, as a matter of fact, he did. Said he'd made a mistake."

"That I would believe. Whether that mistake was what he said it was, I would doubt."

She shakes her head, clearly skeptical that what Declan said to me that day was true.

"It doesn't matter, Nonna. That was a long time ago. I learned a hard lesson, which was only reinforced afterwards."

"You and I learned different lessons from that tragedy, Calliope," she says. "I was reminded to live every day to the fullest, to value family above all else. Having you with me helped me do that."

"You worked very hard in the restaurant, Nonna. I'm not sure that was living life to the fullest, even if I was there a few hours a day."

"Ah! But that's where you are wrong! I met so many wonderful and interesting people there, from our friends who worked with us to the people who enjoyed our food. All those times I encouraged you to check in with our diners, to see how they enjoyed the food — that wasn't just to ensure we were cooking things people loved to eat. It was to bring them into our lives, and us into theirs. That's why they came back time and time again."

"Until they didn't," I say, still a little bitter about Nonna losing the restaurant to condominium space. And I immediately regret it, because she gets quiet. She sips at her chocolate, looking sad.

"I'm sorry, Nonna. I should not have said that. I know you miss it."

"I do, granddaughter. But I refuse to let that loss steal my enjoyment of life. And that, I fear, is a thing you have lost yourself."

"I like my life, Nonna. I like cooking. And I am doing everything I can to learn, to gather up the knowledge I will need to have a successful restaurant of my own someday, and to begin saving up to do that."

"And a wonderful restaurant it will be, with you cooking in it, *cara mia.*" She pats my hand encouragingly. "There will come a time when you find the thing that makes your heart sing again. And when you put that passion into your food — when those two things finally come together once more... Then I will rejoice for you, *angelica*, because then you will know what true happiness is. Then, your life will be full once more, like it was when Arturo was here."

I'm careful to turn away from her when I roll my eyes. Nonna's belief in Declan was unexpected in that moment. That she seems to retain it after all these years, after what he did... what he said... Well, there was a reason I never really told her. She was always a romantic, always wanting more for me than life seems to want me to have.

But, thankfully, for now at least, she's dropped the subject of my self-imposed limitations. I've got just a few weeks with her before I have to head back to New York, and I want this time to be pleasant for us both. I'm not sure when I'll be able to make it back to see her again. I've got to get back for this next job, because I've finally got a line on a sous-chef position and I'm hoping this will be exactly the step up I need.

"Tell me again about how you met Nonno," I prompt, knowing it's a topic she never tires of talking about. She may have lost him decades ago, but this, I think, is where she comes by her romantic notions of fate and eternal love. I'm glad she had that, even if it's not in the cards for me.

"We met on the boardwalk, you know... Not here — in New Jersey. It was a bright summer day, and Nonno was working for a gelateria, carrying a cooler full of gelato and little paper cups. Mama wouldn't splurge on such an expense, of course. A day at the beach was a luxury she could only barely justify to begin with. But Mama loved the ocean, and she knew I loved it, too.

And I was the last of her children — the youngest, and the only one to survive both the journey from Italy and the war itself... So she was inclined to spoil us both with a day here and there, sitting on the sand, enjoying the sunshine."

"But not the gelato, right Nonna?"

"No. She'd gotten so used to rationing sugar, and the pennies she earned, when it was so hard for immigrants from Italy to find good work..."

"But you caught Nonno's eye, didn't you?" I smile, able to enjoy this little bit of second-hand romance, because I see how much her face lights up with the memory.

"It was love at first sight, *angelica*. He was the handsomest boy I'd ever laid eyes on, and he was instantly smitten with me, too. So, he took his tip money that day and bought me a gelato."

"Cherry vanilla, right?"

"Yes. I don't know how he knew it was my favorite. But he did. It was..."

"Fate..."

"Yes."

I start, coming out of the memory in a lukewarm tub of water redolent of those scents of Nonna's garden. That's what the house smelled like the next time I came home — like roses and rosemary, with the garden in full bloom almost six months to the day later. I gathered dozens of blooms to place on Nonna's grave. It had been so sudden. I hadn't gotten the chance to see her, talk to her in person, again after I left that winter.

By the following one, I'd cleared out Nonna's things and put the house up for rent while I waited for my replacement to start at the Mexican fusion place where I'd been working as a sous-chef. The house went on the market in the spring, while I looked for a possible spot to open my own restaurant, and as soon as the summer rentals were done, it was time for settlement.

I listened to Nonna's fountain one last time, sitting on that bench where she used to tell me about the nymph and about the Great Bear in the sky. And then I shut it off, plucking a single crimson rose to join the potted rosemary bush in my new apartment above the restaurant space.

It took all fall and winter to outfit the kitchen and dining room, to hire staff I trusted to help me beat the odds and make my restaurant a success in its first summer season. If we didn't, that would have been the end of it all, and I'd have had to find a cheaper rental, take a sous-chef position somewhere to make ends meet after risking and losing all that Nonna had left me.

Well, no — not all she had left me. I had her chef's book. And that, and all of what I'd learned in my time in New York — I parlayed it all into a menu that kept the dining room full from the first day of May and well into the fall. And even then, we were busy, building a local clientèle that let us survive that first winter season and thrive once spring arrived again. And now... Now I need the space to expand our dining room, and I need a recipe that will ensure I can make it happen.

What I don't need is thoughts of Declan running through my head, let alone the image I have on my phone. Which is exactly what will happen if I don't find something to keep me busy. By the time I'm dressed once again, this time in shorts and a T-shirt, my brain is running in circles again. I need a distraction. Something to take my mind off... Yeah.

I can't bother Siobhan while her studio is open. And she's going to want to talk about Declan. Lyric might, too, but I can make dinner for her and the kids, maybe make cookies with the kids afterward, so she can take some time for herself. That'll be good for both of us, and the kids.

And, if Declan does decide to come back, I won't be here. Perfect.

# CHAPTER 25

## RAISINS

### *An hour later*

Tommy sniffs at a piece of elbow macaroni. He gives it a second look, another sniff, carefully places it in his mouth and chews.

Lyric exhales a sigh of relief.

"Oh, my gods — Callie, you're a miracle-worker! If I didn't know better, I'd say you were a kitchen witch!"

I choke on a brussels sprout. Clearly, Lyric hasn't talked to Brighid in the last twenty-four hours.

"I usually can't get Tommy to eat anything but the stuff with the powdered cheese."

"Mommy? What's this green thing?"

"It's a brussels sprout, Aria. Kind of like a tiny little cabbage." Aria looks dubious.

"What's the rule, Aria?"

"Try something at least once before you decide you don't like it."

"Correct. And these are Auntie Callie's brussels sprouts."

"And Auntie Callie is a chef, which means her food is super-special, right?"

I giggle a little, and Lyric smiles at me.

"Yes, it is. People go to Auntie Callie's restaurant when they want a special meal, because everyone thinks her cooking is so good."

Aria spears a sliver of sprout on her fork, gives me a look out of the corner of her eye, then closes her eyes and sticks it in her mouth, and chews.

Lyric and I are holding our breath, waiting for her reaction.

Her eyes pop open, and she lights up.

"That tastes amazing, Auntie Callie!" she says. "Like potato chips and green beans had a baby!"

I nearly choke on a bite of macaroni. Out of the mouths of babes... and rockstars. So much for keeping my mind off Declan.

"This is incredible! How do you make macaroni-and-cheese taste so good?" Lyric asks. "And you have my kids eating brussels sprouts! I'm seriously calling you an unofficial kitchen-witch."

I ignore the reference to my magical skills in the kitchen and focus on my real talent.

"It's all in the flavor combinations and cooking techniques. Soggy, overcooked brussels are horrible. That's why most people think they hate them. But sliced thin and roasted or flash-fried, they get nutty. And mac-and-cheese is all about the sauce."

"I don't think Tommy even realizes the nuggets aren't from a box."

Tommy's got a brussels sprout on his fork and a breaded chicken strip in his other hand. He nibbles at the edge of the sprout and then puts it back on his plate, seeming unimpressed. He lays down the chicken, too, and then pulls the browned outer leaves off the sprout, leaving them in a pile on the plate.

"He won't eat anything that's browned past a certain point," Lyric explains with a sigh. "Those are the best parts, buddy!" she tells him, shaking her head. "I think you could fry up a batch of loose leaves and I'd eat them for a snack," she says. "Mom never boiled ours to death like everyone else's did, but this is a new level of yum! Thank you so much for cooking dinner for us! You really didn't have to, though."

"I needed a break from the restaurant, the kitchen... myself..." I admit.

"What's going on, Callie? Is this more Declan stuff? I swear, sometimes I wish I'd never offered to do the handfasting. The impact it ended up having on you... But I was such a romantic, even at 20..."

"It's fine, Lyric. You did us a favor, even if it didn't work out. You couldn't have known. I mean, I didn't have a clue..." Tears spring to my eyes, and I busy myself with my food. Her hand grasps mine, gives it a squeeze. "I'm sorry — I really don't want to talk about it. I just wanted to take a break, and give you one, too. So, once we're done, the kids and I will take care of the dishes, and you can go take some time to write, while we make some cookies! How does that sound, guys?"

"Awesome!" Lyric says. "What kind?"

Tommy glances across me, which is as close as he usually gets to agreeing with anything, so I take that as a second vote of support.

"Do you like oatmeal cookies?"

"With raisins?"

"I thought we'd do chocolate chips."

"Pshew," Aria says, relieved. "I don't like raisins."

I lean over close and whisper in her ear.

"Honestly, I don't either. Except golden raisins."

"What are those?"

"They're like regular raisins, except they're made a little differently, so they've got a fruitier flavor, and they're not quite as hard and dry."

"That sounds better."

"I agree. So, how about we make them with chocolate chips this time, and the next time we'll try them with golden raisins instead?"

She nods enthusiastically.

"Are you sure you want these heathens on your hands while you're baking?" Lyric asks. "It was enough you kept an eye on them while you made dinner."

"Nonsense! We had fun, didn't we, guys?"

"Yes! I stirred the macaroni, Mama! And Tommy put the salt in the water!"

"He did?"

"He did," I confirm. "I gave him a little bowl with the salt for the pasta water, and he added it and stirred it in for me, before I put the pot on to boil."

"That's awesome, buddy!" She puts her hand up for a high-five, and he looks over at her hand and then goes back to his food. She shrugs, like it's no big deal, but I can see she's disappointed. "He's been doing it about half the time, lately. I'd hoped this might be one," she says. "He's coming out of

Tommy-world a little more often, with all the work we've put in over the summer."

"That's good, though. And he did help with dinner."

"I can't believe you got him to do that, too! I'm going to have to start asking him to help more. I just want him to be a little more self-sufficient, you know? I mean, it's just me... and I..." She's the one tearing up now, and I return the hand squeeze. "If I'm not here for him..."

Ah. Now, I see. She's worried about what happens to Tommy if something happens to her, which has to be all the more real to her after losing his dad so suddenly. It's hard enough being a single mom, but knowing that your child is extra-reliant on you and could be for the rest of his life...

"The next time I'm over, we can start working on some simple cooking tasks — making toast, or Pop-Tarts, maybe? Frozen waffles with peanut butter, sliced bananas? Something that's not risky but that will let him feed himself in a pinch?"

"Yeah..." she says, not sounding fully convinced. "Yeah." She sounds a little more certain the second time.

"Go — write, take a bath, watch a movie. Whatever you want. I've got these guys for the next hour or two."

"Thank you, Callie. Really."

"Happy to do it. I really did need the break."

## *The next morning*

A break from my routine was exactly what I needed. And I got to give Lyric a break while I was doing it. Win-win.

A fresh start this morning, waking up blessedly alone in my bed, no sign of... him. Then straight down to my office to give Nonna's book another look.

"Is it safe?"

There's an arm with a white cloth — wait, is that an apron? — waving in the doorway. With rings on all the fingers of the hand and a heavy leather bracelet on the wrist.

"Depends. Are you alone?"

"Sadly, yes. Always alone. Quite pathetic, in fact."

"Get in here."

Alex peeks around the doorway, as if he's not entirely sure I won't hold his bandmate against him, but he grins at me, and any thought I had of asking him to take a break from his lessons falls away.

"So, I'm welcome?"

"So long as you don't mention your bandmate."

"That was part of our original agreement. But are you sure you don't want a sympathetic ear from someone who knows exactly how much of a pain in the ass he is?"

"Not today. Probably not tomorrow. Maybe not next week, or next year."

"Got it. So, what's on tap today?"

"I'm still trying to pick a dish for Taste."

"Ah. No individual lionfish for every attendee?"

"Uh... no. Wow. What a nightmare that would be."

"It was delicious, though."

"Thank you."

"Do you mind letting me look? Maybe a set of fresh eyes on what you're drawing inspiration from will help?"

I don't usually let anyone look in Nonna's book. But Alex isn't a chef. Not anytime soon, anyway. And I've gotten comfortable with him in my kitchen.

"Sure."

"I won't steal any recipes. I promise," he says, holding his hand up in what looks suspiciously like a scouting salute. Somehow, I doubt Declan was a scout. And there he is, taking up space in my head. Again.

I hand Alex the book as he sits down on the other side of my desk. He flips through the stained pages, marked with paperclips and notecards inserted here and there, where she made notes later on for recipes that already filled the page.

"'Stir clockwise only'?" he asks with a raised eyebrow.

"Nonna was always particular about how things were done. Most of the recipes I've drawn from, she taught me how to cook them so long ago that following instructions like that is just second-nature to me when I cook them now."

"That makes sense… it's just…" He hesitates, as if he's afraid I won't want to hear what he's got to say.

"What? Spit it out. I won't bite your head off. You're not… him." He chuckles.

"Somehow, I'm not sure he's the only one whose head you've bitten off for annoying you in the kitchen."

Brighid said something once about Alex's intuition. He seems to read people well, if nothing else.

"You would be correct. But I mostly snap at people who should know better."

"Well, I'm still learning, so I hope you'll forgive me if this is a step too far. But — was your grandmother a witch?"

"What?" This has to be the strangest thing anyone's ever asked me.

"It's just that — I've spent enough time with Brighid that I know that clockwise thing is sometimes a witchy thing."

"Brighid's not a witch."

"Yeah… she says that, but it's the same kind of magical, folksy stuff, with the herbs and the tarot cards and stuff. I know she considers herself a priestess first, but there seems to be a lot of overlap."

It's not a thing I'd ever considered before. Brighid had said something about Italian folk traditions when I'd first asked her about sourcing some of my culinary herbs, but… I mean, it was Nonna — other than that one odd comment about letting me cook when I was eager to see Declan, she was mainly focused on whatever she was cooking, whether it was what was right in front of her on the stove or what she planned to feature on the menu next week.

Was Nonna doing magic right under my nose and I never even noticed?

Sitting in the office of my kitchen, Alex has given me some serious food for thought, and he did it without mentioning… his… name.

"Is this arrabbiata sauce the same as yours?" he asks, stopping on a page early in the book.

"No. Nonna's is a good bit spicier. As a matter of fact, one time…" I stop myself as I realize what I was getting ready to tell Alex.

"What?"

"Nothing. It's nothing. Just remembering a time when hers was too spicy for a customer. She cut it with mine, and it turned out it was the perfect combination. That's actually what my arrabbiata sauce is based on."

"It was amazing with the arancini the other night. Hey — what about the arancini? You can make them small enough that they'd be easy to serve to a crowd. You can make the risotto ahead and fry the arancini on-site, so they'll be fresh."

Alex has no idea what he's suggesting, especially after the other night, when Declan asked for the arancini specifically, on top of what I'd already planned to serve him.

"OK... That was not the response I expected to get," he says.

"It's just... Arancini are a very common Italian appetizer. I'm looking to serve something unique, something that's very much my own." It's a reasonable excuse. I don't have to tell him that I'd rather not make them right now, let alone let the future of my restaurant ride on them.

"Well, you've already got your own amazing sauce. What about doing a unique version just for Taste? Add some of your special herbs?"

"I don't know." Well, yes, I do. I know I don't want to make arancini right now. Because of...

Oh, just fuck him. Now he's keeping me from even considering what Alex is suggesting. I refuse to let him control me. Especially when he's not actually trying.

"Maybe some shiso... or papalo..." I'm reminded of Declan's reaction to the corn-fungus tacos, which were accented with the Mexican herb.

"What else is uniquely yours?"

"Nonna and I both focus on seafood. The local seafood is too amazing not to highlight it on my menu."

"So... seafood arancini? With papalo?"

"And shiso."

Now that we've laid out these flavors, my brain is sparking with ideas.

"Lionfish and blue crab arancini with papalo, shiso and arrabbiata sauce. Local crab, environmentally friendly fish, with the herbs and my not-too-spicy sauce."

"That sounds like you on a plate..." Alex says. He frowns. "OK. That came out wrong." He chuckles. "I'm glad someone else wasn't here to overhear that. He'd think I was hitting on you."

"You and me both. Being glad, I mean. If for different reasons. And he's got no right to an opinion about anyone hitting on me, including you."

"But you have zero interest in me."

"Are you trying to make me feel sorry for you, Alex? First the comment about always being alone, and now assuming I'm not attracted to you." I'm teasing him, but he's serious.

"Well, we both know you're not. But that's OK. I already know why." He's smug about it but doesn't elaborate.

"OK — I'll bite."

"If you're going to bite, I should get Declan back in here..." he jokes. "Oops! Sorry," he adds after I glare at him. "But that's why. You're hung up on him. Have been for a long time, I'd wager."

"I don't want to talk about it. And if you want more cooking lessons, you'll leave it there."

"Fine," he says. "But you aren't going to put the past behind you by pretending it never happened."

"That past was *so* far behind me — *so* far. Until it burst into my kitchen that day a week or so ago."

"Why do I doubt that? Especially after the other night."

"I've got it all in hand now. That page has been turned."

"That's the thing about history books, Callie — you can always go back and re-read, learn new lessons from things that have already happened. Sometimes, those things change what gets written on the blank pages ahead."

Those blank pages are scary. Especially right now. I'm used to being the one writing the story of my life. I have been since I was 17. Having someone else writing parts of my story isn't at all what I had in mind. And yet here I am.

But this is my kitchen, and I'm taking back authorship of my life.

I close Nonna's book where it sits in front of Alex on my desk and put it away in the drawer.

"So, you want to help me test out this new recipe of ours?"

"Yes, Chef!"

# CHAPTER 26

# RUMOR HAS IT

### *Three nights later*

"Chef? Chef? Chef!"

"What?" I shriek at Nate.

"The fillet is supposed to be medium-rare, remember?"

"Fuck!"

I pull the steak out of the pan and set it on a plate. If I'm lucky, someone will order it medium-well in the next few minutes. If not, I'll be having filet mignon salad for my dinner tonight.

"I've got it," Nate volunteers.

"No — I've got it! Don't try to run me off the line in my own kitchen, Nate, or it'll be the last time you're cooking anything in here."

Nate blinks, but his surprise just makes me angrier. They know better than to interfere when I'm cooking. I can handle cooking a fucking medium-rare steak. I am not a first-year culinary student.

"Nate, you're on salads for the rest of the night."

Nate starts to reply but seems to think better of it.

"Yes, Chef!"

I throw another filet in the pan, making sure the heat's a little lower this time so I can monitor the sear more closely.

"Callie..."

"Don't say it, Drew. Just don't. Now is not the time."

"When's a better time? When you've lost another line cook and Raquel is doing the risotto solo?"

"Fuck you, Drew. Just leave off. I've got it handled."

"Yes, Chef," he says precisely, the words clipped, making it clear that I've got a talking-to coming later. He knows he's the only one who could do it and not get fired on the spot.

It doesn't help that the last few nights have been crazy. Not crazy busy, but crazy as in diners leaving after appetizers, plates sent back to the kitchen, tables sitting empty. And that's not including waitstaff snapping at hostesses, hostesses snapping at bartenders, runners and bussers colliding in the kitchen doorway because they're using the wrong side... We've had one fistfight and two verbal arguments in the dining room, one of which still required calling the police to remove the customers involved.

Fuck. *Diners. Patrons.* I'm not even meeting my own standards that I'm teaching to an 18-year-old culinary student.

And then there was the amorous couple in the ladies' restroom, who got so loud that every single other diner in the place was staring. A family with young kids walked out, their bill unpaid. I had to knock on the restroom door twice before the couple — in their 60s! — broke it up and came out.

"Chef—"

"What?" I shriek again. Only this time, it's at Raquel I'm shrieking at, and she visibly shrinks. I'm not sure if her mother yells at her, but I instantly feel horrible. She didn't deserve that. Nate knows better. But Raquel...

"Sorry, Raquel," I tell her, genuinely apologetic. I flip the filet and take a deep breath, calming myself as best I can. "What do you need?"

"There's a table out here — they've asked to speak to the chef. When you get a minute. It's not urgent. They wanted me to make sure to tell you that," she says, looking a little uncertain.

I raise an eyebrow at her, hoping she parses my silent question. She shakes her head in the negative. I'm not really surprised. Declan hasn't shown up at the restaurant since that night, not since I left him stranded, naked, in his bed. And I'm not sure what to make of that either. And I've been wondering about it. A lot.

"How busy are we out there?"

"Everyone has either gotten their check or has at least ordered entrées. There's no one waiting for a table or anything."

"At nine o'clock? On a Friday?" OK. That's a little shrieky, too. But it's not directed at Raquel, and she knows that.

"Yes, Chef."

"Where in the service is this table?"

"They've finished their desserts. The check is paid."

Well, this is either very good or very bad.

"Drew..."

"I've got the filet. Go." He assumes my place at the stove. "Not a moment too soon," he says under his breath as I pass by. I take another deep breath and let it out slowly as I head to the dining room, rebuttoning my coat along the way. The current debacle is no excuse for looking sloppy.

Raquel takes the lead, heading toward a table far out of the way, but on the opposite side of the dining room from where Declan had been sitting. There's what seems like a mile of empty tables between where we started and where we end up.

"Brighid? Siobhan? Rory? Lyric?" I do a double-take. "Where are the kids?"

I have to ask that, because as far as I know, Rory, Brighid and I are the only ones Lyric ever lets stay with the kids, and I've mostly only done it when Lyric was also at home.

"They're with David Carter and Piper, David's girlfriend," Brighid volunteers. "Piper's expecting, and I think she and David wanted to get a little experience in, so when I asked, they agreed."

"I like Piper. She's sweet," Lyric says. "And David said he's on the autism spectrum himself, so I figured he'd be more patient with Tommy."

"Declan mentioned David had a baby on the way... Piper's the engineer?"

"Yes. She and David are running the studio now. David's a part-owner."

"Wow. Declan didn't mention that. I take it they're planning on setting up here when he's not on the road?"

"We're discussing that. It's looking likely. David and Hunter both have homes here now. Well — David's staying with Piper until they get their own house built. And Hunter's staying with me, of course."

"So, the band's putting down roots in Mystic Beach?"

The idea is both alarming and... well, guilt-inducing. Could it be that Declan was sincere about wanting something long-term with me? It certainly would be a lot more feasible if some of the other band members are making this their home base. But then, those two girls at the hotel...

"It's an evolving situation," Brighid says. "We're also talking about me going on the road with Hunter when the next tour starts."

"Wow. OK. That's... that's a lot of change."

"It is," Brighid says. "It's the kind of thing that could put you off balance if you weren't prepared for it, if you didn't have a supportive partner you knew you could rely on for the long term."

O... K... That was pretty clearly pointed at me.

"So, you all came out tonight to have a nice girls' night out?" I say hopefully, knowing there's next to no chance that's the case.

"Yeah. No," Lyric says. "You needed a consult. We're providing one."

"By 'consult' you mean 'intervention,' right?"

"Six of one, half a dozen of the other," Siobhan says, that eyebrow ring of hers raised at me again.

"I appreciate the concern, but this really isn't a good time."

"Why not?" Siobhan asks. "Your dinner rush appears to be quite well over."

Ouch. OK. Fine. It's true. But that still hurts.

"We brought Rory with us for two reasons," Lyric says. "First, we thought you should know that rumors are spreading widely around town."

"What kind of rumors?" This is truly alarming, especially in the wake of my brush with posting naked photos of my very famous ex.

"Word on the street is your food isn't quite as good as it had been," Rory says.

Ouch. Again.

"People gossip about that kind of stuff?"

"You'd be amazed how word spreads, especially among the locals. A day or two, tops, and everyone knows everything that's going on around here, whether it's someone having an affair, a business closing, or one that's struggling."

"And people are saying Castalia is struggling? After a few days? A week or two?"

"A few days is enough, as you should be able to tell by your dining room tonight," Rory says.

"So, what? You're doing a story on a failing restaurant?" I don't mean to be hostile to Rory, but she is a journalist, which I guess is how she hears stuff like this. That's also why having her aware of potentially damaging information is extremely dangerous. Though, I have to say, she was in on the behind-the-scenes stuff between Brighid and Hunter, and she didn't publish a word about it, other than big news from the press conference the band held.

"No. They asked me to come tonight for a different reason."

Whatever it is, she doesn't look too pleased about it. At least, I hope that's why she seems so serious, and not that she hated her dinner so much she's frowning at me like that.

"You've got a problem, Callie. And I'm the only one they knew who could confirm the nature of that problem."

"My problem has a pretty face, an ego the size of Mars, pants he can't seem to keep on and a name that starts with D."

"That's the catalyst for the problem. It's not the problem itself," she says.

"Rory's an empath, Callie," Lyric says. "She feels other people's emotions, reads them like I read sheet music or you interpret a recipe. We wanted an expert opinion on whether what Brighid, Siobhan and I suspected is the case here actually is. Rory's the expert."

"Lyric said your grandmother was a chef, too? Born in Italy?" Brighid asks. "Did she raise her own herbs? Did she do odd things that might have seemed superstitious? Harvest the herbs at a certain time of the month? Keep jars of oils around? Have a ritual for stirring soup?"

I finally pull a chair over from an empty table. There are plenty to choose from. Ugh. But I don't want the few other diners left in the restaurant to overhear this conversation, even more than I didn't want anyone hearing the rest of it, so I lean in and speak quietly, just to the four of them.

"Alex needs to learn to mind his own business."

"Yes, he does," Brighid says with a chuckle. "But this has nothing to do with Alex. And now I'm curious as to why you might think it does."

"He didn't talk to you about Nonna's recipes?"

"No. I haven't talked to Alex in more than a week. After the other night, I knew you were giving Alex cooking lessons, but that's all I was aware of. Why? What did he say?"

"He spotted a few recipes in her chef's book — her cookbook — that specified stirring clockwise and things like that."

Brighid exchanges a glance with Lyric.

"She wasn't a witch!"

"And neither am I," Brighid says. "Doesn't mean I don't follow some rules and habits that are rooted in folk magic."

"Well, I *am* a witch," Lyric says. "Unabashedly, second-generation," she adds. "And while that's not for public consumption, with my job and everything, I own the term. And I can tell you — it sounds like Nonna was some kind of kitchen witch. And it also sounds like she handed that talent down to you, along with her recipes."

"I. Am. Not. A. Witch. I don't even believe in all that stuff."

"Even now? After what happened the other night?" Brighid asks.

"I've got it under control."

"A — if you don't believe in it, how is it under control? And B — we can definitively tell you that it is *not* under control."

"That's why we came tonight, to verify our theory."

"Oh? And what is this theory of yours?"

"You're a kitchen witch," Lyric says. "A largely untrained and unaware one, but still, a kitchen witch."

"And you've got some kind of kitchen-witch empathy thing going on," Rory adds. "I can feel the emotions even from the kitchen, and they're carrying over into the food."

"Amber suggested it might be some kind of enchantment, like she does with her jewelry," Siobhan says, "or like my tattoos."

"Wait. Your tattoos are enchanted?"

Siobhan, Brighid and Rory exchange looks. I decide to ignore it.

"How did you think Hunter's broken hand healed up so fast?" Brighid finally says.

"I figured it was your herbal stuff. Some kind of bone-knitting tea or something."

"You watch too many movies," Siobhan says. "It was the tattoo, and Brighid's healing ritual."

"Divine intervention," Brighid adds.

And I'm the one who watches too many fantastical films?

"This is all nuts. Just nuts."

"Is it nuts that you've had numerous incidents of people acting out of character while dining at your restaurant since Declan showed up here?" Brighid says. "It wasn't just the four of us and the couple at the next table the other night."

"The police reports come across my desk on a daily basis," Rory says. "You've had two calls for unruly customers in just the last week. And not a single one before that."

"And it's changed the quality of your food, Callie," Lyric says. "It's usually insanely good. But now..."

"It's not bad, certainly," Siobhan adds. "But..."

"What we had the other night, with Declan, was some of the best food I've ever eaten," Brighid says. "But he was behaving himself better than I've ever seen him — undoubtedly for your benefit — and you were feeling affectionate, passionate, toward him that night."

"And Drew said there was a couple that had a fight on a previous night, when they were sitting next to Declan while you were torturing him in your own special way," Siobhan says.

I look back at the kitchen door and glare at Drew, even though he can't see me do it through the wall.

"Don't get mad at Drew — I asked him if anything else weird had happened recently, and he's just trying to help. You may not believe this is real, but we're not the only ones who've experienced it enough to know something strange is going on. I don't know if Drew has any experience with magic, but he recognized something paranormal when he saw it. If you don't, it's because you're in denial about the depth of the problem you're causing."

And now we're back to the core issue. Whatever this is, whatever has been going on, it seems to be my fault. Well, mine, and also Declan's, if indirectly. And now I've got an entire coven sitting in my dining room, telling me to clean up my act.

"Assuming you're right — and I still don't really believe any of this magic stuff — how do I fix it?"

"Making up with Declan wouldn't hurt," Lyric says. I frown at her.

"You need to resolve your feelings about him, one way or the other," Siobhan adds.

"Beyond that — I'll suggest what I suggested to you before: we can work on a binding spell that might keep your... abilities...

under control," Brighid says. "Or Amber can try an amulet. She said she's willing to do it, if that's what you want. But either of those things has to be done with your consent. I won't invoke magic on someone without their consent."

"I will," Siobhan volunteers.

"Same," Lyric adds.

I look over at Rory.

"I'm not a witch. Really," she says, glancing at Brighid. "I mean, I don't have any problems with anyone who is, but I'm just an empath. The rest of this stuff is over my head. So, if you want a magical solution, I'm not it."

"That implies there's a non-magical solution."

"I can teach you to control and contain your emotions so they don't bleed over into the food you're cooking, and into your customers."

"Diners," I correct.

"Diners, customers, five-legged octopuses — I don't care what you call them. I sat here tonight and watched people grow increasingly uncomfortable the longer they were here. Couples snapping at each other, kids misbehaving, some of them just flat-out depressed. And it's not the food itself, even if that's not up to your usual standards. It's the emotions you're cooking into it, and what you're broadcasting across a pretty wide space around you."

She looks uncomfortable, frowning before she continues.

"I didn't realize I had this empathy skill until a year or so ago. My grandmother — she used to call it 'Knowing,' like I'd know things about how people were feeling that I shouldn't realistically know. I just figured I was adept at reading body language. But I've had plenty of proof in the last year that it goes beyond that. And I've had to both hone the gift and learn to keep it under control. And, if you agree, I'll teach you what I know, and we can see if it impacts your cooking the same way as it does regular empathy."

"I don't have time for this! I've got a competition to prepare for, a restaurant to run!"

"Taste of the Culinary Coastline?"

I look at her in surprise. Maybe she's not just an empath, but a mind-reader, too?

"I'm a reporter. We cover it every year," she explains.

Oh.

"Make the time, Callie," Brighid urges. "Or I'm not sure you're going to have a restaurant to run."

She gestures to the now-nearly empty dining room. Just one couple waiting for their check. And it's not even nine-thirty.

I heave a sigh, unable to argue Brighid's point.

"I'll meet you here tomorrow morning at nine," Rory offers, though it sounds more like an order than an offer. Since when do reporters sound like generals?

"I'm supposed to be working with Alex on the Taste dish."

"I'll let him know you're taking a day off," Brighid says. "I suspect he'll understand all too well why."

Lyric grabs my hand and squeezes it supportively.

"You can do this. We're here to help. But you're going to have to put the effort in to deal with this problem — and your emotions. Especially where Declan Carter is concerned."

Rory winces.

"Ouch," she says. "Yeah — we're going to work on that. Don't be late. We've got our work cut out for us."

# CHAPTER 27

## HERE COMES THE GRUMP

### Declan

"What's up, Dec?" Hunter asks, standing in the doorway to my bedroom.

"I really wish you all would stop saying that. Isn't twelve years enough for the amusement factor to wear off?"

"Ha! The 'aMUSEment' factor!"

"That wasn't on purpose."

"Brighid and I make cartoon jokes all the time. Even in bed."

"I did not need to know that."

"You'll live. Provided Callie doesn't kill you," he says, clearly in-the-know about something Callie-related. And since I haven't heard a peep from her and I'm still trying to be the mature, patient Declan, I'll take any information I can get on that front.

"What do you know? Because you wouldn't be talking to me about her if you didn't know something."

"The girls were staging an intervention tonight."

"Oh? What kind of intervention? I don't believe for a minute that Brighid's going to try to persuade her to talk to me so I can finally explain what I didn't do."

"Nope. I haven't seen any pigs flying by lately, either." I roll my eyes at him. "No — this is a magical intervention."

"Oh." I have no idea what to say about that.

"They even asked David and Piper to stay with Lyric's kids."

"Lyric? Why does that name sound familiar?"

"She's an old friend of Callie's, from back when they were teenagers, apparently. She was homeschooled, so Brighid and I didn't know her back then, just like we didn't know Callie because she was just a summer kid. I think Lyric lived next door to Callie's grandmother."

Now I know where I know that name from... Lyric is the friend who married us. Wow. Twelve years later, and all this stuff is coming full-circle.

"Why didn't you tell us you knew Callie? I mean — I know you were dating a Callie back when we first started the band, back in the busking days. I just didn't realize she was the same one Brighid knows now."

"She was the one..."

"The one? Like *the one*? Wait — is she the girl you cheated on that night?"

My look is so pathetic that it answers his question, I guess. Because he doesn't wait for me to say anything else.

"Wow. OK. Brighid told me she was an old girlfriend you'd dumped, but I didn't realize it went that far back."

"You're one of the only people who knows that happened that night, Hunt, because you were there, you and Dave. And I filled Alex in on some details. But I don't want it going any further than that. I didn't even tell Callie the whole story. Then, or now."

"So, you just dumped her out of guilt and that was that? No wonder the girl hates you. You never gave her a reasonable explanation. No closure."

"I don't want to talk about it. I'm not proud of it. I'm not proud of how I handled it, or what I did afterward, once I was officially single again."

"Yeah. You and I both went a little nuts for a while. I'm not proud of that, either. Especially when Brighid was aware of a lot of it."

"Tell me something, Hunt — did Brighid forgive you for that? I mean, did she really get past it and put it behind you? Or is she still holding it against you in the back of her head, or expecting that you might cheat if you're not here, with her?"

Hunter takes a deep breath, giving it some thought.

"I think she has. We've been doing therapy, individually and together, trying to get past... well, the past. It wasn't always kind to either of us. But we've... we've had some experiences since we got together that… Well, I'm not going to get into it, but I'll just say that we've cemented our bond beyond anything I've ever experienced, and I'd never even consider cheating on her, and I'm pretty sure she knows that. She seems to. I haven't gotten the impression she even worries about flirty waitresses anymore."

"That's good, because you flirt with everyone."

"Not you, too! Brighid said that," he explains, seeing my curious look. "I don't do it on purpose. I'm just a people person! It's been good for our careers, if nothing else. It helps if I play the gregarious guitar player. It offsets the grumpy diva we have for a lead singer."

"I'm not grumpy."

"But you are a diva?"

"Sometimes."

"Well, I hate to break it to you, Dec, but you come off as pretty grumpy a lot of the time. Even the girls backstage on the last tour, you were a little gruff with them."

"I had my reasons."

"Callie being that reason?"

"Partly. Maybe."

The look he gives me says, "Oh, really?"

"OK. Fine. Mostly Callie, though some of it is indirect."

"You've been pining over her for more than a decade. Is that what you're telling me?"

"No! That sounds pathetic."

"No less pathetic than Brighid waiting for me for all those years."

"Wait. What?" Is he really calling his fiancée pathetic?

"I know you thought she was pathetic, waiting for me like that."

"She loved you, you idiot. I never thought she was pathetic. She was following her heart. And it turned out she was right — you were in love with her all along, which we *all* knew, even if you didn't. I can't imagine holding out for that long, just because I loved some… one…"

My words come to a halt.

"Someone who didn't think they were good enough for me." I look up to see him smiling at me. "I see what you did there. Well-played."

"At least Brighid wasn't a dick to everyone for all those years she waited for me."

"Yeah, well… I didn't wait for Callie. I went into rockstar player mode."

"Different response. Same motivation. And I'd be curious to know which pattern Callie followed."

"A combination, it seems. Like, bitchy nun mode."

Hunter barks a laugh.

"You're not telling me Callie waited for you for all these years? Seems pretty unlikely."

"I'm not talking to you about this. Did Brighid wait for you?"

"No comment."

"I thought as much."

"Mace fucking Mason," he mutters under his breath.

Now it's me laughing. Not at Hunter's situation so much as his reaction to it.

"Did she ever definitively confirm or deny?"

"No comment."

I'll leave them to sort that out. I've got enough problems of my own. And I really, really don't want to give Brighid additional reasons to aim her witchy warnings at my dick. I'm still hoping Callie and I can enjoy making use of it some more. Like for the next sixty or seventy years. We missed too much time together. My fault. It's all my fault. And I desperately want to fix it, fix all of it. Or at least as much as I can at this point. I can't undo it. I've got no time machine. But I'll do whatever I need to do to fix this for her, for us.

"You haven't talked to her since the other day?"

"No. I was advised to give her some time and space."

"Probably wise. She's kind of the opposite of Brighid in a lot of ways."

"How so?"

"Brighid gets in these brain spirals, where everything that worries her starts to reinforce itself, even if there's nothing to worry about. If I let her go on like that, she'll worry herself into a frenzy, convince herself her worst fears are true. But if I talk to her, communicate with her, openly, honestly, directly — she's very calm, reasonable, wise even. And that's something I appreciate, because I'm not always great at thinking things through, seeing the longer-term implications of what I do."

"No kidding."

"Hey! You don't exactly have a lot of room to talk."

"No, I don't. I got myself into this mess, and I'm going to have to clean it up, once Callie lets me. And, you're right. They're kind of opposites that way — at least I think Callie is still enough like she was when I knew her that I can say that. Callie's hot-tempered. She has to blow off some steam before she can communicate, or think things through. That's why I had to let her torture me with her food for a couple meals before I could start getting to know her again."

"She tortured you? With food?"

"Ever eaten a muskrat?"

"No..." he says slowly. "I mean, no, I haven't. But also no, she didn't do that to you. Right? I mean, surely..."

"Oh, yes she did."

"I mean, I know some people around here eat muskrat. I grew up here. But... wow. She really was angry with you."

"I seem to have a talent for making women angry with me."

Hunter chuckles.

"That you do. And that's coming from me, the guy whose ex blackmailed him and tried to ruin him and his actual girlfriend. But Brighid's never threatened to make my dick fall off."

"I imagine that would be counterproductive for her these days."

"Indeed it would." He's smug about that.

"I like seeing you all happy like this. I mean, I'm jealous, but it's still great to see it."

"Callie wouldn't be this pissed off at you if she didn't still care, Dec. And now that I know she's the same girl..." He looks me directly in the eyes. "You never forget your first love. If you're really lucky, they're also your last love. I'm an incredibly lucky man. Incredibly lucky to have Brighid in my life, still, and like she is, and incredibly lucky knowing that we're it for each other. She's my person and I'm hers, and nothing can change that."

That's the thing. Callie's my person. Until things blew up the other day, she'd been proving that, showing me in all these little ways that she still cared, that what I did and said interested her, just like it did when we were teenagers. I mean — I've got a lot of people who pay attention to everything I say or do, from my favorite bands to the conditioner I use. But it's in an oddly detached kind of way. I'm not real to them.

But, to Callie... I'm real. I'm that kid who rejoiced in seeing her smile, the one who took her for frozen custard and dunked her, laughing, in the ocean, the one who was never happier than the moment she agreed to marry me, even if we couldn't do it legally. I'm also the guy who hurt her. Badly. But in those moments we had together this past week, over her food, I could see that girl who'd loved that kid, and I could see the woman she'd become start to maybe, just maybe, forgive that kid and see a grown-up me who would never hurt her like that.

Until I had. Even if it wasn't real and it wasn't on purpose. And I need that back. I need back that moment when the grown-up Callie lost herself in grown-up me, offering me not just her body, but her trust. It wasn't a gift I took lightly or for granted. And maybe I hadn't fully earned it yet. Maybe that's why it was so easy for her to take it back. But I want to earn it. I want to know I've really earned it, that she won't ever take it back again because she'll finally know she's safe with me. For good.

Teenage Declan fucked up, and he lost her trust. Grown-up Declan has to earn it back. I have to do that. Me. And I've got to figure out a way to do that. One that makes it clear to her that I'll put her first from this moment forward, and never do anything ever again to make her regret trusting me.

# CHAPTER 28

# HIGHER GROUND

## Callie
### *The next morning*

"Ground, Callie. Root your sense of self in the floor. Straight through the floor and into the dirt. Well, I guess it's more like sand here," Rory allows, "but same difference."

"I'm trying. But how do you know you've done it when you can't actually see it?"

"You'll be able to tell. *I'll* be able to tell. And you haven't gotten it yet."

"Every time I think I've got it, you talk to me, and I focus back up here on you."

"There you go... That's the start."

"What?"

"You said you focus back up here — it wouldn't seem like I was back up here if you weren't starting to get that sense of shifting into the ground. Keep going."

OK.

"I feel completely ridiculous."

"Dismiss that. It's pointless, counterproductive. It's the rational mind telling you things you've been taught your entire life, about what is real and what isn't. At some point in our childhood, we all get told the fairytales aren't real, the magic is an illusion, that Santa and the Easter Bunny are only symbolic."

"You're telling me they're not?"

"I can't comment on Santa and the Easter Bunny, because I haven't met them. But I can tell you that the fairytales are real, and the magic — real magic, not stage magic — exists. I've seen it with my own eyes. I've seen things with my own eyes that I didn't believe at first, either. And a few of those things have tried to kill me, so I know exactly how real they are."

"What? Is this stuff dangerous? What am I getting involved in?"

"You're fine. Your problems are exactly the problems we've been talking about — your cooking and your emotions, and what they do to other people. The stuff I've dealt with has nothing to do with you. But I wasn't left with any options about accepting that these things are real. And you're not getting any options for the things you're dealing with, either. Ignoring it for the last week or so has only let it get further out of control. We need to get this sorted out now."

"I should be working on my arancini recipe."

"Do you have any idea what serving your arancini to a giant tent full of hungry foodies would do? To them, and to your reputation?"

"No."

"Honestly, neither do I. But I've got a decent guess, and it's not pretty. You've got no choice here. You need to stay out of the kitchen and not cook for anyone until you've got this under control. Otherwise... I suspect I'll end up with a story I have no choice but to cover, since there's decent odds police will be involved."

Put that way, her concerns seem important, if not necessarily valid to my logical mind.

"You know what? Let's go down to the beach. Putting your feet in the sand may make this easier."

"Fine. But I need to stop in the kitchen on the way."

"Get out!" Drew orders, pointing me out the back door.

"You can't kick me out of my own kitchen!"

"I can and I have. You are banned from this restaurant until we know you can be here and not cause problems — for yourself and everyone else. It's bad enough I'm dealing with the fallout from empty tables and thin tips, now I've got to find someone to replace Nate."

"Nate quit?"

"Yeah. You snapped at him one time too many, and then demoting him to salads? Not OK, Callie."

"Fuck."

"Yeah, 'Fuck.' You fucked us over good there. First Eddie and now Nate. We're down two line cooks in a week. Both because of you and your temper."

"Right when you're getting ready to go on paternity leave."

"And when you've got Taste coming up, with you and at least two other cooks needed off-site that day."

"Fuck."

"Exactly. So, get this sorted out, Callie. I don't care what it takes — get it sorted out. If you want me to come back from paternity leave, you need to resolve your issues with Declan." I cringe at hearing his name. "Don't give me that look — I have no more pity to give here. You took a difficult situation and made it worse, for yourself and everyone else. So, resolve your issues with him, get your shit together and start acting like Chef Callie again. OK?"

"Yeah. I'll see what I can do."

"Love you, girlfriend, but we've reached the point where tough love has to just be tough. So, get out!"

"Good. I can feel that connection to the earth. Keep it solid. Focus."

I hear a couple kids giggling from not far away.

"Ignore them," Rory says. "You're here to attend to some serious business. Because it's your business on the line. Treat this as seriously as you would a critic coming to review your food. Because I can tell you right now, that if one showed up this past week, you'd be on your way out of business."

I don't remember Rory being quite this pointed with Brighid when we had our little intervention during her troubles with Hunter. But then I guess Brighid's business only affected her and Hunter. This... not so much. If I can credit it as being real.

"You lost focus. Try it again," she says.

I wiggle my toes in the sand, sinking my awareness into the center of the earth, deep below the sand, the water table, all of it. It feels like my toes are growing into the ground, like the roots of a tree.

"There. Now send all that messy, chaotic emotional energy into the earth. You don't need it, and it won't help to have it stored up in your mind and body. Feel the chaos leaving, feel control taking its place... Good. Now start to bring the energy back up, but picture it as cleansed, purified, like you'd run it through a filter and all the messy bits got left behind. The earth is a huge organism, full of salt and metals. It can disperse what little you've sent into it, and you'll do a better job living on it when you're not dealing with out-of-control emotions."

"You know how silly that sounds, right?"

"I'm a journalist, Callie. I deal in fact. Even when facts are up for debate, they're largely tangible things. None of this is tangible, but I can promise you it is absolutely real. And you need to treat it as real, and important, if you want your life back under your control. Now, focus — feet into the ground, messy energy out, clean energy back in... Good. Remember how that feels. Cement that feeling in your mind so you know when you've done it successfully in the future. Now, pull that clean energy up into your center — the part of you where you feel like your essence sits. For most people, that's the center of the body, around the heart or solar plexus."

"Like this?" I'm picturing a glowing blob of energy in the middle of my chest. I still feel ridiculous, but at least I can picture it.

"Yes. Good. Again, cement that feeling in your mind. You'll want to be able to call that state back at will. This is being centered. It's the thing that will keep you from going off-balance, even when chaos is happening all around you. Good. Now send that energy out, to your fingertips and your toes, the top of your head. Gently, just a little push to disperse it. You've got it."

I'm feeling a sense of accomplishment here, but I can't fully credit why, since it doesn't feel fully real.

"You're losing focus."

OK. Maybe I should accept that something is really happening here, because Rory seems to know what's going on inside my head. Huh.

"Picture that energy spreading evenly across your body, out to your limbs, around your head, circulating, just like your blood circulates around your body. Good. That's nicely even, solid. No chaos. Now it's time to learn to shield — this will help you keep what's you from spreading out to everyone else and keep everyone else's stuff from filtering inside. You don't have to worry about that as much, I don't think. But it's good to learn, regardless."

"So, is this like some sort of superhero psychic bubble?"

"Yes and no. A simple shield can be like that. I was taught to layer my shields, to allow for varying degrees of filtering, and I think that's your best bet. Moreover, I think you're going to like the imagery for this technique. Picture an onion..."

"Alright... you've got some decent layers established. It's a good start. But you need to be able to keep it up, even when things are chaotic, whether that's inside you or outside. It needs to be automatic. Tell me about your favorite thing to cook."

"Nonna's pasta, from scratch."

"Describe it to me, the process..."

"Well, you make a well with the flour, and you crack the eggs into the well..."

"Good. Now keep going, but focus on keeping your feelings within the shield. I'm feeling warm, homey feelings, a familiar process... Keep those inside. Reinforce where the layers feel thin. That's better. Good. Now, tell me about Declan Carter."

My eyes pop open.

"Yeah. That's what I thought. Take that chaos, that pain, the passion, and ground it. You're thinking of Declan, but you need to purify that feeling, take control of it, manipulate your feelings and energies like they're... like they're flour and eggs. They need to do what you tell them and go where you direct them. Make them do what you need them to. Good. Nice. Tell me about your grandmother."

"She was wonderful. She taught me so much about cooking, taught me how to develop my own recipes, about using fresh herbs in my food... she told me stories from mythology and about the stars. She said Declan reminded her of King Arthur — a flawed king with tremendous potential for good. She called him 'Arturo.'"

"Good. There's that warm feeling again. Not just her... You've got to find that feeling where he's concerned, let it temper, offset the negatives. Oops! Yeah, there they are. Sink them back into the ground, take charge of them. Temper them with warm memories. No one is perfect. No one is all good or all bad. Losing sight of that leads to loss of balance within ourselves, because sudden reminders of the good or the bad throw us off. Find the balance within yourself. Find the balance of love and hate, warmth and pain, wound and healing. It's all there. Now, tell me about Declan Carter."

I try to do as Rory asks, pulling up long-ago moments when I was full of warmth, feeling safe in his arms, marveling at his talent with music, proud of what he was accomplishing. And, really, he's gone on to accomplish so much. I am proud of that, even if it took him away from me, left me alone to deal with my pain and the loss...

"That's good, but you're losing balance again. Put it in perspective."

Nonna was there. Nonna made sure I had a roof over my head, that I got to school, that I graduated, that I could go on to culinary school. She was there when I needed a shoulder to cry on, about Declan, about...

"Whoa. Whatever that is, Callie, find a positive to offset it. Just for the moment. You don't have to banish all the difficult feelings. But you do need to be able to find balance for them when it's not the right time to deal with them."

I picture sitting in Nonna's garden, listening to the fountain gurgle, the fountain we used to call Castalia, in honor of the goddess, the spirit of inspiration. As far as I know, it's still there. I didn't want to leave it behind when I sold the house, but where would I have put it? Better to leave it in Nonna's garden, even if it wasn't technically Nonna's anymore. The sound of the waves transmutes into the soft murmur of the fountain, and I'm sitting on Nonna's garden bench while she tells me stories, following her around the garden to harvest her herbs.

"Not that one, *cara mia*," she says. "It won't be ready to harvest for another two weeks, when the moon is full. Everything in its own time. Now, this one — this one is perfect to gather today. Come help me and I'll show you how to ensure it will continue to prosper, even after we take parts of it to enrich our food."

Did I really forget that? Nonna *had* harvested her herbs according to the cycles of the moon, and she'd taught me to do so as well. How had I forgotten that? I guess, with all that happened those last couple years here, those last couple of summers, and that final year before culinary school...

And that's when Rory's point sinks home. I've lost things, memories, that meant so much to me. I put them away and forgot them, rather than deal with the more difficult moments of loss and pain. I've stripped myself of feeling — except when I'm cooking, when all of that starts to bleed back out of my mind, my heart, and goes into my food. The warm moments of Nonna's care and sharing. The passion and love I felt for Declan. The pain and hatred of losing him, of knowing he wasn't there when I needed him the most. It has all been going into my food. A chaotic mélange of feelings that can make my food amazing, or ruin it for the diner, even when the food itself is well-prepared.

And if I'm going to win Taste... Heck, if I'm going to keep my restaurant open at this point, after the challenges of the last few days... I'm going to have to find that balance and make choices about what I put into my food. Because it's clear now that it's about more than just the ingredients in the pot — it's how I feel about them, and about my life. And I've been feeling bitter about that for far too long. Declan's awakened that feeling in me, fresh and raw, but he's also reminded me of the sweet moments of first love and the fiery passion when those feelings are rekindled today. I need to use all of that — weigh it all carefully, balance it — just like I do the flavors in my food.

"Whatever that is — hold onto that," Rory says. "That's where you need to be. If you can find that in the midst of chaos, everything will be fine."

No. It'll be more than fine. It'll be amazing. Full of flavor and passion and... maybe even love.

"No. I don't care what you think you've figured out. You're not coming back in this kitchen. Not today. If you want to cook, do it in your apartment. Work on the Taste dish. Take what you need from the restaurant stock, but take it upstairs to your loft and work with it there. I'm not risking losing any more staff, and I need to see what the dining room looks like tonight without you here. Come back in a couple days."

"But Drew..."

"No. End of discussion. Out!"

I could overrule him. I could walk right into my kitchen and start pulling tickets, preparing entrées... I could do it. But I won't. He's got a point. And his idea about working on the Taste dish is a good one. But I'm going to need some help, someone to give feedback as I go. Help I can't pull from the kitchen — not tonight, and not until we hire at least one new line cook.

Callie: *Want to come help me cook some arancini, or are you too busy being a rockstar?*

Alex: *I'll be right over.*

Callie: *Come up to my loft, up above the restaurant. Stairs are in the back.*

Alex: *Should I make him jealous, tell him you invited me to your apartment?*

Callie: *No. I'm not ready to deal with him yet. Don't invite trouble.*

Alex: *He has a hard time not being trouble, so best not to invite him. Yet. He's working on it, though. I'll be there in ten.*

# CHAPTER 29

## BETWEEN

### *Three days later*

"This is it. I just know it."

Alex takes a bite, nodding enthusiastically, and chews. His expression is thoughtful. I can see he's analyzing the flavors, seeing if I finally got the balance exactly right. It's been three straight days of making risotto, tinkering with the flavors of the rice, adding varying amounts of herbs and seafood, modifying the seasoning of the breadcrumbs ever so slightly. This has to be it. I'm so close... well, I'm so close I can taste it.

Once Alex finishes, that is.

Then I'll try it again myself, taking his response into account.

"It's really excellent, Callie. I can taste the contrast between the lionfish and the crab, and the papalo adds something vital that wasn't in your original recipe..."

"But?"

"It's too much shiso. It's overwhelming the richness of the rice, cutting into it too much..."

"And?"

"And I kind of want something a little more... textural. It's got the crunch of the breading, and the smooth creaminess of the risotto, but while I'm tasting both the crab and the lionfish, I think they're too indistinguishable from the rice."

"So... add more pieces to the rice right before it's ready to be breaded, make sure it doesn't break down too much?"

"Yeah. I think that would solve the problem. It's the mouth feel. Once you've gotten through the crust, it's just too smooth. It needs some more interest in terms of mouth feel."

It's a plausible solution to the problem, and over the last few days I've come to trust Alex's palate just as much as I trust Rick's and Devon's. He really could be a chef, if he ever retires from the music business. It's amazing to think that degree of culinary talent is hiding inside this rocker, with his rings (all tucked in his pockets while we're cooking) and his glam fashion style (partly hidden under an apron). You'd never know that food is an equal passion for him, until you got to know him inside. It's just... surprising.

"Oh, my god! I've got it! You're brilliant!"

I give him a spontaneous hug, and he's looking at me like I've lost my mind. OK, fine, I'm not a touchy-feely kind of person. Haven't been since I was a kid. But he's *so* earned that hug, just for being him!

"I'm happy to take the compliment, and the hug — which I will not mention to Declan until he's annoyed me excessively," he adds with a grin. "But what exactly did I say? Do?"

"You tucked a foodie inside a rockstar! It's a surprise! See, Alex — the texture problem. It's not just that the fish and crab breaks down within the risotto. The arancini needs a surprise! You bite into it, and it's crispy and then creamy, and then it's all about the flavors. But what if we stuff a lump of crab meat in the center?"

"Wow. OK, now you're talking. We'd need to set aside the biggest lumps. Do we have enough to do that?"

"We'd need to do that for our test batch, but I've got a supplier who'll sell me their best lump crab meat at a decent price, so I'll have plenty to stuff in the center for Taste!"

"Well, then let's do this! Dial back the shiso, keep the crab and fish as intact as possible when making the balls, then insert one lump, seal it up, bread it and fry it. Serve it up with your sauce!"

"I think this is it, Alex. I think this is the recipe that'll put me in contention."

"I think it'll do more than that!"

"No! Don't! You'll jinx us. Temper expectations so we can enjoy the win."

"Alright, but I still think you're going to win."

"Alex! Ugh. Go — outside." I give him a push toward the door. "Walk around the building three times, backwards, and then throw some salt over your shoulder."

"I thought that was for mentioning that play in the theater. And wasn't it spitting, not salt?"

"Maybe. Doesn't matter. Go — do it. Right now!"

"Are you sure you're not a witch?"

"Pretty sure."

Even if the girls all think I am.

I pour a handful of salt into his palm and send him out the door. Then I take a moment to absorb what we've done. We've transformed my traditional arancini into something truly unique — local, environmentally-friendly, and, most importantly, uniquely delicious. Now I just need to make sure it works as well as I think it will.

# Declan

"So where the fuck have you been?"

"And a pleasant 'good afternoon' to you, too, Dicklan."

And just like that, all the frustration goes out of me. OK — most of it. But Alex calling me out on being a dick serves as a reminder that I'm trying *not* to be that guy. If I'm going to get Callie back, I can't be that guy. She won't take him back, won't give a guy who's a dick to everyone a second chance. Or maybe even the time of day.

"Sorry. I'm just... frustrated, I guess. I hoped I'd hear from Callie by now, that she'd let me explain."

Alex is staring at me, jaw dropped, eyes wide.

"What?" And again, I'm probably more terse than I really should be.

"I'm just surprised to hear you utter that word."

"Which word?"

"'Sorry.' I'm not sure I've ever heard it come from your lips."

I nearly tell him to go fuck himself. But A — he's probably right; and B — I'm trying not to be that guy. So I keep my mouth shut, hoping he'll answer my original question.

"Wow. Now I'm *really* impressed. That was an incredible display of willpower on your part," he says, nodding in approval. "As to where I've been... You mean today?"

"And the last couple of days. I mean, I know you're waiting on me to finish this song, because everyone is waiting on me to finish this song, but..."

"I was with Callie."

Fuck. Fuckity fuck fuck. Fuck. I was afraid of that. Is it possible Callie actually prefers Alex to me? I mean, they've got the food thing in common. And he's... well, he's less of a dick than I am. And he didn't dump her when he was 17. We're almost exactly the same height. Both of us have dark hair, even if his is darker and longer. And right now, he's probably coming off as more put-together. But then Callie seemed to like scruffy me, with the longer hair and a day's growth of beard. Maybe she likes guys with longer hair, period?

"In her apartment," he adds while I mentally compare the two of us.

I close my eyes, take a deep breath, exhale.

"Well, that was impressive."

I give him a questioning look.

"I've never seen you get steamed about something and then rein it back in without exploding. She really is a good influence on you."

"I'm trying to be the guy she needs me to be."

"I think she needs you to be yourself, Declan — the Declan she fell in love with. As opposed to the Declan we've been seeing since... well, since I joined the band anyway. You weren't honest with her about why you broke things off, so the Declan who dumped her isn't you, either. And she still doesn't hate that guy as much as she loves him. The guy who was hanging out with groupies the night before he went to see her — she still kind of hates him. But I think if you can explain that to her in some way that doesn't make you seem like a player, she'll forgive you."

"So you think I'm safe to go see her now?"

"Not on your life."

Crap. Got my hopes up there.

"She's got this competition coming up — that's where I've been the last few days, testing her dish with her, tweaking the recipe. We're getting down to the wire."

"And does she have it? Did she find the recipe that will let her win?"

Alex nods.

"I think she may have. It's a uniquely Callie twist on a classic, and, well, you'd really have to taste it to appreciate it."

"Callie made it. Whatever it is, it's going to be good. So what is it?"

"I can't give you the details. She wants to make sure it's kept secret until the event."

Oh... OK. Alex is keeping Callie's secrets. I just hit a new level of jealous and frustrated.

"Can you give me a hint, at least?"

Alex looks at me, considering. *I've been being a good boy, Mom. Don't I deserve a reward?* I usually hate the family-role designations Billy gave us when we first hired him as our manager. I'm not the grumpy dad. Not really. But Alex plays band mom to perfection, keeping us all in line. Mostly. When we let him, anyway.

"You have been awfully good lately, despite that opening line earlier... OK — I'll tell you that it's something you ordered the night we had dinner with Hunter and Brighid. And that's all you're getting out of me."

"That's enough — thanks."

It is enough, because I only ordered one thing that night, aside from my drink. The first thing Callie ever cooked for me — arancini. That she's cooking arancini for the dish she's wagering the future of her restaurant on... that means something. Is it a message to me, that she still remembers our past fondly? Or is it a reminder to herself of what she once felt for me, and might feel again in the future?

It doesn't matter. Because I've just figured out how to prove to her that she can rely on me, now and in all the days to come. It's going to be brilliant!

# CHAPTER 30

## DESPERATELY WANTING

### Callie
### *A week later*

"How am I going to do this with one assistant?"

"You'll figure it out," Drew says, clearly still in tough-love mode. "The fact that we're short on line cooks is totally on you. Have you tried getting Nate and Eddie to come back?"

"I apologized to them both, offered them a modest raise. But they've both taken jobs in other kitchens. They accepted the apologies, but they aren't coming back. No luck on hiring anyone?"

"We're close to the end of the season, and the college students are already starting to head back to school. It's a good thing we're not as busy as we had been, or we'd have been overwhelmed, especially with you off the line."

"I could have come back. I'm happy to come back." My expression is a hopeful one, but Drew's not biting.

"No. Not yet. Even if I trusted that we wouldn't get a repeat of that last week you were in the kitchen, you've got too much on your plate with Taste. Focus on that. We'll revisit after the competition. And, for that, you've got Devon. I can't spare you another line cook. If you need a third set of hands, your best option is going to be Raquel."

"Well, crap."

I love Raquel. I want her doing prep for us as part of her internship when the new session of her classes start. But she's not ready for this. And she doesn't know the recipe. I've briefed Devon on the changes I've made, and we're on the same page. Raquel would have to catch up, and she's not even scheduled to work until Saturday — the day of the event.

"She's not ready."

"What about Alex?" he suggests. "He's been helping you during the development process. You've told me how good he's gotten. Can't he pitch in to help you and Devon?"

I really don't like relying on an amateur cook for an event that's this important. Alex is great, but serving food on location, with a makeshift kitchen, to hundreds of people, maybe a thousand or more? It requires a familiarity with the setup and professional food service. Alex hasn't even worked as a line cook.

"No... I'm better off with Raquel. Lessons from me for a few weeks doesn't equate with Raquel's months of training, even if she hasn't started working for us in the kitchen yet."

"Well, give her a call and see if she's free to help with prep, learn the recipe in the next couple days. She's eager to get into the kitchen. I'm sure she'll go for it."

## *Two days later*

I have to admit it. Drew was right. Raquel's plunged into this project whole-heartedly. I think she might be able to cook it by herself at this point, even without a written recipe. It took Alex more than a week to get to that point. Between the two of them and a few hours going over things with Devon, I actually feel like we're ready for today.

Alex is planning to attend the event, eager to taste food from all the other local restaurants he hasn't made it to yet. It'll be interesting to hear what he has to say, even if I think he's a little biased by now.

My phone rings as I put my knives in the front seat of the car, ready to go back for the rest of what I need to take with me.

"Hello?"

"Callie — it's Raquel. I am so, so sorry, but I—" I hear coughing in the background, sounding like it's muffled from a hand placed over the phone. Oh, no... Please tell me she's not— "I seem to have come down with something. I mean, it's mostly sneezing and coughing, but I did throw up a couple hours ago."

This is a problem. A big problem.

"I don't think I can cook today."

"No. No, you can't. We can't have you cooking or serving. Not at Taste. And it's better if you just stay home, honestly. I don't want anyone at Castalia getting sick, either."

"I'm so very sorry, Callie. I know you were counting on me, and I was really looking forward to being able to cook for everyone at Taste, but..."

"No. Don't apologize. You can't help that you're sick. Get some rest, lots of fluids, and don't worry about us. Devon and I can handle it. I've got all the risotto prepped." I don't mention to her that I'd made some additions to our plan, just as backup. But now it seems like the backup I need isn't for the food, but for Raquel.

I've got one option left. It's not a bad one. But I hate asking at the last minute like this.

"I thought you were going to pre-cook the risotto and then make the arancini on-site. What's all this for?" Alex asks as he loads a box of ingredients and supplies into my car. The fryer and a stove are already set up at the site of the event, and there's a prep table, as well as a service table decorated to match the restaurant and with the logo on a sign above it.

"A little birdie told me they're expecting heavy attendance today, now that the weather forecast has cleared. The last tickets were sold overnight. I'd planned for a moderately heavy attendance, based on past years, but a sold-out event? I don't want to run out when people are still tasting everything. No tastes, no votes. No votes, no prize money. So I'm going prepared, just in case we start to run low."

To offset the bad luck of losing Raquel as an assistant, I got lucky in that one of the organizers owed me a favor after I donated a gift card for Castalia to her fundraiser. She warned me about the tickets getting sold out, with that last-minute rush of anticipated attendees I'm not sure the other chefs will be prepared for. So, I've got backup ingredients in case we need to make more arancini than the amount of risotto we'd prepped in advance can make.

"Alright. Better to be overprepared than come up short. I get it. That's our practice philosophy," Alex says, indirectly reminding me of his bandmate.

"You didn't... You didn't tell him where you were going today, did you?"

"No. But he knew it was coming up, and he's usually pretty good with dates. Don't be surprised if he shows up."

Great. That's all I need. Why couldn't Declan Carter be scatterbrained, as well as ego-maniacal and slutty? OK. I take that back. I won't slut-shame him. He was single during all of this time apart. He was free to sleep with whomever he wanted. That I didn't do the same is on me. I just wish he hadn't gone out with groupies the night before he came to see me. It undermined whatever it was that he'd hoped to accomplish with me.

"Callie?"

There — I've gone and done it again. I got lost in thoughts about Declan when I need my focus to be laser-sharp and firmly on my food. Ground. Center.

"Hmm?"

"I asked where Devon is."

"She went ahead to make sure the set-up was ready and to load in the ingredients we'd prepped in advance. This is actually my second trip this morning, with all the extras."

"OK. Is this all of it?" he asks, sticking one last box in my car.

"Let's hope so, because if I can't feed everyone who wants to try my arancini, I don't know if we stand a chance of winning. Every vote counts."

# CHAPTER 31

## DICE, RICE, BABY

### *Two hours later*

"Well, this isn't the problem I expected to have."

Not by a long shot.

"I'm sure they're just scoping out all of the options before they decide what to try first," Alex says. I like his optimism. But I'm not sure it's realistic.

"The event started half an hour ago."

We've handed out about half as many arancini as I'd expected to at this point. Maybe less, because I expected an early rush from those who arrived before the tent even opened to attendees. People are cruising past the table, registering Castalia's name and taking in what's on offer, but mostly not taking us up on it, even though they've got enough tasting tickets for a sample from each table.

"OK — I've got news, but you're not going to like it," Devon says, returning to our space after having taken a turn around the tent to survey what the other restaurants are offering and how people are responding. "The rumors about the quality of our food having gone down have spread, and if anyone hadn't heard it before they got here, they've heard about it now. A lot of them are reluctant to 'waste' a ticket on Castalia's arancini. And seeing everyone passing us by for other tables is only reinforcing that."

No, I don't like that news. I've sunk my own ship. My insistence on cooking when I was off-balance because of Declan torpedoed my reputation as a chef at exactly the moment it should have shined. Even Drew kicking me out of the kitchen for the last week didn't repair the damage.

"Don't get down about it. We're not out yet," Alex says. "We just need people to give your food a chance. Once they see other people enjoying it, they'll flock over here to get some of their own. This is some of the best food I've ever eaten," he adds loudly, getting the attention of a few people nearby who approach the table.

"Aren't you Alex Winters? From aMUSEd?" one woman asks, while the other deposits a tasting ticket in the box in front of Alex and picks up one of the little plates.

"I'm just a kitchen assistant for this amazing chef over here, Callie Martin from Castalia," Alex says, giving the women a wink. "Will you try our arancini? It's made with local crab and environmentally-friendly lionfish, which are an invasive threat to coral reefs."

"Ooh... This is really good, Marcie!" she says. "Try it."

The second woman looks dubious, but Alex is winning her over, and her friend's encouragement tips the balance. I'm not sure if she buys that he's not the famous keyboardist, but she drops a tasting ticket in the box and picks up her own serving. Her eyes open wide in surprise.

"Is that lump crab in the middle? What a great idea! I totally wasn't expecting that, and it emphasizes the creaminess of the rice and the fresh seafood flavor. What fish did you say was in this?"

"Lionfish," I answer. "They're beautiful in an aquarium, but deadly to reefs, so eating them is good for the planet, as well as delicious."

"I'll say," the first woman says. "I'll take another one."

She hands a ticket to Alex this time, obviously flirting with him. I won't tell him not to make use of his celebrity to bring us more takers for the arancini. I'm past that point now. This first half-hour has been humiliating, and I'll take whatever help I can get to get people actually tasting the food, rather than relying on rumors that I've lost my touch.

"What about you, love — would you like a second taste of the perfection that is Chef Callie's special arancini?"

That's not Alex. It's Declan, who's come in from out of nowhere to stand at the front corner of the table closest to me.

"Oh, my god! It's Declan Carter!" the first woman exclaims loudly, drawing what must be every eyeball in the place to the aMUSEd frontman. "And here you told me you weren't in aMUSEd," she adds, chiding Alex, who just shrugs before looking helplessly over at me.

Because Declan's turning on the charm, loudly praising my food while a crowd gathers around him, like he's a carnival barker or something.

Did I say I'd take whatever help I could get? This wasn't what I had in mind. Not at all.

"Who hasn't tasted Castalia's new, environmentally-friendly lionfish and blue crab arancini? You? Have you tried it? No? Well, come on up! We've got a fresh batch right here, waiting for you. Just remember to drop in your ticket so this amazing dish gets your vote!"

"And by dish, I mean you, angel," he whispers into my ear, grinning widely.

"Declan — you can't do this," I hiss back at him. "This is unfair to the other chefs. No one else brought a celebrity to hawk their food. It's bad enough I've got Alex here helping me!"

"I agree. It's bad enough you had to ask for his help. That should not have happened. And that's at least partly my fault. So, I'm going to make up for it. You didn't ask for my help, but I'm here to lend my support anyway. And you don't need any extra hands back there, so I'm doing what I do best!"

"How are you today, ladies?" he asks another set of women gathered around him. "Do you like amazing twists on traditional Italian food? You do? I've got something you just have to try, then... I'm told I taste wonderful..." The women both giggle. "Oops! Did I say that? I mean I've got wonderful taste!"

He ushers them over in front of the table, where Alex hands them each a plate and they dutifully drop their tickets in the box.

Soon, we're handing out arancini faster than we can make more to replace them.

"Declan — you've done enough. Thank you for your help, but we can handle it from here," I tell him quietly.

"Does that mean you'll sit down with me and listen to what I have to say after all of this is over?" he asks.

"I'm not discussing this right now. You can't use your fame and sex appeal—

"You think I'm sexy?" he asks, sounding entirely too pleased at my slip. I ignore the question.

"—to sell my food, and then expect it to erase my very real issues —" I drop my voice down to a whisper "— with you sleeping around with groupies hours before you came to see me."

"That's not what happened. And I need you to hear me out so I can explain. Please."

I frown and shake my head, agreeing to nothing.

"This isn't the time or the place for this."

"Well, this *is* the time and place for eating amazing food!" he declares, using that booming voice of his that gets him pelted with panties on stages across the world. "Who hasn't gotten the chance to try Chef Callie's arancini? Hand over those tickets, folks — you don't want her to run out before you get a chance to try it for yourself. It's one of my favorite dishes!"

"It really is, you know," he says quietly to me. "I'll never forget my first bite of your arancini."

If Declan Carter, rockstar, can make puppy-dog eyes, he's doing it right now, and they're targeting me.

"Devon, can you start a new batch of risotto? I'm afraid we're going to run out if this keeps up," I tell her. We change places, with me taking over the fryer, as well as assembly.

She starts pulling ingredients and sets a second pot on the stove, behind the arrabbiata sauce. Alex works to refill the rapidly disappearing supply of arancini, plating each ball on a bed of sauce so quickly after I pull them from the fryer that I'm afraid people will burn their mouths. At this rate, I could have used a fourth set of hands. What has Declan done?

"I need to get the other cooler, with the stock and herbs," Devon says. "I'll be right back."

I can almost keep up with the demand, rapidly forming the balls, breading them and dropping them into the fryer. All the practice we've had in the last week or so makes this a nearly automatic task for me. My brain goes into autopilot, and my ears tune into Declan's patter as he charms everyone around him.

"It's great to meet you, too! I'm sorry — I'm not signing on skin anymore. But I'll sign your plate!"

More tickets in the box, more arancini handed over to the now eager crowd of takers. I shake my head, in both dismay and wonder. This charisma of his... I saw the first spark of it when he was just 15, and it overwhelmed me, making me fall head over heels for him, even knowing we lived hours apart. He's had more than a decade to hone it, with the spotlight on him.

Is he still singing his heart out, like he did at 16, 17? Is he still giving everyone who watches him a little piece of himself to take home? Does he have any left for himself when his day ends in the wee hours of the morning? Who takes care of Declan Carter when the autographs have all been signed and the groupies have gone home?

Once, the person caring for him was me. And there, in my memory, the vision of that brightly smiling teenage boy, enjoying my food so enthusiastically, overlaps with the sight in front of me, as he tells every single person in this tent how much he loves my food.

"Chef?"

Devon's back, but she's looking worried.

"What's wrong? Is there a problem with the cooler?"

"No. But... I got a call while I was out at the van, where it was quieter. There were a bunch of voicemails already, and I didn't get a chance to check them before the phone rang again."

She hands me the phone, stepping in to deal with the arancini while I find a spot out of the way.

"Hello?"

"Callie — it's Simon. I'm really sorry to do this, but Drew won't listen to me, and I'm afraid the only one he will listen to right now is you."

"Is Drew OK? Is everyone OK?"

"It's Maria, Callie — she's gone into labor. We've been at the hospital for nearly two hours, and things are moving fast. I'm afraid Drew is going to miss the birth if he doesn't leave for the hospital right now. I told him you'd understand. You've been pushing him to take all of his paternity leave, so I was sure you'd understand. But he refuses to leave the restaurant. He says he's too short on cooks to leave."

"That pig-headed, ego-maniacal..."

"You're not talking about me, are you?" Declan puts in from way too close to me. I smack his shoulder and shove him to an arm's length away.

"I'm sorry, Simon — I shouldn't be talking about your husband like that, but of all the..."

"It's not the first time it's been said, Callie, and it's usually me saying it."

"I'll send Devon back to take Drew's place in the kitchen. We can handle things here at the festival. We've got it under control. It'll all be fine. And he'll be there with you shortly."

"I can't thank you enough, Callie. This... this is such an important moment. I don't want him to miss it."

"And he won't. I'll make sure of it. Let me know when that little bundle of joy has arrived safely and is in his dads' arms, OK?"

"Will do."

The moment the line goes dead, I hand Devon back her phone, my expression worried and weary. But it doesn't matter how I'm feeling. Drew needs to go see his son born. I take out my phone and call Drew's cell. He knows better than to ignore my call when he's on the line and I'm not. If it wasn't an emergency, I'd call the landline at the restaurant.

"I'm not leaving, Callie. We've got a decent crowd tonight, and I need everyone working who isn't already up there with you, including me."

"I'm sending Devon back, whether you agree to leave or not. Alex and I have this handled. We'll be fine."

"Alex? What happened to Raquel?"

"She's sick. I told her to stay home."

"So, it's just you and Alex? You can't spare Devon. It'll be fine. Dads miss their kids' births all the time. It's what happens afterward that counts."

"And that is the biggest piece of bull you've ever served up, Drew. I'm sending Devon back now. She'll relieve you and you will go to the hospital to be with your husband and your baby when he's born. Period. If I find out you didn't leave the moment she got there, you're fired."

"You don't mean that."

"Actually, I do. You've lectured me too many times about not living my life, about putting all of my time and energy into the restaurant, to the detriment of my own happiness. And that lecture has finally sunk in. So, I'm telling you — take care of your family first. We'll be fine. Everyone will step up and do what needs to be done. You're not irreplaceable. And I will fire your ass if you don't get there in time! You hear me?"

"Yes, Chef!"

I hang up.

"Devon—"

"Get back to the kitchen as fast as legally possible and relieve Drew, even if I have to corral all the bussers into physically removing him from the building."

"Exactly."

"Yes, Chef!"

She takes off at a run, and I turn around to see Declan standing behind our table now, a set of food-prep gloves on as he plates and hands out arancini while making small-talk with everyone who comes up to the table. Alex is making arancini as fast as he can, but he's not as fast as I am, and I'm already seeing spots where the bottom of the container is shining through what's left of the risotto. We need to make more, right now. OK. I can do this. With a little help from Declan, we can do this.

"OK — Alex, we need to prep another batch of risotto. I'm going to need the onions diced fine, just like we did in practice."

"Yes, Chef."

I step up to take his place at the fryer, realizing I'm leaving Alex to make risotto on his own.

"Scratch that. You stay at the fryer. I'll start with the onions and help you with the arancini while the risotto is cooking."

"Risotto has to be stirred constantly, Chef," he reminds me, as if I needed the reminder.

"I've got the onions," Declan volunteers. "How small a dice?"

"Since when do you dice onions?" Alex asks, a look of astonishment on his face.

"You said you hate onions," I remind Declan in the same breath.

"I can handle dicing onions. Trust me," he says, looking me deep in the eyes. And I know he's talking about more than just his kitchen skills. "How fine?"

"The size of a grain of rice."

"Yes, Chef!"

Alex and I watch in amazement as Declan peels an onion and then a second, and starts to dice them into tiny pieces. I give the onions a closer look as they start to pile up on the cutting board. They're cut precisely to the size I specified, perfectly even, every single piece.

"When did you learn to do that?" Alex asks.

"A while ago," he says.

"How?"

"I watch when you cook," Declan replies.

"No, you don't. Half the time, you're not even in the kitchen when I cook."

"I'm a fast study, a visual learner, a dicing savant."

Alex scoffs, shaking his head. And I just watch in amazement as Declan Carter out-dices half the trained cooks in my kitchen.

"What's next?"

"They need to be sautéed, then I have to add some more ingredients... I'll let Alex take over here, if you'll go back to plating."

"No — I've got it. Sautéing onions."

"You can't overcook them, Declan. It'll throw off the flavors. I'll take care of it."

"Trust me," he says slowly, begging me with his eyes and the tone of his voice to do just that. "I can do this."

Don't ask me why, but my gut tells me he can, and I can. I can trust him with this.

"The butter's in the cooler with the stock."

"Yes, Chef."

## *Two hours later*

"And that's the last of them," Alex says, handing a final plate to a young woman who's clearly smitten with him. She's too young for him, and he's not encouraging her, but it's cute. "Enjoy!"

"Awww!" rings out in a disappointed chorus from the people gathered behind her.

"Sorry, folks!" Declan says, resuming his role as barker. "You've totally cleaned us out of those amazing arancini. But Chef Callie will have them on her menu starting next week. Make sure you stop by, for lunch or dinner! Her food is truly magical!"

I glare at him, and he winks at me.

There's a half-hour left to the event, but even the backup supplies I brought with me, just in case, have been exhausted. Declan cooked the risotto with a minimum amount of instruction from me, and that was mostly a question of ingredients and proportions. If it didn't defy any reality I've ever known, I'd think he'd cooked risotto before, as well as dicing onions and everything else he needed to do.

"Fess up, Declan. You've been cooking behind my back, haven't you?" Alex accuses.

"When would I have had time to cook somewhere where you wouldn't see, hear or smell it? I mean, I'm a natural talent, clearly, but I'm not a magician."

"Not funny," I tell him, frowning.

"You're not going to tell me, are you?" Alex says.

"Like I said — natural talent. And you're clearly a good enough cook that my brief moments of watching you have paid off in spades. Congrats!"

I'm not buying it for a moment, and neither is Alex. We exchange a look, mystified, and then both shrug off the mystery that is Declan Carter, sous-chef.

"Wow, Callie! That was amazing!" Margaret proclaims, coming up to the table to greet me while Alex and Declan work together to clean up the prep area. "Seems like those rumors that you'd lost your touch were totally wrong! That was delicious, local and environmentally-friendly. Genius. And your handsome assistants! What a brilliant move that was! I had no idea rockstars could cook!"

"They're full of surprises," I reply, giving Declan a look.

"We have to wait until the event's officially over before we tally the votes, but I can see from your overflowing box that we're probably going to be sending you home with a check!"

"It was a very busy day, and I'm glad we could offer something everyone would enjoy, while helping raise money for the food bank. One of my staff is a student in their culinary program, and it's a cause near to my heart."

"What's your plan for your portion of the prize money, if you don't mind my asking?"

"I'll wait until we've officially won it before I start spending it," I reply with a chuckle.

"Well, I hope you're prepared to be swamped at the restaurant — not that you weren't already," she adds, despite knowing full-well that we've been much less busy recently than we had been. "You're going to have everyone coming from around the area to try this new dish. I'm so glad to see it'll be on your menu so soon!" She gives a nod to Declan, who smiles and nods back.

If I hadn't planned on putting the new arancini on the menu, I'd be in deep trouble now. I can't decide whether I want to kiss Declan or kill him.

"And on that note, I'm happy to present this check to Gabrielle Santos, representing the food bank! Thank you all for supporting this worthy cause." Margaret poses with Gabrielle while several photographers take photos.

"And now it's time to announce our winning chef for this year's Taste of the Culinary Coastline: Callie Martin of Castalia in Mystic Beach!"

I go up to accept the ribbon and the check, expecting Alex and Declan to follow me, but when the flashes from the cameras stop blinding me, I look back to find Alex standing alone in the crowd, Declan nowhere to be seen.

# CHAPTER 32

# LOVE LIKE BOMBS

## *A week later*

"What are you two — you three, I mean — what are you doing here?"

"Drew is not here to work, that I can promise you," Simon says.

"We just brought this little guy out to meet Auntie Callie after his very first doctor appointment," Drew says.

"He's precious! And Andy is a perfect name for him! He looks like an Andy."

"Andrew Simon Garner-Williams," Drew pronounces.

"The Andrew part was my idea," Simon says.

"And the Simon part was mine," Drew adds.

"You all are so cute! A perfect family! And how is Maria? Is she doing OK? It's got to be hard being a surrogate."

"We sent her and her husband off for a week in the Bahamas," Simon says. "She came through the delivery so easily. Apparently, that's often the case when the surrogate has had prior children. And her kids are off with their grandparents while they're gone, so everyone's getting a fun vacation."

"Except us," Drew notes, and I finally see the cheerful veneer of the new dad crack to reveal a very tired new dad.

"He's been a little colicky. The doctor advised us to change his formula, see if that helps."

"He's been keeping us up at night, in the meantime," Drew says. "I'm going to need every bit of my paternity leave just to recover from this first week."

"Good thing I'm happy to play house-husband and stick to writing in between baby duties," Simon says.

"And what about you, Callie? What's the plan now that you won the contest?" Drew asks, having a fair idea what I'm going to say, I suspect.

"We're overflowing with diners again, and I can't get the lionfish in fast enough. We've been running out of arancini halfway through dinner most nights."

"And the expansion?"

"I gave the landlord the deposit on the bakery space the day after the contest. The contractor had a project that got put on hold while they wait for a public hearing for permit approval, and he said he'll have ours done by next week. So I also ordered more tables, chairs and linens."

"Do we have any money left?"

"We do. With Taste selling out completely, the prize was even bigger than usual. We have enough to pay the new line cooks with the hiring bonus I offered to get them on board, and a good bit to tuck into the bank to cover the expansion expenses and additional rent. By the time you're back from leave, we should be running like a well-oiled machine, just with nearly twice the tables."

"And no more... incidents?" Drew asks.

I give him a look, glancing at Simon.

"Oh, Simon knows all about it. His last book was a look at modern witchcraft in the context of historical Paganism."

"Oh... But I'm not a witch."

"Honey, I don't care what you call it — your cooking has always been magical. And that's all I need to know," Simon says with a smile.

"As long as we don't have any more incidents," Drew says.

"Nothing so far. Just a dining room full to bursting and people begging for reservations."

"Which we don't take. Except..."

"He hasn't been in. I haven't seen or heard from him since the contest."

"A little birdie told me he not only turned the tide on people trying the arancini, that he actually helped cook it?"

"He did," I admit. "Alex and I were flabbergasted. Alex had told me Declan cooked steaks. But apparently this whole cooking thing was a surprise to Alex, too."

"Weird," Drew says. "I mean, weird enough that Alex is an amateur chef in his spare time, but how'd his bandmate manage to sneak up on you both like that, with those skills?"

"I have no idea. But I'm going to find out."

"Uh-oh..." Simon says, whistling. "I'm not sure I'd want to be Declan Carter with Callie on my trail."

"Maybe that's exactly where he wants her." Drew suggests, smirking at me.

Baby Andy gives a big yawn, stretching his tiny hand out toward Drew's face.

"Naptime!"

"I don't want to see you again for two weeks, Drew! Not even to visit. Enjoy the baby, because we're going to have a lot of work for you when you come back."

"He'll be begging me to let him come in to work in a week," Simon predicts.

"Too bad. You set a precedent, Drew. If you can ban me from my own kitchen, I can keep you out until you're supposed to be here."

Drew looks at me in mock outrage, and Simon waves as they walk back out the kitchen door.

I take a deep breath, the peace of the empty kitchen hitting me. But it's not as satisfying as it was a few weeks ago. I've gotten used to scrounging for that winning recipe, practicing it with Alex, with Raquel and Devon. And, before that, fencing with Declan with words and with food. Everything in my life is back on track. Why is it that it feels like something is missing?

## *Two days later*

"A special request for the regular arancini and Frutti di Mare, Chef," Raquel says.

That's odd. No one's asked for the old version of the arancini since Taste. And Frutti di Mare hasn't been on my menu in more than a year. Must be an old customer looking for their favorites.

"I can do that," I tell her. "I'll throw the risotto in the blast chiller, like we did at Taste, using the cooler instead. It'll take an extra five or ten minutes, though."

"I'll let the diner know."

She's got me curious now, and as soon as I've got the risotto in the chiller, I take a peek out into the dining room, to see if I recognize any faces I haven't seen in a while.

I gasp.

Raquel is chatting with Declan, who's sitting at his usual two-top out of the way of the rest of the diners. Why didn't she tell me he was here? Why didn't he have her tell me he was here?

Arancini and Frutti di Mare... Why that combination? Why does that feel familiar?

Nonna. Nonna made him Frutti di Mare, after I served him my arancini. It was the first time they met, and the first time I'd cooked for him. Arturo...

There's a warmth, but also a longing, that comes with that memory now. A special meal, a special day, young love at its sweetest, moments of lightheartedness, a sense of family that extended beyond Nonna, because Nonna considered him family. And then the losses... Declan first. Nonna more recently. So much loss. I want it all back. I want to be 15 again and sitting in Nonna's kitchen, cooking for Declan, holding hands, having her smile knowingly over us.

I plate the arancini and shake my head at Raquel when she goes to take it to him. I'll do it myself. It's past time I talked to him again, after his disappearing act at Taste. And maybe I can get to the bottom of the mystery while I'm at it.

"Arancini, traditional style."

He smiles up at me.

"Hi, Callie."

"Hi."

There's silence, a tentativeness to both of us.

"Thanks for going off-menu for me. Again," he says.

"I could accommodate the request pretty easily. I didn't have to send anyone out for muskrat this time."

He chuckles, and it's warm, relaxed, losing that little bit of tension that was there before.

"So... do you want to explain how it is that you cooked risotto like you'd done it a hundred times before?"

"Not particularly. But I will, if you'll let me explain about that photo, and the girls."

That's the last thing I want to talk about right now. I'd half-forgotten about it, won over by his efforts to help me and Castalia in ways that involved time and effort, rather than the money he undoubtedly has piled up in his bank accounts. It showed a respect for me that throwing dollars at the problem wouldn't have. He was supportive, a champion proudly touting my skills, helping with the skills he had, rather than just running roughshod over me and flaunting his financial success.

"Not now. I've got a couple hours left in the kitchen, and I don't want any... incidents."

"I think you've got a handle on it now."

"Maybe. But I don't want to take that risk. Drew's on leave for another two weeks."

"How's the baby?"

"Adorable! And colicky, apparently. They named him Andy."

"Like the kid in 'Toy Story'?"

"After Drew — his first name is Andrew. They gave him Simon's name as a middle name, so he's named after both of them."

"That's sweet. I'm happy for them."

"You're really not going to tell me how you know how to cook? And risotto, at that?"

"To do that, I'd have to explain about the girls, and you won't let me do that. It's all part of the same story."

"Fine. Keep your secret," I tell him, mildly irritated but vastly more curious. *Ground. Center.* "Eat those before they get cold."

"Thanks," he says mildly, seeming just a little sad.

I turn my attention to the Frutti di Mare, enjoying making the familiar dish for the first time in a while. Jack and Reed are masters on the line. I won't be able to keep them long, not with the path to sous-chef blocked by Drew, who's established as my right hand. Devon and Rick rule the brunch and lunch shifts, and no one is displacing them. Once Drew's back, it'll be obvious to Jack and Reed that they'll have to go elsewhere if they aspire to move higher than line cook. The only other course would be to promote Drew to chef de cuisine and move myself into an executive chef role. And I'm not ready for that. I love cooking too much. And would Drew want chef de cuisine with a new baby at home? Seems unlikely. Oh, well. Cooks come and go in every restaurant. Castalia is no different.

I add the linguine to the pan full of seafood and arrabbiata sauce — milder, like the revised combination Nonna served Declan that day — and give it a stir, waiting for the sauce to marry with the pasta. Then, onto a wide pasta plate. Raquel arrives just in time to run it out to him, and I decide to let her this time. I don't think Declan and I have much to say when I'm not ready to have him explain about those girls and he's not willing to explain the mystery without also doing that. I'll let him eat in peace, enjoy a little culinary trip down memory lane.

A half-hour later, Declan's working on his dessert — a more traditional chocolate mousse with chili. No ghost peppers this time. I force myself to take a break from the stove, going once again through Rory's mental exercises. When I'm feeling balanced and peaceful, I peek out at the dining room, surprised to find Raquel sitting with Declan at his table, chatting animatedly.

It's her break, and one she was overdue to take, so I can't fault her for sitting down. I just didn't expect her to be sitting with Declan. I mean, he's been very friendly with her from the first time they met. And she seemed sympathetic to his case when I refused to talk to him. But she's only 18, practically a kid... Could it be Declan's given up pursuing me, in favor of a starstruck teenager? I catch myself before jealousy kicks into full gear, returning once again to my calming exercises.

I look back out at the exact moment Raquel looks toward the kitchen, and she instantly looks guilty. Is it just that she thinks I'm monitoring her break? Or is there something more going on that has her feeling guilty? She excuses herself and heads toward the kitchen.

"Did you need me, Chef?" she asks.

"No, Raquel. I was just taking a break myself, and I wanted to see how Declan liked his dessert."

"Quite well. He was very complimentary about the whole meal."

"I see... Well, that's good to know."

"Would you mind if I left a few minutes early tonight? I've got my class, and I have a friend who needed to ride up with me."

"Sure. That's fine. You didn't take your break until late anyway. And things are under control. I'll be happy to get you into the kitchen here in a few weeks, I'll admit. You did a great job helping prep for Taste."

"I'm so sad I missed it. Rotten timing for a virus. I'm glad it worked out, though," she says.

"It did. Yeah — go ahead and head on out, give your friend that ride. I'll see you tomorrow."

I grab an order while Raquel gathers her things from the break room. But I don't miss the guilty glance she gives me when she leaves — not through the back door to the kitchen, but through the dining room. She gives Declan a nod as she passes, and he smiles back at her. There's nothing untoward about the exchange, but there's a tingling sensation in my spine, and I'm suddenly on edge. That feeling ramps up when Declan drops a wad of cash on his table and leaves without saying another word.

"Reed? Take this steak order over, will you? Medium-rare, with the asparagus and potatoes, please."

"Yes, Chef!"

I walk through the dining room to the front door, nodding at diners as I pass. I'll check in on my way back to the kitchen.

Raquel pulls her car up in front of the door, into the take-out parking spot. Did she forget something? And then Declan crosses the sidewalk and gets into her car, smiling and chatting before he's even buckled in.

Declan's the "friend" she was giving a ride to? I'd assumed she was picking up a classmate. Or maybe she's not headed to class at all. Maybe he's taking her to see the studio... and his room there.

No. He wouldn't. Would he? She's 18! He's almost 30. I mean, it wouldn't be unheard-of, but I wouldn't have expected it from Declan, no matter how many young groupies he's undoubtedly encountered in his life.

The questions are bouncing around in my mind, like popcorn kernels in hot oil.

"Reed, I'm going to get some air. I should be back before closing time. You all OK if I go?"

"Sure. We've got this," he says with a cocky grin.

"What was that?"

"Yes, Chef!"

I'm in my car and double-parked a half-block down from the restaurant before Raquel has pulled out of the take-out spot. I pull out two cars behind them, feeling utterly ridiculous as I execute my first "tailing" of a vehicle. I've watched enough TV to know I need to stay back, out of sight, and not follow lane changes and turns too closely.

But the bulk of their route is straight down the highway — past the studio, I note with a sigh of relief — with a single turn inland after about fifteen minutes. I know she also lives up in this neck of the woods, but it looks like she could legitimately be headed for her class at the food bank. The question is why is Declan with her? Was he curious about the program and decided to tag along?

When she pulls into the parking lot at the food bank, I keep driving, going a few blocks past it before making a U-turn. I pull into the lot just in time to see the two of them heading inside, Declan giving Raquel a squeeze around the shoulders as they continue their conversation. What is going on here?

# CHAPTER 33

## SPOONMAN

## Callie

I peek into the kitchen, which is filled with young would-be chefs, many of whom come from the same kind of disadvantage background as Raquel. This is their chance to get training that will enable them to get good jobs without having to spend four years in college, or even travel to a major city to study at a big culinary school. It's on-the-job training, without the high pressure of a restaurant kitchen, which they'll all likely experience soon enough. In exchange, they're helping the food bank cut costs by preparing the meals that will be delivered tomorrow to seniors and other homebound residents. And that means the food bank can afford to stock more items for food-insecure individuals and families, who are all too plentiful in the larger area, despite the prosperity of the towns near the beach.

I know how lucky I am. If Nonna hadn't bought her house outright so many decades ago, I not only wouldn't have had Castalia, I would have been scrounging for an affordable apartment twenty minutes inland, all while trying to save up money for my own restaurant. I might not have been able to go to culinary school, which was an expense Nonna supplemented with money she hadn't had to pay in rent, since the mortgage was paid off.

And I knew plenty of people in culinary school who'd had brushes with the law, or had parents or siblings in jail, often as a result of generational poverty or drug addiction. Getting hired with a criminal record is hard, and even harder with a reputation as an addict. I'd gone out of my way to find Jack and Reed, who'd taken part in a culinary training program while transitioning out of prison. A few of these kids, too, had been in trouble with the law. Raquel was facing tough financial circumstances, along with her mother's addiction. Programs like this are their salvation, as well as vital supports in a community.

Declan emerges from an office attached to the kitchen, dropping an apron over his head. What is he doing?

He gestures to the students, calling them over to the teaching station, with its mirror overhead so the students can all see what the teacher is doing.

He plucks an onion from a basket on the table and proceeds to peel and dice it, just like he did at Taste. He then does the same with a head of garlic, smashing it instead of dicing it. Then a batch of mushrooms, sliced thin. Soon, he's got stock boiling on the stove, the vegetables sautéing in a pan, and a bowl of rice at the ready. He's making risotto.

No — he's not just making risotto. He's teaching the students — including Raquel — how to make it. And it's not even my risotto recipe! Nor does he have a cookbook or notecards nearby to consult for the recipe. He's cooking it from memory.

"He's been very gracious to share his time with us," someone says from behind me.

I startle a little, until I recognize who it is.

"Hi, Gabrielle. Uh… this is a little awkward…"

"I take it you know him? Or did you come to check up on Raquel? She's doing wonderfully, by the way. She'll be ready for your kitchen in a few weeks."

"Great."

I look back into the room, and Declan's teaching one of the students his technique for dicing an onion.

"I know everyone hates chopping onions, because they make you cry," he says. "I had a point where I never wanted to see another onion again. Our tour chef had finally caved in and offered to teach me a few things. And, of course, the first thing she did was have me chop onions. Baskets full of them. And this was on a gig night, when I had soundcheck in like an hour."

The students follow his lead on dicing the onions in front of them, listening intently. I can only imagine what they're thinking, with this well-known rockstar telling them about what life is like on the road. Only, it seems maybe Declan's life on the road is a little different from what I thought.

"By the time I was done, I could barely see, my eyes were so swollen and watery from chopping onions. I think she was testing me, making sure I really wanted to learn and that it wasn't just some spoiled rockstar whim that I'd get past the moment the work got uncomfortable. But I got them all chopped before I had to go to soundcheck. Only, like I said, I couldn't see very well, and when I got backstage to wash my face, I walked straight into the dressing room, walking in on Alex and his girlfriend — I think that one lasted three weeks? Anyway, since I didn't want anyone knowing I was trying to learn to cook, I couldn't exactly tell him — especially not Alex, who was already an incredible cook — that I'd been chopping onions all afternoon. So, I told him I'd come in hoping for a threesome with his girl, which he thought was hilarious, but the girl didn't. He knew I was joking, since I don't do that anymore and she was, however briefly, his girlfriend, not just some groupie..."

And now I know the story about the onions and the threesome. And it wasn't at all what I'd suspected when he'd mentioned it so casually that first morning at Castalia, playing it off as a little scandalous. I'm starting to wonder if any of my assumptions about this grown-up Declan are true.

"It's not exactly the ideal teaching style, but they seem to enjoy it when he tells them about the experiences he's had, from the rockstar treatment to cooking in food banks and soup kitchens in Chicago, L.A., D.C., Paris, South America."

South America? Declan's cooked in soup kitchens in South America?

"He's been teaching the class? For how long?"

"Come back to my office. We'll go in the door from the hallway and you can watch from there."

She settles down behind her desk in the office Declan had come out of, propping the door open so I can see and hear Declan, though the angle means it's unlikely he'll see me, thankfully.

"He is a friend of yours, right? I mean, he mentioned your name when he first showed up, asking to help out. I assumed you'd sent him, since you'd been monitoring Raquel's training."

"An old friend. But I didn't send him. When exactly did he first show up?"

"Oh, a few weeks ago. I was teaching them how to debone a chicken that night, so that would have been... that Friday? About three weeks ago?"

The night before he'd come to see me at Castalia for the first time. The night he'd taken the photo with the groupies.

The pieces start to fall into place. His cooking skills, and why he'd said they were intertwined in the same story as the photo. Though what the connection is between them is still beyond my comprehension.

"I'm not sure I should say any more about it, since you didn't send him after all. We all signed a non-disclosure agreement, as he asked. And his monetary donation was very generous as well, so I didn't argue. And the students — once they realized he was going to be helping teach them, they all signed the NDA."

"Why did he say he wanted that?"

"In confidence?"

I nod, and she continues.

"He didn't want anyone knowing he's been volunteering like this. It was kind of odd. He said it was penance, and if he took credit for it, it wouldn't be penance anymore, because it would look like a publicity stunt to rehabilitate his reputation. I'm not really sure why he'd need that. Other than a few off-color stories, he's been incredibly generous and easy to work with. The students love it when he shows up."

"How often has that been?"

"A couple times a week. He's taken a shine to Raquel, though."

I give her a look.

"No — not like that! She doesn't seem to be awestruck over him, unlike most of the other girls were at first. But he worked with her that first night he showed up, talking to her at length about her internship. Honestly — that just reinforced for me that you had to have sent him. She told him all about working with you. She really looks up to you, you know?"

"Oh."

I look back into the kitchen, watching Raquel help one of her fellow students just as Declan helps another.

"You ditch your security detail again tonight, Declan?" the student asks.

"Nah," he says. "Gryff had me followed to the club that one night. His guys aren't nearly as subtle as they think they are. But as soon as I got into a hotel room, they backed off. That's the great thing about establishing a pattern of behavior — after a while, no one suspects you're doing anything other than what you let them think you're doing. So, Gryff assumes I'm in a hotel room with some girls, and I've got the evidence to confirm that, at which point I leave them to enjoy the room and room service, and I can cut out to do whatever, without anyone following me. That'll teach him to put tracking software on my phone."

"You're not worried about some stalker coming after you, or some girl showing up in your bedroom?"

"They worry about that stuff while we're on tour, or even in New York, but not here. And I've got a girl. Don't need or want any more in my bedroom or elsewhere. That's been the awesome thing about being here — I can just be me. Except when we're performing incognito, of course."

"When are you playing out next? I want to see you before you finish the album and leave."

"Probably a few weeks. I got a little caught up in other stuff, and I haven't felt much like writing songs. But things seem like they're getting better, maybe. I've got some ideas. Being able to cook for other people, where I could see them enjoying the food — that was awesome. It's like the creativity of the kitchen sparks the music in my head. Now, you ready to add that to the pan?"

I look back at Gabrielle, dumbfounded by what I've heard.

This whole time — who knows how many months or years before now — Declan's been ditching his security detail, during a tour, to go cook in soup kitchens and teach students in food bank culinary programs. And he's been hiding this "penance" behind a subterfuge of groupies, pretend threesomes and faux trysts in hotel rooms.

What does he even need to do penance for?

I wonder that, but as soon as I do, I start to get the feeling that I already know.

# CHAPTER 34

## IF I WERE A CARPENTER

### *An hour later*

Nothing is what I thought it was. I was prepared to humiliate Declan over photos of him with girls he was never even interested in. And while I was condemning him as a player who'd go from groupies to proclaiming his serious interest in me in the space of a few hours, he'd been chopping onions and teaching disadvantaged kids the skills that will pull them out of poverty and keep them out of jail.

And it wasn't the first time he'd done it. He'd apparently made a pattern of it, all around the world. All with no one the wiser, because he wanted it to be a selfless, anonymous act of penance.

Out of remorse over having hurt me when we were still teenagers.

That has to be it.

I have no doubt he had his wild times as a rockstar at some point between our breakup and when the band arrived in Mystic Beach. Maybe even as recently as just before Brighid's and Hunter's engagement party. But at some point, something changed for him. Alex said he'd been looking for me from the moment he'd seen me that night. And Declan had found me within hours of talking to Raquel at the food bank.

Declan's done some stupid things, but he's not a stupid man. He had to have known that the local culinary program would have students placed in my restaurant, if not currently, then certainly at some point in the past. And he'd not only sought them out, apparently hoping to find me, he'd stayed, and he'd made a donation — of both money and his time. And even after he got the information he'd been looking for, he'd kept going back, following that same pattern of volunteering with no public recognition desired.

If Gabrielle hadn't clued me in to what had happened, if I hadn't overheard him say those things to the students, with no idea I was listening... I'm not sure I'd ever have believed it. I'm still having a hard time believing it. But it makes sense. It all makes sense. In fact, the only thing that doesn't make sense now, in the wake of these revelations and his actions at Taste, is the fact that he dumped me all those years ago.

It didn't make sense then, and it doesn't make sense now. I'd had to learn to accept it, and I'd hated him for it, for abandoning me to go off and be a rockstar. But if I'm honest, I never got over him, never stopped loving him, even if I hated him in the same breath. And now I'm wondering if it was the same for him, if he never got over me, never stopped loving me. That makes sense, too, in the context of what he told me that morning he showed up at Castalia and of his behavior since then.

I can't resist the pull any longer. I check in on the kitchen, having been gone for more time than I'd ever anticipated. But Jack and Reed — they've got it all in hand. I'm going to have to give them both bonuses after this.

"You sure you're OK to close without me?"

"Yes, Chef!"

"Seriously, you two — no concerns?"

"We've got this, Chef. Really. It's almost closing time anyway. We'll button things up and it'll be fresh and ready for you in the morning."

"Thanks."

I head up to my apartment, going straight to the closet where my oldest possessions are stored, in boxes buried deep in the back. It takes some excavation, but I finally locate the fabric-covered box I used to store keepsakes in. I take it out and set it on the coffee table, not quite ready to open it. It's been so long...

Finally, I take a deep breath and open the top, taking out the album that sits atop all the little mementos.

"Our Wedding," it says across the front.

I'd hidden this, even from Nonna, concerned that she might tell my parents that Declan and I had gotten married, even if it wasn't legal. Their response would have been... Well, I'll never know. But I can safely say it wouldn't have been positive. They might not have even let me come back to visit Nonna again. As it was...

I open the album cover, tracing my fingers across the red, green and white ribbons, still tied together with the same knot that Lyric had tied around Declan's and my joined wrists and hands that day in August. Almost exactly 12 years ago. There were no witnesses. Just Lyric and the two of us. We'd have needed witnesses for a legal ceremony, but that wasn't what we had in mind that day. We knew it wasn't legal. It didn't matter. It was the promises we made to each other. To love each other, care for each other. Forever. For eternity.

And then...

I shake my head free of the knowledge of what would come to pass not long after that happy day. I want to stay in the moment, enjoy the memories while they were still sweet.

# Declan
## *Twelve years ago*

I can't even see her face, and already I'm just floored by her. The dress highlights her curves, narrow at the waist, full to her knees. I half expect to see a halo over her head instead of the crimson and cream roses she has tied into the back of her hair, which flows down her back like warm brown silk. Her sandals lace up her ankles, which I'm really tempted to get down on my knees to kiss. She looks like a princess as much as she does like the heavenly vision she was the first time I saw her.

And this girl agreed to marry me?

I must be the luckiest guy on the planet. She's so far out of my league. Maybe someday I'll be worthy of her, but it'll take the kind of success I've only dreamed of to make that happen. And I'm not waiting that long to make her my wife. Even if our parents insisted waiting was the least we'd have to do.

But I'm not letting a matter of months keep me from making this thing between us real. So what if we can't have the piece of paper that makes it legal? We'll get that soon enough. For now, we'll make our promises to each other, in front of her friend Lyric and the universe as our witness, and that will carry us over until next summer, when we can make this marriage real in a way no one will be able to deny. Not even our parents.

"You ready, angel?"

She turns to face me, the fountain in Nonna's back yard a perfect backdrop for her glorious smile, and my knees threaten to buckle. *Hold it together, Declan. You're going to marry this girl in about ten minutes. You can fall at her feet during your honeymoon — all two hours of it.*

Yeah, it's hardly a traditional honeymoon on a tropical beach, but we're 17, and we have to keep the wedding secret from our parents, and even Nonna and Dave. I'll save up my gig pay, and we'll go on a real honeymoon once we'd made it legal. Maybe I'll take her to Italy so she can see where Nonna was born. Yeah. That's what I'll do. For now, we've got a few hours before she's got to go to work at the restaurant, and I want to make love to my wife before that happens. The ceremony will be simple, quick and just between the two — well, three — of us. And that's OK. What's between Callie and me is all that counts.

"Yes. I am. I really am," she says, raising her bouquet to show me.

It matches the roses in her hair, cream and crimson, tied with a white ribbon.

"You are breathtaking, Callie. Just... wow."

"Thanks. I was hoping you'd like it. I mean, it's just a sundress. It's not like it's a real wedding dress."

"But it *is* a real wedding dress," I tell her. "We're getting married, and it's the dress you're wearing. That makes it a wedding dress."

She smiles again, seeming bolstered by my reminder that this is, as far as I'm concerned, entirely real.

"You look handsome, Declan," she says.

I've just got on a plain button-up shirt and some khakis — clothes I brought this summer, like usual, just in case we went out somewhere fancy to eat. We haven't, since Dad's been tied up with business most weekends anyway and hasn't been down but a couple times. Mom's irked, especially after the whole marriage thing blew up. Boy, was that an ugly argument they had over the phone.

And Callie's parents weren't any happier when she called to tell them she wanted them to give her permission once they got here. That nearly blew up right in our faces, when they threatened to come take her home to Philadelphia early, like they did last year, when they realized we were sleeping together. Nonna calmed them down, promising she wasn't going to sign any papers for us either, though she didn't seem entirely happy about it.

"Thank you, angel. But you're so radiant, no one will even realize I'm there."

"Well, I will. It's hard to have a wedding without a groom," she teases.

"True. I guess I'll have to make up for it by being extra-loud when I say, 'I do,'" I tell her. "Which is fine, because I really, *really* mean it when I say I want to marry you."

I put my hand behind her neck and pull her to me, pressing my lips firmly against hers.

"That's it! Right there!" a voice calls from behind me. "That'll be the photo!"

"Hi, Lyric," Callie says. "Thanks again for doing this, even if it's not legal."

"Well, it may not be legal," the blonde girl, just a little older than Callie and me, says, "but it is very much real. I want to make sure you both understand that — when I marry people, it sticks. So, if you're not a hundred percent sure, you need to tell me now. We can call this off—"

"No!" Callie and I say simultaneously. Why am I not surprised? Not only that she's just as opposed to calling off this wedding but that we'd answer the same way, in the same breath.

"Alrighty then!" Lyric says. "But even if we go ahead with it, you should make sure that you really want to make this a 'forever' bond. I can still do it for a year and a day. That way, if things change, we don't have to worry about longer-term repercussions. You'll have a year to re-think things—"

"Absolutely not!" Callie and I both say, this time exchanging a grin, because the odds were against it this time. But we do this brain-sharing thing, so...

Lyric chuckles.

"OK. I get it. I just want to make sure you understand — after a year and a day, I can renew your vows. So, next summer, you could just extend it if you want. I can do a year and a day, a lifetime or forever. It's up to you two to decide what you promise each other. So, which do you want?"

"Forever." I'm not surprised when we say it together this time. She and I both want this so badly. There was no way we'd want to promise each other anything other than forever.

"Then I've discharged that responsibility, and we can go ahead and do this. Did you want to do it here in the garden?"

"We were thinking about the beach," I tell her, taking Callie's hand in mine.

"Perfect," Lyric says. "It's a beautiful day, and I know just the spot — out of the way but with the ocean as a background for the photos."

"I'm happy to take some photos for you, if you like."

An elderly gentleman offers to lend a hand when he sees Lyric trying to take photos as she's performing our ceremony. He smiles, exchanging a look with the woman next to him.

"Young love," she says. "I remember when we were that age, so eager to get started with our lives together."

"And now, here we are, sixty years later, almost to the day," he says, kissing her hand.

"Congratulations," I tell them, squeezing Callie's hand. This was fate. Again. "And please. We'd appreciate it."

Lyric hands him the camera, and he moves to stand between me and Callie, just far enough back to get the three of us into the shot.

"Do you, Callie, take Declan to be your husband, for as long as time would bind you together?" Lyric asks.

"I do," Callie says, tearing up.

I slide the simple white-gold wedding band onto her ring finger.

"Do you, Declan, take Callie to be your wife, for as long as time would bind you together?"

"I do." And she slides the matching band onto my ring finger.

We both agreed we'd take them off afterward, to ensure none of the official adults would freak out. Callie's got a chain to put hers on, and mine will go in my wallet. Just for now. Once we're 18...

"I now pronounce you husband and wife," Lyric says.

She doesn't get a chance to do the "You may now kiss" thing, because I pull Callie hard against me, squashing her bouquet just a little in my eagerness. That's OK. I'll buy my girl — my wife — all the flowers she could ever want once we're signed to a record deal. And I don't think that's too far off. All the little pieces of the life I want are coming together.

"Oh, Frank — look how happy they are! Just like we were at their age! Capture that look on their faces!"

Mrs. Frank is right. I'm happy, and Callie's happy — which is the really important part. From here, there's no limit to how far we can go. Together.

## Callie
### *Present*

To look at them today, the images look like anyone's wedding photos, if less formal and with all three of us clearly being younger than the norm.

And, as far as I was concerned... as far as the three of us were concerned, it was a real wedding. I'm certain of it. Whatever Declan said when he broke up with me, I know when he said those words to me on our wedding day, he meant them.

Lyric treated the role of officiant as a sacred duty. She and her mom were classic hippie-dippy granola types, with her mom having a girlfriend and their house full of crystals and jars and dried herbs hanging from rafters, and I didn't think much of it, of the ideas of witchcraft and goddesses. To each their own. But Lyric was older, and she'd married people before, just as her mother had before her. She was a legal officiant, registered with the state. All we were lacking was a piece of paper and a couple of witnesses to sign it. And, in the end, that didn't seem to matter so much. We made our promises, and Lyric declared us husband and wife.

These two deliriously happy kids... No idea how things would go wrong in the days and weeks to come. Smiling brilliant smiles at each other with the backdrop of the Atlantic Ocean, thinking they had forever ahead of them, forever together, tied together soul to soul, as sure as their hands were with those ribbons.

Tears escape my eyes, and I wipe them away. I know what's in the back of the album, and that's only going to make it worse, so I refuse to turn the pages. Instead, I flip back to the front, savoring the happy moments and the feelings the photos of them still hold for me. My fingers absorb the smooth, satiny feeling of the ribbons, recalling how they felt that day. Like we'd done something good, and permanent, and lasting. Something that could be relied upon.

There's a knock at the door. I know it's probably Jack or Reed, coming to tell me everything's locked up for the night, even though they don't need to do that. I set the album aside and open the door.

"Hey, Callie."

It's not Jack or Reed, of course. It's Declan. Of course.

"Can I come in? I think we need to talk."

There's a quiet, calm intensity to him that's different from what I've grown accustomed to with him, both as a teenager and in recent weeks. The chaos and the ebullient energy of the performer, the ego... It's gone, or at least parked somewhere out of the way. This is a more mature Declan, serious, thoughtful.

"Sure." What else can I say? He gave me time to deal with my anger, my resentment, and once I'd done that, I discovered some — maybe all — of it hadn't been justified. I owe him the chance to explain, and I think maybe I owe us the chance to clear the air, get rid of some of that baggage I've — we've — been toting around for more than a decade.

I close the door behind him, only then realizing that the album is still sitting on the sofa where I'd left it. I scramble ahead of him, snatching it up and tucking it behind the throw pillow before leaning back against it. If I'm lucky, he didn't see it.

"What did you want to talk about?" As if I don't have a good idea...

# CHAPTER 35

## BIGGER PICTURE

### Declan

"I saw you leaving the food bank tonight."

Her expression shifts from cautious to guilty? Embarrassed? I don't know.

"The 'I pull over for pasta' bumper sticker gave you away," I tell her. "I kind of have the back end of your car stuck permanently in my memory, after chasing it for a block," I add wryly. "I just went out to get some air while the students stirred risotto until their arms about fell off, and I spotted that familiar back end. The car's — not yours." Clarity is important in relationships.

"Oh," is all she says.

"How much did you figure out?" I know it's probably more than I would have told her on my own. But maybe that's for the best.

"Most of it, I think. The onion story, the bit about slipping your security detail. Gabrielle filled in some of the rest, before she realized I wasn't already aware of it."

"So you know about the photo — about the girls at the hotel?"

"Yeah."

She doesn't seem mad. She seems... almost sad.

"I danced with them for a little while. I took them to the hotel room. I ordered room service. We took a selfie, just like I always do when I slip away from Gryff's guys. Makes it more plausible... But then I excused myself and caught a ride to the food bank."

My tone is earnest, and I know I need to give her more than just this explanation.

"I'll be honest. I went there mostly in hopes it would help me find you — at least that first night." I give her a small smile, hoping she'll understand what my priorities are these days. "But as I guess you now know, I do that pretty regularly — helping out in soup kitchens, teaching the kids in the early culinary classes, the ones who can't afford to go to the CIA or Johnson & Wales, let alone the Cordon Bleu."

"Why cooking, Declan? Why food-focused non-profits? You weren't into cooking when we were younger."

"I was *very* into *your* cooking."

"Is that why? Because I was planning to become a chef?"

"That was what sparked the idea. But when I got into that first food-bank kitchen and saw all those kids, some just a few years younger than me, but struggling to make their lives — their families' lives — better, and doing it by acquiring a skill that you'd learned at your Nonna's side... I admired them. And I wanted to help them — and other kids like them. Help them get jobs if they'd gotten busted for drugs and gotten clean, help the ones facing a lifetime of poverty or abuse if they didn't find a way out. They needed a hand up. And I was in a position to give it to them, after our album charted and especially after I'd gotten some training that I could share with them."

"It's very noble of you," she says. I don't like thinking of it that way. It makes me really uncomfortable, which is why the NDAs have always been part of this deal.

"Noble? Hardly. I figured this was something I could do in your honor, you know? I've got a lot to make up for, a lot of karma to shift back into the plus column."

"Why do you think that?" She asks the question, but I suspect she knows already. The core bits, if not the details — the details I still don't think I can tell her.

"Because I hurt you. The one person I loved with every part of me. The person I'd promised forever. Until I realized I wasn't built for forevers, not with the career Dave and Hunter and I had been building. I knew I'd fail you — probably sooner, rather than later. And I couldn't bear to do that. I thought maybe it was better to break things off at that point. I've come to suspect that I might have been wrong about that, that I might have robbed us both of something we can't get back now, and that I probably hurt you more badly than if I'd been truly honest about my reasons for it."

"It never made any sense. It came totally out of the blue."

"I realize that now. But I was 17 and I was stupid. And in the middle of trying to do what I thought was the right thing, I kind of panicked. I said things I should never have said. Things that weren't true. I figured if you could blame me, hate me for what I was doing, that it would be easier for you, easier to get past it, move on, find some guy who'd be better for you, especially as a husband."

"I never wanted anyone else, Declan. Not then. And not since. And, frankly, I stopped trusting people. Especially men. I'd trusted you to be there for me, just like I'd planned to be there for you, whatever happened, no matter where life took us."

"And then I threw it away. The best thing I'd ever had, and I threw it away."

Tears stream down her face, and I'm a moment away from losing it myself.

I reach around behind her, pulling out the thing I saw her stash behind the pillow, clearly hoping I wouldn't see it.

I run my fingers across the title on the front of the album.

"'Our Wedding'... You really kept this all this time? Even after what I did?"

"I couldn't bring myself to throw it away. The glue wasn't even dry on the paper bits. I've had a few times I was tempted to burn it, but I just couldn't do it. So, it's mostly sat in the back of my closet."

I open the cover, finding the ribbons knotted just as we'd left them after the ceremony, slipping our hands out, rather than untying them or cutting them. Lyric had said it was symbolic, that the bond we'd made wouldn't be undone or severed. And yet I had. Well, I'd thought I had. But would Callie and I be here right now if that bond had truly been severed?

I turn the page, flipping through the photos. There's that happy Declan. The kid thrilled to have married the girl he loved, the kid making solemn promises that he had no business making but still did so, with total conviction. And the guy who looked back at me in the mirror in Callie's bathroom what seems like months ago but is more like a couple of weeks. The guy who woke up in the bed of the girl he'd loved for his entire adult life, even if he'd decided early on that he couldn't allow himself to keep her.

"You were so beautiful that day…" I tell her, touching the image of her face captured in the moments after it was all said and done. "I don't mean you aren't now. I already told you you're even more beautiful than you were back then."

She blushes, and it's enchanting and frustrating all at once. Has no one ever told her that? Not since I left her? Someone should be telling her that every day, at minimum. Dare I dream she'd ever allow me to be that person?

"But the light in your eyes… That was the moment I knew I'd done the right thing. No matter what our parents said, I knew I'd done the right thing when I saw your eyes light up. You were joy incarnate, and I wanted to hold that against my heart for the rest of my life."

She looks away, and I can see that this visit to our past is bittersweet for her, just as it is for me. But the real question is what the next part of our story will be.

I turn pages, glancing over the images of her bouquet, Callie standing serenely in front of the ocean, looking devastatingly beautiful that that dress, even though it was just an everyday dress and not a fancy official wedding dress.

Then there are the other mementos of our summers together — a mini-golf scorecard (she kicked my ass), tickets from the amusement park, a flattened wrapper from the frozen custard we shared, a few of the emails we'd exchanged between those summers, the fortune from the fortune cookie she got one night when we ordered Chinese ("Fate isn't always kind. It reveals its ends in its own time"), the movie ticket stubs from the one time we managed to pull off something resembling a real date, courtesy of Nonna. Despite that, there aren't a lot of pages, and before I realize it, I'm at the end of the album. Faced with a photograph of two people I never met, but who hated me nonetheless.

"That was the last photo I got from them, on that trip to India that same summer. They were due to come home the next day, but Mama stuck that photo in the mail. I think she wanted the postmark to mark the end of the trip in some tangible way. She'd done that before, with their trips to Greece and Italy, Egypt…"

Suddenly, I have this terrible thought.

"What happened to them, Callie? I know they weren't mentioned in Nonna's obituary. Did they find out we got married and you ended up estranged? I mean, I know Nonna liked me, but I—"

"They died. That day Mama sent the photo. There was a car accident, on the way to the airport."

Stunned is not a sufficient word to describe it.

"That was..."

"About a week after the last time I saw you."

# CHAPTER 36

## HERE COMES THE RAIN AGAIN

### Declan

"Oh, god... Callie... I..."

Declan Carter, frontman, is rarely at a loss for words, but me — I've got none right now. Not one.

"Nonna took me in, and I lived with her during my senior year of high school." She says it very nonchalantly, as if we're talking about what classes she took that year and not the fact that her parents had died a week after I broke her heart. "We both worked in the restaurant. Me part-time and her full-time. I saved up for living expenses I knew I'd have in New York, once I got to culinary school, and afterward, while I worked my way up the ladder."

"What about your parents' estate?"

"There wasn't a lot, as it turned out. They'd been making minimal payments on the mortgage, but we were living on an adjunct professor's salary, with a little bit from my mother's art restorations. And they traveled. A lot. It wasn't inexpensive, but they prioritized that, with my father's research and her focus on art."

"And not you."

"Not so much, no. I mean, they weren't bad parents, and I'm sure neither of them expected to die before I'd even graduated from high school. But I'd been the surprise baby they had during college — the one who'd derailed my mother's graduation and her career plans, extended the time it took my father to earn his master's degree, who forced them to move out of the dorms and get an apartment that cost a lot more... And the thing that kept them from traveling, like they'd both dreamed of doing once they'd gotten their degrees. Now, it seems obvious that there was this disconnect, and why. They both resented me — no, it's OK, I've had to accept that," she says when I start to object. "And they didn't understand me, so they stood in my way anytime I found something I wanted, whether that was culinary school or..."

"Or me."

"Yeah." She sighs. "But Nonna *got* me. We were so much alike."

"I noticed that the first time I met her. You looked a lot alike, but it was your spirit, and your passion for cooking, that I noticed was so similar."

"I don't think Mama liked that, that I was so much like Nonna and so different from her. She'd lost her independence because of me. And here I was wanting to get married before I'd even finished high school, with no desire to get a degree — just the training I needed to become a chef. I think she kind of looked down on Nonna, actually, like cooking was a domestic chore that was beneath a modern woman, and there was no way she'd have her daughter follow in her mother's footsteps, working in a kitchen."

"I thought Nonna was your father's mother. I called her Mrs. Martino that first day we met."

"And she told you to call her Nonna, without correcting you. Nonna — she was Aoede Valentina D'Agostino Molinari. Mama named me after her, which goes to show just how much Mama changed after I was born."

"But you're Calliope, not Aoede."

"Aoede's my middle name."

"I'm lost here... I thought it was Angelica!"

She laughs.

"No — Nonna called me '*Angelica*' all the time. It was her pet name for me, because I was her angel."

Well, I feel kind of stupid now. I married the girl, and I didn't even know her middle name. But it fit her, that pet name. It felt like part of her.

"You were my angel, too, you know. A blessing I let go, knowing you were too good for me."

"Why do you think that, Declan?" She looks both concerned and curious.

For half a second, I consider coming clean, telling her the truth I'd avoided when I broke up with her, still trying to protect her. Looking back at it, I realize I'd been as reluctant to tarnish the memory of what we'd had as I was to admit I'd slipped, even accidentally. And, truthfully, I still am. We've got enough baggage. Confessing that ugly truth now won't make that load any lighter, but it would likely change how Callie sees me, and our brief marriage. And even if she never wants to see me again after this summer, I can't bear the idea of her thinking even less of what we had.

"Oh, you know — the rockstar lifestyle, choosing to pursue that instead of being a husband," I say. It's a partial truth. "I was stupid enough to think I couldn't have both. And then, once I'd hurt you like that... It confirmed I was that guy I'd been trying to protect you from."

"You could have given us a chance. We had another year of school to go, another summer."

"I never came back, Callie — by the next summer, the band was getting popular, and I stayed in Virginia with Dave and Dad while Mom had the beach house to herself the entire time. And I couldn't risk running into you again, because I knew seeing you would be too painful, and I — I didn't want *you* feeling that pain, either. So I never came back here, not even once. Until now."

"And then it turns out the mutual friends neither of us ever realized we had were getting married."

"Yeah." I catch her gaze, make sure she's looking at me. "Never in a million years did I think you'd be here, Callie. I assumed you'd be a sous-chef at some fancy restaurant in New York or Philly."

"I only went back to Philly to gather up my stuff, what I wanted to keep from among my parents' possessions."

"It's still a little strange that we were both living in New York, at least for a few years. And I never ran into you."

"It's a huge city. And I didn't exactly socialize — well, at all, let alone in the same circles you do."

"And we've been on the road so much since our first album dropped, it's unlikely I'd have run into you even if you had."

"Do you even feel like you really live in New York?"

I shrug.

"It hasn't been important. My main home for most of the year is a tour bus. I've barely slept in my own bed for the last seven years."

OK. That's awkward.

"But lots of other people's? she asks.

"No, not really."

"I see — quickies with groupies in the dressing room, right? A little mutual release, an autograph, a selfie, no phone numbers?"

"No, actually. Not for a long while."

"How long has this penance been going on?" Her expression is intense. "How long have you been faking trysts with groupies to get away from your security?"

"About six years."

"And before that?"

"I was a very busy boy. But still not sleeping in other people's beds."

"Dressing rooms, right?"

"Dressing rooms, hallways, restrooms, a bunk on the bus... I wasn't picky."

"And neither were they, I guess."

"Hey!" I complain, just a little offended.

"I meant about the settings, not you, rockstar."

"Again — part of the lifestyle. But it hasn't been like that for most of us for a while. Hunt's mostly been off groupies since Brighid walked in on him."

"And onto models and influencers instead, apparently," she says dryly.

"For a while. I still think he was avoiding anything that smacked of commitment. Otherwise, why date multiple women at the same time? And he'd been dodging them when they showed up at shows, too, though I don't think any of us realized that until we got here. Appearances can be deceiving, as I've proven. I'd suspected Hunt was hung up on Brighid, but I had no idea he was so deeply in love with her. I don't think *he* did, actually. That's why it was so messed up between them for so long and so very messy when the blinders came off. Literally."

"So, that's what you've been doing, too? Avoiding commitment?"

"Other than the band, Callie, I've made one commitment in my entire life. And I broke that. But it didn't change how I felt about you. I figured I didn't deserve that kind of happiness, with you or anyone. So I never tried."

"So, anonymous encounters instead?"

"For a while. But, honestly, cooking a meal in a soup kitchen has been much more fulfilling than getting off with some stranger ever was."

"Hence the duplicity with the security team and social media."

"I faked what they expected of me so that I could do what was important to me."

"And take no credit for doing it."

"I don't want any credit. I don't deserve it."

"Just like you don't deserve to find love, to be happy…"

"God, you get me way too well after twelve years apart."

"You forget — I saw the guy under the would-be rockstar, the one who felt like his parents would never be proud of him, no matter what he did, the one who lit up when people watched him perform, whether it was two people or twenty, the one who lit up nearly as much when Nonna called him part of the family."

I'm a little stunned. That was something I'd never told her. When it happened, we were still too young, too new, for me to be thinking in terms of marriage, even if Nonna seemed to have other ideas.

"I envied you, honestly. I mean, I figured out later that your parents weren't much different from mine. But you had Nonna, and I'd never really known either of my grandmothers — one dead when I was just a baby, the other living overseas, out of contact with everyone. It was the first time I'd really seen a grandparent dote on their grandchild. In the same moment that I wanted it, I was so glad that you had it. And I think a little part of me was hoping that it was something you'd eventually share with me."

"I would have. Gladly. But, in the end, she was all I had."

It's like a candle flame guttering, then gone. The warm memories of Nonna's kitchen, of the warmth between them, the sunshine of her smile — all extinguished in a moment. And I know I'm the one who did that.

"What happened, Callie? You still know me so well, but..."

"I'm different than you remember? Harder? Colder?"

I've seen so many emotions in her in these last few weeks. I recognized the passion, the pride in her work, even the anger. But there's also an almost brittle hardness to her at times.

"Declan, I lost three of the four most important people in my life in the space of two weeks. One day, I'd been a happily — if secretly — married woman. The next, I was the girl who got dumped, with an explanation that offered no closure. It might not have been my first instinct to run to my parents at a time like that, considering how they'd disapproved of our entire relationship, but I would probably have thrown myself into my mother's arms the moment she got here."

"But she never did."

"No. And, again, someone I'd counted on to at least be present in my life was suddenly ripped away. Nonna — she was surprisingly stoic about it, about losing her only child. And it might have seemed natural for us to comfort each other, but it was a while before either of us could bring ourselves to even talk about it."

"What did she say about the breakup?"

"I never told her exactly what happened. I actually didn't even tell her we'd had the wedding ceremony until a few months before she died, and she just accepted it then, like it made total sense to her. But she knew that first day that my heart was broken. I don't think she knew what to say. She'd believed in you and me almost as much as I had. She'd trusted we'd end up together, and I'd trusted that, too, with the promises we'd made to each other. But she and I were both disappointed."

I can barely look at her. I see what little hope I had for us making this work start to slip away.

"So, I buried myself in work, in school, in getting ready to go to culinary school. Nonna was focused on the restaurant, and half the time we ate together, it was in silence, because neither one of us knew what to say to the other."

"You didn't know Brighid in high school?"

"No. I mean — I know now that she was there, that the girl everyone called Ellie was her. But I was a new kid coming into senior year. No one there knew me. Lyric was homeschooled. And between work and the fact that I was in mourning over too many losses to bear..."

I cringe. If I'd had any idea...

"I wasn't exactly a social butterfly. I barely talked to Lyric... And, honestly, it's taken a while to rebuild our friendship from that. She was hurt, naturally, that I'd pulled away. She had every right to be. She hadn't had a ton of friends, either — I mean, her mom is kind of... odd, and she homeschooled. But I didn't want to talk about how I was feeling. I didn't want to go to see a movie or talk about boys or hang out listening to music." She shakes her head. "No, definitely not that. Eventually, she stopped trying."

"That must have hurt."

"Honestly? I was relieved. I'd realized that the reason I'd been hit so hard when everything happened was because I'd let myself rely on people. I mean, you should be able to rely on your parents, but they'd gone off on their own, with barely a thought for me, over and over again. I'd been an unwelcome burden, and I knew it. Them dying so suddenly was just one last bit of distance between us. A permanent one this time."

"And you'd relied on me."

"I had." She nods. "More than I'd realized, I think. We'd talked about college, culinary school, finding time to be together until I finished school and could get a job, either here or in Virginia."

"And I'd asked you to marry me."

"I didn't say yes on a whim, Declan. I didn't tell my parents what we wanted to do, knowing they'd flip out, without giving it some serious thought. They nearly packed up and came home, until Nonna assured them we couldn't get married without parental permission. And I didn't take Lyric up on her offer to do the ceremony thinking it was something fun to do as part of a 'summer fling,' as Mama had called it."

"I meant it when I asked you," I tell her emphatically. "I meant it when I asked my parents for permission, the same as you did yours. And I meant it when I made those promises in front of Lyric."

"And then you took it all back."

I can practically hear her heart shatter all over again. I swallow, hard, and look down at my hands, fingers laced together between my knees and so tight it's almost painful.

"You're supposed to get cold feet *before* the wedding, Declan, not after! Getting married isn't like buying a television or a car — you don't get to claim buyer's remorse and act like it never happened!"

"It wasn't like that — not in my head, anyway. I promise you that. I botched that conversation as badly as I've ever botched anything." I take a deep breath, knowing this explanation is long overdue. "You remember I said earlier that I'd lied to you that day?"

She nods slowly, cautiously, as if she's afraid of both the lie and whatever I might reveal is the truth.

"Callie, I loved you the moment I saw you that first day on the boardwalk — your eyes lit up with excitement over the music, your smile so open and full of joy, your hair tucked back but with a few strands here and there that had escaped your ponytail and curled against your skin where you'd started to sweat just a little."

She rolls her eyes at me.

"It was cute! I assumed it was from running down the boardwalk in the sun to hear us play. I figured out later that it was from being in the kitchen, cooking. But I was done-for in that moment. I half expected a heavenly chorus to join in on our song in celebration of the arrival of an honest-to-god angel. And later, when I met Nonna and she called you Angelica... It seemed like some kind of benediction from above, a sign confirming that you were the one for me, that you were it."

I sigh.

"From that moment, I was head-over-heels in love with you." Surprise registers on her face. "I mean — I played it cool." I chuckle. "At least as cool as a 15-year-old guy can play it, anyway. But I wanted to spend every spare minute I had with you. Those hours you were working, every moment I wasn't performing, I wanted you with me. And even when I was performing, I wanted you there, watching, so I could sing for you like I had that day we met."

"You never said any of this to me. I mean, I figured it was just me, romantic teenage girl, crushing on the cute musician."

"You thought I was cute?" That's 15-year-old me smiling back at her.

"You know you were cute. You've never been lacking in ego — definitely not since you went from cute to devastatingly handsome."

"You think I'm handsome? *Devastatingly* handsome?" That's 29-year-old me gladly accepting that I've got at least that much going for me as I try to win Callie over again.

"Declan..." she groans, rolling her eyes at me. "You're getting off-topic."

"So I am... You'll have to forgive me for wanting to relish you telling me you're attracted to me."

"And always have been... yada yada."

"Right... Anyway — I loved you at first sight." Skepticism takes over her face. "Truly. I'm not being schmaltzy or selling you a bill of goods! I wanted every moment of every day to be spent together, and I always felt like something was missing when you weren't with me."

"Me, too." With those two words, I start to wonder if maybe, just maybe, I have a chance to fix this.

"When we left at the end of those two summers, went back home and to school — I was never a great student, but I was in a constant state of distraction, waiting for your next email, waiting for school to end so we could come back here, where I could see you, touch you, spend time with you, play songs for you. I think I said some of that, but by then, I think we both knew this wasn't just a one-sided crush for either of us."

"Yeah. Nonna knew, too."

"I think she did. That's why she always encouraged us, gave us extra time together..."

"Got me on the pill, because she knew it was inevitable that we'd start having sex."

"You were so gorgeous... I couldn't believe how lucky I was that you wanted to be with me."

"And I'd managed to catch the eye of the future rockstar."

"Not my eye, Callie — my heart."

"And you told me you loved me. And you married me. And then you took it all back." She says it so matter-of-factly...

"That was the lie, Callie. Me telling you I'd never really been in love with you — that was the lie I told you that day. The one I never should have spoken. It wasn't true. Not even a bit."

"Then why? Why say it? Why break up with me? It still doesn't make sense."

"I'm not sure I can make it make sense. Not now. Not to you. I just know when I needed to tell you I couldn't fulfill my promises to you, I wanted it to be, 'It's not you, it's me.' I didn't want you to think it was your fault, something you'd done, something you were missing. And in that moment of sheer panic, realizing how badly I was hurting you, the only thing that came to mind to say was that I'd made a mistake, that I'd been stupid and jumped the gun on us, on the wedding, that I'd been immature and impetuous, and I was owning that mistake."

I take her hands between mine, looking her in the eyes.

"I was wrong. *That* was the biggest mistake I made. Ever. I was a stupid, panicked 17-year-old boy, and about the only true thing in all of that was that it was my fault. Because you were... You were perfect, Callie. It was like the universe had peered into my head and taken notes on what my perfect woman would be like and crafted you to match. I loved you from the moment I saw you. And... I never stopped. Not for an instant."

I wait for a response. Something. Anything. But she's frozen, her body, her facial expression. Finally, she looks away, avoiding my eyes, pulling her hands free. She stands up, pacing in the space beside the coffee table, and I'm terrified that I've messed this up by moving too fast.

# CHAPTER 37

## SHE TALKS TO ANGELS

## Callie

I don't know what to do with that. I don't know what to say in response. He's always loved me? He still does? How do I even begin to absorb that, let alone deal with it? He said he made a mistake before, but maybe the bigger mistake is the one he's making now. And I'd be making an even bigger one if I let him.

"I'm not the same person I was at 17, Declan. And I'm not deluding myself for a minute in thinking you haven't changed. Probably a lot. But I know I'm different." I start ticking off points on my fingers, taking a few steps before turning and taking a few more in the other direction. "I don't let people in. I don't trust. I don't ever expect anyone to have my back — not even Drew or Lyric. I know I can't rely on anyone but myself. Not where my life is concerned. Everyone who I ever relied upon has either failed me when I needed them most or was taken from me, or both. And I knew at 17 that I couldn't let that happen again."

Declan's quiet, waiting for me to finish, giving me time and space to say what I need to say to him. It's both wonderful and terrifying, and I leap blindly into it.

"I spent a lot of years building up that protective shell around me, learning to keep people at a distance, to not get attached. I watched other people's lives go on around me — the relationships, the marriages, the friendships — and I knew that wasn't something I could have, because I'd tried for it once and fell flat on my face. And the damage that did wasn't scrapes and bruises. It was soul-deep, Declan. I'm a hollow shell with a block of ice for a heart and a knife where my hands should be."

"I don't believe that for a minute," he says, his jaw set. He shakes his overgrown hair out of his eyes, and I know I'm in trouble. That hair, those eyes... How many times have I seen them in my dreams? "I've seen you — with Drew," he says, "with your staff, Raquel... And the girls — they love you. They're your friends. They've been there for you, even if you didn't think you needed them."

He's right about that. Even Rory, who I barely know at all — she'd taken time out of her life to teach me something she felt I needed to know if I was going to save my business, and maybe myself. And it worked. As much as I'm still trying to bend my brain around this stuff, I have to admit that it worked.

But none of this was what I'd intended — not these new friendships, not letting Lyric so close again, not getting so attached to Drew, and now his little family. And Raquel... Our circumstances were different, but she does, I have to admit, remind me of me at that age. Even that tough outer shell. She's just done a much better job of letting people in.

And now... Declan. Who isn't the man I'd thought he was. Not the player. Not anymore, anyway, if I can believe what he's said — which for some reason I do. And not the egomaniacal rockstar who doesn't care about anyone besides himself. Not even the shallow, immature kid who threw away our marriage, or at least who I thought threw away our marriage because he was shallow and immature. He may have said he had never loved me, but as I look in his eyes now, full of concern, caring... I see that boy I loved more than anything, and I want that back. I want it so badly.

And that, if anything, is reason to keep my distance. I take a step back, away from him. Hurt flashes across his face for just a moment, then compassion, and it nearly breaks me. I turn my back to him, look at a blank section of wall, trying to find that calm, quiet space that Rory showed me. *Ground. Center.* A deep breath. Then a second. By the time I've made it a third, I'm calm enough to face him again. His expression is nearly the same, with an added trace of determination.

I am in such trouble.

The hard, impenetrable protective shell I built for myself at 17 and continually reinforced for the last twelve years — it's cracking now, like Declan's fingers are the only thing that could pry it apart. And underneath is that onion-layer shield Rory helped me build — the one that filters, rather than acting like my own personal prison. I feel vulnerable, and I don't like it. At all. A wave of fear washes over me, and I know it's coming from within me, not from Declan or anyone else.

"You have no idea how many times I've wished for a time machine, especially since that night at the engagement party," he says. "I know this is my fault. But I want to fix it. I want to prove to you that it's OK to trust, that you can rely on the people who love you, whether that's me or Drew or the girls, that we won't abandon you or leave you to fend for yourself."

He stands up, approaching me slowly, carefully, like he's afraid I'll crumble, or explode. I don't know which, but still he moves ever closer.

"But most of all," he says, "I want to prove to you that you can trust yourself — that your feelings don't have to be stuffed deep inside, away from the world, like they don't exist, and that you can express them, act on them, and still be safe. Because you have people who love you, heart and soul. And I know that because I'm one of them. And after twelve years, it's past time I told you that. Because that's the truth. It always has been."

## Declan

She falls into my arms, like gravity returning an object to earth, to the place it always belonged. And I finally feel like I can take a breath. This odyssey of ours isn't over. Not by a long shot. I'm not so cocky as to think it is. But we've taken a big step today, dumped some of this really heavy baggage we've both been carrying around for a long time. It starts to feel like maybe there's a path forward — not just to safety from the middle of the minefield that is our past, but to a place where the future is one we can create, together.

"You know — I don't want to talk about this anymore," she says suddenly, stepping away. "I've had too much of this heavy stuff weighing on me for too long."

"I know the feeling."

"I bet you do... Otherwise, I can't imagine how that sweet guy I married ended up with a reputation of being a gargantuan dick to everyone." She pokes me in the ribs, making it clear she's teasing me, and my body finally starts to relax again. But she's right.

I take her hand and pull her back to the sofa with me, sitting close, but not quite touching.

"I lost the thing that made me happy. For a while, I tried to distract myself with the band, girls..." I meet her gaze, hoping she'll understand. She doesn't look put off. Maybe she's just come to accept that those crazy days were a part of my life. My past. "But it was all a little hollow, and every day I became just a little more bitter, acted out just a little more. The band, building our fanbase, going on tour, signing our recording contract — that was the only goal I had, and as soon as we'd taken one step, my focus was on the next one, and then the next one."

"What step is ahead of you now? What's left for Declan Carter to achieve?"

I chuckle, mirroring the reaction I'm afraid she'll have to my answer.

"Don't laugh... But I want to be as big as Mace Mason. Bigger. I want people to look back in twenty or thirty years and say, 'Freddie Mercury, Robert Plant, Jim Morrison, David Bowie, Chris Cornell, Declan Carter — the best rock singers of all time. Legends.'"

She's not laughing.

"That's some impressive company there. Even being on par with Mace would be a major accomplishment." She hesitates before she continues. "Keep in mind that I know next to nothing about the music industry, other than the music I loved before I was 18. But how does one get to that top tier? How do you become a legend?"

"You keep making great music and putting on great performances. You sing your heart out, leave your guts on the floor after every concert. You bleed for them — the people who love your music, who get what you're doing on a musical level and what you've been through. You tell them your most personal stories, knowing that they've been there, too, for the highs and the lows."

She's quiet for a moment, serious.

"What's left for you after all of that, Declan? Once you've dumped the highs and lows of your life into a song and laid it out for everyone to hear? What's there to fulfill you, make you happy?"

There's a reason I said Callie gets me. I don't think anyone's ever asked me that question. Not even in the context of "Is not being truly happy what's making you act like such a dick?" Certainly, no one's ever asked what I want, what it would take for me to be happy. Don't get me wrong — I'm satisfied with my life. But just that — satisfied. Happy? That's another thing entirely. And after all she's told me tonight, I want to open up to her, too.

"I get a lot of satisfaction out of performing, touring."

"Satisfied isn't the same as happy, Declan. You talked about me not stuffing down my emotions. What brings *you* joy?"

"The sound of the crowd after the last encore."

"Nothing else?"

"Knowing I've helped someone learn a skill they can use to make their life better."

"Are you doing that because it makes you happy or because you feel like you still have to make up for hurting me?"

I shrug. "Both."

"Well, I don't want you to feel like you owe me anything."

"I owe you more than I could ever possibly repay, Callie." I take a deep breath and plunge ahead. "You want to know what gives me joy? The look on your face when you know I've enjoyed the food you've prepared." I run my hand down her cheek. "Your expression when you come, and you finally let go and just let the pleasure carry you away." She blushes, and I'm tempted to make that happen again, right now. But there's more. "That radiant smile of yours when you're remembering all the good times, the sweet moments, the love..."

"I want to find the sweet again," she says, interrupting me, giving me hope that she really heard me earlier. "I really do. I want that back in my life. I stuck these memories in a box in the back of my closet, because losing all of that hurt so badly that I couldn't think of the good parts without feeling sad, bitter or angry. I want to be able to remember the good bits and have them just be good again."

"I'd like that, too. For you, and for me."

"Then let's do that," she suggests. "You tell me a memory that made you happy, and I'll tell you one of mine. We'll let everything else just fall away."

Her stomach grumbles.

"Callie — did you eat tonight?" I can't help but laugh.

"No. I normally bring something back up with me when we close up for the night. I got a little distracted tonight."

"Can I cook dinner for you?" It's a spontaneous offer, and I should be done with cooking for the night after working with the culinary students, but at this moment, I want nothing more than to show Callie how much I care about her... how I want to care for her... and to do it through food.

"You don't have to do that. I can pull together a salad or something."

"I want to, Callie. Will you let me do that for you?"

"Can you cook something other than risotto? I think I need to take a break from rice for a while," she says, laughing.

"Your wish is my command. Any requests?"

"Surprise me. I trust you." Those three words... they're the second-sweetest three words I've ever heard, and I nearly fall to my knees. The other three... Maybe we'll get there again. In the meantime, I'm going to cook something for her, and I'm going to put my heart into it, just like she does every night.

# CHAPTER 38

# HEART AND SOUL

## Declan

"**D**id you seriously cook me grilled cheese and tomato soup?"

She laughs loudly, it's instantly one of my favorite sounds. Actually, I guess it always has been... It's just been too long since I heard it. I made her sit on the sofa while I worked in her kitchen, and we reminisced, just like she'd suggested, recalling our favorite parts of our summers together. After the first three times she started watching me and I made her turn back around so I could surprise her with my culinary skills, she finally settled in and just talked. Now, she's sitting on a tall chair at the island and it's the moment of truth. And I'm dealing with a skeptic.

"I did indeed cook you grilled cheese and tomato soup."

"It's the height of summer, Declan."

"It's comfort food, Callie. It has positive associations with warmth, caring, simple, easy times. Besides — you haven't had my grilled cheese and tomato soup! This isn't the stuff from a can, 'Just add water,' and I got more creative than throwing some 'cheese food' between two slices of buttered bread! Come on — you should try everything at least once, remember?"

"Fine. But my expectations are low."

"Then you'll be pleasantly surprised. I promise."

She looks dubious, but she picks up her spoon, giving me one last skeptical glance before she brings the soup to her mouth. I wait for her reaction, holding my breath.

"OK. I take back any suggestion that you'd gone softball with this cooking thing tonight. Wow. If Nonna had made tomato soup — which she never did for me, because I was always here in the *summer*, when tomato soup is *not* commonly served — she'd have made it like this. As a matter of fact... Is this... Is this Pappa al Pomodoro?"

"Indeed it is! You had everything I needed, including the slightly stale bread and fresh basil. It's canned tomatoes, of course, but I knew you'd have the best ones."

"San Marzano all the way! Nonna had tomatoes in her garden, but that's the next best thing. And as for the bread — I've been busy. I kind of forgot I even had that loaf."

"Kismet! It's like the bread gods knew I'd need to cook you a traditional Tuscan soup!"

"Don't get cocky, rockstar. The jury's still out on your grilled-cheese skills."

"Luckily, you had fresh focaccia..."

"Did you... Did you turn it inside-out?"

"I did. More flat surface area to caramelize in the butter."

"You're scaring me, Declan. Where did you learn to cook like this?"

"At first it was like I said — I begged lessons from Aurelia, our tour catering chef. Snuck them in whenever I could. I picked up more basics in the soup kitchens and food bank kitchens. We didn't get much downtime, but whenever we were in New York for a few weeks, I hired a guy from the CIA to teach me some more advanced stuff, give me some ideas about flavors."

"The culinary institute, right? Not the intelligence agency? Because it seems like you've also acquired some super-spy skills along the way, with the eluding your security and creating alibis..."

"You do what you have to," I tell her, shrugging. "Now, to quote award-winning Chef Callie: Eat, before it gets cold."

She picks up a triangular half of the sandwich and, after giving it a cursory examination, takes a bite, chews, pauses, chews some more... The suspense is killing me.

"Is that rosemary butter?"

I nod. "Goes with the focaccia."

"The cheese... I know I had some Brie in the fridge. And pear?" I nod again. "Prosciutto? And there's something else..."

"A light drizzle of honey-mustard."

She takes a second bite, chewing thoughtfully again.

"I may need to put this on my lunch menu," she finally says. "And the soup. Wow."

"You enjoy that. I'm going to clean up after myself."

"I think I'm in love..." she mutters, taking a third bite of the sandwich after dunking it in the soup.

"What was that?" I ask from the kitchen, hopeful.

"I said I'm in love with your soup and sandwich combo."

"I see."

I drop it there. It's not a huge leap from her loving my food to loving me again.

"You remember that time Nonna dropped us off at the amusement park, and we spent the entire afternoon trying to obliterate each other with bumper cars?"

"You should not be allowed to drive outside of a bumper-car track," she says. "Every time you ended up in reverse, you just drove around that way, like a maniac!"

"It wasn't me who was the maniac! Who was it who purposefully T-boned that 9-year-old just to chain-react my car?"

"Well, she was in my way!"

"And you made her cry, so we had to leave before they threw us out!"

"And we ended up playing the frog-pond game, only you were so excited about landing one frog on the lily pad that you leaned too far over the side of the pond and fell halfway in!"

"Not my finest moment," I admit. "But that game is hard!"

"Hey — you remember ordering a pizza and having them deliver it to us on the beach?"

"You're the one who didn't want to leave the shade of the beach umbrella to get lunch!"

"I didn't want to get sunburned waiting for them on the boardwalk!"

"Hmm... That *was* a very small swimsuit. Probably better that we didn't risk additional sun exposure to your very fine ass... But that delivery guy couldn't take his eyes off you."

"And you stiffed him on the tip, after he walked across all that sand!"

"Hey, if he'd kept his eyes on where he was walking and off my girlfriend, I'd have given him a great tip."

"Mmm... I remember those days, sitting on the beach, you rubbing sunscreen into my shoulders..."

"And other areas..." I remind her. "Come here." I gesture for her to scoot over closer to me on the sofa, turning her so her back is to me."

"Declan..." she says, her tone chiding.

"I'm just going to massage your shoulders. I promise."

"That sounds heavenly, actually."

She leans back into my chest, and muscle memory kicks in. With all the time she spent on her feet in the kitchen during those summers, a massage was one of my favorite ways to help her wind down at the end of the evening. Well, a favorite for both of us, really. And by the time I'd gotten halfway decent at it, it became foreplay, too. So easy for hands to migrate from shoulders to breasts, from tops of thighs to those lovely places between them... But I promised. Shoulders only.

After a few minutes, Callie's head is slack, leaning against my shoulder. It's more than the bonelessness of a good massage. I carefully peek around the side of her head and confirm it. Her eyes are closed, her breathing slow. She's asleep.

As teenagers, we never had many times like this, where we could just relax together at the end of the night. At 16, my mom was keeping too close of an eye on the clock, unless we had a rare formal gig somewhere. And I wasn't bold enough to ask Nonna if she'd let me sleep over, even after she'd taken Callie to get on birth control. I kind of felt like we'd been gifted with her blessing on our relationship, and I didn't want to push my luck too far.

It's hard to believe that that kid became the guy known for quickies with groupies in his dressing room, threesomes in hotel rooms. And sitting here with Callie like this tonight, reconnecting with her and with our past selves, it's the time in between that seems almost unreal. I feel like I'm that 17-year-old again, head over heels for an amazing girl and wanting nothing more than to be planning a future with her. I mean, I wanted the band. I wanted us to be successful, get famous. I wanted that, too. But if you'd told me at 17 that I'd have to choose between a normal life with Callie and the exciting, sometimes surreal, life of a rockstar... I know which I'd have picked.

Now that I know that Callie lost her parents so soon after our breakup, my mind is full of what-ifs, ideas about what I could have done differently, what I *would* have done differently if not for that one night...

Nonna wouldn't have held us back from getting married. I know that. As soon as I turned 18, I could have moved to Mystic Beach and gotten a day-job delivering pizzas and gigged with Hunter at night. Hell, Dave was already 18. He could have come with me.

We could have gotten an apartment, the three of us. Hunter wouldn't have had to leave Mystic Beach to get away from his dad. He could have stayed here with Brighid. And Callie could have moved in with me, like a real wife, or stayed with Nonna until she was ready to go to culinary school, then come back and moved in with me. The band would have built a following here. It might have taken us longer to get discovered and signed, but I know we'd have gotten there. My parents would have pitched a fit about college, but they did that anyway, and Hunter paid the price for that, ending up out on his own for a while, at 18.

Fuck. Where is that time machine?

I know I can't go back and undo what happened. And I know if I'd made different choices, it might have changed things just enough that nothing I've accomplished would have happened. We might be playing backyard parties instead of arenas and stadiums. Without her self-imposed isolation, Callie might have met someone at culinary school and divorced her teenage husband back home.

I'm not sure Brighid would have even left Hunter to go to college, let alone sold her yarn art for enough money to start her own business. Or she could have ended up falling in love with some frat guy and settling down in Virginia, and Hunter... I suspect Hunter would have self-destructed at some point. He was on the cusp of heading down a bad road when an overheard joke pulled Brighid away from him — and that was the thing that woke him up, made him start to change his life for the better. Just like I'd grown out of my self-destructive, self-punishing phase and found a way to feel like I was redeeming myself. Was that for me, or for Callie? Maybe it really was for both of us. I don't know.

What I do know is that I wouldn't exchange this feeling... of having Callie relaxed in my arms, feeling safe enough to fall asleep, her belly full of my cooking, air cleared and our minds full of sweet memories... I wouldn't trade that for anything. Not millions of dollars, millions of fans, all the awards and accolades. Not even having my name mentioned among the legends of rock.

I don't know where we go from here, but I know I want to move slowly, carefully, so I can avoid making the kinds of mistakes I've made in the past. I want to savor this time with Callie. It's a second chance I never thought I'd get. Never dared dream I'd get. But tonight, it actually feels like that dream could come true.

I slide my arm under her back, the other under her thighs, and carry her to her bed. She's solid, not feather-light, but I spend enough time in the gym that I can manage. I always loved her body — athletic but with ample curves, which have only been enhanced now that she's a grown woman. She's truly grown into her beauty. I lay her down gently, but she seems to be a light sleeper, and she stirs before I can cover her with a blanket.

"Declan?" she says, still half asleep. "Did I fall asleep on you? Sorry..."

"It's fine. It was nice, just sitting quietly with you."

She blinks, still groggy.

"I'm sorry I wouldn't listen when you tried to explain about those girls..."

"It's OK, Callie. It's all sorted out now. You know the truth. That's what counts."

"And I'm sorry I took that other photo... I was just so angry. But it's you who should be angry with me — not listening to you, almost making a huge mistake like that..."

"I'm not angry, Callie. I don't blame you at all. You were acting on something you thought was true. And now we both know where we stand."

"Yeah... Too far away. Come get in bed." This sleepily coquettish vibe from her makes me smile.

"Tempting, but no."

"No?" She's starting to wake up now.

"I'd love to see that look on your face again, when I suck your clit until you can't stop coming..."

She moans.

"But not tonight. I'm going to head back to the studio." She pouts. It's so cute and out-of-character for grown-up Callie that I almost change my mind. But I want something else even more right now. "Callie, I want us to try again. I want to see if we can put the past behind us, start with as much of a clean slate as we can get, taking just the best memories into the future, and try to build a life together, like we used to talk about."

"Then why are you leaving? I don't understand. Did I do something?"

"No! It's nothing like that. I just want us to take things a little more slowly than we did the other night. I want to do the things we never got to do — go on real, grown-up dates, spend some quiet time together without worrying about parents or the end of summer..."

"But you're supposed to be leaving soon..."

"Not *that* soon. We're way behind on recording this album, and I've been kind of stuck on the songwriting. The album will get done when it gets done. Dave's a part owner of the studio now, so we'll get some extra leeway there, and the label's been generous. Anyway — the bottom line is I've got some time, and spending a chunk of that time with you might be just what I needed. I want to do that. I don't want to lose any more time than we already have. But I want to do it right this time."

"OK. But we've already slept together. Why are you trying to backtrack on that? I know I'm a little rusty... You can be honest with me."

I stop her right there.

"I hurt you once with a lie, and I'm promising you now — I will always be honest with you. And the honest truth is you are glorious. Everything I ever dreamed of, and all the more amazing for the fact that you're back in my life. But I want you to be really sure about this, about us. I don't want this to be something we do because it's comfortable, familiar. Or because we're horny." We both chuckle, and it's good to see her relax again. "Callie, I'm serious. I really want this — us. But I promised you forever once, and I messed that up. This time, I want us to be forever for real. And I don't want to start forever with a quick fuck when we're both tired and feeling nostalgic. I don't want to feel like we're taking any of this for granted just because we've done it already. I want to take you on a real date, like a normal couple working to build a relationship that's going to last."

"OK."

"OK?"

"Yeah. OK. My next night off is Sunday. But I'll warn you..."

I wait, getting concerned about what she might be set to lay on me.

"It's going to be very hard for you to beat grilled cheese, tomato soup and a shoulder massage. You may end up having to put out."

Oh, that smile of hers... the lightness shining out from her now that she's starting to feel safe with me again...

"I'll put some thought into it, come up with something creative, something special."

"Why do I suspect time with you is going to feel special no matter what we do?"

"I don't know. But you're not the only one who feels that way."

Looking down at her, I remember everything I ever loved about that girl, and the rapidly growing list of things I love about this woman. I lean over and kiss her forehead.

"Goodnight, Callie. Sleep well. I'll see you on Sunday."

"Goodnight, Declan. 'Til Sunday."

I slip out her door, locking it on my way out. I pause on the landing, inhaling a deep breath of fresh ocean air and marveling at the stars sparkling in the midnight blue sky. Ah, there it is — not the Big Dipper, but the Great Bear. The symbol of the legendary king who let his kingdom crumble but who, it is foretold, will return to build it anew.

# CHAPTER 39

# ONLY THING MISSING WAS YOU

## Callie

It's the third time this week that there's been a knock on the door before I've even gotten down to Castalia. The first time, I kind of hoped it was Declan, wanting to get in a little morning fun, despite what he'd said the other night. Instead, I was greeted with a large bouquet of roses, their white petals edged in red. And there's a card...

> *The red rose whispers of passion,*
> *And the white rose breathes of love;*
> *O, the red rose is a falcon,*
> *And the white rose is a dove.*
> *But I send you a cream-white rosebud*
> *With a flush on its petal tips;*
> *For the love that is purest and sweetest*
> *Has a kiss of desire on the lips.*

*I didn't write this. John Boyle O'Reilly did. But when I read it in English class senior year, it made me think of you. I wanted to send you roses like this, flowers as purely beautiful and sensual as you are. So now I'm making up for lost time. Be ready to go out at noon on Sunday. Dress for fun!*

*— Yours, Declan*

Declan must have been paying attention to the things I'd put in our wedding album. Despite his mention of wanting an "adult" date, it wasn't a fancy restaurant we went to, nor even a movie, let alone something rockstar-extravagant, like a day-cruise on a yacht or something. No, we went to the amusement park, spending hours trying to obliterate each other with bumper cars, laughing all the while. Declan won that insanely difficult frog pond game (without falling in this time), and awarded me the prize of a giant teddy bear. It came down to the wire, but I edged him out in skeeball, adding to our haul of cheap stuffed animals that instantly became very valuable to us both.

We took a break for a late lunch, getting a table at a bar that wasn't hopping yet on Sunday afternoon, and being left blissfully alone, despite the fact that the waitress clearly recognized aMUSEd's frontman when she saw him. Then it was mini-golf, where I again dominated Declan, even winning a card good for a free game when I sank the ball into the clown's mouth at the end of the course.

"We'll have to do this again," he said, smiling that seductive smile of his that seems to merge the 17-year-old boy I loved with the sexy rockstar.

"Maybe next time you'll actually win!" I teased.

"I think I won enough today, just being with you."

And he kissed me, sweetly but deeply, like a vision from the past had been brought to life.

We held hands on the carousel, his black horse and my white one racing side by side in circles that I instantly wished would go on forever.

It was a quick dinner of fish tacos and margaritas, and then a walk along the beach, getting our feet wet in the ocean, Declan scooping me up in his arms when one wave washed up higher and faster than we expected. And then another kiss — deeper, more passionate, exploring, promising more. So you can guess how surprised I was when we arrived back at my apartment and I got a chaste peck on the mouth and a brush of his lips across the back of my hand, right before he walked back to the studio.

"Thank you for the best date I've ever had," he said in parting. "I hope we can do this again. Soon."

"But..."

"*Soon*," he said, his tone full of meaning, before turning and walking back down the steps from my apartment door.

But the next morning, there was that knock on my door again and another bouquet of roses, this time with a single red rose at the center.

*Thank you again for a perfect date. I'm working on a new song today, feeling inspired. I'll see you tomorrow. Sometime. It'll be a surprise.*
*— Yours, Declan*

And now, this morning, a third bouquet, in a glass vase, with two red roses at the center.

*Have a good day at work today. I'll see you later. Can't wait!*
*— Yours, Declan*

I take the flowers down to Castalia with me, setting them on the ledge behind the host stand, where everyone can enjoy them. Thoughtful of him to include a vase this time. I used my second — and last — one with yesterday's bouquet, now sitting on the kitchen island where he'd cooked me the most amazing sandwich and soup I've ever had. I'd told him it was good. But, honestly, I undersold how good. Declan's an amazing cook. I'm even curious now to try *his* risotto.

Many hours later, we've hit the height of the dinner rush, and there's no sign of Declan. Maybe he plans to show up at closing time and do a late-night date? Dare I hope he might be looking for more than a chaste kiss goodnight? That one night together kicked my libido back into full gear, like it hadn't been a decade since I'd had sex. And if he hadn't been so sweetly insistent that we take things slow, I'd have pressed the issue that night we cleared the air and reminisced. I don't know what the future is going to bring us, since eventually he will go back to his life in New York and on the road. It's not like I can pick up and abandon Castalia to go on the road with them, like Brighid's talking about doing.

"It's nice to hear you humming while you cook again, Chef," Raquel says. "You used to do that all the time when I first started working here."

"Oh? I never even noticed."

"Yeah — you stopped for a while there..."

"When Declan first got here..."

"Yeah. But now you're doing it all the time, even more than you did before. It's nice. It makes the kitchen... more welcoming, somehow."

"That's good to know." I shrug. I never even realized I did that. Maybe during all those years avoiding music, I'd sublimated my love for it into my cooking instead. I mean, apparently I'd sublimated my emotions into my food, too. So maybe those two things just go together.

"You have a diner who'd like to speak with you when you have a moment, Chef."

A-ha! That has to be Declan! I'm going to have to think up something special for his meal tonight.

I finish up the simple cacio e pepe I'm working on, adding the fresh pasta to the butter, which I've spiced with three kinds of pepper and a dash of za'atar, and stirring in an effusive amount of Pecorino and Parmesan. A bit of marjoram, and it's ready to serve.

It was Fatima who suggested adding the za'atar to the traditional Italian dish, when I was working in her and her husband Khaled's restaurant in New York for a brief time. The Palestinian American couple split cooking duties — she handled desserts and breads, while he took charge of the rest of the menu. I was fascinated with the ingredients they sourced from Palestinian farmers, including za'atar, and Fatima had noted the Italian cuisine's staples of pasta and rice, while her own relied on bread and rice. From there, it was only a small leap to use the za'atar she used on her taboon or mana'eesh bread on my pasta.

I send the dish out with Raquel, then head straight to Declan's usual two-top.

"Good evening, Chef," he says, that sexy smirk of his belying the formality of his words.

"What can I do for you tonight? Steak? Fish?"

"You can sit," he says, standing up and gesturing to the second chair at the table.

"I wish I could, but we're slammed right now."

"Never fear — I have brought backup!" he says, gesturing again to the chair, insistent that I sit. Perplexed, I do it anyway. A minute off my feet won't hurt. Much.

"Your apron, please," he says, holding his hand out.

"Declan, what is this? I can't disrupt the dinner service."

"Hand over the apron, Callie," says a familiar voice from behind him.

"Drew! What are you doing here! You've got another week of leave left!"

I start to get up to give him a hug, but Declan pushes me back down into the chair.

"Apron, please," he asks again.

"Just give it to him," Drew says, rolling his eyes. "I needed to get out of the house. Simon and I were driving each other nuts. So we agreed to each go out on our own at least once a week, let the other one enjoy some daddy-and-me time with Andy."

"And you wanted to work?"

"Yeah, I was starting to get a yen... But you'd banned me from coming in until my leave was up. And then Declan called and asked me if I'd be willing to come in for half the dinner shift tonight."

"You didn't!" I say to Declan, more than a little irritated with him.

"Don't get angry with him!" Drew interjects. "Like I said, I needed some time out of the house, and I've been having a yen to cook. This was perfect!"

"And I arranged for David and Piper to watch Andy tomorrow night so Drew and Simon can do their own date-night," Declan adds. "Big Bro and his little mama are trying to get some practice, prepare for what they're in for in another eight or twelve months or whatever. So it worked out perfectly."

"Your brother and his girlfriend just volunteered to babysit a newborn?"

"I may have promised him that I'd spend the next four mornings working on songs with him, instead of sleeping late. He's getting a little antsy about getting the album done, and Piper wants to run live sound for us again, which she can't do until we have more songs to test out on audiences."

"And you're ready to write?"

"Definitely. Feeling very inspired of late." He gives me a look.

"Alright, you two — since I'm here, I'm not going to waste time watching you two make goo-goo eyes at each other when I could be making a plate of short ribs."

"You should try Drew's short ribs, Declan. They're amazing."

"Maybe I will. But not right now." He holds out his hand again. "Apron."

I hand over my apron, expecting Drew to take it, but as soon as I'm seated again, Declan puts it on.

"What are you doing?"

"Drew's taking over for *you*. Meanwhile, I'm preparing *your* dinner myself."

"In my kitchen?"

"Yup."

"He's going to mess up the flow, Drew," I warn, skeptical.

"He'll be fine. I'll set him up at the end of the line. And, apparently, he's quite familiar with commercial kitchens, if in a different context."

I raise an eyebrow at Declan, wondering why he's decided to let Drew in on the secret that I don't think he's even told Alex yet. But then I guess getting Drew in on this plan might have taken some convincing.

"He signed the NDA," Declan says with a shrug.

Drew smiles, turns around and heads into the kitchen. Declan drops a kiss on the top of my head and follows him.

Well, huh. This is not at all what I expected when Declan said he'd see me tonight.

"Can I get you something to drink, Chef?" Raquel asks.

"White wine. Let Jared pick something."

"Yes, Chef!"

And so I sit back in my chair, like I'm just another diner, in my own restaurant, waiting to see what culinary magic my once-, and *maybe* future, boyfriend will whip up.

"Prince Edward Island mussels, steamed in butter, white wine and garlic, with crispy garlic focaccia." Declan puts the deep, wide plate in front of me.

"Where did you get PEI mussels? My supplier ran out this week!"

"I have my ways," Declan says cryptically. "Which may or may not have involved hiring a courier to fly them down here on short notice."

"Declan..." I shake my head. The extravagance of it...

"I made sure he brought enough to fill your usual order, once Drew told me the report from the kitchen was that you were out. That should tide you over. You can put them back on the menu. Now, eat."

I give the dish a detailed examination. Every single mussel is perfect. Medium-large, no cracked or broken shells, open just enough that you know they're done but not tough.

"I made sure they all snapped closed before I cooked them," Declan says, setting down a separate bowl for the discarded shells. "They're all fresh and safe to eat."

I should have known he'd make sure they were still alive before he cooked them. Giving me food poisoning wouldn't be a great way to start this very unique date.

I take the tiny seafood fork and dig in.

The mussels are tender, sweet, with that pure ocean taste of fresh seafood. The garlic and...

"Shallots?"

"Milder than onion," he says, giving me a wink. Ah, yes, all those onions he's chopped over the years. It's funny now that I know the story.

"Pancetta?" Now that a few of the shells have been added to the second plate, I can see the little bits in the sauce.

"Gives it a subtle, rich smokiness."

"And parsley and thyme."

He nods.

I pick up one of the pieces of toasted bread and dip it into the sauce, catching a piece of pancetta.

"Oh, my god — I'm going to have to brush my teeth first to get rid of the garlic-breath, but I'm going to have to kiss you when I'm done eating this!"

He snatches up a piece of focaccia and dips it in the bowl, savoring the flavors of the butter, garlic, wine and herbs soaking into the crisp bread. I want to jump his bones on the spot, just from watching the raw sensuality of it. Instead, I take a long sip of wine, swallow, carefully put down my glass and only then look back up at him.

"No worries about garlic-breath now, my dear," he says, leaning over and giving me a breathtaking kiss that pushes the boundaries of acceptable PDA in my restaurant.

Have I said the man is hot?

"I'll have your entrée out shortly," he says, pulling away just as I'm tempted to grab him and yank his lips back to mine.

I fan myself with my napkin and have some more wine. He's going to wreck me if he doesn't come up to my apartment with me tonight. Dinner has barely started and I'm already ravenous, and I don't mean just for his food!

A few minutes after I finish my appetizer, he returns, looking a little pleased with himself.

"Foraged mushroom and spring pea risotto with Parmesan and roasted shrimp."

He places the plate in front of me, and it's like a dish I'd get in a starred restaurant in New York, beautifully plated, the rice having given up just enough of its starch to turn the sauce creamy, slivers of beautiful Parmesan across the top, the bright green peas peeking out amidst the dark brown of the mushrooms and the pretty pinks of the fresh jumbo shrimp I did manage to get in.

"Foraged mushrooms?"

"I know a guy," he says, shrugging. "And he knows his mushrooms."

"Good to know you're not going to poison me..."

"You had a chance to poison me — several, in fact — and despite the fact that I probably deserved it, you didn't."

The smile on his face now isn't that cocky smirk, nor the smoldering one of the sexy lead singer of a rock band. It's sweet, wistful and longing. Asking for something I'm not sure I know how to give. Something I may no longer be capable of giving. But seeing it on his face, I want to. I really, really want to.

"Bon appetit," he says finally, giving me a nod and heading back into the kitchen.

The taste of the dish matches up to its visual beauty. I close my eyes and mull over the flavors of that first bite. It has the savory, umami notes of mushroom, and the bright green accents of the peas, a soft undertone of shallot and, yes, onion, plus the herbal bite of thyme and earthiness of sage, the smoothness of white wine and the intensely rich flavor of the best Parmesan.

Darn it! It's better than mine!

I try to take that realization in stride, deciding to just enjoy every spoonful, savor every morsel of rice and vegetables, the snap and saltwater of the perfectly cooked shrimp.

As I scoop up the last few bites, Raquel returns with a second glass of wine.

"It's good, isn't it?" she says, her smile small, controlled, like she's afraid to let it loose. "It has to be even better with the shrimp and foraged mushrooms, right?"

And that's when I remember that the dish Declan cooked with the students the night I discovered his secret was a mushroom risotto.

"That's right — you've had this dish before..."

"Not like this, but it was still amazing."

"It's better than mine, isn't it?"

She mulls over the question longer than I'd like.

"It's close, but... no — I like yours better. I think it's your stock. It's a little richer."

"I roast the bones first," I tell her, feeling a little relieved. Declan can make a risotto that gives mine a run for its money, but mine can still win, at least with Raquel.

"Chef — I'm sorry I didn't tell you about him being at the food bank, but he was so nice, and the NDA... I really respected him wanting to keep it quiet, who he was and that he was there, helping out."

"It's OK, Raquel. I know how persuasive he can be. He's had that charisma since we were 15."

She does a double-take.

"You've known him that long?"

I nod.

"And you two were..."

"He was my first boyfriend. My only boyfriend," I admit, keeping my voice low. "And I hadn't seen him in twelve years when he showed up here that first morning, after the food bank."

"First love... I remember it well..." she muses.

"I would think so, considering how young you are." I chuckle.

"Hey — I had my first boyfriend at 14! That lasted three months. And I've had a few since, which I now know is something you cannot say for yourself. So, don't act all sage and jaded about it."

"You're right." It's tough to admit, but she is. Where Declan is concerned, half the time I feel like I'm a teenager navigating dating my first boyfriend. Because he was. Is. Is-ish. "Spending time with him like this, it's like we picked back up where we left off... well, before the breakup anyway."

"Who dumped who? Or was it mutual?"

And that's when I realize I've already said too much. Too many people know too much of this story now. And if Declan and I are going to have a chance to really pick back up from when things were still good, I need to put everything in between behind us.

"You were the one who told him where to find me, weren't you?" I ask, instead of answering her question.

There's that look of guilt I've seen on her face a couple times since Declan first showed up here.

She nods, slowly.

"I'm so sorry, Callie — I mean, Chef," she hastily corrects. "He said he knew you, that you'd lost touch over the years, and that he owed you an apology 'and then some.' I figured it was just a matter of time before someone else told him where you were, or he hired a P.I. or something."

"And he'd won you over with that rockstar charisma."

"Actually — no," she corrects me. "It was the expression on his face when he talked about losing touch with you, about wanting to apologize. I'm not sure I've ever seen someone look so... lost, I guess. It seemed like maybe the universe was trying to fix something that was broken, maybe in both of you."

I want to argue with her, tell her I wasn't broken, that she had no right to interfere in my personal life... But, looking at her face, I can see she's utterly convinced that what she's said is true. And that makes me wonder if it just might be.

"Dessert is served!" Declan says brightly from behind her, and it's a relief, not having to answer that question, to her, to Declan or to myself.

"It's fine, Raquel," I tell her. "No harm done."

"Candied peach crème brûlée, with local peaches, cardamom and basil," Declan says as she picks up my very empty risotto plate.

Again, the dish is beautiful, with thinly sliced peaches, browned underneath the hard caramel. It looks like sweet summer in a ramekin.

"Alex went shopping for clothes and jewelry this morning, so I had the kitchen to myself for a change — just long enough to make the custard," he says, proffering a spoon. "I have no idea why he thinks he needs more of either of those things, but they're his thing, aside from keyboards and cooking."

Alex has been scarce since Taste, saying he was working on some things at the studio. And I know the band has been trying to get some writing done now that Hunter's hand has healed. However that happened. But I kind of miss those morning lessons. I kind of miss Alex. But maybe he's just giving Declan and me some time to get to know each other again. That seems like something he'd do.

I take the spoon from Declan and crack the caramelized sugar, noticing it's a little softer than usual for a crème brûlée, probably from that juicy peach. I dig out a sliver of candied peach from the top and scoop a little of the lightly spiced and peach-infused custard from beneath and put it in my mouth.

I can't believe it. He's done it again!

"I may have to hire you, if you get bored with being a rockstar sometime soon."

"Alex will be devastated," he says with a smirk. "I think he had his eye on Drew's job."

"With the second dining room full every night now, I may need to open a second restaurant," I joke. And then I realize it's true.

"Let me know if you need a chef," Declan says with a chuckle. "Or an investor," he adds, his tone shifting from the joke into something else. "I've been looking to finally set down some roots. Especially now that Dave's wanting a break from touring and Hunter's getting married."

His tone is still light, but the look in his eyes is serious, earnest.

I know what I think he's telling me, but I can't bring myself to consider the ramifications. I tuck it away in the back of my mind and tuck into the crème brûlée instead.

"Sit," I tell him. "You've more than earned a reward, Chef," I tell him with a nod of approval, and he takes the other chair.

"And what might that reward be, Chef?" Now his tone is suggestive.

"Well, I was going to say it's getting off your feet, but you've probably earned dessert, too." I hold the spoon out to him, full with another bite of custard and sweet peach, and he leans forward, wrapping his lips around it and slowly pulling back, savoring the dessert. I nearly come on the spot. Then he licks the spoon that my sex-addled mind has left hanging in the air in front of him. And... I think I did just come.

I close my eyes and take a deep breath, letting it out slowly. Ground? Center? What's that? My entire existence is centered between my thighs right now, and I'm desperate to get Declan down there, too.

"It's really good," he says slowly. "But I've tasted things I like better."

We're brain-sharing again, I know. Or maybe it's just that we both want each other so badly right now that there's no question what we're really talking about.

"You getting off anytime soon?" I ask him, teasing him about his temporary chef job.

"Oh, I really, really hope so," he drawls, the double-entendre I didn't intend made utterly clear when coming from his lips. "But, ladies first..."

He stands up and holds out his hand for mine. I take it, ready to run out the door and into my apartment, but I know I should check with Drew first. So does Declan, it seems, because he pulls me toward the kitchen.

"Chef — we've had a lovely evening, but my shift is complete," he tells Drew. "And I need to give some personal attention to this very demanding customer."

"Diner!" Raquel corrects.

"Diner," Declan repeats.

"The diners are always our top priority at Castalia," Drew says. "Get right on that!" he adds with a smirk.

"Yes, Chef!" Declan replies. "I fully intend to," he growls into my ear.

"Can I finish your crème brûlée?" Raquel asks.

"You've more than earned it, kid," Declan tells her before I can respond. And, you know, she really has.

# CHAPTER 40

## HANGING BY A MOMENT

## Callie

"I think an amazing dinner like that deserves a special reward, Chef," I tell Declan as I lock the door behind us.

"Your enjoyment of the food is all the reward I need, Chef," he says, his smile coy, for what I suspect could be the first time ever in his life.

"Nonetheless, I think you've earned something special."

"I think I've already got that."

He pulls me into his arms, kissing me sweetly, and I can't do anything besides sigh. This is the sweet boyfriend I remember from when we were 17. This is the man I married. I'm not sure where we're headed right now, and I won't let myself get caught up on that. I pull him with me to the bed, where I've longed to have him for days now. I sit, unbuckling his belt where he stands. He strips off his shirt, looking down at me with such adoration on his face...

There are times when I wish he wouldn't call me his "angel." I don't want to be that innocent girl I was at 17. She was naive, and she got blindsided. And maybe if she'd been a little naughtier, a little more experienced or aggressive — maybe then he'd have decided to try, to try to stay together...

I undo his jeans with determination. I may be far out of practice at this and lacking much experience in it at all, but I want to show him I can do it. I want to show him how much I want him. Because I do. I wanted him even while I pushed him away. Wanting him was never in question. Being open to having him in my bed, let alone my life, was always the difficult thing. And then he broke open that shell of mine and climbed back inside my heart. Onions be damned. There was no shield that would have kept him on the outside. Not once the illusions had fallen away and I saw the real Declan again.

And now... here he stands... that soft expression taking on a heated edge as I pull his boxer briefs down and lean in... and panic. It's been too long. Do I even remember how to do it properly?

"Callie?"

When my eyes connect with his, he looks puzzled, concerned. Can I even explain? Will any explanation I offer him do anything but make this worse, emphasizing how much different I am from even the briefest of his rockstar conquests?

"What's wrong, angel?" he asks. And it pushes a button I'd only just realized existed for me.

"That's what's wrong, Declan! You keep calling me 'angel,' and it just reminds me how little experience I have... Just you... And it's been so long..."

"Callie, it doesn't matter to me if you've been with one man or a hundred, whether you feel you're out of practice or want to try something new — I think I proved that already," he says, chuckling, and I blush, remembering the words that lured him in for my planned revenge. "Anything you want to do, I'm happy to try, and I don't care if you feel like you got it perfect on the first try or want to try it a million times until you think you've reached an expert level."

"But all those women..."

"Are not my wife. Are not my Callie, my angel. There is no comparison. Anything you ever do to me, for me, with me — it's always going to be special, because it's you. And I'll let you in on a little secret," he says, pulling my hand to his cock. "There is no such thing as a bad blowjob. As long as you don't bite me — hard, anyway," he adds with a chuckle, "having your mouth on me is going to feel very, very good. Possibly too good, because even the idea of it is really hot, frankly, and I'm not sure how long I'll last. But I'm happy to find out!" He crouches down, looking into my eyes. "Assuming you want to do it. Because that's all I really care about — is whether you're enjoying whatever it is you're doing to me."

"I want to," I tell him. "I really want to. I just maybe need some practice, I think."

"Then I am your very willing test subject," he says, standing back up. "Have at it." He strokes his cock, leaving it bobbing in front of my face. And he gives me what is simultaneously a very eager and very silly smile.

And I crack up.

"OK — now that's not really the response a guy wants to get when he suggests his lovely wife go down on him. I know you're out of practice and everything, but this is an expert tip: You should never laugh in the face of a man's dick."

I'm officially rolling with laughter, even if it's on the bed and not on the floor.

"Alright. I see how this is going now. You require a little reset, a little mood-setting to get you back on track," he says, nodding. He grabs the waistband of my pants and pulls them straight off, taking my panties with them.

"You see — this is not entirely unlike the skill you want to practice here," he says, kneeling down and pulling my thighs apart. "The aim is a skillful application of mouth and tongue, with judiciously applied suction." He sucks on my clit. "And carefully directed touches of the tongue." He licks around the sides and then across in a zigzag pattern. I gasp. "On the other hand, even the most direct and seemingly clumsy move can serve a purpose," he adds. And he sticks his tongue in my opening, lapping around the edges. My hips ride up, and he presses them back down to the mattress.

"So — does that give you an idea? Or do you require more demonstration? I mean, I recall you being a visual learner, so if you'd like me to make a short video, I could do that. I'm not sure I should post it to YouTube, though... This seems like the kind of thing for a private subscription service," he says, only making it that far before we both crack up.

"Someone has too many clothes on," he finally says. "It's time to get naked, woman, and you've got way too many buttons going on there."

I strip out of my coat, shirt and bra the fastest I've ever done it in my entire life.

"God, you're gorgeous," he says. "I'd apologize for the fact that I keep saying that, but it's both true and astounding every time I see you, so I take no responsibility for excess enthusiasm."

"You're not half-bad yourself, rockstar," I tell him. "I start to see why you've got so many groupies."

"Fans. I have fans," he corrects. "The moment I saw you again, I stopped having groupies. And they'll all just have to adapt."

"Speaking of which... You think I could work on that practice thing?"

"You sure? You don't have to," he says.

"Definitely. I do remember enjoying it. I'm just out of practice and feeling a little intimated."

"You have nothing to feel intimidated about," he says. "I remember having your mouth on me with great... fondness."

"Fondness?" That doesn't seem like the right word.

"Fortitude? Felicity? Fellatio! That was it!" Now he's smirking at me again. "It was great fellatio. Fantastic fellatio, in fact. You can jump right back on it, with confidence."

"As opposed to jumping on it with my mouth..."

"Whichever you prefer. I'm good either way," he says, standing back up, erect in both posture and penis.

And darned if he hasn't completely diverted my attention from my self-consciousness. How does anyone not realize this man has an amazing sense of humor? And a really amazing set of male anatomy. To which I am now applying my mouth.

"There you go... Perfect... See — you've got this. And me," he says, panting slightly as I surround him with a hand and then pull the rest of him into my mouth. Maybe it's muscle memory. Maybe I just read Declan really well, but it doesn't take much before he's thrusting gently into my mouth, his fingers wrapped up in my hair. "Callie — as much as I'm loving the feel of your mouth on me..." He pulls free, taking a series of deep breaths.

"Did I...?"

"No — stop there," he says. "That was perfect. I mean, look at me."

I do. He's very... erect.

"And we will practice the whole swallowing thing at some point in the very near future, if you want — I promise. But I have been waiting to make love to you for days, and I think you've been waiting, too, based on your reaction the other night when

I suggested we wait. And then tonight... So, I'd really, really, like to do that. Now. Like, right now."

I slide back on the bed and flutter my eyelashes at him. It's a parody of the sex-kitten I'd like him to see me as, but Declan doesn't seem to mind.

"Mee-roww," he says, leaping on top of me. "Where's that last condom?"

I pull it from the drawer of the bedside table, and he tears into it, putting it on himself this time, and I just sit back and watch, eager to have him inside me again. Twelve years was too long. This last week has seemed just as long. I don't want to think about the future, whether that means a few days of busy life, months on the road or... He's crawled inside my heart, and my body's unwilling to go without him now, either.

"I have more in my wallet. Don't worry," he says, noting the concern in my expression. And that's all I need to let go and just let come what may.

"Make love to me, Declan... I want you. Now."

"Whenever you want, angel. Whenever you want."

He brushes his lips against mine, then slides down, taking a nipple into his mouth.

"Your breasts are just astounding, Callie," he says before moving to the other. "I could live in your cleavage and be a happy man."

"I'd rather you were living between my thighs," I tell him, caressing his cock and guiding him toward where we both want him to be.

"Then we'll both be very happy here in just a moment," he says.

He presses himself against my opening, pushing in an inch at a time until he's fully seated within me.

"Fast or slow, Callie?" he asks, tracing his fingers across the place where we're joined. "You're wet for me..."

"Fast and hard, Declan... I want to feel you in me hours after we're done."

He groans.

"I'll never be done with you, angel. But I'm happy to oblige. Hold on," he warns before pulling back and then slamming back inside. He works hard against me, propped up on his strong arms, and then grasping me hard against him as he continues pounding into me. We become a single unit, pushing against each other, panting and grunting at an ever-increasing pace. He bends down to nip at my breasts, and I pull my legs up, wrapping them around his ass and pulling him into me even harder.

"You close, angel?" he asks, panting hard now. "I'm not letting go until you're coming."

He brushes his thumb against my clit, just about where we're joined, and that's all I need.

"Fuck me, Declan... Now. I'm coming!"

He times his thrusts with his caresses, until neither of us has any control over our movements, bodies operating purely in response to the sensations we're giving each other, and then exploding together. I collapse into the mattress as his hips ride out their frenzy, pressing him deep inside me before he collapses on top of me.

"Give me just a minute," he says, panting in exhaustion.

"There's no way you're ready to go again that fast," I tell him in pure disbelief.

"I meant the condom," he says. "But I'll be ready to go again in ten minutes, tops," he says. "God, you're sexy when you let go like that. It's a good thing I'm not having to do a show every night. I'd be too worn out to do more than crawl out on the stage."

It's a reminder of an inevitable separation that I don't want to even think about yet. But it also reinforces what he's been telling me — that it's me who matters to him, in bed and out, no matter how much catching up I have to do in the bedroom.

"That whole swallowing thing — you mind waiting until the next time to work on that?" he asks. "Because I'd like to go through at least a few more condoms first. I mean, it can wait an hour or two, right?"

"An hour or two?"

"It's been a while for me, too, Callie. We're both making up for lost time. And I've got a lot more orgasms I want from you."

"I'm not going to be able to walk tomorrow, am I?"

"Not if I can help it, no. But you'll enjoy getting that way. Trust me."

And, for some reason, I do.

# *An hour later*

"I could live off those sighs," Declan says as I settle back into the bed for the third time, already a little sore, but, yes, in the best way possible. "If angel food had a sound..."

He kisses me again, this time taking my lower lip between his teeth and nibbling at it. I wrap my arms around him pulling him in for a deep kiss.

"You'd think neither one of us had eaten tonight," I tell him. And then I realize... "Wait! Did you eat? You cooked for me, but I never..."

He shushes me, putting his finger over my mouth.

"I did a dry run with Alex before I left for Castalia," he says. "He and I taste-tested everything."

"Wait — you cooked with Alex?"

"Well, I did the cooking. Alex and I both ate."

"And..." This I can't wait to hear.

"He was impressed. Again."

Now his expression is both coy and proud.

"Did you make *him* sign an NDA?"

Declan laughs.

"I should maybe have made *you* sign one, but I think we're way past that point," he says. "We'll call it spousal privilege."

I'm still working on girlfriend/boyfriend. Jumping back into husband/wife is a little intimidating. But it's a little less terrifying than it was a week ago.

"Did you tell Alex how it is you know how to cook?"

"Do you think I'd do that when I could continue to torment him with the mystery?" he asks, smirking at me.

"I start to see where your reputation for being difficult comes in," I tell him, chuckling.

"Just difficult? Most of the time, people call me a dick."

"I think you've got a... challenging sense of humor," I tell him. "And I don't think everyone understands that about you."

He stares at me, and then tilts his head, considering.

"You really are my person, aren't you? These guys have known me for more than a decade, and I'm not sure they get that. Heck — I'm not sure Dave does."

"Do they assume you're just being an ass when you say things like that?"

"Usually."

"That's their loss if they do."

It's also very sad for Declan. If he hadn't already decided I was "his person," I'd still feel compelled to offer him some understanding. I also start to see why it is that he's thrown himself into his work with the food banks and culinary programs. If they've welcomed him as warmly as the local one has, it has to be an incredible relief to him — no star treatment, worshiping at his feet, and no expectations formed on his reputation for being difficult. I mean — what "difficult" celebrity shows up at a food bank, asking to help out with the unglamorous work of cooking hundreds of meals for those in need, with the caveat that no one know they'd even been there?

"I try not to let it bother me," he says. "In fact, I try not to let anything bother me. Not really, I mean. I'll complain when the lighting isn't exactly right on stage or when they mess up the requirements in our riders, because we don't need to get off on the wrong foot for a gig because Hunter's pitching a fit about getting the wrong orange soda or Kier's homesick for real Irish butter on his bread."

"And you're not picky about stuff like that?"

"Not as much as my reputation would suggest," he says, shrugging. "The lighting, yes. Because I don't want to be blinded when I'm trying to connect with the audience. My mics, the mix in my in-ears — yeah, I'm picky about that. It's a key part of the show we deliver to an audience who paid a pretty penny to get in. And I may be picky about my shoes, my clothes — but that's a practical thing with 'costuming.' Alex cares about clothes whether he's on stage or off, because it's who he is. I just keep focused on our image."

"You're not at all who people think you are, are you? The playboy, the egotistical lead-singer. That's all misperception — intentional and otherwise, isn't it?"

"Some of it, at least," he says. "The manwhore image is old news. I outgrew that a long time ago, figured out how to channel my frustration in more productive ways. I just let that notion of me persist. Maybe it was a bad idea, but..."

"Your reasons for doing it were good ones, worthwhile ones."

"I think so, yeah. I knew the label, the security guys — they wouldn't have let me go out on my own, not to neighborhoods like the ones I frequently end up in, especially for the soup kitchens. And the moment I turn up with a security detail, those NDAs are all but useless. It changes people's perceptions of me. They don't relax around me, don't see me as a person."

"And that's important to you."

"Yeah. Especially in that they let down their guard and really see me. No one sees Declan Carter, Rockstar, and listens to what he has to say about roasting garlic or food insecurity. I become a circus sideshow, and that doesn't really help — not in the direct kind of way that I really want to. Hunter's only been able to do some real good with mental-health issues because he had a tragic story to tell. If it was just a cause he supported, the message would get lost in the celebrity factor. It had been, until things came out this summer."

"And you need to feel like you're making a difference."

"Not just a difference — a difference for real people, individuals I can see with my own eyes."

"You're a good man, Declan Carter. Rockstar or not. I'm glad somebody besides me can see that."

"I haven't lived a perfect life, and I'd never try to pretend I have, but doing this — it makes me feel like I'm setting some of those wrongs right again."

"Just don't do it for me, OK? Not anymore. Promise me."

"I don't know that I can," he says, his expression guilty. "It's not that I'm refusing, Callie. I just don't want to promise you something I can't be sure I'll deliver on. The two things are still entwined in my head, and I'm OK with that. So I hope you can be, too."

"As long as you're doing it because you want to. For you."

"I am. That much I can promise. I get a lot out of the work. If I didn't, I wouldn't have worked so hard to make sure I could do it."

"Then I'm happy for you, happy for this man you've become. You've learned a lot, but you've given far more."

"You have no idea how much it means to me to hear you say that," he says, kissing me again and pulling my back against his chest.

It's a position I'm getting used to, Declan spooned up against my back, both of us worn out in our pursuit of mutual pleasure, but both of us also feeling connected, relaxed, at home. It makes falling asleep easy, pleasant, with the promise of more pleasure when we wake. I snuggle into him, looking forward to it.

# *The next morning*

I wake, rested and relaxed, in a way I can't remember feeling before. At least not as an adult. Maybe I slept this soundly as a child, awoke this refreshed, but I can't remember the last time I did.

Declan...

Isn't here.

I stretch, reaching across the bed and finding it empty.

And the emptiness is profound.

Did I mess up last night, after all? What would have gotten Declan out of my bed at this hour if something hadn't gone wrong? I wrack my brain, trying to remember anything that might have bothered Declan, and I'm at a loss. Even that slightly delayed practice seemed to have gone really well. Unless it was the fact that I needed to practice at all...

There's no note. There isn't even a single sign that Declan was here last night, aside from me waking up naked, with my clothes in a pile on the floor.

That's the realization that gets me moving. I can't lie here in bed all day, wondering and waiting. So I get in the shower, get dressed in clean clothes, throw the others in the laundry. As I toss the laundry basket back into the closet, there's a knock at the door. There he is!

Or not...

"Delivery for Callie?"

It's the same florist, but a different delivery person. Once again, a large bouquet of crimson-tinged cream roses with a cluster of crimson roses in the center and a fancy crystal vase. And more this time — a woven basket full of goodies from Suzi's bakery: croissants and blueberry preserves, a quiche Lorraine, a fresh loaf of focaccia and another of country-style Italian bread, and a tall cup of... steamed milk with sweet vanilla syrup. A caffeine-free alternative to coffee, which Declan clearly remembers I don't like the taste of.

It's a twist on our beach brunch. A clear statement of "no hard feelings" on that front, with an overriding tone of caring. And there's a note:

*Hated to leave a beautiful angel alone in her bed, but I'm working on being the guy who fulfills all his promises, no matter what. And I promised Dave I'd work on songs this morning. Enjoy a leisurely breakfast for once. You've earned it. (Hope you're walking OK, even if it means I fell short there. If so, I'll gladly keep working on it.) I'll be thinking of you all day, and I'll see you after your work is done.*

*— Declan*

I've got time to eat, even after sleeping later than I'm accustomed to. That I slept at all is astounding, after how much I struggled to sleep with Declan in my bed the last time. How much has my life changed in this short time that it now feels strange to awaken *without* Declan in my bed?

A hefty slice of quiche, a croissant with blueberry preserves and one vanilla steamer later, I put away the rest of the bounty and head down to Castalia, fortified for a full day and only a little sore. The day goes smoothly, and I catch myself humming while I work — a habit I notice now that Raquel pointed it out. There's no sign of Declan by the time I lock up, but I refuse to let it worry me. Much. I'm sure he just got caught up in work. I'll probably get a text in an hour or two, or a visit in the morning.

I'm distracted enough, though, that I don't notice that something's different until I've locked my apartment door behind me and dropped today's coat and pants into the laundry.

It's the scent that catches me, finally. Savory, with a hint of spice. It's coming from my slow-cooker, which I know I didn't leave sitting on the counter this morning, let alone full of... chili? It's switched over to the warming setting, ready to be eaten. I grab a bottle of water from the fridge, finding that it, too, offers dinner fare — a big salad of fresh greens with a carafe of green goddess dressing.

Clearly, Declan wanted to make sure I didn't have to make dinner tonight when I got off work.

"Angel?" a voice calls sleepily from my bed.

Speak of the devil...

"Did you make me dinner?" I ask him.

"*Us*. I made *us* dinner. Something that could sit for a while and be just as good when we got around to eating it."

"'Got around to eating?'" I ask, curious.

"Well, I've got some more work to do if you're walking around that easily..."

And that's when I realize he hasn't just been asleep in my bed — he's been sleeping naked in my bed. Declan Carter, keeper of promises...

I laugh. And then I strip off my shirt, bra and panties, climbing into his lap.

"Welcome home, angel..." he says before taking possession of my lips, and the rest of my body.

## *An hour later*

"Are we really doing this?"

"God, I hope so. As often as possible," Declan says with a smirk, running his hand along bare skin, from my thigh to my ribs.

"No — I mean this thing—" I clarify, gesturing between the two of us. "Us."

"Like boyfriend and girlfriend?" Declan asks.

"Yeah — that."

"Are you up for that?" he asks.

I think hard, wanting to be sure.

"I think I might be... Yeah, actually."

"I should throw coins in fountains more often," he says.

"What fountain have you been throwing coins in? This isn't Rome, you know."

"I could fly us over there tomorrow, if you want to change that... We could take in the cuisine first-hand, get some ideas for that second restaurant."

It's another extravagant notion from the rockstar, and my initial response is silence, my mind blown. But it's too extravagant to consider seriously, and I've got a business to run. I can't just take off for parts unknown. Or known, really. And, whether by plane, train, boat or automobile, going to Rome would mean traveling, and that's a thing I'd long ago resolved never to do. As for the second restaurant... It's just too soon. It's all too soon. Too much, and too soon. We've made enough progress that I can get myself to agree to trying a relationship with Declan, but the rest...

"Maybe we can talk about all of that once Drew's back full-time."

"Deal."

"And I haven't decided to open a second restaurant."

"But you will."

"Why are you so certain of that? I haven't even really thought about it, let alone discussed it with anyone. And I'd have to take out a business loan. That contest money is a drop in the bucket of what I'd need."

"I'll fund it," he says, so casually that my defenses are triggered.

"I don't want your money, Declan. I told you that before. I want the restaurant to succeed on its own."

"That's the thing, Callie — it has. You need a second location because you've done such an amazing job of building Castalia up from the ground, of making it a success. No investor in their right mind would turn down the chance to invest in a second restaurant with you as chef, or executive chef, if you want to keep working at Castalia and give someone else the head chef job... or even take some time off, travel... maybe come on tour..."

Again with the travel. I'm starting to have an anxiety attack even thinking about it.

"I don't travel."

And now that's caught Declan's attention. Maybe it's sunk in that I've said that before.

"Why is that, Callie?" He's curious, but clearly sympathetic. He wants me to say it. Fine.

"My parents died while they were traveling. I mean, they were coming home, and they died just trying to get to the airport!"

"And I could get hit by the town trolley tomorrow."

Well, that's a horrifying image that I won't be able to get out of my head now.

"That doesn't help. Especially when you already said you basically live on a tour bus..." Images of horrific tour-bus crashes replace the one of Declan smacked to the ground by a little trolley bus.

"Sorry," he says, seeming to mean it. "My point is that life is always a risk. But how can you really value it if you aren't enjoying it, using it to experience new things, new *foods*? We talked about this before... about you limiting your life to such narrow confines..."

"The morning you showed up in my kitchen..."

"Yeah. Listen, Callie — I've made a lot of mistakes in my life. I've had a lot of experiences, too, and I wouldn't want to go back and undo seeing the Parthenon or the Taj Mahal..."

"You've been to India." My voice is flat, merely observing a fact.

"Yes. And pretty much every major country in the world," he says. Again, so casually. "I don't always get a chance to do the tourist stuff, but I try to find the time to try the local cuisine, as well as helping out a soup kitchen or something."

"You've been to India..." I repeat.

"Oh..." He suddenly realizes what he said. "Callie — I'm sorry. I didn't think."

"No — it's OK. I just... I'm sorry — I don't really want to talk about this right now."

"OK. But I do want to talk about it later, when you're ready. OK?"

"Yeah. Just..."

"Give you some time."

"We're brain-sharing again," I tell him with a smile, eager for the change in subject.

"There's nobody I'd rather share a brain with," he says, chuckling a little. His demeanor shifts to tender, and he strokes my cheek, kisses me softly on the mouth.

"Me, either."

"You have no idea how good it is to hear you say that."

"I think I have a clue..."

"So, we're doing this thing?"

"Yeah." I nod definitively. "We're doing it."

"Ooh... That sounds like an excellent suggestion!" He says, his smile lascivious.

"Declan! We haven't even eaten yet!"

"Are you saying it's not?"

"Well... now that you mention it..."

# CHAPTER 41

## ANGELS

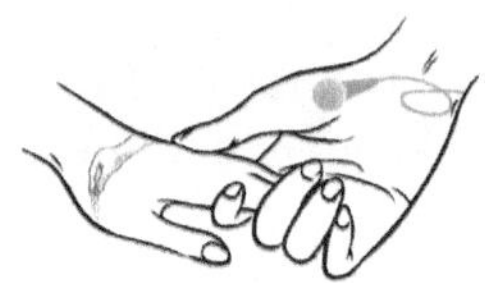

## Declan
### *A week or so later*

I can't remember the last time I was nervous about performing. Hunter's a pacer, and he used to practically wear a hole in the floor of the dressing room when we were getting ready to go on stage. He doesn't do it much anymore, but that's the thing I think of when I realize it's me who's pacing this time.

I shouldn't be nervous. I have no reason to be nervous. I live for this, for being up on stage, singing my heart out in front of a crowd of strangers, giving them this music, our music, my music. The song I really wanted to do tonight — it's not finished. It's close, but I'm known as a perfectionist for a reason. So, instead, I added a new cover to our setlist.

And I guess... I guess that's really why I'm nervous, because it's a song I usually only sing when I'm alone. I stopped singing it the moment Dave walked into the room that night when I was commiserating with a bear. In fact, this is the song that's symbolized Callie to me for most of the last decade. An old tune by a musician from Belfast by the name of Gary Moore. You may have heard of at least one band he was in for a while. A little group called Thin Lizzy. You might even have heard their song "The Boys Are Back in Town." Now, he'd left the band at that point, as he did a couple more times later on. But it's actually one of his solo tunes that grabbed me by the balls the first time I heard it.

Clapton covered "Still Got the Blues (For You)" as a tribute to Moore, and that should tell you how amazing the guitar part on that song is. Kieran, of course, already knew it like the back of his hand, with Moore being from Belfast and part of the legendary Dublin-based band, even though it was first released when he was a toddler. And, honestly, I think if we ever recorded this one, he'd give Clapton a run for his money on the guitar part.

The vocals — that ball is in my court, which is probably why I'm pacing now. OK — it's half the reason I'm pacing. The other one being that Callie's here. For the first time since it was just me, Dave and Hunter busking on the boardwalk, Callie's going to be in the audience to watch me perform. It's the main reason I wanted to do this song tonight. But singing this song, in front of her...

"Still Got the Blues" is a straight-up torch song. The singer is lamenting a long-lost love that he never got over, never stopped loving. It's full of pain and longing and lessons learned, the chief of which is that losing his girl has left a gaping hole in his chest. Kind of like the one I'd had in mine for twelve years.

In that time, I've written songs about being the kid who could never please his parents, who rebelled against the future they mapped out for him, and who kicked ass when he did. I've written songs about life on the road — so many faces with names I never knew or remembered, crammed into a moving motel room with four of my sometimes-unwilling adopted brothers and my frequently-unwilling actual brother, no roots and no anchor. I've written songs about the pressure of the spotlight, the drive to do better, get better with every single concert, song and album, of wanting to be a legend.

What I haven't written is a single love song, sad or happy.

Dave writes those. Which, in retrospect, is kind of weird, considering he'd never had a regular girlfriend, at all. But I guess he's proven to us all now that he was always a romantic at heart. He just needed to find the right girl. And now, probably not coincidentally, he's written his first real ballad. Hunter had years of writer's block without Brighid there to inspire him, so now, naturally, he's got love songs pouring out of him. Alex has even written a few, which I guess makes sense, considering how fixated he's always been on everyone else's love lives.

But me? No love songs. Not one. Until now. But like I said — it's not done yet. The story I want to tell in that song isn't done yet. So it'll have to wait. Instead, it'll be Gary Moore's words that tell Callie what it's been like for the last decade and change, missing her, lamenting the choice to let her go, wishing things had been different. His words, my vocals. And as any aMUSEd fan could tell you, my vocals can tear hearts out with the best of them. But they've never hit this close to home.

"Dec, you OK there?" Kieran asks. "I've never seen you pace before, and you're wearing a right hole in the floor."

"Can you wear a left hole in the floor?" Rhys asks, with typical Rhys randomness. Alex doesn't smack him on the back of the head this time.

"I thought pacing before a gig was my thing!" Hunter says. "You stealing my moves, Mr. Legend?"

"He's nervous because Callie's here," Dave says.

"And because he's singing that song for her," Alex adds.

"I need some air," I tell them, walking out of the dressing room and straight to the edge of the water. It's not the ocean, and I'm not Dave, with his king-of-the-sea impression, but there's more oxygen out here or something, because I'm instantly about ten times calmer. Or it might be because Callie's standing behind me.

"You OK?" she asks, laying her hand on my arm. "You looked a little... green there for a second."

It could be Callie *is* my oxygen. Because the moment she lays her hand on me, I'm no longer in danger of flying out of my body and careening away at full speed. Instead, I'm sinking into her, like she did into my arms that night we jettisoned all that baggage we had.

"Just needed some air."

"Uh-huh..." She's dubious, which makes sense, since she and I are brain-sharing so much now that we're back together.

Did I mention we're back together? I mean, we haven't run off and eloped, but I'm liking that idea quite a lot now that I thought of it. But the important thing is we're back together. Other than rehearsals for this show and spending time in the studio, writing with Dave and working on recording Hunter's stuff, I'm spending all my time either with Callie, in her restaurant or in her apartment, waiting for her to get off work. Drew's leave is nearly up, and he's been transitioning back in with half-shifts, which has taken a lot of pressure off of Callie, so she's been extra-relaxed — happy, even.

Or that might maybe have something to do with me, and the fact that we're back together, and the fact that I've been giving her amazing orgasms morning, noon and night. Don't look at me like that. She went a decade without having sex. I've got to make that up to her! It's a difficult job, but someone has to do it.

"Are you thinking about sex again?" she asks, smirking at me.

"Maaaybee..." I admit. "Is that brain-sharing, or do I have a tell?"

"You have a certain smile that starts creeping across your face, but it was just a guess."

"So, both then." I pull her into my arms, my forehead to hers, now letting that smile take over my face. "I could go kick the guys out of the dressing room..." I suggest. "Bending you over the sofa in there would do wonders for my nerves."

"So, you are nervous! I thought that might be it."

"I don't get nervous. That's Hunter."

"I wouldn't know. I've never seen aMUSEd perform before. And you did seem a little anxious there."

"*Fine*. I'm nervous. *Was* nervous. Not anymore. Seems there's an instant cure for stage-fright, and it's called Callie." I kiss her gently, then deepen the kiss as she opens up to me. Man, I could do this all day...

"Don't you have to go on in a few minutes?"

"Maybe. But you're so hot it won't take me long to take the edge off."

"And leave me hanging?"

"Never. I'd go on late for that. The audience won't mind. You get a little loud when I go down on you. They'll think it's the opening act."

"Declan!" She's outraged, but she's really not. I can tell. Yeah...

It's amazing how much we've settled in with each other in this short time. It's like we've been transported back in time, into our 17-year-old selves, and then downloaded an instant update with the grown-up parameters. See — it turns out I didn't need that time machine after all. And I got to keep the chart-topping singing career, with no worries about butterflies flapping their wings!

Now I just need to finish getting Callie over her fear of traveling... and get her on board with letting me invest in her second restaurant. But, hey — I'm Declan Carter! I can be charismatic and persuasive when I want to be!

"You," she says, giving me a peck on the lips, "need to get backstage and get ready to come out with your band. If you were any taller, I wouldn't be any good hiding that pretty face of yours from this crowd, and there are a *ton* of people here tonight."

"Yeah. I think Hunter and Brighid's little scandal and them going viral clued in a lot of people that we were here, even though I had them put us on the marquee as The Flu Fighters tonight."

"That was you? It sounds like you're a PSA for vaccinations!"

"No — see, Dave Grohl comes here sometimes..."

"The drummer from Nirvana?"

"Well, yeah, but he has his own band now, and he's their lead singer, plays guitar..."

"And that has something to do with this ridiculous fake name you're using for the band?"

"They're called Foo Fighters."

"What does that mean?"

"You know what? I have no idea. I should maybe ask him that the next time I see him."

"You've met him? The drummer for Nirvana?" She's visibly starstruck at the idea.

"You realize the lead singer of chart-topping band aMUSEd just offered to go down on you in a dressing room, right? What am I? Chopped liver?"

"I kind of forgot for a minute. In my brain, you're still mostly my 17-year-old boyfriend."

"And you like 'em young, eh?" I waggle my eyebrows at her. She smacks me on the arm.

"You know what I mean!"

"I do. And you're so cute when you're like this. Reminds me of a certain 17-year-old girl I had this *huge* crush on."

"That's one lucky girl," she says, smiling slyly.

"Nope. I'm the lucky one. I was an idiot, and she still gave me a second chance." I kiss her forehead.

"Smart girl."

"I think so. The smartest."

"Well, this smart girl is reminding you that you're going on stage in like a minute now, so you'd better go join your bandmates."

"Awww... Do I have to?"

"Yes. Otherwise I won't finally be able to see aMUSEd perform."

"And you don't want to miss that. I can promise you that. I've even got a surprise just for you."

"Oh? Why am I frightened?"

"Because you know your boyfriend is a recovering idiot and jackass, and he might find a way to screw things up again?"

"Nah... He's a good guy. He just made some mistakes early in life. I'd like to think he's learned his lesson."

"Well... now that you mention it..."

"What?"

"Just wait... You'll know it when you hear it."

"O... K... Now I really am frightened."

"Love you, Callie." I give her a quick kiss and take off without waiting for her response. Not hearing those three words coming back at me would totally throw me off for the gig. I'll let her find them in her own time.

# Declan

"Good evening, ladies and gentlemen and non-binary folks of all ages!"

Alex told me it was not trans-ally behavior to say just "ladies and gentlemen." So I expanded. He's got that socially-correct thing down pat, except for the occasional off-color joke among friends, usually involving handcuffs or something (which should, in retrospect, have been a clue that he'd have keys handy). Me — I've spent so long being an asshole to everyone when I'm not on stage that it didn't even occur to me that my intros were exclusionary. But now I know better, and it fits right in with my new-and-improved not-a-dick Declan, so I'm all for it.

"We are The Flu Fighters, and we're here to amuse you!"

Dave glares at me. I'm not sure if it's because of the fake band name or the oblique reference to our real band name.

"'Fire in the Head!'" a woman yells over the opening applause.

Dave gives me a death-glare.

Yeah. Someone requesting our first big hit as aMUSEd is probably a good indication that the jig is up, though it looks like this lady's in the minority, because a lot the people in the audience are just staring at her, looking confused.

I catch a glimpse of Brighid, sitting at a table with Callie and some of the other girls, and she's shaking her head in disapproval. Sometimes Hunt's girl says things that you only find out later are true, and I suspect she called this one. Oops.

"Don't know that one — sorry," I say into the mic. "Let's try a classic!"

I launch into "We Will Rock You," like we've started every show with since we've started doing these gigs, doing my best to give Freddie a run for his money, which even I'll admit is like climbing Everest. Harder, really, because no one's ever getting there. But I'm content to stand at his feet.

Callie looks a little perplexed as a bunch of the crowd gets to its feet and sings, claps and stomps along. But she knows this song. After a second, she joins in. Oh, my girl… if I can reawaken that love of music in her, give her back that connection that she'd clamped off an eon ago… if I can do that, I can do anything.

The thought sends me soaring, carrying me through five more songs. Early on, I give Callie a saucy little wink during "Brick House," which also sets Hunter to making goo-goo eyes at Brighid. We're a pair of saps. I admit it. Happy saps, though. And even though she's listening to all of us to tailor the mix for the audience, Piper's tapping her feet to Dave's bass beats during a pair of Red Hot Chili Peppers songs.

That's when I realize half our band is now spoken for. Billy's going to pitch a fit, with so much of our fan appeal off the market. Rhys, Alex and Kieran are in for it. And Kier's already put his foot down about the groupies. Rhys will have to pick up the slack.

Now it's time for "Spoonman," and I'm in seventh heaven. I love this song. I loved it when it was Cornell singing it, and I love to sing it even more. I even love the break, with Rhys taking the spotlight for a minute and then Dave joining him. Then it's back to me, and I almost forget I'm not standing on stage in Madison

Square Garden or something. It's just me pouring myself into the mic, engaging with the fans…

Whoa. That's actually a lot of fans for this little bayside bar. In fact, the whole dance floor is packed, and without even thinking about it, I've been grasping the reaching hands from the front row, just like I usually do when we've got people that close to the stage. But that's when we have security lining the front of the stage to keep things under control. And we don't have that here. Unless Gryffin has his guys "secretly" tailing me again. One of those hands grabs for me when I start to lean back and retreat from the crowd a bit, grasping hold of a few strands of my hair, which has gotten even longer in recent weeks, since Callie seems to like it. I'm liking it a little less myself when the woman doesn't let go, and my hair gets yanked.

But I'm a pro. I just lean forward again, not missing a beat with the song, and grab her hand with my free one, like I'm going to squeeze it supportively, but then I slide it off my hair and into my palm, which I then slip free of her grasp.

"I love you, Declan!" she screams.

Yeah. I'm fucked. Whether it's my fault for the band name thing or Hunter's because of the social media spotlight on us here, they — at least some of them — know we're aMUSEd. And that's knowledge that is only going to spread.

I'll worry about that later, though. Other than the handsy lady, everyone else seems to be behaving themselves. No one climbing up on stage or anything. I keep back out of grabbing range, though, just to be safe. I glance at the other guys, and they all seem to have noticed that little incident. Alex signals to the venue security and exchanges a few words with one of them without missing a note. A minute later, there's a guy on the floor by each corner of the stage, ready to deal with any further problems. Which is good, because it's time for me to really do my thing.

I slide the mic back into the stand and shake my hands to loosen up and fling away the unfamiliar wave of nerves that is coming on.

"Thank you all so much!" I say into a raucous round of applause and some whistling.

"I love you, Rhys!" a woman shouts.

Rhys does a "Who? Me?" and a flourish on the drums. At least he didn't confirm it directly.

"You all have been a wonderful audience tonight, and we've got something special we want to share with you now. If you want to grab that someone or someones special, this would be a great time to bring them onto the dance floor," I say, hoping it might help break up the crowd at the front of the stage. It does. A little. I turn my focus squarely on that one face in the crowd that makes me feel like I can do anything, with just a glance from her. She looks a little overwhelmed back at the table with her friends, but she smiles, and I'm ready to sing a tale of a heart that's felt empty for so long, but that now feels full again, thanks to her.

"This one's for Callie. Thanks for making my blues finally go away."

Kieran lights into the blazing opening guitar riff of "Still Got the Blues," and I settle in to sing the only ballad I've ever sung in public. There's a quiet beat, and then I pour my heart out to Callie. Because she's the only person who exists in this place. No, on this planet. It's just her and me, with those steel-gray eyes of hers warming and melting as I tell her just what it's felt like to be without her all these years.

By the time I hit the chorus, she's got a hand to her mouth, her eyes glistening, and while I don't like seeing those tears forming, I know it's her way of telling me she gets it, that she's hearing the pain I've felt for twelve years leaving me in a rush, making room for all the love she's started pouring back into me, even if she hasn't said those words back to me yet.

And then she does... as the final chorus draws to a close, she mouths them at me, clear as day. Those three precious words. Our eyes lock, and it feels like I'm levitating off my feet. I half expect to fly across the deck and land in her arms. It doesn't happen, but it feels like I might as well have, because I'm full to overflowing, and I haven't even heard her say it yet. But this is enough. It's what I've desperately longed to have come from those sweet, seductive lips of hers since that horrible day I messed up so badly. Not said in anguish, but with promises of a life together — one we can both commit to having now, with all of that put firmly behind us.

She truly is my angel, regardless of what her middle name is. And she's my muse now, too. She'll know that soon enough, because I'm going to show her, in a way that'll let her know I'm in this forever — for real this time, and nothing's going to get in the way of that ever again.

# CHAPTER 42

## FRESH FEELING

## Callie

Wow.

Just wow.

I mean I knew that the band had gotten huge. I knew they played shows to sold-out crowds in large venues. But at no point did I envision what that would look like from the audience, let alone in a small venue like this.

Nor did I fully account for the fact that I was no longer the only woman under Declan Carter's charismatic spell. That fact became abundantly clear when some woman grabbed onto his hair and refused to let go. I was halfway out of my chair to drag her away from him when Brighid grabbed my arm and pulled me back down, shaking her head no. And by then, Declan had gently freed himself from the woman's grasping hands, like it was nothing... something that happens to him all the time. And maybe it is. Maybe women scream "I love you!" all the time, too. He certainly didn't seem to take much notice of her declaration. Even Rhys brushed off the woman who yelled out to him.

This has all been incredibly eye-opening.

Thankfully, there are a couple security guards stationed by the stage now. I mean, the crowd doesn't seem all that unruly overall. But it makes me feel better to know that it's unlikely anyone will put their hands on him again. There's no question that a lot of these people know who they really are. Maybe not all of them, but enough that once the music dies down enough to talk, nearly all of them will know.

But my attention is pulled away from them and directly to Declan again when he pauses to thank the audience, drawing all eyes back to him. When he invites them to bring their special someones up to dance, the crowd in front of the stage gets blessedly thinner and I relax a little bit. But that moment is short-lived.

"This one's for Callie. Thanks for making my blues finally go away."

And I about die on the spot.

Brighid squeezes my hand, but I barely notice, my gaze locked in with Declan's. The world shrinks to just the two of us as he sings his heart out directly to me. Loss. Pain. The torment of loving someone you can't have back.

I don't think this is one of aMUSEd's songs. The sound is too different from the few I've listened to in the last couple weeks, in the rare moment I wasn't working or spending time with Declan. This is a blues song. A rocking one with an almost metal edge to it, but still a blues song. And when Declan sings about that empty place in his chest, the full depth of what he's been telling me hits me.

While I built a shell of armor around the broken bits of my heart, never letting anyone in after that horrible day, Declan tried filling that space with meaningless encounters. But they never came close. It made him bitter, jaded, a cranky asshole, as Alex had described him. The guilt and pain coalesced around the little spark of love left in his heart for me, turning it into something like a black hole — sucking in every bit of happiness and joy like it had never existed, leaving him scrambling to find something that would keep it from dragging the rest of him with it.

What he grabbed onto was this — his music, turning his soul inside out on the stage for the whole world to see, striving constantly for the next hit, the next sold-out show, even greater acclaim... It elevated him, and his band with him, to the incredible heights they've achieved. But when that still wasn't enough, he searched and searched, until he finally found one thing that stemmed the constant leeching away of his enjoyment of life: his penance, serving others in my honor, trying to make up for the hurt he'd cause me in the only way he could, through the medium of food.

But now — now... we've put that behind us — my armor, his guilt, and the pain both of us have suffered the whole time we've been apart. I opened myself to feeling again, to trusting again. And he's absorbed every bit of the reawakened love I have for him. Because that's what it is — love. He's absorbed it and filled his heart with it, enabling him to forgive himself just as I've forgiven him. And instead of guilt sucking away the joy around him, he instead is pouring it out onto others. And most especially onto me.

He tossed those words at me earlier, without a care as to whether I said them back to him. He gave me the space and time to do that on my own, when I was ready, when I could admit to myself, to him, to the world, that I still love him, that I never stopped.

But how could I not love this man? I loved the boy once, and he broke my heart. But he broke his own in the process. Now, he's healing us both with his love for me, our past tossed away, no longer weighing us down, and instead, the lightness of love lifting us both up. Together. With a love like this fueling us, is there anything we *can't* accomplish together? A second restaurant is an easy thing to do when we do it together. Heck, we could conquer the world together! The world I've been terrified of venturing into for my entire adult life, no matter how much I've loved exploring other cuisines and cultures. And right now, with the bottomless love showering down on me from those deep blue eyes, I know I could do it. With Declan, I can go anywhere and do anything.

Because he loves me. And I love him. I love him.

I mouth three words to him, knowing he can't hear me but that, whether he reads my lips or gets the message via our little brain-sharing thing, he'll understand me. And when I see his face light up, even without the benefit of the stage lighting, I know he does. And it's the greatest moment of my life.

"We'll have to go back to the dressing room to see them," Brighid says, the smile she's giving me making it clear that she knows something significant has happened between me and Declan, even though he was on stage at the time.

"I'll take you back," Piper says, looking a little dismayed at the number of people crowding the deck. "I won't be able to break down anything until the crowd clears anyway, and the security guys know me."

I couldn't even tell she's pregnant, as petite as she is. Her curves hide any suggestion of it, at least for now. But she has a definite glow to her. Maybe it's the pregnancy. Or maybe it's just being in love. That much is clear just looking at her as her eyes follow David off the stage and she smiles radiantly.

Do I look like that now? Do I look like a woman in love? Can everyone who sees me tell?

It makes me feel a little self-conscious. But I follow Piper and Brighid back in the direction Declan had come from earlier, trying to fight off his nerves. And now I get why he had them. He'd planned to dedicate that song to me, knowing he was pouring out every bit of his pain on that stage, and then his love...

He loves me! And I love him.

It feels so right, like a dislocated joint finally popped back into place. Or a heart restored to a chest it was pulled from long ago.

And then the physical manifestation of that feeling envelops me, as Declan grabs me up, dodging past the security guards at the dressing room door to pull me back in with him.

"I'd much prefer to be alone with you right now, but that's not happening," he says, nodding at his bandmates, with Brighid now tucked in under Hunter's long arms and Piper looking cozy with her own arms wrapped around David's shoulders and his around her waist, his chin resting on her head.

"Well, guys, that was a close one!" Alex says.

"No flipping kidding!" Rhys says.

"'Flipping'? Since when do you say 'flipping'?" Alex says, looking concerned.

"Since Mom called to tell me she'd seen my last interview and that I had too large of a vocabulary to need to use profanity outside of an emergent situation."

"So, you're going to start saying 'Flip' instead of fuck? What's the next waitress who gives you her number going to think when you tell her you want to 'flip' her?" Kieran asks.

"Mom suggested I use 'flibbertigibbets' instead of the F-word. So, I guess, that."

The other guys exchange looks, and Brighid's having a hard time not cracking up. I can tell.

"I think that's a noun and not a verb, Rhys," she finally says. "So, it probably works as an exclamation, but not so much for telling a girl what you'd like to do to her..."

"I dunno, Bridge... I'm kind of looking forward to taking you home for some flibbertigibbets," Hunter says, with some serious smirking.

"That'll have to wait," she says sternly as he pulls her back up against his chest, wrapping his arms around her waist. "You all can't go back there until that crowd has started to break up."

The guys all look at Declan.

"What? I was just doing what I always do! I can't help it if some woman decides to take advantage of the fact that I don't have a steel barrier and five retired Marines between me and her!"

"Maybe — but you could have not invoked the band name in your intro again, like I told you after the *last* time, Dec," David says. "And 'The Flu Fighters'? Really? People are going to start checking the marquee for Grohl and Telltale Signs references."

"We'll see..." Declan says. "I've already got an idea for the next one." His smile is mischievous, and I'm both amused — no pun intended — and terrified at the thought of what he's come up with.

David just rolls his eyes.

"How much hair did she pull out?" Alex asks Declan.

"A couple strands, maybe."

"That was a smooth move with the hands there, Dec," Hunter says. "I'll have to remember it the next time some woman grabs my hair."

"Brighid doesn't count, Hunt," Declan says.

"*She* can grab my hair all she wants," he replies. "Or any other parts of me she wants to pull on..." he growls, looking down at her.

OK. This is almost as embarrassing to witness as the security video from that night the dining room at Castalia went haywire.

"Behave, you," she says. "Or I'll have to follow the doctor's orders..." There's a threat in there. A sexy one, by the sound of it, but still, a threat.

"Doctor? Brighid are you pregnant?" Piper asks, seeming to miss the sexual context I had no trouble picking up on.

Brighid's smile falters. Hunter kisses her on the top of her head. But she recovers quickly.

"No. Not yet. But it's only been a little over a month. Nothing to worry about... But the doctor — Hunt and I have been doing the therapy thing, and they had some suggestions for us," she explains. "And I will leave it at that."

"Ooh... sexy therapist suggestions," Rhys intones. "Now I want to have flibbertigibbets with a therapist..."

Everyone cracks up, except Rhys.

"What? Hunter said it first! Why is that funny? I mean, as long as she's not *my* therapist, can't I do that?"

"Yes, Rhys. I just don't think you should call it that," Brighid tells him with a smile.

"Oh."

"And don't scream 'Flibbertigibbets!' when you come, either," suggests Declan.

Another round of laughter, and I start to see the band dynamic here. They really are like a family. Something I haven't had since Nonna died, and only her for a long while before that. But then maybe Drew, Devon, Rick, Raquel and my other staff are a kind of family, too. They've certainly stepped up to help when I've needed them this summer.

All of a sudden, it feels like I have family all around me — my staff, the girls, and now Piper, too, and this aMUSEd family. Declan said he'd hoped to be part of my family, with Nonna, when we were younger. He never really got that, but he's built his own family, and now it feels like I'm the one being invited inside. And I have to say, that feels almost as good as having Declan tell me he loves me again.

"Should I peek out and see if the coast is clear?" Brighid suggests.

"Go for it," Declan says.

After a minute, she comes back in the dressing room.

"It's not empty, but the crowd's down to manageable levels. I think most of the fans decided you weren't coming back out and left. There's still a few out here, if you want to schmooze."

"I need a shirt that says, 'This is my schmoozing shirt.' And I can wear it after every show," Hunter says.

"And now you've ruined your Yule present," Brighid chides with a soft smile.

Everyone laughs, except Hunter, who gives Brighid a look.

"You didn't!"

"I did. Ordered it last month."

"And you thought *we* brain-shared..." Declan says quietly into my ear as the rest of the band shakes their head at how in tune Brighid and Hunter are with each other. Or maybe Brighid really is as intuitive as people suggest.

"OK, guys — let's hit it," Alex says. "Piper needs to get started breaking things down, and we do not have the luxury of techs and roadies again tonight."

The band members all moan.

"Hey — I thought *I* was your *unofficial* roadie!" Brighid says.

"You are, babe." Hunter replies. "Always have been," he adds, giving her a brief kiss.

She's talking about carrying heavy equipment like it's an honor. And I realize I could have been part of that, if things between Declan and me hadn't fallen apart. Maybe they're long past the days of hauling their own equipment under normal circumstances, but tonight, at least, it's a flashback to their earlier days, and that is something I don't want to miss being part of again.

"So, what do we do first?" I ask Declan.

"You? Go get a drink. I've got a lot of work to do before we can go home."

"I want to help," I tell him. I'm also wondering what he meant by "home." Could he mean my apartment? And he didn't say "*We've* got a lot of work to do," meaning the band. He meant *he* was going to do the work, and then *we* — meaning him and me — would go home. Together.

I'm liking that word more and more every time I hear it. *Together*. Amazing.

"You sure?" he says. "You don't have to."

I nod eagerly.

"This is your work, just like the restaurant's mine. And if we're going to be partners in this new venture, I want us to be partners in this part of your life, too, even if it means I'm hauling amps and microphone stands or whatever."

"Woman, you have no idea how good it feels to hear you say that," he says pulling me to him and kissing me hard.

"What part? Me wanting to haul equipment, the restaurant thing or being partners?"

"All of it, angel. All of it."

By the time he finally breaks off our kiss, I've nearly forgotten there were still people waiting outside, hoping to meet the band.

Brighid was right. It's way less crowded than it was, but people are still lingering outside the invisible barrier provided by the security guys in their yellow T-shirts with "SECURITY" spelled out in bold letters on the back. So weird to think of my boyfriend as needing security...

"Declan, can we get your autograph?" a woman asks.

It's not the woman who pulled his hair, thankfully. And she seems to be with a boyfriend or husband, so her hitting on Declan seems less likely. Good.

"I'm going to go help Brighid and Piper," I tell him, not wanting to seem like I'm hovering. This is his job, and I have to let him do it.

The girls are only a few feet away, Piper under Alex's keyboard — better her than me or Brighid, since it's tight quarters down there. She may have to ask for help getting things off the top shelf at the grocery store, but Brighid and I would have a hard time getting in there amongst all those wires and metal boxes.

"Hand me that case over there," Brighid says, gesturing to a stack of round fabric cases behind me. I hand her the one on top and grab the next one.

"I'll take that one," Rhys says.

I hand it over and watch as he and Brighid each lay a drum inside a case. It seems like Brighid's done this before. And no wonder. Rhys' drum kit is the biggest, most elaborate one I've ever seen.

"Grab that next one, Callie," Brighid says.

I go to hand it to her, but Rhys hands me a drum instead.

"Go ahead. Just don't drop it," he says. "Glinda's my favorite tom."

"You name your drums?"

"Yeah! How else could the techs tell them apart?"

It's a good point. I think. Maybe. Or it could be that it's just Rhys, who seems a little... odd.

The three of us have the massive drum kit broken down in no time, while Piper keeps ahead of us to take the mics off each of them and pull a bunch of colorful cables out of the way.

"It helps to keep track of which drum is going into each connection on other end of the drum drop," she explains when she sees me looking curiously at the rainbow of wires. "Then we take those feeds and put them into the board. Not that I use the board much these days. It's all on my iPad. But the brain is still inside the board. For now."

I have no idea what any of that means, but I'll take her word for it.

Brighid has moved on to helping Kieran pack up his guitars, all the while repeating phrases back to him in what I guess has to be Irish, like he's quizzing her. Piper is helping Alex put his keyboards in their cases. I wonder if each of them has a name, too — the guitars and the keyboards.

"We've got it for now, Callie," Alex says. "Piper's already got Declan's mic and stand put away. You can help us load stuff into Brighid's car once it's all packed up, if you want."

"OK. Cool."

Declan's just finishing up with one guy who's talking animatedly with his hands, finally shaking Declan's hand and taking a signed vinyl album away with him. I didn't even know they made vinyl records anymore... must have had a revival at some point in the last decade. I barely remember CDs.

Declan's got a woman waiting to talk to him, but I figure that won't take long, so I slide into hovering range, exchanging a smile and a nod with the nearest security guard. He doesn't object, so I move up behind Declan so he can stay focused on his fan but will have me waiting for him when he's done.

With the things we said to each other tonight, verbally and otherwise, I want nothing more than to get him alone. I want to hear those words come from his lips again, and I want to give mine to him in return, where they can fall on his ears for the first time since we were 17.

I try to put the last time I said them out of my mind, recalling all too well that I said them in desperation, begging him to change his mind and give us a chance, or at least to give me some kind of explanation for his sudden change of heart.

We've promised to put all that behind us now. No more secrets, guilt or bad memories. Just honest communication going forward, focused on the future and no baggage weighing us down. The future seems full of possibilities, and moreover, full to overflowing with love and trust reestablished between us. I feel warm and safe for the first time in a long time, and it's all because of Declan.

# CHAPTER 43

# POLICY OF TRUTH

## Declan

"Oh, my god! Declan! It's been almost 12 years to the day since I last saw you!"

I'm trying to remember if I've even seen this woman before. Where would it have been? On the boardwalk? Is she a friend of my parents?

"At that bar in O.C, when you all were still the Carter Brothers Band?"

In my head, I'm trying to reverse the impacts of twelve years of aging on her. Light blonde hair. Clearly out of a bottle. Wait...

"You were amazing that night. I knew you'd be a superstar someday, and I wanted to be able to say I'd been with you when that day arrived... We sure had some fun in that hotel room, didn't we?"

She smiles, clearly enjoying the memory.

In contrast, my face is blank, any expression wipes away as I realize who this is... *the* blonde — the one I got drunk with and cheated on Callie with the week after we got married.

I turn quickly, hoping desperately that Callie is still talking to Brighid or Piper and didn't overhear this shameful walk down Memory Lane with a groupie I was barely old enough to legally sleep with...

When my eyes find her, standing behind my left shoulder, Callie's face isn't blank. Her expression is horrified. And then furious. And then gone. Because she turns on her heel and, once again, runs away from me as fast as her feet will carry her.

"Callie! Wait!" I call behind her, knowing it's long past time I come clean about what happened that night and exactly why I broke things off with her all those years ago, if it's not already too late to fix this final fuck-up of mine. I should have just told her. This one last thing. We'd put all the rest of it behind us. Why didn't I trust that she'd understand? But the blonde grabs my arm, stopping me from chasing after her. I start to pull free, but her next words freeze me in place.

"That's Callie? Your girl who stopped me from sleeping with you?"

"Wait. What?" I turn back to her, grabbing her shoulders and shaking her lightly before I get control of myself again. "How do you know about Callie?"

The blonde looks confused, and a little alarmed.

"You called out her name that night. Don't you remember?"

"I don't remember anything from that night except helping you to the bed and then waking up naked next to you the next morning."

"Oh."

"Oh?" I repeat, outrage creeping into my voice. "That's all you've got to say? That night changed my entire life — I broke up with her because I cheated on her, and she deserved better. And you're telling me we didn't actually sleep together?"

"No, honey..." she says, looking remorseful as my words sink in. "I woke up with you asleep next to me, in just your underwear, and I thought we'd headed into the bedroom to have some fun, then passed out before we got the chance. So I finished taking off my clothes, and... well, I thought we were both into it, so I started kissing you, and you responded, so I stripped off your underwear, and I was about to... you know... And then you murmured, 'Callie.' And the way you said her name — it sounded so full of love, so enraptured with her... I just couldn't do it. Even if you'd been into it, I couldn't have done anything with you at that point. I'd have felt horrible being the other woman.

"My husband cheated on me," she confesses, "and that was a wild time in my life, after I found out. I slept with a lot of guys, but I'd never have slept with a married man. Not ever. And, clearly, married or not, you were already taken. I knew that the moment you said her name. So I crawled back to my side of the bed and went to sleep. Passed out, really. I'd definitely had too much to drink. Didn't wake up until nearly noon."

"So we never slept together? Never did *anything* together?" I ask, desperate and incredulous at the same time.

"No. Like I said — I kissed you, and you kissed me back. But it was pretty clear pretty quickly that you thought I was her — your Callie. So I backed off. Her name stuck with me all these years, just because of how much love was in your voice when you said it."

"Fuck."

"You didn't know that? All these years you thought we'd... that you'd... that you'd cheated on her? On your girlfriend?"

"My *wife*. We were married about a week before that."

"Oh. Good thing that I... Oh!" she exclaims, her eyes going wide. "You thought you'd cheated on her — on your wife — with me, and you broke up because of that? Because of me? Oh, my god. I'm so sorry! If I'd known..."

Yeah... if she'd known. If *I'd* known. If I hadn't just assumed and then made the worst decision of my life — as it turns out, based on a false assumption... and then lived the next decade thinking of myself as the cheating rockstar who'd destroyed his marriage over a groupie... punishing myself with brief, meaningless encounters and then... secret penance in food bank kitchens across the world.

That one night had made me who I am today, or was... or maybe am again — a dick, weighed down by guilt, trying indirectly to make it up to the woman I loved that I'd cheated on her, trying to somehow balance the scales of the huge mistake that, it turns out, I never actually made. Only I made a second, *bigger* mistake — breaking up with Callie, telling her I'd never really loved her, when she was... *is*... the only thing I've ever loved more than being out on that stage in front of our fans.

I've spent the last handful of weeks trying to make up for that, trying to make up for the damage I did to Callie all those years ago, and the ways her life changed as a result. And now, with one chance encounter with *another* woman I hadn't seen in twelve years, I discover that all of it — all of it! — was a misunderstanding. But Callie has no idea. She now thinks I cheated on her all those years ago, just like I have for the last decade plus. Wrongly.

Oh, just fuck me... Flibbertigibbets!

I hear murmuring next to me, and my brain won't make sense of it. The shock of hearing the truth of what happened that night... I shake my head, try to focus.

"...and I told Sharon that I'd come *this* close to sleeping with the lead singer of aMUSEd, back before they were even signed to a record deal. And she said she'd heard a rumor that the band was back here on Delmarva, playing these secret shows, and we had to come out to see if it really was you and if you remembered me... and I said, 'Sharon, it was twelve years ago. He was barely more than a kid. I'm sure he won't remember me...' But she insisted, and that's why I'm here."

She beams at me brightly, as if expecting a pat on the head, or an offer of a selfie in honor of old times.

But I feel as if she's just kneed me in the nuts.

I force myself to take a deep breath, and I walk away. I spot our manager a moment later. Good, it's time for him to do his job.

"Billy? See that blonde over there? In the red top? I need you to get her contact information."

"I thought you and Callie..."

"No! It's not like that. I just... I may need her to testify to something that happened a long time ago."

"Should I call the lawyers?"

"No — not like that, either. Just get her info and file it away in case I need it, OK? Give her front-row seats to a future show, if you need to — just no backstage passes, OK?"

"O...K..."

"Thanks, man. Oh — and have her sign an NDA. Nothing we talked about tonight can be repeated to anyone, OK? Now, can I borrow your car?"

"I don't know... are you sober this time?"

I can't even begin to explain to Billy how sober I am right now. Even if I'd been drunk, I'd have gone stone-cold sober after that conversation, and now knowing I have to explain this all to a very angry, hurt Callie.

"Yes. Give me the keys," I demand. "Please," I add, desperate.

"Be careful, Dec. I don't want to be pulling broken bits of you out of a pile of wreckage in a couple hours."

"That's exactly what I'm hoping to avoid," I tell him. "If it's not already too late."

# CHAPTER 44

## STOLEN CAR

## Callie

I t *all* makes sense now. All of it. Finally. Declan breaking up with me, telling me he didn't love me and never had, talking about groupies and blowjobs and the rockstar life he had ahead of him... and, more recently, saying it had all been because he wasn't good enough for me.

Of course he wasn't! A week after we'd gotten married, my 17-year-old husband went from promising me forever to fucking women nearly old enough to be his mother. Maybe. Maybe she just hasn't aged well... What am I even thinking about?

He'd cheated on me. Twelve years ago, Declan had cheated on me. And then he'd apparently run straight to me to break things off.

Was it because I wasn't good enough in bed, wasn't experienced enough? Maybe he realized he wanted more experience himself before he got tied down. Our marriage wasn't legal, so it's not like he had to worry about a divorce or an annulment. Cold feet. Buyer's remorse. Whatever it was, that night in Ocean City seemed to have given Declan a taste of what was to come, and apparently, he liked it. Because it seems they sure had some "fun" together.

*Together.*

No. Not the same anymore. It's like the word has changed its meaning in the space of an hour.

I realize I'm driving down the highway at sixty-five miles an hour, in a fifty, driving into Mystic Beach proper, where the speed limit is thirty-five. I hit the brakes, then realize I should have checked behind me first. Luckily, no tailgaters. But I pull off onto the shoulder of the road. I've got to get hold of myself.

So a rockstar cheated on me twelve years ago. So what? So my boyfriend lied to me — by omission, if nothing else — in nearly the same breath as he promised to be honest with me. I say again: So what? So, he'd offered me forever. Twice. And then spoiled it all with this rockstar nonsense — fans and groupies and women pulling on his hair, yearning to have him touch them, just for a second. So fucking what?

"It's not something to get into a car crash over," I tell myself. Flibbertigibbets!

Then I realize what I just said. No, not flibbertigibbets — a car crash. Wouldn't that have been ironic? Or is it fitting? Doesn't matter. Me, dying in the same manner as my parents, almost twelve years *to the day* later. What a cosmic joke that would be. Well, the joke's on you, universe — I'm going home and I'm going to... I'm going to...

Change the locks!

There we go. That's got it. Brighid did that when Hunter was persona non grata at her place. I can do that. I'll have to go to the hardware store first, though. Hmm. Kind of late for that right now. But I can put the chain on the door, and even if Declan does come chasing after me, with the key to my apartment that I so stupidly gave him, he won't be able to get in. I can hide in the bathroom and pretend I'm not home. He'll go away after a while. Siobhan may have to threaten to call the cops, but... Nevermind. Siobhan would just kick his ass herself and send him crawling back to the studio.

Now there's a visual I can enjoy.

Siobhan! I can hide out at Siobhan's! But then Declan will see my car and know I'm somewhere nearby. He found me. He'll find Siobhan. And then I'll have the same problem — Declan Carter on my doorstep, begging me to forgive him. Again. Making promises he can't keep. Again. Redefining "forever" as something more along the lines of a week...

"Callie?"

I look up and realize that I'm parked in my usual spot behind my apartment. And I don't even remember pulling into the alley. Some super-spy skills *I've* got!

I roll down the window for Siobhan, who is looking Brighid-level intuitive right now, showing up just when I was thinking about her.

"What's wrong? You look like you've seen a ghost!"

"Yeah — the ghost of jackass boyfriends past..."

"What did he do now? Do I need a shovel for the body? Brighid's got that fenced yard now, or we can take him and dump him in the swamp. There's a rumor that the swamp monster is back."

"Swamp monster?"

"Yeah. You never heard that story?"

"No."

"Not important. What did he do?"

"He cheated on me!"

"That bastard. Brighid warned him not to hurt you again or she'd make his dick fall off! This happened tonight? I wanted to be there, but I can't refuse a regular client when she asks for a late appointment."

"No. Not tonight. Twelve years ago!"

"Wait... your boyfriend of twelve years ago cheated on you twelve years ago, and you just now found this out?"

"Yeah. He'd said he wasn't good enough for me..."

"Well, he was right! I'll go get the shovel."

"No. It doesn't change anything, Siobhan. Not really. It just finally makes sense, after all these years..."

"Oh! That's why he said he didn't love you! He didn't want to admit that he'd cheated on you!"

"I think so, yeah. And I... Oh, god... He's bound to be chasing after me to try to explain this away. Just like he did with that groupie photo. And I can't, Siobhan. I just can't..."

"OK. He's got a key to your apartment now, right?"

"Yeah. How'd you know that?"

"I saw him let himself in the other night when I was just getting home myself."

*Home*. Another word that now means something new, and unpleasant.

"I don't even want to go home right now," I tell her.

She takes a deep breath, thinking, and then exhales decisively, like she's got a plan. That's good, because I don't.

"You're going to go up to my apartment and lock the door. Don't open the door unless I use the special knock."

Oh, how appropriate that seems right now, the chorus from "Rolling in the Deep."

"I'm going to take your car and drop it off over in Brighid's driveway. I'll call her, let her know it's there but you're not, give her the upshot of what happened. She'll make sure Declan gets a talking-to if he shows up there."

"A talking-to? A minute ago, you needed a shovel to bury the body."

"Or clock him over the head with. Both, probably. Yeah. But *Brighid* won't do anything worse than yell at him in Irish. She'll let him think it's a curse on his itty, bitty little penis..."

She looks at me, questioning.

I shake my head gravely.

"OK — his really big, woman-pleasing, magical penis..."

I can't help it. I laugh. And then I start crying. I loved that penis. Not too big, not too small. Just perfect for me. I'm going to miss it, just like I missed him all these years, even if I couldn't admit it to myself. And now that I have... he goes and ruins everything. Again.

"Oh, honey... Don't cry! He's not worth it."

"Yes, he is! He told me he loved me. He sang me a sad song about loving me and how his chest was empty."

"More like his skull..." Siobhan mutters.

"No, it was a beautiful song! And it made me realize why he tried so hard to find me once he saw me at the engagement party. And then working at the food bank..."

"He worked at the food bank?"

Oops. Well, *I* didn't sign an NDA.

"He's been doing penance. For years."

"For what? Did he pee in a vessel of holy water or something? These rockstars, I tell you — worse than any twelve drunk bikers... And I can say that from firsthand experience."

"No! He's been doing it because of me! He learned to cook, and he worked in soup kitchens and food banks and teaching disadvantaged kids..."

"Declan Carter. Lead singer of aMUSEd. We're not talking about some other Declan Carter, are we?"

"No!" I wail, my emotions running wild at this point.

I want to kill Declan. I also want to kiss him and have this all just go away again. I want to have Brighid make his manly bits fall off, and I want to defend him when Siobhan thinks badly of him. How screwed am I right now?

"OK. We can discuss Declan Carter, his dick and his dickishness later. Right now — here. Take my key. Go make yourself at home. Just..." She looks at me, scrutinizing. "Just promise me you won't cook anything. I can live if my kitchen goes up in flames, but if it spreads to the studio, I'd be pissed. So don't do that, OK?"

I nod.

"Now get out of the car. I'm going to go move it before the soon-to-be dickless wonder shows up."

I follow her order. It's easy enough. I don't have to think, make decisions, contemplate a life without Declan. Again.

Nope. Running now! Up the stairs. I open the door and lock it behind me, throwing every bolt, latch and chain Siobhan's got on here. And boy... I just now realized how many locks Siobhan has on her door. It's like a dozen or something. OK. Half a dozen. But what the hell is she expecting is going to try to get in here? A zombie horde? In tiny little Mystic Beach? OK. Nevermind. It's Mystic Beach. I've seen — and apparently done — enough supernatural stuff in the last month or so to know zombies are not entirely out of the question here.

Then she's knocking on the door while I picture Adele stomping on her ex's face with high heels clacking in time to the beat.

"It's me! Open up!"

It takes a while, but I get the door open for her.

She looks back proudly at me when I give her a questioning look about all the locks and latches.

"What? It's good personal safety!"

"I thought that's what the self-defense classes were for."

"Never hurts to be prepared!" she says, cryptically. I start to wonder exactly how bad that big breakup of hers was...

"Now, you stay here. No cooking!" she warns again. "I'm going to go swap the deadbolts between our apartments."

"You can do that?"

"In my sleep."

Well... OK, then. I guess we'll sort it out with the landlord later.

"I'm going to go get my toolbox out of the studio, then I'll make the change. Go put something distracting on the TV. No romances, no heavy dramas. Why don't you try that 'Leverage' show? Piper raved about it."

OK. Why not? It'll give Piper and me something to talk about since we could possibly, eventually, end up as sisters-in-law...

Oh.

Yeah. That's not happening now, is it?

Well, that's depressing. Still, I search for the show. "Leverage" or "Leverage: Redemption"? The second one sounds grittier but uplifting, like you could turn around the worst things that happened to you. Which seems right on par for my day. I start the first episode.

OK. That's a woman in mourning... and a grave. And I probably should have gone with the other one, especially with jokes about vents and stealing things going right over my head. What is this show? I mean, it's clearly funny, good acting. Wait — is that the guy from "Angel"? The evil one? I like the longer hair. He's cuter like that. Not as cute as Declan, but...

Oh, flibbertigibbets.

But now I'm invested. So I turn on the other "Leverage." And there's a heist and some ass-kicking and a doublecross. Man, I know kind of how that feels, things not being what you were led to believe. And then C-4. Lots of C-4.

OK. Now I see why Piper likes this show. Snappy dialogue, clever characters. Parker's kind of... odd. Reminds me just a little of Rhys, actually.

Flibbertigibbets.

"OK, sorry that took so long, but here's dinner," Siobhan says, rushing through the door, handing me a takeout bag from Castalia. "I told Drew you're taking off until further notice. He commandeered someone's order of short ribs and what I have to say looks like some really delicious little rice balls."

The arancini. I'm going to have to kill Drew.

"Did you tell him why?"

"Just one word: 'Declan.' He rolled his eyes and sighed. And then he handed me the rice ball thingies. Oh, and a really nice steak."

What the fuck, Drew? Steak? The one thing I knew Declan could cook before his whole ruse got exposed, and Drew sends me steak for dinner? Tonight?

"But I'm eating the steak," Siobhan says. "Unless it's really emotionally important to you, because — wow."

"The filet mignon?"

"Is that what it is? Not a big slab but super-thick?"

"Yeah. That's filet mignon. Enjoy it. You've definitely earned it."

"Well, I will have once I swap the deadbolts. Now, before I do that, and before Declan shows up, do you need anything from your apartment? I've got an extra toothbrush. Well, lots of them."

*What?*

"And my oversized tanks will fit you fine, even with your curvier curves. And I've got some yoga pants. Might be a couple inches too long, but it'll be fine."

"Siobhan — you're kind of rambling."

She stops. Take a deep breath. Exhales.

"Sorry — I went into emergency mode there. But this is just a nice guy who wants to get you to listen to him, right? He's not going to break down any doors, right?"

"You were going to dump his body in a swamp fifteen minutes ago. And now he's nice?"

"Well, *you* seem to think he's nice. Are you sure you don't want to actually talk to him? Maybe he's got a good explanation. Or at least a gift for groveling... as well as a mighty fine magical penis..."

I snort a laugh.

"There you go... See — not a tragedy requiring digging a really big hole. But if that changes, you let me know. I've got a really nice shovel."

I start laughing, and I can't stop, until it crosses the line from hilarious into hysterical, and then so do I.

Siobhan sits down next to me, tossing several feet of white-blonde hair behind the back of the sofa, and pulls me into her shoulder.

"I'm not good at this touchy-feely stuff, you know. That's kind of Brighid's thing. Or Lyric. But then she's got the kids. She didn't go out to the gig tonight, did she?"

"No. Brighid and I were going out, and you had that appointment. And I guess she'd started letting Piper, and David..." I trail off, unable to finish the thought.

"It always comes back around to Declan, doesn't it?"

I nod solemnly.

"I know I said it before, but fate has a funny way of putting you through your emotional paces before it sets you down where you're supposed to be. Just ask Brighid. Or Piper and David."

I give her a questioning look, not privy to Declan's brother's story.

"Not my tale to tell," she says, shaking her head. "But he's a nicer guy than his brother. No ego. Quiet. Keeps out of trouble— Uh... nevermind."

OK. I'm going to need someone to tell me this story at some point.

"So, if you don't want to drop Dick-lan in a very deep hole or feed him to the swamp monster, what do you want to do? Amber's got those torches in her shop. We could tie him up, torture him a little. Someplace it wouldn't show... You still attached to those manly bits of his? Because we could..."

"No!"

She smirks at me.

"Besides, I don't think he'll let me tie him up again after the last time."

"The last time? Girl, what have you two been up to these last few weeks?" She shakes her head, the little braids mixed into the loose strands sliding back over her shoulder. "Well, if you ever need a pair of safety scissors or a cuff key, you know where to come," she says.

I shake my head. She's got so much more sexual experience. Maybe not a lot more *relationship* experience, but *sex*? Yeah, Siobhan's got that mastered, I think.

"I've got a set of keys, but I left the cuffs with Declan. *On* Declan, actually."

"OK. Now this I have to hear..."

I'm still in that funny no-man's land between proud and guilty over that incident. So I tell her what happened.

She's quiet for a minute. Is she appalled at what I did? I mean, it seems hard to believe that the woman who just offered me safety scissors would think I was too extreme.

"Where's that photo?"

Uh-oh. This doesn't sound good, regardless of what she's thinking.

"No! I'm not sending it out. Even if he did actually cheat on me at one point."

"I've got a VPN and an anonymous email. I'll do it."

"No. It's not right. I mean, it's not legal, either, apparently. But I just wouldn't feel right doing it."

"What's changed? You went from thinking he functionally cheated on you to *knowing* he did."

"Yeah. But he hadn't cheated this time, the more recent one. And the other one — it was twelve years ago. And now I get why he broke things off like that."

"So you got closure, finally, and now that you did, you're less mad than you are sad."

"I think so, yes. I mean, I'm still mad. I'm just..."

"Disappointed. Yup — you've hit Stage Four."

"Stage Four?"

"The stages of grief: denial, anger, bargaining — like you arguing with me on whether or not he's a good guy — and now depression. Well, they weren't really supposed to be stages of grief anyway, but it applies in this case. And you were very efficient at it, I have to say. It's been what? Fifteen minutes? That's an express train to being OK again. Next stop: acceptance."

"I don't know if I *can* accept it."

"You don't have to forgive him or forget what he did to accept that it happened. You just have to let it go enough that it doesn't consume your life. And you've got to give yourself time to do that before you think about forgiving him," she says, her eyes flicking briefly to the door, "which I'm saying right now because..."

"Callie!" I hear Declan bellow through the door, the walls, the expanding universe. Forget brain-sharing. Declan could transmit messages to the moon yelling like that. He sure knows how to use his voice. And then I remember him singing that song to me tonight. Unless Declan's a far better performer than I gave him credit for, that was real — that pain and heartache.

"Calliope Aoede Martino! You open this door right now, or I'm letting myself in!"

"Calliope Aoede Martino?" Siobhan asks quietly. "I thought Callie was short for Callista or Charlotte or something."

"My family had this thing with the muses..."

"Muses like the aMUSEd logo?"

Huh. Well, I hadn't thought of it that way, but wow, that's a coincidence. Maybe there's something to this fate stuff...

"Well, yeah. But..."

"Callie! Come *on*! We've been doing so good with communicating! Don't shut me out!"

"You know Declan named the band, right?" Siobhan says.

"You don't think he named the band after me, do you? I mean Calliope's a muse, but up until a couple weeks ago, he thought my middle name was Angelica." She gives me a look. "Nonna called me her angel. In Italian," I explain. "He just assumed it was my middle name and not a pet name."

There's a rumble and then a soft bang, and I know Declan's used his key to let himself into my apartment.

"I have to talk to you about this, Callie! It wasn't what it looked like! It wasn't what you thought it was. It wasn't even what *I* thought it was."

Now I'm curious. But I can't deal with this right now. Maybe he'll explain it to the walls while he looks for me, but barring overhearing that one-sided conversation, I'm not open to discussing it.

I can hear him close the bathroom door to make sure I'm not in the tiny linen closet behind it. He's desperate, or he would realize I'd never fit in there.

"And Martin-o? Not Martin?" Siobhan asks, still keeping her voice down.

"I changed it after I went to New York. I didn't want to get tagged in culinary school or the restaurants I worked in as being Italian. It would have boxed me in in some people's minds. And I wanted to learn every cuisine I could get close to. And, honestly, between my parents and Declan..."

"OK — I get wanting to make it harder for Declan to find you after the breakup. But what's that got to do with your parents?"

"Fuck! Fuck fuck fuckity fuck! Fuck!" I hear Declan growl through the shared wall, followed by the slam of a door. Not as hard as he could have. He took some care with my door, even as emotional as he clearly is right now. And another rumble that I assume is him locking up after himself. A real asshole would have slammed the door and left it unlocked, my belongings unprotected. Or left it wide open for opportunists.

But Declan just wants to talk to me. I wish I could. But I can't. Not yet.

"Flibbertigibbets!" he screams into the air outside my door.

I crack a smile. We're going to be stuck with that, both of us, aren't we?

Siobhan's got that eyebrow raised again, the ring in it emphasizing her expression.

"Rhys," I explain.

"Enough said."

I guess Rhys' reputation has preceded him. Much as Declan's has with the population at large. Only, nothing with Declan was what it seemed from the outside. He's not the womanizer he once was, and even that was out of some weird kind of self-punishment. He dealt with his heartbreak in the polar opposite way to what I did. Then he faked it to cover up volunteering with those less fortunate than either he or I had been. Just so he wouldn't get the credit for it.

He did it all for me. Because he'd cheated on me. Once. At least once. But I have to assume it probably wasn't more than that. I accused him of more than that when I threw him out of Nonna's house that day. It was easier to think I'd been fooled all along by him, that he was a player and I'd gotten played, the summer fling when he was away from home. But the more I think about it, the clearer it seems that something happened that night before he broke up with me. Something that scared him, or at least woke him up.

That sudden change in him, in how he said he felt about me, about us. *This* was what he was covering up, that he'd cheated on me. I don't know what happened that night twelve years ago, and I probably won't know unless I decide to let him explain. But I've seen inside Declan these last weeks, and I know that whatever happened shook him up to the point where he abandoned all hope of a life with me, even though it sentenced us both to years of unhappiness, loneliness.

All it took for him to try to reverse that, even though it had been twelve years, seeing just a glimpse of me across a room. From that moment on, he'd done everything he could to try to show me that he really did love me, that he always had. And maybe... just maybe... that he wanted to live up to that promise he'd made to me so long ago.

There'd been so much standing between us — a painful history, and time and space — until he blew into town and did his best to sweep it all away, like magic. And I'd wanted that. I'd wanted him to erase all the hurt and resentment, the barriers I'd erected around me to keep me safe. And he had. All but the one thing he'd never been honest with me about. And now, that's the one thing standing between us.

Now, the question is this: Is there enough good, enough love, in our relationship, before and now, to keep the weight of all of our baggage — its contents now known to us both — from dragging us back into a past that tore us apart?

And I honestly don't know.

# Chapter 45

# A View To A Kill

## Declan
### *An hour later*

"I'm not judgmental! I just know when someone's wrong!" Brighid says, her voice raised nearly to shouting levels. I can say that, because I'm standing outside their house and I can hear her and Hunter arguing, quite clearly.

After driving around a while, looking for any sign of Callie, I finally found her car parked in their driveway. But I now suspect that was a ruse, because I can't imagine Brighid and Hunter having a fight like this if Callie was taking refuge with them. I'm not sure I've ever heard them argue, actually. Some crazy shit's gone down between them over the years, but raised voices?

"Babe, I should never have told you. It wasn't my secret to tell. And, honestly, I thought you knew already! I figured Callie told you when she first talked to you about Declan."

"Clearly, Callie didn't know at all, Hunter! Who does that? I mean, clearly Declan Carter does, but who tells a woman they love that they realized they never actually loved her at all? And to do it to cover up that he'd cheated on her with some groupie!"

"I know you aren't fond of the groupies to begin with, Bridge, but we were 17, and we were all sloshed that night. Except Dave."

"Of course! Because David Carter is the only mature one amongst the three of you! And even then he nearly gets himself killed..."

"Hey! I've matured a lot since then. I was very stupid, I admit. Declan was just a little stupider!"

Well, he's got me there.

"Wait — Dave was nearly killed?" Well, that slipped past both me and Hunt there for a second. "When was this? What haven't you told me, Bridge?"

"I'm sworn to secrecy. That just slipped out because I'm so upset with you..."

"Not with me! With Declan!"

"Well, I'm mad at both of you right now, and I'm even angrier now that you've made me say something I swore I'd never speak of."

"So you're not going to tell me?"

"I can't."

Yeah, Dave and I are going to have a little talk later. As soon as I get things sorted out with Callie. Mom'd kill me if I let him get killed.

"Well, *I* can't condemn Declan for something that happened twelve years ago, when we were 17! And I'm a little surprised that you can!"

Alright! Hunter's in my court!

"Give me one good reason why I shouldn't! Just one!"

"You didn't see his face when he realized what he'd done."

They're getting quieter now, so — using those super-spy skills of mine — I walk up on the porch and sit down on the bench in front of the window. Yes, I'm eavesdropping! They're talking about me! And the woman I love! And, I suspect, whether Brighid will be carrying out her threat to unman me. Literally. I've got to know what I'm facing before I actually knock on the door.

"Realized? Realized what he'd done?" she asks. "You say that as if he didn't have any control over what happened that night!"

"He was plastered, Bridge. I mean — I know he drank at parties at home, but he didn't go through a crazy phase like I did, and I had a few times when *I* didn't fully remember what I'd done the night before!"

"I hated that. I hated seeing you coming home before dawn, barely able to walk into your house."

"And the girls..."

"That, too."

"It's in the past now, Bridge. We're putting all of that behind us. That's what Dr. Apple is helping us do, so we can move forward and have a healthy relationship. Don't you think Declan deserves a chance to do the same with Callie?"

Well, I've overheard more than I wanted to. Prying into their stuff wasn't part of the plan. But it isn't really anything I couldn't have guessed at.

"You didn't cheat on me!"

"No, I didn't. But I wasn't as careful with your feelings as I should have been, and in some ways that's almost worse."

"Don't do this, Hunt. Don't keep punishing yourself for things that happened fifteen years ago."

"It wasn't *all* fifteen years ago! I don't even want to think about how long I stayed on that path, how close I came to losing you, maybe my relationships with the guys, with Mace, messing up my career. If you hadn't read me the riot act, if Mace hadn't threatened to tear my head off for hurting you..."

"He did? He told me he'd backed off when he realized you were hurting, too."

"He did. But he did threaten me first. And I'd earned it! And it still took me a while to get myself straightened out, to decide which Hunter Graves I really wanted to be, and then to figure out how to get there. *Here. This* is what I wanted — you, us. And even though I didn't realize it for a long time, I'd have been devastated if I'd realized it and then had the past pop up again to destroy it!"

"And you think that's the case with Declan..."

"I do. Other than that one day — when you were already pissed at him because of what Callie *had* told you — you didn't see him when he was looking for her. He was driven, obsessed — but in a good way. He'd realized what he'd wanted, and he was finally giving himself the chance to have it — to *earn* it, by being that better version of himself, just like I have with you. And you've seen how he is now — asshole Declan is all but gone. He's happy. For the first time since that night twelve years ago, he's happy."

Yeah. I am. Was...

"I've seen him go from carefree 17-year-old with a girl he loved," Hunter continues, "to a guy who gave up on finding real happiness because he'd messed up. Once. One mistake. One night. And a fuck-ton of booze we had no business even being in the same room with. And it crushed him. He was trying to do the right thing when he broke up with Callie. Because after one mistake, one night, he felt he didn't deserve her anymore. And, yeah, he fucked up the actual breakup part, but he was 17 and she was his first girlfriend, and, man... that shit's never easy. I mean — look how badly I botched it. And I'm 29!"

"You did make a giant mess, didn't you..."

"I did. And then I made a mess trying to clean up the mess. Honestly, I give 17-year-old Declan kudos for trying to do the right thing, and I give 29-year-old Declan some props for trying to fix it all, all these years later. And he'd done it! He'd gotten her to trust him, to open up to everyone."

"And now she'll never trust him again, because he still wasn't honest with her about why he'd broken up with her back then."

"But do you understand why, Bridge?"

"So he didn't have to take responsibility for what he'd done. Because he knew she'd never forgive him."

"No. That's not it. Bridge, he didn't want her to look back at their time together as teenagers and have it tainted by that one night. He wanted her to have a stupid kid to blame for breaking her heart in a clumsy way, not this idea that she wasn't enough for him or that he'd wanted someone else more than he'd wanted her, when that wasn't true — not for a minute."

"He told you this?"

"In so many words, yeah. Then and now. And I read between the lines a bit, because I know that in his shoes, at 17, I might have done the same, just to know you hated me, good and clean, and could move on with someone who'd deserve you, who'd make you happy."

"How easily you forget," she says. "You tried that one on me."

"I did, didn't I?" He sounds a little sheepish. "Didn't work."

"Because I was head-over-heels in love with you. And I'd seen enough in my visions of our life a couple hundred years ago to know that you might eventually pull your head out of your ass and claim your wife of several lifetimes."

OK. Whoa. I *so* shouldn't have heard that. But I did. And now I know why he asked her to marry him "again."

I mean, at this point, brain-sharing, fate, magical cooking — what's a little past-life memory added to the pile of stuff I didn't really believe in before I got here? This town is... odd.

"I had to see it for myself, Bridge. I felt the connection we had even at 6, but I couldn't let myself risk that for a relationship."

"Until you got tricked into looking at me that way, whether you wanted to or not."

"I'll never be grateful for what Holly did, but she forced me to face what I'd been denying for a long time. And that's what put me in a place that, when I did see our past myself, I couldn't deny it. Not for a moment."

OK. So now *Hunter* is having visions of past lives. And Dave nearly died. I kind of feel like we need a band meeting or something. Probably inside one of those salt symbol circle things.

"And still you tried..." I hear her laugh a little.

"I'm a fuck-up, Bridge. You know that."

"You are not a fuck-up! You made mistakes because you'd been hurt, traumatized, and you turned that in on yourself. And you're learning how not to do that anymore."

"And Declan seems to be working really hard not to fuck up with Callie now that she's given him a second chance. This is old mistakes coming back to haunt him. Not truly new ones. And, if nothing else, I think this will teach him to always be honest with her. You and I know how important that is. You said it. Dr. Apple said it. And if Declan can learn that... Can you imagine the two of them, happy like we are now? No more salty chef, and no more Dick-lan."

"I'd feel better if I didn't know he'd cheated on her..."

"But I didn't!" I yell, bursting in through the front door.

"Declan! How long have you been out there eavesdropping?" Brighid asks, outrage warring with concern.

"Since you were being judgmental."

"Holy fuck."

Well, that's a new one from her, at least from what I've heard. She's usually all "Mother of twelve gods" and shit.

Brighid closes her eyes, takes a deep breath, and I duck behind Hunter, afraid those twin violet laser beams of her glare will slice me in two.

"Declan, you can't keep hiding behind me when you piss off my fiancée," Hunter chides.

"You will say *nothing* of this! You hear me, Declan Carter?" she growls at me.

But I've withstood Callie-grade anger, and I'm marginally immune now, as long as no one is threatening my dick. Because I need to tell Callie what really happened and hope she'll forgive me for not telling her the truth that wasn't really the truth. And after that, much fucking. And lots of love-making. Maybe a few days with my head between her thighs...

"Declan, the lady's waiting for an answer. I'd suggest you give her the one she wants," Hunt says.

"Fine. I won't say anything to anyone about the visions or past lives, or therapy."

Brighid rolls her eyes. Hey — at least they're not eye-lasers!

"And about your brother?"

"Can't promise that. We're brothers, even if we annoy the shit out of each other. If Dave died, I'd be in a heap of trouble. So he and I will have to have a little chat soon. But I'll spare us all and promise not to tell Mom."

"She'd blame me," Hunter says.

"Probably," I admit, nodding.

"Fine," Brighid says, harrumphing at me. "Now what's this about 'You didn't do it'?"

"I didn't cheat on Callie!"

"Dude, I was there," Hunter says, dubious. "I was hungover, but I was in the room when you were standing there, naked, ranting about being drunk and waking up with that blonde, who was also naked."

"And you offered to trade for the brunette!"

"Fuck! That was a joke, Declan!"

Brighid rolls her eyes at *him* this time.

"That much is water under the bridge, boys," she says. "But someone needs to explain how naked Declan woke up with a naked blonde in a hotel bedroom, after a night of drunken debauchery—"

"I feel it necessary to remind you that Dave was neither drunk nor debauched," I interrupt.

"Did he suddenly remember seeing you sleeping in a different bed from the naked blonde?" she asks pointedly.

"No. That would have been useful at any point before tonight. But the blonde — she was at the gig tonight, and she was reminiscing about when we'd met twelve years ago..."

"Is that how Callie found out you'd cheated on her? From the other woman's own lips?"

Brighid is building up a head of steam again, and I can't help but marvel how I bring out this side of her when she's normally so calm and wise... But...

"Yes! But Callie only overheard *half* the conversation! And she made the same assumption I'd made — that we'd *all* made — twelve years ago: that I'd had sex with that woman!"

"Are you telling me you did not have sexual relations with that woman?"

Why does that sound familiar? Nevermind, I can't get off-track here.

"Yes! I did *not* have sex with her!"

"You woke up *naked* in the same bed."

"It's a long story, but the gist of it is that when she put the moves on me, I was so far out of it that I thought she was Callie, and this woman could *tell* that I loved this Callie, just from how I said her name. *That's* how much I loved her! I was all but passed out and I was *still* thinking of her, still expecting no one but her to have stripped me naked!"

"I'm not going to ask how you ended up totally naked without realizing it wasn't Callie."

"Wet jeans!"

"OK. Nevermind," she says, shaking her head in dismay. "Is this woman willing to tell Callie what really happened? Or rather, what didn't happen? Because I'm not sure Callie's going to take your word for it after you lied to her about the real reason you dumped her."

Yeah.

"It was stupid — but Hunt was right! I thought I was doing it for the right reasons. I was really stupid then, and I was a little stupid when I decided not to tell her again now. But she and I had agreed to leave the bad stuff behind, to relive only the good stuff together — that's why I took her to the amusement park for our first date!"

"Now? Not twelve years ago?" she asks.

"Yeah. Why?"

"Nevermind. I was going to question your maturity again, but if Hunt had taken me on a date to the amusement park, I'd have loved it."

"You would?" he asks, seeming genuinely surprised.

"Yeah. Good memories." She smiles softly, and I recall both times Callie and I did that together.

"And lots of darkness to make out in on the Haunted Mansion..." Hunter says suggestively.

"Now why didn't I think of that? We just destroyed each other at bumper cars!" I feel like I missed a key opportunity there.

Brighid and Hunter exchange a look.

"What?" There's no reply. "Anyway — we'd agreed to leave the bad stuff behind and celebrate the good stuff, bring it forward in to our second chance. And me thinking I cheated on Callie was definitely in the bad-stuff category. So I decided it was better left in the past. But now I know I didn't do it! And once Callie knows I didn't..."

"Did you get a sworn statement?"

"No. But I had Billy get her contact info and have her sign an NDA so this doesn't go viral like you two did."

Maybe I shouldn't have reminded them of that when Brighid's still irked with me. Oh, well...

"And that woman, she was horrified at the idea that me thinking — incorrectly — that I'd slept with her was the reason I'd left my wife..."

Oops.

"Wife?" Hunter says, incredulous.

"OK — I swore not to mention the past-life stuff. You all have to promise that that goes no further than us. There's like only two other people who know."

"Three," Brighid volunteers, raising her hand. Hunter frowns at her. I have a feeling the two of them are going to be having a discussion about all these secrets Brighid's been swearing to other people that she'd keep.

"Who are the other two?" Hunter asks with a sigh.

"Alex, because he was cooking with Callie when I found her again, and I needed to tell someone why I was so thrilled I'd found her. And Lyric, because she was the one who did the marriage thing."

"A handfasting?" Hunter asks.

"Yeah. That's it. We weren't old enough to do it legally. So we did the religious thing — the handfasting."

"A year and a day?" Hunter asks. He sure knows a lot about this stuff.

"No. Forever."

"Oh, crap. At 17? No wonder," he says.

"No wonder what?"

"No wonder you two have been so messed up for the last twelve years! No wonder it took you finding each other again to straighten you both out, let you be happy, live again. You promised her forever! There's no take-backs on that shit."

"Hunt, how do you know that?"

"Who do you think is doing Brighid's and my wedding?"

Oh.

"Lyric?"

"Yeah."

"And how do you think Brighid and I ended up finding each other across time and space when the last time we were married was two hundred years ago, in Ireland?"

Oh.

"So, when Callie and I die... we get to do this all over again?"

"Probably," Brighid says. "Ideally, you'll have learned some big lessons this time out and won't have to repeat those. And there's all kinds of complicating factors. For one, Hunter and I renewed our vows with a goddess presiding."

"In a vision, right?"

"Yes," they answer simultaneously. Weird.

"Just making sure. Because if Lyric is a goddess, I'm going to need lighting-proof underwear. If I can't get Callie to believe me about this first."

"I'd be more worried about Siobhan," Hunter says, his grin a little too gleeful.

"Siobhan has a shovel," Brighid adds ominously.

"And steel-toed combat boots," says Hunter.

"And a number of belts in various martial arts," Brighid says.

"And she threatened to tattoo a middle finger on the inside of my eyelids!" Hunter is still grinning gleefully, so I guess that's no longer on the table.

"Oh! Then I need to talk to her! I have a thing I need."

"Why do I suspect there's a muse involved?" Hunter says.

"Because Callie is my muse."

"Flibbertigibbets!" Brighid says. "You Carter boys and your lifebonds..."

"What?"

"Not my story," she says, clearly dissembling.

"Yeah. Gonna have to talk to Dave once all of this is sorted out."

"You're going to have to get to Callie first. And right now, that road goes through Siobhan. And I should probably warn you — there was some mention of torches and swamp monsters, along with the shovel."

Oh.

"So, this is like the dragon guarding the princess in the tower?"

"A bit," Brighid says.

"That's OK. I've got this, then."

"Why do you think that?"

"Because I'm King Arthur!"

# CHAPTER 46

# TWICE AS HARD

## Callie
### *The next day*

"I'm fine, Drew! Never better!"

"You are *not* fine. You overcooked a filet mignon. You served my short ribs on squid-ink pasta instead of polenta. You reversed the measurements on the mayo and mustard in the imperial sauce. And you added garlic to the tomato sauce twice, instead of garlic *and* onion."

"Fruits of Satan," I mutter under my breath.

"What?" Drew shakes his head. "Regardless of your feelings about onions right now, you can't double up on garlic instead, and you know that! Right now, Raquel would do a better job of serving edible food in this kitchen than you are!"

I drop the tongs I had in my hand, and the sound rings across the kitchen.

"Oh, my god! Somebody grab the fire extinguisher!"

I look around, expecting to see that I've caused some kind of flare-up on the stove by losing focus on the eggplant parm I was making. But it's sizzling along happily, unlike everyone in this kitchen right now, and...

Oh, my god — that came from the dining room!

Drew's already out the kitchen door into the dining room, fire extinguisher in hand.

I'm hot on his heels, clearing the doorway just in time to see him dousing a batch of Bananas Foster that apparently got a little too close to the curtains over the front windows, igniting them. A moment later, the curtains are also extinguished, leaving just a burned dish of bananas and a slightly singed window covering — both spotted with foam — to testify to what could have been a nightmarish accident.

"I'm so sorry!" Drew says to the couple who had been seated at the table. "We'll get you a fresh table setting and a fresh dessert. Your meal is on the house tonight. Thank you so much for your understanding!"

The couple doesn't seem too put-out, just a bit in shock still. As is everyone, I think. That's never happened before.

"Lily — do a quick turn-around on that two-top in the other room that just paid their check, and seat these nice folks there immediately," Drew says, while I stand behind him, dumbfounded.

Our hostess pulls the couple away from the scene of near-disaster.

"Everyone OK?" Drew says, asking around at the nearby tables, where everyone has returned to their seats. He gets a round of nods. "Dessert's on the house, folks. Our apologies for the excitement."

"Phillip — can I see you in Callie's office, please?"

Phillip looks guilty, and a little scared, so I'm guessing he was responsible for the flambé.

"You," he says, grabbing my hand. "You are going to join us, because we're going to have a little chat after we've talked to Phillip."

OK. Now I know how my staff feels when I talk to them in that tone. I am in big trouble.

"Phillip, have a seat," Drew says as soon as we get into my office and shut the door. He gestures to my chair behind the desk as soon as Phillip's seated in the other one. I decide following his request is probably for the best.

"OK. Tell me — tell *us* — exactly what happened out there," Drew says.

"I was doing the flambé with the Bananas Foster, just like usual," Phillip begins. "I've done it a hundred times. We don't get a ton of orders for it, but once or twice a week somebody has a special celebration or they just want a fancy banana dessert."

"We know, Phillip. But what happened tonight?"

"I really don't know."

"Nothing was different? Same measure of rum and banana liquor? Same bottles you used the last time? The lighter worked like normal? Nothing spilled over the side of the dish?"

"No. All exactly the same. And I wasn't even that close to the window. I've done the flambé in exactly that spot numerous times."

"Did somebody open the door? Did the wind blow the curtains?"

"No. It's the weirdest thing. It just suddenly erupted like three times the size of normal."

"OK. Thanks, Phillip," Drew says. "We'll chalk this one up to an act of God. Just be extra-careful the next time, OK? Go ahead and get the curtains down and the mess cleaned up. Avoid inconveniencing the other diners as much as possible, please."

"Got it. Thanks, Chef — Chefs. I really don't know what happened."

"No blame on you, Phillip. You know your job. Just a freak accident. Let's move on."

Drew opens the door and lets Phillip out. And then closes it again.

He sits down heavily in the chair Phillip just vacated, sighing and looking at his outstretched legs. Definitely not at me.

"Callie," he finally says, "You can go home — or Siobhan's or Brighid's or Lyric's or Hawaii, wherever you want — or I can go. But if I go, I'm not coming back."

Whoa.

"So it's come to that, has it?"

"Yeah, Callie. It really has," he says wearily. "I don't want to leave. You'd have to drag me out of here kicking and screaming, except I'm really afraid we're going to end up dragging a lot of people out of here kicking and screaming, with the building on fire."

"I don't know what happened there, Drew."

"I think you do."

"No. Really. I'm fine. Declan hasn't tried to contact me, hasn't sent me flowers, shown up at my apartment — nothing. Brighid said she'd told him he'd have to go through Siobhan to get to me."

"And we both know Siobhan would kick his ass."

"Yeah. So, I guess he realized he'd have to give me space again, let me figure this out on my own, decide what I want to do, if I can forgive him."

"You going to tell me what he did?"

"No. Not this time. I'll say it wasn't entirely a recent misstep that caused this. So, don't hold it against him. Not like that. But our history just keeps bubbling up, and not all of it is good."

"I thought you were putting that stuff behind you. The two of you seemed so happy this last week or so."

"We were."

"Not anymore?"

"I don't know. It's... it's complicated."

"Isn't it always..."

"Drew — don't leave. I've got this under control."

"No. No, you don't, Callie. If it was just burning sauces or sending entrées out with the wrong set, that would be one thing, but that..." he looks me in the eyes. "Somebody could have gotten hurt, Callie. We could have had a massive fire that not only took out the entire building — including your apartment and Siobhan's — but Brighid's shop, too. And chances are if it had gone that way, somebody *would* have gotten hurt. Or killed."

"You told Phillip it was an act of god."

"Unless you're laying claim to your godhood, finally, I think we both know that's not the case," he sighs deeply. "Honestly, I don't care. God, witch, fire-starter..." I glare at him. "Words are just words. But you had gotten this under control, and then things were humming along this last week or so, and I was ready to come back full-time, looking forward to it."

"And now you're not."

"The kitchen's stressful enough, Callie. You know that. It's one of the reasons I kept telling you to take more time for yourself. And you have been — and it's been good for you. But now you're back here, in before dawn, not taking a break, things going haywire left and right, and while I'm in there telling you to go home, arguing with you about it, a fire suddenly and inexplicably erupts in the dining room?"

"Don't argue with me?" I suggest, mostly joking.

He levels a stare at me that immediately negates my thin attempt at humor.

"Fine. Are you ready to come back full-time?"

"More than."

"Without me here, at all?"

"Yes," he says definitively. "We've got this, Callie. Really. You've set us up for success, especially with the two new hires. So, take a tropical vacation. Binge-watch every show on TV for a couple weeks while you sit around in your pajamas. Go to Italy and try out some new flavors. Go grab Declan and jump his bones until you're both too tired to argue about whatever it is that's gone wrong!"

"I knew I wasn't the only one who said that!"

"What?"

"Jumping people's bones."

"It's not exactly the height of modern vernacular."

"I'm a little behind the times on that particular front."

"Vernacular?"

"No, sex."

"All the more reason to go see Declan."

"I'm not ready for that yet."

"That's fine, if that's the case. But make sure you don't take too long to *get* ready. He's going to leave at some point before the weather gets cold."

That's something I hadn't even thought of. It's something Declan and I would have eventually had to figure out. But now... everything's all up in the air. And I have no idea if I should even try to work things out or just be done with it all. For good.

"I'll figure it out."

"I don't want to see you in here again until you do, Callie. I don't care if its two weeks or a month or a year. We've got this all handled. Now you have to go handle your own shit."

It's tough-love Drew again. And I have to admit it: he's not wrong. I just don't know where or how to start.

"Hey, girl! You taking a dinner break?" Siobhan asks, spraying and wiping down one of her work areas.

"No. Drew kicked me out."

"Again?"

"Yeah."

"For how long this time?"

"Until I get my shit sorted out. I may or may not have just almost set the restaurant on fire."

"Do I want to know?" she asks, that eyebrow ring doing its thing again.

"Well, there were Bananas Foster involved."

"Oooh... I love those. Bananas! Rum! Plus — fire!"

"A little too much fire this time."

"You get your measurements off?"

"No. I wasn't even in the room."

"Oh. Then how was it your fault?"

"Drew and I were arguing. He was trying to get me to leave."

"Because?"

"Because I kept messing up the food."

"You don't do that. Ever. Except that one burned batch of sauce."

"Which was also Declan-related."

"You do the exercises Rory taught you?"

"Yeah. It's not working as well as it had."

"Because you're off-balance. Because you haven't resolved your feelings about him. You can't ground when you're focused on two possible choices, over and above your inner balance. Balance first. And you haven't decided."

"No, I haven't. I hate the fact that he wasn't honest with me almost as much as I hate that he cheated on me way back when. But I also understand why he didn't tell me the whole truth — then and now. And I do honestly believe he was trying to protect me, protect what we had — have."

"Or could have."

"Yeah. That, too."

"Do you believe he loves you?"

I sigh, knowing this is one area where I'm very certain.

"I do. And I believe him when he says he always has, that he lied about that when he broke up with me. Misguided as it was."

"Then what's the problem?"

"I had just started to feel like I could trust him again, and now I know he wasn't honest with me."

"So you're feeling vulnerable, and like you got fooled into trusting someone. And it's his fault again."

"Yeah."

"Then I think you have to ask yourself whether you can bring yourself to trust him again. But, moreover, first, I think you have to ask whether you can bring yourself to trust *you* again."

"Me?"

"Yeah. It's not so much that Declan let you down. It's that you decided you trusted your instincts where he was concerned. Again. And — regardless of what happened before — now you're wondering if you should have known better."

"I did know better. I pushed him away."

"But not too hard."

"No. I guess not."

"Because part of you knows that he does love you, and that he wants to do the best he can for you, even if he still makes mistakes."

"Mistakes he thought might actually protect me."

"Yeah. I think so."

"I still hate that he lied to me."

"Yeah. That sucks. He should stop doing that. If only there had been some kind of consequences to him having lied to you... Oh, wait... You disappeared on his ass, and Brighid chewed him out and yet again threatened to hex his dick off."

"She did?"

"Yeah. And warned him that I have a really excellent shovel and some really big boots."

"Those are some hefty boots."

"Steel-toed," Siobhan notes, clearly proud of that.

She's one of a kind, Siobhan. Cargo shorts and combat boots. In the summer. At the beach. And armed with a shovel.

"You think that's why he's staying away?"

"I'd say it's definitely a good reason for him to."

"What if I want him to come back?"

"I think you're going to have to tell him that."

"I'm not ready for that."

"Then don't." She shrugs.

This is why I'm off-kilter. I don't like any of my options right now. I'm not ready to make a decision.

"Hey — I've got a client coming in any minute, so I've got to cut this short. But let me ask you..." she says, seeming a little hesitant.

"What?"

"You still got that picture you took of him?" Her face is full of mischief.

"Siobhan!"

"You do, don't you!" She smirks at me. "You couldn't delete it because you have a photo of a gloriously hot and naked Declan Carter on your phone, and you love that massive, manly, magic penis of his, even if you have to look and not touch right now!"

"Siobhan!"

"What? He's hot. I'd do him. The new-and-improved version, anyway."

Instant nausea again.

And it wouldn't matter if it was Siobhan or a groupie or some pop princess.

"Come on — break it out. Give a girlfriend some eye-candy! I haven't had a naked guy in front of me in months."

I give her a look.

"I mean in a sexual context. Tattooing random guys' asses and piercing their decidedly less-magical penises does not count."

"Do they get more magical after you pierce them?" I'm honestly curious. It's not like I've had a lot to compare.

"Oh, they can be!" she says, nodding fervently. "You've got to fit the piercing to the penis, though. And they've got to abstain for a good long while afterward, to let it heal. Don't ever let a guy with a freshly pierced penis claim he's 'close enough' to being fully healed. They never are. They're just horny as hell with all that stimulation and no safe way to relieve it until they really are healed."

"I wouldn't know."

"Declan isn't pierced?"

"Did you think he was?"

"No idea. But you got him to let you cuff him up, so it's possible he's kinky enough that he'd be into it." She shrugs. "So, you going to give up the goods?"

"You're way too interested in my boyfriend's penis."

"Is he still your boyfriend?"

And there we're back at the core issue. And I still can't decide.

## *Two days later*

"Still nothing?" Lyric asks as I check my phone for text messages.

With all this forced time off, I decided I'd come hang out with her for the day, give her some kid-free hours while she finishes up her lesson plans for the new school year. The summer is flying by. Except the last few days. Because I keep expecting Declan to show up to make his case. And he hasn't. Not a text, call, visit or even flowers.

"No."

"You're noticing it more because you're not at work all day."

"No doubt."

"You ready to break down and admit you miss him?"

"I have no problem admitting that. But there's a big difference between that and deciding I want to give him yet another chance."

"For what it's worth, I'm really sorry I didn't try harder to dissuade you from going with 'forever' all those years ago."

"Why? Do you think things would be different if we'd said a year and a day?"

"I don't honestly know. You're the only couple I've married who split up for any length of time afterwards, let alone so soon afterwards. But I know from personal experience that not being with the person you love is sheer torture, and trying to find someone else who makes you feel that way once they're gone seems like an impossible task. But if you do... then you're faced with the possibility of having that kind of loss all over again."

She says it so matter-of-factly that I check to see if the kids are within earshot.

"They both went upstairs to play in their rooms. They're too old for naptime, but we try to do quiet hours of solo play."

"Are you OK, Lyric? I know it's tough..."

"I really appreciate you coming over, to help with the kids and give me some girl-time, but I'm really not wanting to revisit my loss right now." The screen door gets pulled open in the breeze and slams shut again. She jumps.

Something's up with her. She's not her usual bubbly self. In fact, she's acting more like the old me than the usual Lyric. Maybe it's the pressure she's under. Maybe Brighid was right about sending her for a spa day, if we can just get her to do it. But right now, she's not giving me much to work with. I may have to call in reinforcements.

"OK. Understood," I tell her. "Just know that while I'm on leave, if you need anything, I'm here for you."

I squeeze her hand, because it's the thing you do. But I'm not any better at the touchy-feely stuff than Siobhan is. Maybe I used to be. But I haven't let myself be open to it for so long that pushing myself to not put walls up between me and other people is still pretty foreign. Reaching out is even harder.

"Thanks," she says, smiling thinly at me. "Actually — I've got to start working on the fundraiser for the music department, or we're going to be sharing instruments again this year. If you want to donate a gift card for the restaurant for the silent auction, or maybe a chef-cooked dinner party in someone's home, that would be a huge help." I can already sense the relief in her at that idea. Maybe she just needs to get some help with that fundraiser.

"Sure, I can do that. Probably better if I don't do the cooking thing, though."

"You don't think you're going to burn down someone else's kitchen, do you?"

"Siobhan has a big mouth."

"Siobhan was worried, as much as she pretends otherwise. And I don't mean about you burning down her studio indirectly. You need to find some peace. It's not good for you to continue struggling with this decision, back and forth, angry and sad, disappointed and wistful. Siobhan's afraid you'll end up doing something you'll regret. And I don't disagree. This reunion was a long time coming for you two. This isn't an easy decision because it's a complicated situation in a relationship on a huge scale. You two are tied together, until you both decide otherwise."

"We did! He dumped me, and I was done with him. I moved on."

"But did you really?" she asks, the question punctuated by a rumble of thunder outside.

She looks up, seeming concerned.

"I'm going to have to cut this short. Tommy doesn't like thunderstorms. It's too much sensory stimulation. I need to get him down here and focused on his movie before it gets any worse."

"OK. Like I said — if you need anything."

"Thanks, Callie. I appreciate it. For now, just try to find some peace for yourself. OK?"

"Yeah. I'll try."

# CHAPTER 47

## TEQUILA

### *Later that night*

"Open up, girly! We are here to crank the volume on this pity party to twelve!"

When I open the door, Siobhan has a full bottle of tequila in one hand and a bag of limes in the other. Lyric follows in her wake, seeming in a better mood as she totes a bottle of orange juice and another of... Limoncello? Brighid, who doesn't even drink, brings up the rear, with her giant dog.

"What? Every party needs a wolfhound! Did no one inform you all of the rules?"

My expression is dubious.

"OK. Fine. He was afraid of the thunderstorm. He didn't want to be left home alone, and Hunter's over at the studio, working with the guys."

"I thought he liked to go to the studio," Siobhan says.

"He does," Brighid says. "But he has a habit of singing along when a certain lead singer — who shall not be named — is doing his vocals, and the last time, Crógan didn't restrain himself, even when they had the recording going. And The Nameless One is a perfectionist, so it was not exactly a welcome set of harmonies. He got banished. Temporarily."

"Declan can be a dick, can't he?" Siobhan says. "Oops!" she adds.

"You weren't supposed to say it," Brighid admonishes her.

"How about this? We'll play a game. We'll discuss whatever each of us wants, but anytime someone says the D-word, they have to drink."

"Sounds like you've been doing that already, Siobhan," I tell her.

"I may have had a pre-game round with a client earlier. Who tipped me with this mighty fine bottle of tequila, I might add. This is not the shitty tequila that requires salt and lime. But I have nonetheless brought my own supply, should we find it desirable."

"And I've got your fancy Italian Limoncello for canary shots, and O.J. for tequila sunrise shots!"

"What about Brighid?" I ask, plenty ready to drown my sorrows, even if Siobhan's choice of alcohol reminds me far too much of talking to Declan that first day at Castalia.

Flibbertigibbets.

"You just thought about him, didn't you?" Brighid says. "I think she needs to drink!"

"Excellent idea!" Siobhan says.

"But I didn't *say* it!" I argue.

"No, you thought it, and that proves you're already operating under a handicap," Siobhan says. "You need to catch up anyway."

She pours me a shot and hands it over, and I bow to peer pressure and down it.

"So, what are we going to discuss?"

"How about the hottest guy you've ever dated?" Siobhan suggests. "Or slept with. Or fantasized about. I've got it: when it's your turn, you say the name. If anyone else has dated, slept with or fantasized about the same guy, they drink. Then the previous person will guess which of the three it is for the namer. If they're right, the namer drinks again."

It's a very short game if we're restricted to the guys we've dated or slept with. Because I'm pretty sure Brighid's list is nearly as short as mine. And since when is she drinking?

"I'll start," Siobhan says, pouring out a long line of shots into the glasses she's got stacked inside the pockets of her cargo shorts, "since we all know I have had no shortage of men in my bed. So, Round 1: Jason Momoa."

Brighid groans.

"Did Hunter say something?" she asks Siobhan.

"Not to me. You got some secret tryst you want to fess up to?"

"No. Definitely not."

"So, are you drinking? If it's any of the three, you drink. On three!"

We all grab a shot and down it.

"I'm guessing none of the four of us have had that experience outside our fantasies," I say.

"Our very respectful fantasies," Brighid says.

"Speak for yourself," Siobhan says, laughing. But she takes another shot. "That was an easy one. Round 2! Brighid?"

"Hunter Graves!"

"Ooh! Playing with fire, girl! Your fiancé! On three!"

Siobhan and Brighid both drink.

"Bonus round! Which is it: date, slept with or fantasize?"

"You hadn't better have slept with my man, Siobhan, or we're going to have words!" Brighid says, already sounding a little tipsy. The dog barks, as if to emphasize the point.

"You've dated and slept with him, so that's easy," Siobhan says. "Somebody guess me instead."

"Fantasize," Brighid says, seeming a little relieved when Siobhan drinks.

"Round 3! Callie!"

"I'm going to get it over with: Declan Carter."

"Ding! Ding! Ding! She said the magic words! Down the hatch, Callie!" Lyric says, beaming.

And now I'm catching up.

"OK. Anyone else want to own up to that one?"

"You already know where I stand on Mr. Magic Penis!" Siobhan says, laughing.

"What? Do I want to know?" Brighid asks.

"You really should ask, before you decide to hex that lovely member off," Siobhan says.

"Well, I'm out on this one," Brighid says. "I've known Declan too long. He's like an annoying brother I'd occasionally like to kick where it counts."

"And I'd met him back in the day, so he's always been Callie's territory as far as I was concerned," Lyric adds.

"Ooh... I'm going to take that as a no on all three with both of you," Siobhan says. "That leaves you and me," she tells me.

We both drink.

"Callie's dated and slept with him. And I guess that Siobhan's also fantasized about your man, as well as mine," Brighid says.

"What can I say? They're both hot!" Siobhan says, finally back on track. "Not nearly enough tattoos on either of them. But, boy, wouldn't it be fun to add some more!" She laughs uproariously.

"He doesn't have any tattoos." I realize my mistake a moment later and facepalm.

"Drink 'em up, Callie!" Siobhan calls out.

"Fine." I down another shot, and Siobhan refills all the empty glasses with tequila and Limoncello.

"Even David's got ink now," Siobhan volunteers.

"Oh?" I'm still waiting for people to tell me this secret story about Declan's brother.

"Ooh! She just thought about him again!" Brighid says.

"Drink! Drink!" Lyric chants.

"Fine. But I'm going to end up passed out on top of your dog, Brighid."

"He won't mind. He's a big cuddler."

"Kind of like Hunter, right?" Siobhan says.

"No comment. We've already done the Hunter round."

"Spoilsport!" Siobhan charges.

"So what's David's tattoo?" I ask.

The curiosity is killing me.

Brighid and Siobhan exchange a look.

"Come on! What is this big secret no one will tell me?"

"Sworn to secrecy, sadly. Can't break that oath," Brighid says, making a zipping motion over her mouth.

"But the tattoo's not secret. She could see it for herself, if he had his shirt off," Siobhan says.

"True," Brighid replies.

"OK — it's bad enough we're talking about Declan—" Lyric says.

"Drink!" I gleefully tell her.

She downs a shot.

"But his brother is with my kids right now, so I'm not getting into what the guy looks like with his shirt off, especially not when his girlfriend is with him!"

"So what's the tattoo?"

"He's got the aMUSEd muse logo on his left shoulder now," Siobhan says.

"Like most of the guys in the band," Brighid adds. "And Siobhan matched that design with the one she gave Piper, which has a seal and ocean waves in it."

"Oh. That's nice. So they have matching tattoos."

"Five muses down, one to go!" Brighid says.

"What's that mean?"

"Five of the guys now have that muse logo tattooed on them, on their arms or shoulders or backs," she says.

"And I started customizing them when I did David's," Siobhan adds. "His muse looks like Piper."

"Because *she* is *his* muse," Brighid says, as if that was an explanation in and of itself. She catches my confused expression. "The artist who did all the other guys' ink when they first signed their record deal — Olivia — she left the muse's face indistinct, mostly just black and white."

"Blackwork or black-and-grey, Brighid. Black-and-white is for photos."

"OK. That. But she left it that way so that the guys could adapt the design as their lives evolved. And they're mostly customized — Hunter's has his green guitar, and David's, which Siobhan did from scratch, has the seal and the ocean, and he had her do Piper's face for the muse."

"And the others?"

"You know — I don't know," Brighid says. "I honestly haven't seen all the guys with their shirts off. I just know they have them."

"Well, we know who didn't get one," Siobhan says.

"Who?" Lyric asks, though I'm avoiding even thinking of the answer because I don't want to have to drink again, and she seems to be able to tell when I'm thinking of...

"I can't say, or I'll have to drink," Siobhan says.

"I wonder why," Brighid replies.

"I have a theory," Siobhan says.

"Which is...?" I ask.

"Nope. I'm keeping that one to myself!"

"Oh, come on!" I object. "You all and your secrets... He's *my* boyfriend!"

"Drink!" Siobhan says, a satisfied smile on her face. And I'm not sure if it's because I have to drink without even having said his name or whether it's because I called him my boyfriend.

"Round 4!" Siobhan announces as soon as I've downed that shot. I'm feeling at a decided disadvantage here. "I'm stealing Lyric's turn, because inquiring minds, and all that..." She has a Cheshire Cat grin on her face, and I'm instantly worried about what she's going to say.

"Mace Mason!"

Brighid groans again.

"I hate you," she says to Siobhan.

Siobhan cackles, immensely pleased with herself.

"You know you want to clear the air on that rumor! Hunter told me Rhys used to tease him about Mace and you."

"What did you say to my fiancé to get him to tell you that?" Brighid asks her.

"Trade secret."

"Well, I can't answer that one, by drinking or otherwise."

"Ooh... the plot thickens!" Siobhan says. "You are just full of secrets, aren't you?"

"Many of them not my own, Siobhan. And ones I'm sworn to keep. Remember that."

"It's like playing a drinking game with a Catholic priest, only you keep asking him about what was said in the confessional. Maybe he cracks. Maybe he doesn't..."

"I haven't had a drink in years, Siobhan. This isn't playing fair."

"Fine," Siobhan says. "You sit out this round. Callie, Lyric and I will play. You can do the bonus round. So: Mace Mason."

All three of us drink.

"And it's fantasize for all of you," Brighid says, sounding triumphant. Siobhan drinks. Lyric drinks. I drink. "Yeah, that round probably wasn't fair either, considering that Brighid seems to know a good bit about Mace Mason and his secrets.

"Next! Alex Winters!" Lyric says.

"You're going to get us all in trouble if we keep putting the guys' names in on this," I say.

"Alex Winters!" Siobhan repeats. "On three!"

Siobhan downs a drink, and Lyric, Brighid and I look expectantly at each other.

"It's just me?" Siobhan asks, shrugging.

"He's attractive," Brighid says. "But, again, he's kind of like a brother at this point. If a less annoying one than He Who Shall Not Be Named."

"He's a friend," I admit. "And objectively, quite attractive. But still, just a friend."

"Too glam for me," Lyric says. "He's got better taste in clothes and jewelry than I do!"

"I'm going to have to start being more selective with my fantasies if I don't want to end up passed out while you three are still half sober," Siobhan says.

"Did Declan have a problem with you and Alex being friends?" Brighid asks suddenly.

"Drink!" Siobhan says, handing Brighid a shot.

"Mother of twelve gods... I forgot."

"Drink!" Siobhan repeats. "Lightweight."

"That's the first time anyone's ever called me that," Brighid says, laughing and downing that shot with a grimace.

"Oh, girl — you are gorgeous. Serious Earth Mother vibes!" Siobhan tells her.

"I don't really care what anyone thinks," Brighid says.

"Except Hunter."

"Yeah... He's gorgeous, isn't he? With those eyes, and all that hair..."

"I drank on that one, don't forget," Siobhan says, waggling her eyebrows at Brighid.

"Callie only has eyes for what's-his-face," Brighid says, sounding increasingly drunk.

"Declan," I say.

"Drink!" Siobhan says.

Oh, boy...

# CHAPTER 48

## TEQUILA SUNRISE

### *Eight hours later*

"Oh, gods... shoot me now," Siobhan moans from the sofa. "No more pre-gaming for me."

Brighid's dog snores loudly on the floor in front of the sofa.

"Five more minutes, Hunter. You kept me up all night..." Brighid murmurs from her spot draped across the dog.

Siobhan and I exchange a look.

"They're both very hairy," she says. "She may get them legitimately confused."

She and I both laugh as quietly as possible.

"Pain meds?" she asks.

"Top cabinet, far end," I tell her, pointing to the kitchen. "I'm just glad Lyric got home OK."

"Responsible mama genes," Siobhan says. "She cut out on us early so she could be semi-sober by the time she got home. Good thing it's not a long walk. Even if she'll have to come back for her car."

She does one of those martial-arts kick-up moves and ends up with her feet on the floor at the end of the sofa, leaning heavily on the arm.

Even hung-over she's coordinated and strong. And she's managed to get clear of the sofa without stepping on or over Brighid or the dog.

"Hey, Callie—" she says from the kitchen. "Is this your phone charging over here on the counter? I mean, I have to assume it is..."

"Probably. Why?"

"Because it's not locked. And it's got a very lovely picture of a very hot, very naked Declan Carter on it."

"Drink!" Brighid chirps from the floor, giggling to herself.

I launch myself out of bed and across the room, snatching the phone out of Siobhan's hand.

Sure enough, that very embarrassing photo of Declan is now the wallpaper on my phone.

"You did not see that," I tell Siobhan.

"Sorry, hon, I cannot *un*-see that, nor would I want to. Wow. I can now testify that the penis does indeed appear to be magic."

"Siobhan!"

"It's not like I looked on purpose! It was sitting here, charging, unlocked! And you have like, what? Three total apps on there? It's not like the manly bits were hiding under a Tinder icon."

"What's that?"

"Oh, gods... You really are totally out of the loop on social media. It's a dating app. Well, more of a hook-up app. Commitment-free is their specialty. Hence the aptness if that fine specimen of manhood had been hiding under the bushel that is the Tinder app icon."

"The bushel thing is actually a Bible reference, you know," Brighid mumbles into a large pile of dog.

"Totally inappropriate then," Siobhan says. "Just like that photo."

"Does she really have a naked photo of Declan Carter on her phone?" Brighid asks, sitting up.

"Naked and chained up to his bed, by the looks of things."

"Whoa," Brighid says. "And I thought Siobhan was the kinky one."

"Hey — don't forget we let you get away with not answering that question about Mace."

"No comment."

"Spoken like a true star of viral social media."

"Ugh," Brighid moans. "I'm feeling lousy enough right now. Don't bring up my virality."

"How? What? When? Who?" I'm still staring at my phone. The words come pouring out of my mouth without conscious thought.

"This feels familiar for some reason," Brighid says.

"Spit it out, Callie," Siobhan urges.

"I didn't put that on there!"

"Well, I happen to know that you had it on your phone, because you told me you'd taken it."

"I had. But it was just in my photos app. I'd never have put it on there... like that..."

"We were all pretty sloshed last night. And we did keep coming back around to Declan," Siobhan says.

"And that led to getting even more sloshed," Brighid notes.

"I don't remember you showing it to me, if that helps any," Siobhan says. "It's nice that I still got to see it, though," she adds with a smirk.

"Maybe you just accidentally set it as your wallpaper," Brighid suggests. "It's like two clicks."

"Maybe." It still feels really unlikely, though.

"Just be glad it was only the four of us last night," Siobhan says. The dog snores loudly.

"It could have been a dozen of us passing your phone around with that picture on it!" Siobhan adds.

"I've got to take him out," Brighid says. "I can't believe he didn't wake me up before now. What time is it? Come on, boy! Up!"

"Half past nine," Siobhan says, pulling her own phone from one of her many pockets.

"Thank the gods Molly was opening the shop today," Brighid says. "I've got to get going, get him home, fed. Whoa... Ow," she adds, holding her head. "This is why I do not drink. Mostly. Are you feeling any better about things now, Callie? We figured you just needed to let loose, get your mind off..."

"Oh. My. God. Declan Carter!" Siobhan says.

"Drink!" Brighid replies with a giggle.

"No! I don't mean that... My phone. Oh. My. God. I'm so sorry, Callie!"

"What?" I grab her phone from her hand, only to see the exact same photo staring back at me. "Did I text this to you? How drunk was I?"

"No. You didn't text it to me. That's my Twitter feed."

"What? No!" Brighid says, grabbing Siobhan's phone out of my hand. "Oh. My. God. Declan Carter!"

"Drink!" Siobhan says. "You're going to need it," she tells me.

"I cannot un-see that. Ever," Brighid says, shuddering, before handing the phone back to Siobhan. "No offense, Callie. But I *so* didn't want that image of Declan in my brain."

"You may not be alone in that Brighid, but you would be in the minority, based on how many likes and shares that image has gotten. And that's even with the 'sensitive media' settings keeping it hidden from huge swaths of people."

"But I don't have a Twitter account!" I object. "I never even made an Instagram account. How did the photo from my phone get onto Twitter?"

"Could you have gotten hacked, Callie? Does anyone else know you had that photo?" Brighid asks.

"Just Drew. And Declan."

"Neither of whom would have any reason to post that photo. Declan would have every reason *not* to. What account is it posted to?"

"It's under DeclansBiggestFan. Brand new account," Siobhan says. "My guess is it's a fan, looking to get Declan's attention. Which I imagine it probably has, if he's awake or any of the other guys are."

"David's a morning person," Brighid says.

"Oh. God. No."

"I'd bet Billy and the PR people are losing their minds right now." Brighid says. "But they can get it removed, Callie, since the poster won't have had Declan's permission. But it's going to have been saved and shared all over the place by now. This was posted hours ago."

"This is all my fault." I sit down on my bed, demoralized.

"You didn't post it. No one's going to blame you," Siobhan says.

"But it wouldn't exist if I hadn't taken it, intending to post it."

"You were going to post this?" Brighid asks.

"I was angry. Declan had pictures posted with groupies."

"All the guys do."

"It was in a hotel room. The night before he came to see her the first time, right after he found her," Siobhan explains.

"Oh. Kind of glad I didn't know that the last time I saw him. In person, anyway," she adds, shaking her head like she's swallowed something sour.

"It wasn't what it looked like," I tell her.

"Yeah — you explained that, but you didn't ever explain what Declan is doing in food banks."

"Declan's at a food bank?" Brighid says.

"Not now. And that's not important right now, either. I've got to apologize to him for this."

"It's not your fault," Siobhan says. "I'm going to keep saying that until you believe me."

"Not helping," I tell her.

Because I know this is my fault. Declan is going to hate me now, thinking I'm some kind of angry, obsessed, vengeful purveyor of private pictures. The whole band is. The whole world is!

Oh, my god — I can forget a second restaurant. Not only will there be no Declan in my life to fund it, I'll have no diners left to sustain it. And the only way I could possibly keep Castalia from tanking after this is if I let Drew buy me out before anyone realizes it was me who took the photo, and me who let some unknown person get hold of it and post it all over the freaking internet.

Flibbertigibbets!

This scandal will destroy me professionally. And all I can do is try to salvage the restaurant for Drew to run. And I'll have to do that this morning if I'm going to stand any chance of doing it at all.

But I have one thing I have to do first. Something I can't put off for another minute, even if it's going to destroy me personally to do it.

# CHAPTER 49

## MISSION IMPOSSIBLE

### Declan

"**D**ec! Dec! Wake the fuck up, Dec! Don't make me pour water on you like I did Hunter!"

My eyes peel open just enough to see red curls falling into brown irises, about two inches from my face.

"What the fuck!"

I sit bolt upright, smacking my forehead into something hard. Very hard.

"Ow! Flibbertigibbets!" the voice says.

"I repeat: What the fuck?" I demand, rubbing my forehead and trying to pry my eyes open just enough to make sense of what is going on here. I'm in my bedroom at the studio house. Check. The light coming in through the sliding glass doors onto the upper deck is blinding, being as they face out on the ocean and it's a ridiculously early hour after a very late night. I look at the clock on the wall.

"It's nine o'clock! Why the fuck is anyone waking me up?" I demand, swiveling my head back toward the door and the apparent source of the other expressions of pain and cursing. If oddly mild cursing. Like if Mary Poppins was pissed off that she'd smacked foreheads with a rockstar.

"You've gone viral, Dec!"

OK. Now it all makes sense. Rhys.

I flop back in the bed.

"I'm always viral, Rhys," I explain wearily. "Every time I post a photo on Instagram, it goes out to a million people. If I take a photo of a jar of pickles, it goes viral. Why is this news worth waking me up at zero-dark-thirty?"

"Well, it's closer to nine-thirty," he points out. Helpful as always.

"Fine. But why are you *Waking. Me. Up?*"

"It's not a jar of pickles."

"What? In English, Rhys."

"The photo — it's not of a jar of pickles. And, actually, it's on Twitter, not Instagram, because Instagram doesn't allowed nudity. I mean, I guess you could call it a photo of *a* pickle, but that might confuse people who'd think it was a literal pickle and not your naked penis."

OK. Now I'm awake.

"You woke me up to tell me that there's a dick-pic of me. On Twitter. And it's viral?"

"Yup."

"I bet Billy's having a coronary right about now."

"He's on the phone with Dave. And Malcolm. And some bigwig at the label."

"And not with *me?* It's *my* dick!"

"That's why I'm here."

"Because it's *my* dick?"

"No. Because they're on the phone. You've got your phone on silent, I guess. So I came to wake you up and — I'm quoting here — 'Tell Mr. Carter the Younger to get his naked, narcissistic ass down here to the office so we can have a strategy meeting about yet another viral aMUSEd scandal! But it had better be clothed, or he's going to be *wishing* it was a bed he was handcuffed to!' I think that was it." He looks up, thoughtful. "Yeah. That's what she said."

She? Uh-oh.

"I think you'd better come with me, Rhys. And bring your phone."

"Why?"

"Because I have a feeling you're going to need an alibi. And I'm probably going to need a witness to testify in the trial for my murder."

Three minutes later, and I'm pulling a T-shirt over my head as I get to the bottom of the stairs from the first floor to the ground floor.

"I'm off the hook, Dec," Rhys says, smiling, as I reach the studio control room. "I showed Dave, Billy and Malcolm that I really did delete that photo from my phone. And Billy said he'll be happy to witness your murder."

Heh. I just bet he would be...

Distracted by Rhys, by the time I get to the office, I'm just pulling my shirt down over my abs.

"Thank you for joining us, Mr. Carter. And additional thanks for taking the time to put on some clothes first."

"Good morning, Marina," I say coolly, glancing at the video conference display on the wall.

"Ms. Matthews to you, Mr. Carter," she insists, her demeanor getting visibly chillier. Our label CEO is a hardass to start with. And she's apparently of a mind to be hard on *my* ass, in particular. Oh, this is going to be a fun meeting. Not.

"Have a seat, Declan," Billy says. He, Dave and Malcom are already sitting down, facing the monitor, like they've been discussing this with *Ms. Matthews* for a while now. Extra fun. I love people discussing the disposition of my naked ass — and other parts — while I'm not even in the room.

"OK — would somebody care to tell me exactly what's going on? I had a late night last night, and I was trying to catch up on sleep so that we could get some work done in the studio today. Next thing I know, Rhys is waking my ass up and telling me to get down here ASAP."

"Ass is right," Dave mumbles from my left. I give him a look. I get a quirked eyebrow in response. Alright. Dave's not on Team Declan right now, whatever this ballgame turns out to be. Got it.

"Billy?" prompts Marina — because I'm not calling her Ms. Matthews in my head, not until she gains the power of telepathy and starts monitoring my thoughts.

"At 5:43 a.m. today, someone going by the handle 'DeclansBiggestFan' posted a photo to their account, in which they tagged..." Billy pauses while he checks something "...Declan's personal account, the official aMUSEd account, several fan-run *un*official aMUSEd accounts and a number of official accounts for various music publications. That photo..." he clicks around on his laptop, adding to the video of Marina Matthews on the conferencing screen.

Wow. It's a lot... bigger on that giant monitor than what I'd imagined when Rhys told me my dick had gone viral. I narrowly avoid smirking at the double-entendre.

"Mr. Carter! This is nothing to be smirking about!" Marina says sharply. OK. Maybe she is telepathic, because I was certain my facial expression hadn't changed. "This is a public-relations catastrophe!"

There's a long moment of silence that stretches nearly to breaking while she waits for my response.

"I'm not sure I see the problem."

I'm going to have to play this cool if I'm going to keep Callie out of trouble.

Dave's eyes go wide, his eyebrows raised even higher. Billy growls quietly on my other side. Marina Matthews... she looks out of the monitor with an expression somewhere between extreme irritation and loathing.

She opens her mouth to speak and then seems to think better of it.

"Mr. Gryffin?" she prompts.

As his image pops up on the screen next to hers, Gryff's stoic expression is no different from every time I've ever seen or talked to him. Cool as a cucumber.

"The account, and the photo itself, have been very well isolated from their origins," he says. "Not even my best ha—I.T. professional — could trace them to a person or even an I.P. address. Whoever they are, they have some serious tech knowledge, or at least the wherewithal to hire someone with that level of skill."

"So your guys weren't up to the task again, eh, Gryff?" I can't help it. I smirk a little bit this time. After he was such a dick about helping me find Callie, it seems only fitting that his team's inadequacies are on display when dealing with a photo of my actual dick. Dick-lan, indeed.

He takes a deep breath.

"As I said, the person responsible for this image being posted has a very high level of skill. We're not going to be able to trace it back to anyone, not even with the services' cooperation."

"Well, the first priority is to get the image taken down," Marina says. "It's too late, of course — it's already been shared across the internet. We could send out takedown notices to every service and site on the planet and we'd never get every copy eradicated." She looks at me like I'm personally responsible for this and not the person who's naked all over the internet today. "But we can demand the original post is taken down, that account banned."

"I don't see the point of that," I tell her. "If it's out there, it's out there."

She blinks, frowns.

"Are you suggesting we leave it up, Mr. Carter? You really don't have any concerns about your... business... being exposed to everyone who cares to look?"

I look at the photo, where it still sits displayed on the screen.

"No. Not really," I finally answer. "People are going to think what they're going to think." I shrug.

"What about the impact on the band, the band's reputation? Billy?" she asks.

"Honestly, I'm not sure it isn't a net-positive for the band as a whole," he says, musing. "I'm not in the 'Any publicity is good publicity' camp, as we know from Hunter's situation earlier this summer. And, for any of the other guys, this would be a nightmare. But Declan's reputation amongst fans and the general public has always been somewhat... problematic."

"Very diplomatic there, Billy. Thanks," I tell him, giving him a nod.

"What he means is Declan's well known to be a... well... a dick, if you'll pardon the on-the-nose vernacular, Ms. Matthews," Dave says. He looks over at me, as if I'm going to be at all put out about him saying to her the same thing he and the guys have said to me a million times in the last decade or so.

"I've told you — call me Marina, David," she says pointedly.

Ah, so that's how this goes. I see.

"David's point — which I agree with — is that this particular image," Billy says, "while shocking to many, conveys not only Declan's sex-appeal..."

"Which is well-established," I point out. Dave rolls his eyes.

"Yes," Billy acknowledges. "But also an openness — even a vulnerability — that our early analysis indicates will actually improve public perception of him within a substantial subset of existing and potential album-buyers and concert-goers."

"You've got to be kidding me," Dave mumbles, giving me good reason to smirk this time.

"Additionally," Billy says, "the particular... context... of this image has opened up a dialogue among certain more... fringe... communities, which have embraced it — and Declan — with open arms in the few hours since the image first surfaced. He's trending — in positive contexts — within those communities, as well as in the larger social media dialogue. The negative response has been relatively mild and minimal," he says. "Mostly people wondering why Declan would allow a photo like that to be taken, and how it came to be posted."

"Malcolm, you've been quiet during all of this. What is your take?" she asks our producer.

"Honestly, Marina, other than the fact that I've now seen something I can't un-see—"

"You and all of us, Malcolm," she growls.

"Other than that," he continues, "the only issue I have with it is that we've taken time to deal with this when I could have been in the studio with Alex, working on the scratch tracks for his song. We're considerably behind schedule, for any number of reasons, but this is a minor irritation at worst. I'd just as soon forget it happened. It has no impact on the album, as far as I'm concerned."

"Fine," Marina says, sounding disappointed that the report and Malcolm's take aren't more damning. "But those last two issues Billy mentioned are something I would like to have addressed, Mr. Carter. Who took this photo, and can you explain to me why I shouldn't be having my lawyers — and the police — hunting them down for charges under revenge-porn laws?"

And here's where I've got to ensure that Callie's protected. However they determine the image got out there, it still gets traced back to her somehow, because she's the one who took it. I know it, and the guys all know it, and I'm only hoping they'll keep their mouths shut about it.

"I know who took it," I tell her, honestly. "And that person had my approval to have the image in their possession."

"And the posting of it online? You approved of that also?"

I pause, trying to think how best to word this.

"I don't have an issue with it," I finally say. "Billy's made the case that this has been a net-positive for my image, personally, and therefore for the band overall. In another five or ten years, it'll only be a piece of trivia or a 'Hey, do you remember when...?' And a lot of people won't. And those who do, they're not going to be outraged about it — they're going to think it was amusing..." I do smirk at her this time, just over the pun. "...Or that it was sexy, and that doesn't hurt anyone involved. Rather the contrary."

There's silence as Marina looks at me. I could take a guess as to what she's thinking, but she cultivates this air of cool inscrutability, and I have a feeling no one knows exactly what goes on in that very, very sharp mind of hers. If I come out of this conversation feeling like it's a draw, I'll count myself lucky. Especially if that means Callie's protected from the fallout from taking that photo.

"If you don't wish to press charges or sign onto takedown notices, Mr. Carter, my hands are pretty well tied," she says. I narrowly avoid commenting on my own hands having been pretty well tied, too. "I could invoke the right-to-publicize clause of your recording contract and pursue remedies on your behalf..." she warns, and I panic for a moment, fearing for Callie if Marina follows through on that threat, "but it would create more headaches than it would solve. So, I'll drop it here."

I very, very carefully avoid any display of emotion, including relief, even though that feeling is coursing through my veins right now.

"Alright, then — this meeting is over. You all can get back to work. This album had better be great, with all the headaches you all have given me since you arrived there. I'm starting to wonder if it's the band, the studio or the town that is a magnet for trouble. Regardless, I want it to stop. Understood? Mr. Carter?"

"Understood, Ms. Matthews."

I join Billy, Malcolm and Dave in standing up, more than ready to head back to bed. Malcolm won't need me for hours, as early in the process as they are with Alex's new song.

"Mr. Carter — remain behind, please."

Uh-oh.

Dave smirks at me as he shuts the door behind him. I stick my tongue out at him. *Goody-goody.*

I remain standing, hoping it'll convey that I don't plan to stick around for a long lecture. I may be under contract with Siren's Song, but I am a grown-ass adult, and I won't be treated like a misbehaving child.

"Declan—"

Well, that's... intriguing. No more "Mr. Carter."

"I'm not as stupid as you seem to think I am," she says.

"I would never for a moment think of you as stupid, Ms. Matthews, let alone be so stupid myself as to voice such a thought. You're one of the sharpest businesspeople I've ever crossed paths with."

"And your parents exposed you to that world early, did they not? You and your brother?"

"They did."

"That kind of adult demand on a child can be very... counterproductive," she says. And now I'm wondering where she's heading with this. I just nod. "In your and your brother's cases, that seems to have led to a tendency to rebel against parental plans. The band, in lieu of college. Other... interests... favored above education, career..."

"I'm very focused on my career, Ms. Matthews. I always have been. And I never needed college to make that a success."

"Your brother has regretted not pursuing a degree."

"And, as I think you know, he's rectified that," I tell her.

"He's also managed to purchase a portion of this studio, and to begin building a family with a woman it appears he dearly loves."

"I would say so, yes. I'm happy for him. About all of it."

"Are you?" she asks pointedly. "I'm sure you've had your concerns about the impact of those decisions on the band, on you personally."

Yeah, I'm back to wondering if Marina Matthews has telepathic powers. And, based on everything that's happened since we got back to this weird little town, I'm not going to fully reject the idea.

"I have. Dave has mentioned altering touring schedules, or even having us find a touring bassist to replace him when we go on the road."

"That's a natural concern — both his wish to prioritize his new family, and yours about how this impacts you and your bandmates."

"Hunter's settling down here with Brighid. He's fully on board with Dave's wishes."

"And that, I expect, would only make you more concerned for the future of the band."

"I'll admit that it has. A bit."

"It would also be entirely natural for you to feel concern that you're losing the one piece of your birth family that you've been close to for your entire life, and then additionally about possible changes in your adoptive family."

I nod. It costs me nothing to admit it. And I'm curious where she's going with this psychoanalysis.

"And, in that position, it would be very understandable were you to also be looking at your own life, trying to decide what you want for yourself over the long term, what your priorities are," she says. Again, I nod.

"I just want you to know that you have the support of the label, wherever those priorities take you." OK. Now I'm surprised, and concerned. "If you would like to pursue solo projects, we can discuss that. If you'd like to pull together some industry leaders for a collaborative effort, I can help you make those connections." And now I'm alarmed. Is she offering me an out because she thinks aMUSEd won't survive Dave and Hunter settling down?

"And if you find you'd like to prioritize other aspects of your life, I will fully support you in that as well, just as I have your brother and Mr. Graves."

Wow. OK. I'm back to telepathy. It's the only explanation.

"Siren's Song prioritizes the work-life balance of our artists, and I realize the extensive touring schedule aMUSEd has had in recent years isn't something that can be sustained over the long term. That's one reason I wanted you recording your album at Mystic Studios, where you'd be able to get some R-and-R while you work. So, if you were to feel the need to, say, pursue some personal interests or causes, you should know that you would have the full support of the label."

Wow.

"And our *top-notch* security staff," she adds pointedly. "Because we pay these *experts* quite well to ensure the safety of you, your bandmates and your families, and there is nothing that will prevent them from guaranteeing that you are all safe, secure and able to maintain your anonymity in your personal pursuits, should you so wish."

Wow again. Is she saying what I think she's saying? Maybe my super-spy skills aren't quite as good as I thought.

"You should also be aware that your cell phone is one issued to the band through the label, and that the label retains ownership of the phone, its data and its contents. Specifically to ensure that all security concerns are quickly and fully addressed. Not that we would ever invade your privacy ourselves, so long as there were no such security concerns involved."

Oh. I do believe I am busted. On several fronts.

"Am I understood, Mr. Carter?" And we're back to "Mr. Carter" again...

"You are," I tell her.

Telepathy or whatever, she's got me nailed, and I'm getting off easy if all she's doing is telling me she's watching. As is Callie. This could have gone so much worse, for both of us.

And now I need to make sure Callie knows she's off the hook.

And that, from this moment on, she knows she can rely on me to always have her back, to always be worthy of her trust.

# CHAPTER 50

## HEADPHONES

## Callie

I'm sitting on the corner of the bed in Declan's room at the studio. Alex let me in, giving me a smirk that I know means he knows I took that photo of Declan. Oddly, he doesn't seem at all hostile. In fact, he seemed vaguely... amused.

He said Declan was in a meeting regarding PR strategy, and I know that's got to be about me — about that photo. I wish I'd gotten here in time to apologize to Declan before he went into that meeting. On top of being embarrassed by being naked and tied up in a viral photo, he's probably now in trouble with his bosses and the band over having let it happen. He's taking the heat for something I did.

I feel horrible. At my angriest with him, I would have purposely done this to him. As soon as I'd cooled off, I would have changed my mind. Why didn't I just delete that photo? OK, Siobhan may have been right that I liked looking at my boyfriend, naked. But, still, I should have deleted it. And not doing that now means Declan's paying the price. All while I've kept him at a distance over something that happened twelve years ago and that he'd wanted to avoid hurting me by keeping that one secret.

I've kind of earned the fallout from this. And the least I can do is own up to that to his face.

Which is full of surprise as he opens the door and sees me sitting here.

"Callie!"

"Hi." My voice is subdued as he unnecessarily shuts the door behind him. This won't take long, and I'm too mortified by all of this to talk any louder than necessary for him to hear. "Listen, Declan — I can't express how sorry I am about that photo getting out. I mean, I didn't send it out to anyone, so I don't know how it got out in the first place, but I shouldn't have taken it, and once I did, I should have just deleted it. I was angry, but that's no excuse. And I just needed to tell you how sorry I am. If there's anything I can do to fix it, I'll do that. If I need to confess online that I was an angry ex-girlfriend..."

"You are *not* my ex-girlfriend," he says.

"OK. 'Former lover.' 'One-time paramour?' Whatever you want to call it. Just blame it on me being an angry, evil bitch determined to ruin you, tell them I tricked you into it — because that's what I did — and..."

"Callie. Stop," he says firmly.

"Sorry. I mean, if you want to file a police report, I can go sit quietly on the front steps and wait for them to get here."

"Callie," he says, kneeling down on the floor in front of me, grabbing my forearms and setting them down in my lap. "Stop."

I force myself to stop talking.

"First — you are not my *ex*-girlfriend. You are my *girlfriend*. No ex. And, personally, as far as I'm concerned, you're still my *wife*. Have been since that day on the beach."

I look down at my hands. Is he really telling me he still wants to be with me after what I did? What I allowed to happen?

"Second," he says, lifting my chin so I'm forced to look up into those lake-blue irises of his. "Second — no one's filing a police report. I just talked through all of this with the label, our management, our producer, Dave... Who I still need to talk to about him *not* dying on me..."

"What?" I'm confused.

"Nevermind. Not important right now."

"The gist of it was that I told them all that I have no issue with the photo being out there."

"You don't?" He shakes his head. "Not at all?"

"Not really. Nudity's never bothered me. I mean, I posed for that underwear ad years ago, and those things were *skimpy*..."

"You did?"

"You never saw that billboard in New York?"

"No. And it didn't show up on your Instagram, when I was looking..."

"And found that photo of me with the two girls at the hotel."

I nod.

"OK. I've got a lot to explain to you, and I'm going to try to do it as efficiently as possible. I need you to hear me out, because I think once I've explained everything you'll feel much better. OK?"

I nod. I'm so lost here. And he's got all the answers.

"I don't care about the photo. Except maybe that I'd kind of prefer you were the only one seeing me totally naked from this point forward. But I still haven't fucking found that time machine, and, frankly, I'd never risk undoing us getting to where we are right now, because you're here with me, and that's all I really care about."

"It is?"

"It is."

"But what about the label?"

"I told them I had no issues with the photo, and without that, they're not really able to do much of anything. I mean, they could have, but they're not. Especially since it's probably at least as much of a positive for PR as it could be a negative, or so their data says. So, the photo is out there and will stay out there, and that's OK. And I don't want you worrying about it one bit from this moment forward, OK? Promise me?"

"If you say so."

"I do. Now — I owe you an apology. A lot of them, really. But one big one."

"Because you cheated on me."

"No!"

"You're not sorry about cheating on me?"

"No. I'm sorry I didn't tell you the whole truth when we cleared the air and dumped our baggage that night. I shouldn't have lied to you, even by omission. Especially when I'd said I'd always be honest with you. It was another stupid mistake, and probably not the last one I'll make. But I did learn my lesson, and I promise you — really promise — that I will be fully honest with you from now on, and that I will do my best to communicate better, too. Especially if you can try to communicate with me, rather than stuffing down your feelings and blowing shit up."

"You talked to Drew."

"I did. I'm sorry that happened to you. I know being upset about what you overheard is what kicked all of this off, especially when you'd only just come to accept that I hadn't done anything with those two girls in Ocean City. But I'm hoping that — once I'm done explaining — you'll feel secure enough in my feelings for you that you can put nothing but love and passion into your food."

"I need that, Declan. I've gone from shutting myself off from everyone to falling apart, and I don't like that it's finally allowing myself to feel again that seems to be causing it. I don't want to go back to the way things were. But I can't stay like this, either."

"Callie — I have no doubt that you'd have figured it out as soon as you had a chance to get your feet back under you again. You were doing so great, even before we were officially back together, even though this magic shit is totally foreign to both of us. Though, not to everyone, it seems..."

I frown, confused again.

"Yeah — this town..." he shakes his head.

"Now *that* I understand. Mostly."

"Good. Because this — what I'm going to say next — is the thing I really, really need for you to understand." He takes a deep breath. "I know you overheard a conversation that made you think I'd cheated on you twelve years ago, right before I broke up with you."

"I did."

"And I know you may have realized that that was why I broke up with you, though I'm not sure you fully understand what I was thinking at the time."

"You didn't want me to think less of myself or our relationship because you'd cheated."

"Or me. But, yeah, that was it. See — you are my person! You get me. This brain-sharing thing..." He grabs my face in his hands and kisses me on the lips. "Like I said before, in the middle of doing what I thought was the right thing — letting you go so you could have someone who was good enough for you, which I didn't think *I* was after that night — I kind of panicked, said things I didn't mean. I never, from the moment I met you, loved anyone or anything more than you. You're it for me, Callie.

Really. I meant it when I said forever, and I hate the fact that I fucked that up, especially given what I now know."

"Which is what?" What could he possibly say about cheating on me that will make things better?

"I never cheated on you."

"But—"

"What that woman said that night was true — I was drunk off my ass, with a bunch of people, including a bunch of older women, in that hotel room after the gig that night. And, I guess it was fun for a while. I'd been kind of bummed that you hadn't been able to make it to the gig after all, and I drank too much, and... This one woman, she was way drunker than me, and I think maybe she thought we were going to do something, but really, I was just helping her to the bed before she passed out. I was going to the bathroom, and we just ended up kind of leaning on each other to stay vertical. And that's the last thing I remember from that night."

"I see." I'm not sure an "I blacked out and I fell on top of her with my penis" excuse is going to be enough for me to get past the idea that he slept with some other woman.

"No — don't be like that. I promise, this is the truth, and I will prove it to you if you don't believe me when I'm done explaining it. OK?"

"Alright. Continue."

"OK. This woman — she had a drink in her hand, and I guess it must have spilled on my jeans when I put her on the bed, because I ended up passing out, in my underwear, in the bed next to her. And when I woke up hours later, I was naked, and she was naked and passed out, and it seemed like the natural conclusion to draw that I'd been so drunk I'd had sex with her and just didn't remember it."

"Yeah. Natural." This isn't getting any better. At this point, I'm kind of wishing he hadn't told me all of this.

"Callie — I was wrong. I didn't *remember* having sex with her because I *hadn't* had sex with her."

"You just ended up with both of you sleeping naked in the same bed. Drunk."

"Stick with me. I'm almost done."

"Fine."

"I made an assumption, that I'd had sex with her but didn't remember it. And I tried to persuade myself for about thirty seconds that if I didn't remember it, I didn't need to confess to you that I'd done it. I hadn't done it on purpose — that much I knew. But it was a lame excuse, and I... I guess I blamed my subconscious or something. And the bottom line was I'd cheated on you. Or so I thought. And you deserved better than a guy who would do that to you, even if he only did it because he was blackout drunk."

"Siobhan agreed — that I deserved better. She offered to clock you over the head with a shovel and dump your body in the swamp."

He sighs.

"I know. But I don't really care what anyone else thinks. You're my top priority. Always. In everything."

He's looking me deep in the eyes, and I want to believe him. But I did before and...

"So, I botched the breakup. I know that. And I hate how that hurt you, how it changed you, changed both of us. The only thing I can say to explain it — not excuse it — is that I was 17 and I was stupid, and you were my first girlfriend, and I panicked. But I want you to know that I was trying to give you a clean break, even if it meant you hated me."

"Well, it worked. Mostly."

"I know. And we've had to forgive and forget a lot to get to where we were the other night, before you heard what you did. But you only heard half the conversation." He reaches up again and strokes my cheek. "Callie, when you ran off, I was right behind you, ready to grovel like no man has ever groveled before, if only you'd forgive me for not being totally honest with you. But she stopped me. She heard me yell your name when I called after you, and she'd remembered your name, from that night."

"So you talked about me with some groupie you cheated on me with?"

"No. Not on purpose, anyway. The reason she remembered your name was because — as she tells it, anyway — she woke up while I was still passed out, and thinking that we'd gone in there to 'have some fun,' she'd kissed me and taken my underwear off, the rest of her clothes off. But before she could do more than that, half-conscious me assumed it was you kissing me — because you were the only one I'd ever been with like that, and the only woman I'd ever loved..." His eyes are pleading with me to believe him. And I want to... But... "And when she heard how I said your name, how I responded, thinking it was you — only you — she immediately stopped. She'd been cheated on, and she couldn't abide the idea of being 'the other woman,' so she stopped. And she passed out next to me. Naked — but next to me. Where she was when I woke up hours later."

He grabs my hands between his.

"The bottom line, Callie, is that I never touched her in any kind of sexual way, and what little she touched me was a mistake that she never followed through on. We didn't have sex. I didn't cheat on you. I wouldn't have ever cheated on you. I got drunk and passed out in the worst possible place. And I made an assumption when I woke up that seemed logical, but turns out not to have been the truth. Everything that happened afterward was a result of that mistaken assumption..."

"And you spent the last twelve years thinking you'd cheated on me."

"I did."

"But you hadn't."

"I hadn't."

"And that's why... That's why you felt like you had to do penance in my honor. That's why you punished yourself."

"That and the fact that I'd hurt you so badly when I tried to break things off."

"You did do that."

"I did. And I will regret that for the rest of my life."

"No baggage, remember?" I chide him, running my hand along his jaw. He leans into my palm, turns and kisses it. "Keep the bad parts in the past. Only the positive memories coming forward with us. We promised each other."

"We did. But I'd understand if you considered me not telling you what I'd thought I'd done to be a new bad part. Or hearing that I'd cheated on you, even if I hadn't. I'll do whatever I can to make up for that. But I made another promise to you, Callie, and I plan on keeping it, even if we had a huge bump in the road." He kisses my hands. "I'm not the same idiot I was at 18. I have zero interest in ever being with anyone else. Never again. And since I've been here, with you, I've been a different version of me, and I like that guy. I like seeing happy Declan Carter looking back at me in the mirror. I like not being a grumpy ass to everyone, stewing in my own unhappiness, feeling like I've got nothing inside my chest but pain and loss and guilt. I like feeling happy for my brother, and not resenting that he's got something I'll never have."

I stroke his cheek, seeing both the 15-year-old boy I fell in love with and this man I fell in love with all over again as he rediscovered who he was without that incredibly heavy baggage.

"The only thing I want is you," he says, kissing my palm again. "But if you decide you don't want that... I'll have to accept that, I guess."

He looks down, away from my eyes, but I can see tears starting to pool between his lashes.

"What I want, if the universe is gracious enough to give me a second chance at it — is to be happy Declan, married to the girl I've loved since I was 15, and loving her for the rest of my life. No — forever. I promised you forever, and I'm going to keep that promise. No matter what. I can only hope you'll have me, because I want you to be my wife. I want to be your husband, a good husband to you. I've wanted that every day. And if you'll give me that chance, I want it to be in every way."

He shifts from kneeling in front of me to being on one knee. And I remember so vividly the last time I saw him like this.

"Calliope Ange—" He starts and stops again. "Calliope *Aoede* Martino — my angel — will you do me the honor of becoming my wife?"

"It's Martin now. I changed it, mostly so you couldn't find me while I ran away from myself, and from you."

"So I had your entire name wrong this whole time? Or parts of it?" He chuckles and shakes his head. "I know Calliope is the muse of epic poetry. I looked that up long ago. But what does Aoede mean? I know it was Nonna's name, but..."

"Aoede is one of the original three muses. The muse of song."

"Of course she is... who else could she be?" he asks, shaking his head again, a huge smile spreading across his face.

He grabs at the collar of his T-shirt and pulls it over his head, tossing it on the bed beside me. I look down at him and am shocked to realize I'm looking into my own face.

"Except for Dave, the other guys all got one, back when we first signed our record deal. The tattoo artist, Olivia, she told them all as they got their ink that she was leaving it undefined — the face of the muse that's the band logo — because she wanted for each of us to be able to shape the tattoo's image as our lives progressed, because while we were one in the band, each of us was an evolving individual."

He swallows, a flash of sadness across his face.

"I didn't get one when the other guys did. Dave was talking about it. But I told them I didn't want one. I'm not sure why. It just didn't feel like it was the right time or something. But I went back later, to see Olivia, when the guys were all busy doing other stuff before we left on our first headlining tour. I figured I should get it done, a show of solidarity, commitment to the band. But... Olivia — she told me the same thing she'd told the other guys when they'd gotten their tattoos done — that she was leaving the face of the muse blank, so that when we'd each grown enough to be ready to finish it, we'd recognize what our own personal muse looked like, and then we could complete the muse in our skin with her face."

He takes a deep breath.

"I chickened out, Callie. She told me that, and I knew I couldn't do it. I couldn't do it because I already knew what my muse looked like, and I'd already decided I wasn't good enough for her. Getting the tattoo done without your face felt like I was saying I'd find someone else some day. And I knew that wasn't in the cards for me. So, I chickened out and left without getting it. It would have been a painful reminder every time I looked in the mirror that I'd lost you, and I was already living with that pain every day. I couldn't add to it."

Tears spring to my eyes. He strokes my face with his right hand.

"Calliope Aoede Martin-Martino," he says with a chuckle, looking me in the eyes again, the mood lightening and then intensifying. "You've been my muse since the first moment I saw you. You've been in my mind every moment of every day, with every song I wrote or sang, calling on me to be a better man. But it wasn't until I found you again, here, that I knew what that better me looked like, and he's the one who's been writing songs like they were raindrops pouring into a dry lake since that first time I kissed you again, there in your restaurant — the one named for the fountain that's sacred to the muses."

My jaw drops. I didn't tell him that.

"I looked it up. That's when I decided to prove to you that I was in this for the long haul, that I was going to make it forever for real."

"Siobhan did this." I trace my fingers around the edge of the design, not wanting to touch the relatively new tattoo.

"She did. She inked the band logo, the muse — my muse, you — into my skin, the day after you ran away from me that second time. At first, she refused, threatened to go get her shovel. So, I explained to her that I'd been wrong all those years ago." He chuckles, shaking his head. "She didn't take my word for it. She made me make a video call to that woman so that she could tell her, face to face, that it had all been a misunderstanding. And *still* she questioned whether this was a good idea, considering. She called me out on pretty much every stupid thing I've ever done where you're concerned, and then some. And then she inked my muse into my skin, where I could tell her I love her every day, no matter where I am. And she told me to sing to her while she did it, that that was part of what she does."

"Her tattoos — they're enchanted, Declan. They're magic. That's how Hunter's hand healed up so fast after he broke it, or part of how. At least, that's what the girls said. And with everything that's happened, I believe them."

"Good. Then she's made visible the woman who enchanted me from that first day, and she did it while I sang her the first love song I've ever written."

"For me?"

"You're my muse, Callie. That's how it works."

He kisses me sweetly, and I relax into the kiss, all of what's transpired today washing over me and then away, leaving behind only sweet memories, passion and love.

"What would you have done if I'd said no, Declan? That's my face on you, for the rest of your life!"

"Yes, it is. And if I'd been able to have it inked there for eternity, I'd have done that, too. However things worked out with us, you're still my muse. You always will be."

I kiss him suddenly, hard, wrapping my arms under his and pulling him to me. An untold amount of time later, we come up for air, and he gives me the oddest look.

"Uh... Callie?"

"What?"

"You never actually answered my question."

"Which question?"

"That whole 'Will you marry me?' thing?"

"Oh, my god! Yes!" I pepper his face with kisses, each one punctuated with another "Yes!"

He lays me back on the bed, crawling up over me, the tattoo rippling with the movement of his arms. I shake my head, barely believing that he actually did this, not knowing if I'd agree to marry him again.

My smile fades a little.

"What?" he asks. "What's wrong?"

"I threw away my rings! I mean, I went back later to try to find them. But I'd thrown them at you, literally threw them back in your face, and I didn't know where either of them had bounced off to, whether they were even still on the chain after I pulled it off."

"Why'd you go look for them?" he asks. "Especially after that day..."

"After I got the news about my parents... I had Nonna, but at that moment, I wanted you, Declan. I needed you. And since I couldn't have you either, those rings were the next-best thing, the closest thing I had to that feeling of being safe and totally at home, when I was with you. But I couldn't find them — not on the porch, not in the flower beds, not in the bushes or the lawn."

"I'm sorry I wasn't there for you," he says. "I would have been if I'd known. I'd have left home and stayed with you until you felt safe again."

"I know. I know that now," I tell him, and I do. "When I looked for my rings and couldn't find them, I decided it was a sign. That I needed to move on. That you weren't really home like I'd thought you were. But now... Now I know you were always home for me, and always will be."

He kisses me on the forehead.

"It's been the same for me, Callie. Nowhere else has ever been home for me, not since that day, not really. Not even the band. The guys, they're like a tour bus — the place I call home when I'm working — but I've wanted a place I truly felt at home since the day I left you. I honestly gave up on ever getting it, of ever feeling like that again."

I stroke his cheek, knowing we've felt the same sense of loss and being unanchored since that day. But now, maybe we've got a chance to fix that, for each other, for both of us.

"I want to show you something," he says, climbing out of the bed and putting his shirt back on.

I'm perplexed, but a feeling of trust and safety comes over me. Whatever Declan wants me to see, I'll be safe with him. He won't let me get hurt again. And now, even if he wanted to drag me to the airport and hop on a plane for an unknown destination, I'll happily join him. I want to experience life fully, like Nonna talked about, and I want to do it with him.

When he holds out his hand, I take it willingly, eagerly.

# CHAPTER 51

## MARRY YOU

"You drive. I'll navigate," he says.

"Do I—"

"Patience. All things in their own time. As I think we've learned," he says with a smile.

We have. So, we hop in my car and start driving. The streets are familiar. We haven't left Mystic Beach. And then they're even more familiar.

"Turn in here," he says, gesturing to a house on the left side of the street.

"Why are we here, Declan?"

"I told you — I need to show you something. Come on!"

He pulls me up on the porch of the home and opens the door without knocking.

"Declan! You can't just walk into some stranger's house!"

"I've got the owner's permission," he says, pulling me behind him through the foyer, down the hallway, through the kitchen and out through the back door, into a florid garden, lush with summer blossoms and the sweet sound of water spilling from a fountain. When we're next to the fountain, he takes my hand and gets down on one knee again. What is he doing?

"Calliope Aoede Martin, will you do me the incredible honor of becoming my wife? Officially and forever?"

He puts something in my hand, and I look down to realize it's a small stuffed grizzly bear — the same one I gave him so many years ago.

"You kept him? All this time?"

He nods.

"He's gone everywhere with me, traveling around the world, always there when I needed someone to talk to, keeping my deepest secrets and holding my greatest treasures."

My eyes start to tear up again. The sheer sentimentality of it. The romance. This is the Declan I knew at 15. This is the Declan I married. And he's been in there all along.

"I don't understand. I already said yes. Why come here? And why the bear?" I look at the little guy again. He's a little the worse for the wear, his fur rough, like he's been stroked over and over in the same places by someone seeking comfort. And...

"What happened to you, little guy?" I say to the bear. "Looks like you've been through some hard times." I finger the rough stitches in the bear's chest.

"He has. We have," Declan says. "But he's always been there for me, keeping my treasures safe."

"You said that before..."

"Pull open the stitches, Callie."

OK... There are just a handful of them, crude, like a little kid — or a teenage boy — had made them, not wanting to ask for help from an adult. They pop free easily, the thread slightly brittle. The edges of the hole they closed aren't torn. They're cut. I stick a fingertip inside and feel something hard, metallic... It can't be. I grab hold of the object with my fingertip, pulling it free of the bear's chest.

"Oh, my god... You had these? All this time?"

He nods.

"My greatest treasure. Even if you weren't with me, you were. You've traveled all around the world with me already, Callie. Safe and sound, in the heart of the Great Bear. He's kept those broken bits of my heart safe when my own chest was aching and empty. I didn't know it, but he was keeping them safe for the day when I could put them back on your finger, where they always belonged."

He holds out his hand, and I give him the rings. And then he takes the tiny diamond solitaire and slides it onto my left ring finger. And the delicate white-gold band after it, just like he did the day we got married. I grab his other hand, taking from it the matching band, and I slide it onto his left ring finger, just like I did that day.

And he leans down and kisses me, just like that day. And then more, the kiss deepening beyond what we allowed ourselves that day on the beach. Mouths open, tasting, eagerly consuming each other, like we're starving. And we had been. Until this moment, I think, we have starved for each other for twelve years. And I'm not sure I'll ever get enough. And the way he's kissing me, I don't think he will either.

But I suddenly realize we're standing in a stranger's garden, making out like newlyweds on the way to their honeymoon.

"How did you make this happen? How did you manage to get permission to come into the house, into the garden to do this? How did you get the new owners to give you access like this? You couldn't have known I'd come see you this morning. You couldn't have known that we'd be able to work things out between us to where proposing was even an option!"

"OK — I promised no more secrets, so I have to come clean on this," he says. And I'm instantly worried. What else hasn't he told me? "I had a good idea you'd come see me this morning. I'd talked to Brighid that same night you overheard that conversation. I'd found your car, and long story short, I told her what I'd found out, what really happened twelve years ago. And she told me I'd have to get through Siobhan to talk to you."

"The dragon guarding the gate," I confirm.

"Brain-sharing!" he sing-songs at me.

Of course.

"I'd already decided to get the tattoo done, so I needed her help anyway. So, I killed two birds with one stone. Slayed the dragon with Arthur's magic sword."

I raise an eyebrow at him. He can't know how many times Siobhan's referred to his penis as magical.

"Too much?" he asks. He shrugs. "I talked to Siobhan, convinced her of what really happened twelve years ago, persuaded her to do the tattoo. But you weren't ready to talk to me, see me, let me explain. Siobhan confirmed that. I didn't want to force you, but I also didn't want you suffering like that, thinking that I'd cheated on you when I hadn't. So, when Siobhan thought you were nearly there, I gave you a little push."

"What?" I don't like this. It smacks of being manipulated. Even if they were right.

"I don't know exactly what Siobhan did last night. She just said she'd make sure I was on your mind, that she'd make sure you were open to talking to me."

"She got me — and herself, and Brighid, and Lyric, a little — drunk on tequila!"

"Ah! That's why she told me I had to buy her a bottle of tequila! I made sure it was a good one."

"Thank you. I think. My head is still pounding."

He kisses me on the forehead.

"I'll make it better, I promise," he says, that cocky, flirty smile coming out to play.

"And then what? I only came over to talk to you because that photo got out somehow and went viral, and I needed to apologize. I mean, I was pretty much ready to hear you out anyway. But— Siobhan didn't post that photo herself, did she? I'll kill her! I mean, she'll wipe the floor with me, but I'll make a good try at it, and since I now blow up Bananas Foster, I might actually do some damage! How dare she!"

"Bananas Foster?"

"Drew didn't tell you exactly what happened? There was a small fire in the dining room. I may or may not have caused it, from the kitchen, because Drew was trying to ban me from my kitchen again."

"And did he?"

"Yeah. That's why I took leave. He said it was me or him."

"Ouch," he says, commiserating. "I like him," he adds, now smirking at me. I stick my tongue out at him. "But, no, don't go after Siobhan about the photo getting released. That's on me."

I just stare at him for a minute as that sinks in. Then I get mad.

"You! You did this? You made me think I'd destroyed your career, just by taking that photo! I figured once they traced it back to me, Castalia was done-for. I was headed to see Drew to sell him the restaurant right after I apologized to you, just to minimize the collateral damage!"

"Oh. Oops," he says, cringing.

"Oops?"

"How was I to know you'd take things that far? I'd already told you I didn't blame you for taking it! And it's not like you were the one who released it!"

"Declan Carter! I about died from sheer guilt when I saw that picture on Twitter this morning. Did you have Siobhan put it up as my phone wallpaper, too? You had me wondering if I'd sent it out while I was drunk. And I don't even have a Twitter account!"

He chuckles. I glare at him.

"I promise — I didn't ask Siobhan to put it on your phone. I didn't even tell her what I had planned. I was just picking up the ball after her offer to help you finally be ready to talk, so I could clear things up."

"I'm still going to have a strong word with her."

"Just remember — she's the one who helped get us where we are right now. Don't be hard on her."

I look around, look at the rings on our fingers once again.

"Fine. But I am not happy about being manipulated! Don't do it again."

"I promise."

"So how'd the photo get released if Siobhan didn't send it from my phone?"

"You took it on my phone, remember?"

Oh. Right.

"I've got a guy on the road crew who's really good with tech stuff and happy to sell some signed merch if I happened to have some lying around. I had him set me up a new Twitter account, and make sure that it wasn't traceable back to me, or anyone else. Totally anonymous. Unhackable. Even when I posted from it later. Which I did in the wee hours this morning, after he spent most of the night getting it working and testing it for me."

"So you sent it out yourself? You're DeclansBiggestFan?"

"Who else would be? I mean, really?" he says full of mock derision.

"I can't tell if that ego is real or a front now."

"Six of one, half a dozen of the other," he says, shrugging.

"So, you sent out a naked photo of yourself, chained up to your bed, to the entirety of the internet, just so you could ensure I would come see you this morning. Are you insane?"

"Just crazy in love, Callie," he says. "And determined that you not suffer any more, thinking that I'd cheated on you. It was all worth it, now that you know. I couldn't care less about the photo. If I did care, I wouldn't have sent it out. And, like I said — it seems to be a net-positive. Can't say I knew that would happen. But I got very lucky today, in oh-so-many ways."

"I'll say. What would have happened if I'd gone to Drew to sell the restaurant before I came over to see you?"

"I'd have bought him out by tomorrow to give it back to you."

"Of course you would have." I shake my head at him.

"What if I'd slept until the afternoon, sleeping off this hangover?"

"I didn't know Siobhan was getting you drunk. Wait — did you say she got Brighid drunk, too?"

"Yeah. That was weird. Brighid said she doesn't drink."

"She doesn't. There was an... incident when she was in college. Involving a frat party, way too much spiked fruit punch, Hunter flirting with a sorority girl and Brighid half-naked with a frat-boy. It culminated in Hunter busting down a door."

"Wow."

"I'd say you had to be there, but I was there, and 'Wow' is about right."

"Brighid was naked?"

"Half. And Hunter's got really wide shoulders. I didn't see anything... much."

I roll my eyes at him.

"She was in on it..."

"Who?"

"Brighid — she was in on Siobhan's plan. And so was Lyric, I'd bet. She'd been kind of off earlier that day, and the last thing I expected was for her to show up for tequila shots. And she went home early."

"I'd say I owe them some thanks, then."

"We."

"OK. I like that. We. Together. Good words. Inspiring."

"Yeah," I agree, taking his hand, linking our fingers together and pulling him down to sit with me on that garden bench where Nonna used to tell me stories. I don't know how much time we've got here, and I want to absorb those happy memories while I can.

"Did you really think you had things timed out so well that you could bring me here to propose during whatever window you worked out with the new owners?"

"It worked out, didn't it?" he points out. "But, no — I hedged my bets. I got permission to have full access to the property twenty-four/seven," he says.

"That was generous of them. Or did you offer them backstage passes or something?"

"No. Nothing like that. It wasn't a big deal, really. That kind of total access is what they give you when you buy the place."

Whoa. Declan Carter's big gestures aren't limited to the stage, it seems.

"You didn't! Declan! Tell me you didn't buy Nonna's house back, just hoping things would work out so that you could propose to me here."

"I did not," he says firmly. "I put in the offer on Nonna's house right after you took that photo, while I was giving you space."

"When I was still angry with you? Did you think you could buy your way out of me being angry about those girls?"

"No!" he looks genuinely surprised that I'd even think that. "I didn't know you'd sold Nonna's house to finance your restaurant until that night..."

"The first time we slept together... In my apartment..."

"Yeah. I would have given it back to you regardless of what happened between us. I mean, it's *your* house." His expression is earnest, like there's no other way he could have been thinking of it. "But then things were going so well once we finally dumped all our baggage — I decided to give it to you as a wedding present. Because, Callie — since I was 16, I dreamed of being part of your family, just like Nonna said I would be one day. And I'm hoping you'll say that day is today..."

"Oh, Declan..." Now I'm crying, tears streaming down my cheeks. He pulls me into his arms and holds me tight. We sit there for a long while, just holding each other, the summer sea breeze stirring the roses, the musical sound of the fountain the only sound besides the occasional bit of birdsong.

"Was that a yes?" he asks, chuckling. "You have a habit of not actually answering my most important questions."

I smack him on the shoulder. Not the one with the tattoo.

"Of course it was a yes! I wanted that as much as you did, for us to be family, from that very same moment. I just gave up even dreaming that I'd ever have it. And then you show up here, turning my life upside-down, and you stick with me through every torturous mousse, every crazy magical moment, helping me win a contest that assured the future of my business, offering to help me grow it even more... even dealing with having a naked photo of you released onto the internet... I'm a little surprised you still want that."

"There was never any question in my mind. That first moment I saw you again, this was what I wanted."

"And you finally let yourself have it," I tell him pointedly.

"I did. I'm done with the self-punishment. Not the helping out in the food banks and soup kitchens, the culinary programs, and definitely not the cooking. That was never punishment, just a way of expressing my devotion to you, doing some thing good in your honor. But I know now that I'm right where I belong. Anywhere you are is where I belong."

I lean back and marvel at the house, which is so little changed from how it was when Nonna was alive.

"You want to come see inside? See what's different, what's the same?" He pulls me behind him again without waiting for an answer, stopping only when we're back in the kitchen.

I take a good look at what I only barely let register the first time we came through. The kitchen's been completely redone. It's not the simple home kitchen it was when Nonna was alive and cooking in it. But that's OK. Something was going to have to change when other people moved in.

"They'd updated it, but they just used it for a weekend place, so they were willing to accept a generous cash offer to settle immediately. Once that was done, I had it renovated a bit more."

"I'll say."

It's now a cozy but well-outfitted chef's kitchen, with marble countertops, built-in appliances, glass-fronted cabinets. And a single slab of butcherblock atop one section of lower cabinets.

"Is this...?"

"I had them preserve it. It was the one surface the prior owners hadn't replaced. It seemed important, symbolic."

"Declan — were you here when they re-did the kitchen?"

"No. I approved the changes, confirmed they'd done everything to my specifications when they were done."

"So you didn't see this piece of butcherblock when they took it up to re-do the cabinets?"

"No. Why?"

I dip down, craning my neck to make sure.

"Take a look."

"What am I looking at?" he asks, mimicking my maneuver.

"Under the lip, where it hangs over. Nonna had it done special, so she could hang her herbs close to the oven for drying, but with plenty of air circulation."

"I see some holes that look like they've had hooks screwed into them."

"Do you see the pattern? The pattern of the holes?"

"They're not spaced equally."

"They're not. Nonna had that block put in when I was 15, that first summer I lived here. She wanted to teach me all her recipes, and she wanted a proper butcherblock so she could do it. And later, while I was here, she added the hooks. I asked her why the holes weren't spaced normally, and she told me to use my imagination, my senses beyond vision. So, I ran my fingers over the holes. I closed my eyes and pictured how they were laid out. Like stars in the sky..."

"This isn't..." he says, squinting at the tiny holes. "She can't have..."

"She did. It's the Great Bear. And the one piece of her kitchen that is exactly the same — you kept it for me, for us, for our family. And it was the one piece she'd marked with the constellation that reminded her of you, *Arturo*..."

"Are you really sure she wasn't a witch?"

"Not anymore I'm not. And I'm totally OK with that."

Declan stands back up, pulling me into his arms.

"Me, too. I'm kind of partial to kitchen witches, as it turns out."

We've spent the last fifteen minutes going through the house, rediscovering what's the same and examining what's different. The house is beautiful. The things that had gotten worn or outdated while I was gone to New York, when Nonna didn't change much of anything — it's all been updated. The result is airy, spacious but still cozy, with Craftsman details retained and touches of classic beach-cottage style added, and all the windows at the back of the house looking out over Nonna's garden, which has thrived in the years since I sold the house.

At the heart of it is still the fountain. The one I lamented leaving but couldn't justify taking with me. I brush my fingers across the marble. It was Nonna's one big extravagance, other than the butcherblock. It's not a huge fountain, nowhere near as large as the one she conjured in my imagination when she told me the story of the nymph who transformed herself into a fountain and then inspired poets, musicians, dancers and, yes, astronomers. But it's the centerpiece of this garden.

"Is that an engraving?" Declan asks, coming up behind me after I wandered back out to the garden again.

"Yes. She asked for it to be done, special."

"What's it say?"

"It's in Greek. Nonna was Italian, of course, but the stories of the muses inspired her, including their Greek versions, and especially this one... It says, 'Castalia.'"

"Wow."

I look back at him, touched that he gets this, without me having to explain it to him.

"I hated leaving this here, when I sold the house. But I didn't have a real place for it, and it felt like this was where it belonged. I never thought I'd be back here to see it, let alone... like this. Thank you, Declan. I can't thank you enough."

"No thanks are needed. Seeing you here like this... that's all I wanted when I did this."

I trail my fingers in the fountain, and that's when I notice it. A glint of metal in the sunshine, reflecting through the water. A dime?

"Declan — is this the fountain you threw the coin into?"

"Of course! Where else? I mean, we can try it again in Rome, if you want, but it seems like it worked."

"I still can't get over you doing this, not knowing if I'd agree to get married again..."

"I had hope. For the first time in twelve years, I found that I had hope," he says. "I hoped you would come back to me. And I hoped you'd say yes when I asked. And it's a lucky dime! Some guy gave it to me when we were in Vegas. Said Mercury was lucky. I figured this was the perfect place for it, in your fountain, in Nonna's garden. But, regardless of what happened with us, I knew you loved this house, loved the memories and the feel of it. And we had so many good memories here, just the two of us. If you'd said no, if you'd kicked me to the curb, I would have been devastated. But I'd still have given you back this house, because I knew you loved it, and I wanted you to have that love back in your life. I wanted you to have a place that was truly home."

I pull him down to me and kiss him again.

"This is home. But it's a house. You're my real home. Wherever you go, I'll always be home when I'm with you. You've given me both of those things in a single day."

"And you gave me everything I needed in three words. Even if I haven't heard you actually say them yet," he teases.

"Oh, my god! I was waiting until we were alone that night, just so I could speak them into your ear, and then everything..."

"Got a little crazy. Yeah. That happens sometimes. Are you sure you want to do this? Marry a guy's who's on billboards in his underwear and pelted with strange women's panties on stage and grabbed by overwhelmed fans?"

"It's part of your life. I'll adapt. We'll manage. As long as we can be honest with each other, no more secrets," I emphasize, "we can do anything. Together."

"I love that word. Especially now."

"Because we're back together?"

"Yeah," he says. "And always will be. Because we promised each other."

"And we will again." I grab his face between my hands, our eyes locked together. "I love you, Declan Carter. Always have. Always will." And I kiss him within an inch of his life, wanting to cement those words in his head, so maybe they can finish healing the wounds he inflicted on himself and kept open and raw for all these years.

"God, I needed to hear that," he says with a sigh of relief. I can feel the remaining tension melt from him. "I love you, Callie. Forever."

He presses his forehead to mine, and we sit like that for a minute, just absorbing each other's presence. Safe. Home. Together.

"I'll talk to Lyric, ask her to renew our vows," I tell him.

"And we can go get a real marriage license this time," he says, clearly relishing the idea. "Sign our own names to it, no one's permission needed."

"Nope. Just Lyric and two witnesses."

"You know... in Delaware, you can get married twenty-four hours after you get a marriage license..."

"You looked that up, too?"

"I did. Like I said, I had hope..." he says, smiling slyly.

"How late is the office open?"

"You think we have time?"
"If we leave now."
"Then, let's go!"

# CHAPTER 52

# TATTOOS AND TEQUILA

## Callie
### *Two days later*

"Y ou busy?"

"Uh... Yeah?"

OK. Siobhan is currently inking a... Is that a hippo in a tutu? ... on some guy's right butt-cheek. He looks up and waves at me, totally fine, apparently, with me seeing his naked ass. Apparently, carefree public nudity is trending.

"I don't mean this instant. I mean, like, in an hour? Half an hour?"

"Well, I'm almost done with this. Why?"

"We need to have a talk."

"O...K... Am I in trouble? I haven't heard from you in a couple days... Are you going to set *my hair* on fire this time?"

"Depends on whether it's been soaked in tequila or not..."

"Oh." She looks incredibly guilty and resolute, all at the same time. "Uh. Yeah. OK. Sure. Let me finish up with this guy, and I'll close up for a bit. I don't have any appointments until tonight."

Fifteen minutes later, Siobhan sits down on my sofa, looking a little nervous.

"So..."

"I saw Declan's photo is still up online. Like, all over the place," she says.

"You went to look at the magic penis, didn't you?"

"Mostly," she admits with a smirk. "But also to see if they'd gotten it pulled down. The photo, not the penis."

She and I both crack up.

"Is this a good sign? That you're laughing about having your boyfriend's penis floating around online?"

"This is not going anywhere good, is it, this conversation? It's just going to circle around, over and over again..."

"Like your boyfriend's penis on the internet? And, if you're as lucky as I wish I was, around certain portions of your own anatomy?"

"Siobhan!"

"Hey — can't blame a girl for objectively appreciating beauty. Or skill. Whichever it is in his case."

"Both. But that's not up for discussion."

"Darn."

"Did you set the photo as the wallpaper on my phone? Be honest. Because I don't remember doing it."

"No. Honest!" she says when I look unpersuaded.

Maybe I did do it when I was drunk. Weird. But she's still acting strangely. She looks around the room, avoiding my eyes.

"So... Did you ever figure out how that photo got online?" she asks. "Did you drunk-post while we were..."

"Wasted on tequila? Railroaded by one of my friends? Left vulnerable to poor decision-making by one of my friends who got me wasted on tequila?"

"So... I'm guessing you've talked to Declan."

"I have." I nod, not giving her anything else.

"Listen, Callie, I know it was a little extreme, a little..."

"Underhanded? Manipulative?"

She looks thoughtful, analyzing.

"Yup. That fits."

I give her a stern look.

"Sorry?"

"It works better if you don't say it like it's a question."

"Well, I don't want to fall into the 'sorry-not sorry' cliché."

"So, you're unrepentant?"

"Aside from that blazing headache that only went away about three hours ago? Yeah." She shrugs. "Sorry. Ish."

"You did drink like twice as much as any of the rest of us."

"All for a good cause," she says, laughing.

"What I want to know is how you roped Brighid into that. I can kind of understand Lyric joining in up to a point, because at least she drinks. But Brighid?"

"We were worried you wouldn't give him a chance to explain. And that you'd be miserable forever if you didn't. And Brighid was feeling a little guilty because she'd judged Declan unfairly. She and Hunter even had a fight about it, so she was a little put out that Hunter had been right about being sympathetic to Declan and she hadn't."

"So, that was penance on her part?"

"Yes."

"Ironic."

"A little," Siobhan says, chuckling.

"Did you really talk to 'the other woman'?"

"I did. Her name is Maggie. She's actually really nice, if a little ditzy. But she had a rough divorce, cheating hubby and all that. I invited her to join us for self-defense class."

"You didn't!"

"No. I didn't. I also didn't ask her name, so if it's actually Maggie, that would be really extraordinary."

"But not out of the realm of normal for Mystic Beach."

"Nope. Not lately, anyway."

"So... you believed her?"

"Yeah. Declan had their manager get her number and have her sign an NDA, so she can't talk about him or you to anyone. But since he was standing right next to me when she called me at his request, she knew it was cool. And, yeah — if my instincts about people are as good as I know they are, she was telling the truth. Lousy case of him being in the wrong place at the wrong time, too young to be drinking, no responsible adults in the room. Including her. Wow. I mean, I like guys and I'm not one to reject casual sex, so long as it's safe and consensual, but... Wow."

I look down at my feet.

"You OK with that? Did he grovel sufficiently about not confessing, back then and now?"

"Pretty much."

"What'd he do? Did he let you tie him up again? Were there riding crops involved?"

She's picturing this scenario way too easily.

"Siobhan?"

"Hmm?"

"I'm not talking about Declan's penis, or our sex life. Not anymore. You've seen it now. Do you really have any more questions that need answered?"

She considers it for a minute.

"Not really," she says, seeming satisfied.

"You saved a copy of the photo, didn't you?"

"Would I do that?"

"Yes. In a heartbeat."

"You know me well for somebody who kept all her friends at arm's length for so long." She smirks at me.

"Yeah. Sorry about that. I'm trying to do better."

"I know. We all know. We all get it. So... are you feeling safer now that you know he didn't cheat?"

"Safe as houses."

"I always thought that was a weird turn of phrase."

"Literally true in this case."

"What's that mean?"

"You wanted to know if he'd groveled? I said no."

"And then I asked about getting some healthy bondage action in?"

"Yeah. We didn't do that, either."

"So, what'd he do to show he's repentant?"

"He bought me a house."

"No."

"Yes."

"Where? Up on the beach?"

"No. He bought my grandmother's house down the street, and he gave it to me for a wedding present."

"What? He proposed? He didn't tell me he was going to do that! I wouldn't have gotten you nearly as drunk if I'd known you'd end up hungover for your engagement."

"He did." I wave my left hand at her, and she grabs it to look at the rings.

"These are very... understated... for a multimillionaire rockstar..."

"That was very politely phrased."

"Well, he did buy you a house. So, I guess it all works out in the wash. I'm really happy for you," she says, tearing up before she shakes herself and tries to pretend it didn't happen.

"I know. And that's why I have a favor to ask... Well, two favors, actually."

"What?"

"Well, the first one requires you that you're free in about two hours, so you can be my maid-of-honor."

"You're getting married already? Today?"

"Yeah. Lyric's going to renew our vows. And this time, we have an official marriage license!"

"Wait... *Renew* your vows?"

"Did I forget to mention we got married when we were 17?"

"Uh... Yeah! Why didn't you tell me that? Why didn't he?"

"Lyric warned us that when she marries people it sticks."

"You didn't..." I can tell what she's going to ask.

"Promise each other forever? Yeah. We did."

"This all makes even more sense now! I mean, it felt like fate. But you two formed a bond. Nothing was going to keep you two apart forever."

"And the rings — there's a reason they're not a measure of what he's worth today. They were what he could afford after a couple summers of busking on the boardwalk and a few gigs, twelve years ago."

"They aren't!"

"They are. He had them the entire time. His and mine. And they've gone everywhere with him for all these years."

"Your grandmother's house? Your original wedding rings? Why did no one have a clue that dick-ish Declan, lead singer of aMUSEd, was such a romantic?"

"You tell me. You're the one who inked my face permanently into his skin."

"Ah... He did the reveal! What do you think?"

"She looks like me."

"I do a lot of portrait tattoos."

"I'm actually a little weirded out. But incredibly touched."

"It was his first tattoo, and he sat for it like a champ. Sang such a beautiful song to me. I'd have cried if it wouldn't have messed up my sterile canvas."

"So, you did that thing? Like you did with Hunter's hand?"

"And Brighid's back. And David Carter's shoulder."

She looks odd as she says that last bit, like it hits her deeply but not necessarily in a comfortable way.

"I don't do it all the time. Just when the client asks for it, or when it seems like it's what should be done."

"So, no enchanted hippos-in-tutus tattoos?"

She cackles at that.

"No. None of those. So far, anyway. And, I hope, ever."

"If it healed Hunter's hand, what will it do to Declan?"

"That's for you and Declan to figure out. But Hunter's wasn't just my tattoo. They'd done a healing ritual. He just needed the tattoo to finish that, to show Brighid he was committed to her, that he believed in the two of them together."

"And Declan?"

"He said his brother had told him he should show you he was all-in if he really wanted you back. He started with the food. That was to show you. The tattoo — I think it was as much to prove it to himself as it was to prove it to you."

"Did he tell you...?"

"About chickening out on Olivia? Yeah. And he was right. I heard that in his voice when he sang to me. It had to be you, or no tattoo at all. And, I think, by committing to you, he's also committed to the band and to himself."

"He has, Siobhan. He's the Declan I remember, but more mature, deeper. I think being apart aged us both — not like it made us older than our ages, but like wine matures into its full flavor. And we're only just now getting the chance to enjoy that about each other."

"So, was it worth it? All the heartache?"

"I won't go that far," I reply, chuckling. "But all that stuff you said about fate? About putting us through our emotional paces? About it bringing us where we belonged, in its own sweet time? I think that was true."

"So, what's next for you two, then? Playing house at Nonna's?"

"Not playing, Siobhan. We're a family, Declan and me. We always have been. Nonna wanted that for the two of us. She'd invited him in the first time she cooked for him, like she knew he belonged. It's just taken him a long time to arrive. And now... Now he's come home. We both have. And now I need to ask you another favor..."

# CHAPTER 53

# IN THE CLEAR

## Declan
### *An hour later*

"**D**ave — you got a minute?"

He's sitting in the control room, noodling on his acoustic, while Hunter and Kieran run through their parts for Alex's song.

"Take a walk with me?"

He looks confused, but he puts down the guitar.

"Uh... Sure."

We head out through the back door, onto the beach. It's as fitting a setting as any. He's at home here, more likely to be open to talking. It's also the same beach I married Callie on twelve years ago, if a few blocks to the north of that spot. And it's where he offered his little brother relationship advice from the font of wisdom he's gained in the last couple months. OK. That was a little sarcastic, but he gave me good advice. Advice that's stuck with me through some pretty crazy situations in these last weeks. And now I know he was right — I'm all-in. And together, Callie and I really can do anything. And we will.

"What'd you want to talk about?" he asks, seeming a little uncomfortable.

"Have a seat," I tell him, gesturing to the same spot on the sand we'd had our little heart-to-heart about Callie, and about

Dave's plans for the future. We both plunk down, side by side, arms propped on our bent knees. Even with the small height difference, the different eye color and my grown-out hair, no one seeing us like this would question that we're brothers. Despite how different we are inside, too. It's been a wedge between us for a long time, and it's one I'd like to pry free now, with all the changes we're going through.

"I've made some decisions about the future," I tell him. "I talked to Marina Matthews after you all left the meeting the other day, and she's offered me some options, where my career goes, for some personal projects..."

"So you're leaving the band? Just because I said I don't want to tour as much?" He looks both sad and a little betrayed.

"Actually, no." He relaxes a little. "I told her I agreed with you, and with Hunter, that it was a good time to re-evaluate our lives, find some balance. Well — I agreed with her when *she* said it. But same end result." He relaxes further. "She gave me the same green-light she gave you, and probably Hunter, though she's still irked with him, just like she is with me... And I've decided that we should plan on shorter tours, shorter legs, longer breaks in between."

"That's great," Dave says. "I know you weren't happy about that at first."

"If you can get Rhys, Kieran and Alex on board, I don't think it will be a problem."

"Kier's burned out. The groupies were just the tip of the iceberg. But he may want to take some time, go back to New York. He was there years before us."

"Rhys will just do whatever everyone else wants," I predict, and Dave nods in agreement. Rhys is good that way. He's weird and a pain in the ass sometimes, but he's laid-back in his own hyperactive, disjointed, unpredictable way.

"Alex just does what he thinks will make everyone *else* happy," Dave says. "Even if it's not what *they* say they want or what actually makes *him* happy."

"He's so busy living everyone else's lives, trying to fix them, that I don't know if he even knows what he wants. And I think this might be a really good time to give him a chance to figure that out. Take the pressure off, let him stop worrying about everyone else for a change."

"That's a good idea," Dave says. "Take the pressure off — him and everyone else. I mean — we've still got to finish the album, but Marina will give us the leeway to do that on our own schedule while I finish reorganizing the mess that Steve left. With Piper here, Malcolm can come and go as needed. And we can figure out a workable touring schedule for everyone, now that we've got some time to really relax."

"Yeah. I think that's a great idea. Especially finishing the album on our own schedule. I think I'm going to take some time off. Like, go on vacation for real."

"This have anything to do with Callie? You need to get away and get over her?"

"Nope. Not gonna get over her. I've loved her since I was 15, and I don't expect that will change. Especially once we've renewed our vows." I can't help but smile. Playing it cool was hard enough.

"Once you've what? Are you telling me she agreed to marry you? Again?"

"She did. That vacation will be a honeymoon. And, if you're willing, I'd like you to be my best man."

"Wow. Sure. Of course," he says. "I'm really happy for you, Dec. It was hard these last weeks, knowing you were still broken-hearted over Callie after all these years. Even more so once I had Piper in my life and understood what that kind of love felt like. When you and Callie were on the same page these last couple weeks... you were a changed man, and it was amazing. No offense," he adds, realizing how that sounds.

"None taken. I know I've been an asshole for a long, long time. And I'm sorry about that. Really. I owe all of you — and a lot of other people — an apology. But I want to start that by telling you how happy I am for you, that you've got Piper, and that little bass-playing engineer in the making. You deserve every bit of that happiness."

He looks a little surprised, and I feel like a bit of an asshole now, that he knew I resented him at least a little for it.

"Yeah — I *was* worried about what all these changes would mean for me. I was a self-centered bastard about it. And I'm sorry about that. I was also more than a little jealous that you were with the woman you loved, and I was still alone, pining for Callie, thinking I'd be that way for the rest of my miserable life."

"And now you're not."

"No. I am blessedly not. She's agreed to marry me, again. And I even went and bought us a house."

"You didn't! Here? In Mystic Beach?"

"That's where she works. I work all over the place. So, yeah, we'll be here full-time, just a little ways down the road, a few blocks west of Hunt and Brighid, in the house Callie lived in with her grandmother back when we first met."

"Wow. Now *that's* a romantic gesture. Piper and I are just building a house."

"Yeah — where is that, exactly? I haven't even seen Piper's apartment."

"Uh..."

"What? Is it classified?" I joke.

He's not laughing.

"Is Piper a super-spy or something? Is she a super-hero, and I'm not allowed to go visit her secret lair?" I tease.

"Uh... no. But she's had a lot of drama going on, and she's trying to keep that separate from us, from the two — three — of us, and the band."

"Oh. Alright. So, where's this house?"

"We've got a lot right over there," he says, pointing toward the south side of the studio property.

"In that gated community?"

"Next to it."

"So, you'll be right next door to the studio. That's awesome. Convenient for both of you."

"Yeah. That was kind of the point."

"Hey, Dave..."

"What?"

"Anything else you want to tell me?"

He looks a little panicked. I can imagine he'd prefer not to talk about this, considering how secret he's kept it.

"Nothing that I can think of?"

"You didn't want to maybe tell your brother that you almost died recently?"

"Uh. Who told you that?" Dave's not good at dissembling. He's even got the shifty-eyes thing going. Definitely not a super-spy.

"I'm sworn to secrecy." And I'm way better at it.

"O... K..."

"Spill it. Or I'll tell Mom."

"She'll just blame Hunter."

"That she will," I agree, smirking.

"It wasn't a big deal, Dec. I had a little accident out in the ocean, nearly drowned. But Piper found me, got me some help. And pretty soon I was fine."

"Was that when you went off the radar with that 'cold' or whatever for a couple days? 'Staying in a hotel so you didn't get us sick'? Wasn't that what Hunter said?"

"Yeah. That was it. Just didn't want you all worrying about me, trying to keep me from going out on the water again."

I can't tell he's not even coming close to telling me the whole truth.

"You OK now?"

"Yeah. Never better. Really," he says. And that I finally believe.

"Good, because you've got a girlfriend and a baby to stick around for. And Mom would kill me if you got killed on my watch," I joke, though it's pretty much true.

"It's not your watch, Dec. Not anymore. I can take care of myself, Piper, the baby. If nothing else, this whole thing taught me that."

Whoa. It's clear he's not going to tell me the whole story, but there's more there than him nearly drowning. And after what I've seen and overheard since we got here, that doesn't make me any less concerned.

"Good. I want to make sure we get a chance to do some family stuff — you and me, and Callie and Piper, the baby once it gets here."

"Not Mom and Dad?"

"Can you picture them coming back here after all these years, hanging out with a bunch of rockers and their girlfriends?"

"They'd spend the whole time asking everyone about their college degrees, their investment portfolios, ambitions for political office... And looking down on all of us for not fitting their idea of success."

"Exactly. Doesn't matter how many awards we win, how many albums we sell... It'll never be enough. Though, I'm sure they're proud of you getting your bachelor's finally."

"I haven't told them."

"Why not?"

"I haven't told much of anyone, aside from you and Piper."

"I'll ask again: Why not?"

"I'm not doing it for them. I'm not doing it for anyone other than myself."

"Good."

"Good?"

"Yup. The only thing that matters is that it makes you happy."

"Does doing music make you happy?"

"Most of the time," I admit. "Certainly, satisfied. But I was never going to be truly happy without Callie. She's my soulmate. 'Lifebonded,' Brighid called it."

"Brighid said what?"

"She said something about 'lifebonds.' Callie and I promised each other forever, and that's what we got."

He looks pensive.

"You ever feel like you know what Callie's feeling when you're not even with her?" he asks. And now I'm wondering what exactly Brighid was talking about when she talked about the Carter brothers.

"Not exactly. But she and I do this brain-sharing thing sometimes. We say the same things at the same time, using the same words, or finish each other's sentences because we were already thinking the same thing, word for word. It's weird. But it's nice. Now that all the baggage is cleared away, it's like it was when we were together the first time. We just get each other."

"And now you're back together. Getting married. Again." He chuckles at that. "You and Hunter. He still won't tell the rest of us what that meant."

"Does it matter? Does it matter that Callie and I got married before?"

"No. I guess not. It just matters that everyone's happy."

"Exactly."

"So, when's the wedding?"

"In about an hour."

"You're joking."

"Nope. We got married with just the two of us and the officiant the last time. The only thing else we needed was two witnesses and a license. And that's all we're going to have. We got the license two days ago, and we just had to wait twenty-four hours to make it legal. So, you busy?"

"What would you have done if I was?"

"Can you imagine the in-fighting if I had to pick another best man from among the other guys in the band? It'd break up the band. Can't let that happen. So, it's gotta be you."

"So, where are you doing it?"

"At the house this time — Callie's house, her Nonna's. Ours now."

"You're really going to live here, in some decades-old house that's not even on the beach?"

"Yup. You'll get it when you see it."

"Should I bring Piper?"

"Nah. Nothing against your girl at all, but Callie's got her maid-of-honor picked, and we're keeping this small. In fact, I'm swearing you to secrecy. We'll tell everyone else when the time is right."

"I can keep a secret."

"I hope so. I've already gone viral once this week."

# CHAPTER 54

# HEY, BROTHER

## *An hour later*

"You sure you all don't want a big wedding with all the trimmings? Brighid and Hunter are at least doing the invitations-florist-catering-rented chairs-on-the-beach thing," Dave reminds me.

"Absolutely sure. This isn't the same kind of wedding as it is for Hunter and Brighid. They haven't had one yet. Well, sort of." Can't really talk about that, since Brighid might actually hex me if I tell anyone what I overheard them say about their own relationship. "But... Anyway... Callie and I — we had our wedding once, and I think we both want to remember that just how it was. This is just... It's just making it official, finally. She's been my wife for twelve years. I've been her husband for twelve years. We weren't together during that time, but now that we're back together, all the bad stuff behind us, we're just kind of picking up where we left off. With a piece of paper and witnesses. And that's exactly how we want it."

"You're right about the house," he says. "It's got a really cozy, homey quality. I get why you'd like it, want to settle in here. It's warm. Totally unlike..."

"Our parents' house? Yeah. But that's only part of it. It's like Callie and I... we just belong here. Together. It's our home."

"Where *is* Callie?"

"They're over at her apartment, getting her ready. We may be going low-key for this shindig, but she still wants it to be special. They'll be here soon."

"Well, I have to say I like your idea of wedding attire!" he says, gesturing at his linen shorts as he rolls up the sleeves on a loose white cotton button-up shirt.

"We wanted something casual and beachy," I tell him, stripping off my jeans in favor of a similar pair of khaki linen shorts. I pull my T-shirt off and grab my own button-up.

"Whoa!" Dave says, his eyes bulging out.

"What? Have I bulked up that much from all the time I put in the gym when Callie wasn't speaking to me?"

"Uh... No."

"Oh. I thought I'd at least gotten a little more definition in. I'm working on that eight-pack thing."

"Dec..."

"What are you freaking out about, big bro?"

"You seem to have acquired a tattoo since the last time I saw you with your shirt off."

"Which was, not coincidentally, the last time you saw me naked."

"Third-to-last time," he corrects. "I had to look at that photo *twice* — once when Rhys found it, and again when we discussed it at the meeting." He shudders. "*So* did not need to see that. Even once."

I laugh at the absurdity of it all. It really doesn't bother me in the least. I think I came off pretty good in the photo, even if I wasn't fully... prepared. And I *had* been spending a lot of time in the gym, working off the frustration over not being able to find Callie and then working off all those extra calories from making sure I ate everything she gave me to eat. Until the thing she gave me was herself...

"So... that tattoo..." he prompts.

"It was time."

"I thought you wanted to keep your body 'pristine.'"

"A likely story."

"Yeah, it was. So why now and not then?"

"You tell me. Why'd you wait so long? Why'd you get yours when you did?"

He answers without hesitation.

"Piper. She gave me my life — she literally saved me, and she gave me a real, full life for the first time. She's my muse. Just like Olivia told the other guys they'd find and get inked into their tats themselves one day."

"And you've answered your own question."

"Did... Did Siobhan do yours?"

"She did."

"Did you sing for her?"

"I did. Just like Hunt did. Just like you did, I suspect."

He doesn't answer me. And he seems a little haunted.

I wonder exactly what happened to my big brother this summer... A near-death experience. A first love impactful enough to ink the girl's face into his skin after just a matter of weeks. A baby on the way. Buying into the studio. Getting ready to settle down and build a home for his new family. And the first ballad aMUSEd has ever recorded. I'm guessing that's the music Siobhan put into his tattoo. And I'm reminded what he asked me on the beach earlier: Had I ever felt what Callie was feeling when she wasn't with me? Is that what he and Piper have? Is that what Brighid alluded to when she talked about this "lifebond" thing? Is it the tattoo that did it? Or did it exist for them before that, like the connection between Callie and me did?

"I was really worried you might bail on the band, you know," I tell him. "The matchy-matchy tattoos felt a little cheesy to the me who was still bitter and desperately trying to find Callie. But once I realized that you love Piper like I have always loved Callie, I realized that the fact that you'd finally chosen to get the muse design meant you had committed to the band the same way you had to Piper."

"I had. If anything happened to me, I wanted you guys to know that."

"Well, fortunately for everyone, nothing happened. Right?"

"Yeah. Right."

It's a response in the affirmative, but it doesn't quite feel like a wholehearted confirmation. More mystery. Exactly how close did Dave come to dying? And why didn't he — why didn't anyone, including Piper — tell us something serious was going on?

"You feeling better about my commitment to the band, now that I have this?" I ask him, gesturing to my own tattoo as I slide my arm into my shirt sleeve.

"Oddly enough, yeah. I mean, buying a house here, marrying Callie, who lives here — that tells me you're on the same page, with me and with Hunter. I kind of feel like the band's coalescing around the three of us again, just like it did when we first started."

"You think Rhys is next to fall in love with some local chick?" I ask, mostly kidding. Rhys has never had a serious relationship that I know of. His attention span is so short that it makes total sense that he usually ends up with a waitress who'll be staying behind at the diner when our tour bus rolls out.

"If I had to lay a wager, I'd say Alex will be the next man down," he says. "He's been kind of moody since we got here. Especially where Piper and Brighid were concerned."

"Callie, too. Though the two of them have gotten to be friends. Probably even before Callie was open to taking me back."

"He's still smarting over Megan. After all these years," Dave says. "I'm not sure what she did to him, but he's been gun-shy ever since."

"Yeah. I dunno. But he's always been a romantic. And now he's got less than half the bandmates to try to fix up."

"I kind of hope it's him," Dave says. "He spends a lot of time worrying about the rest of us. It'd be nice to see him get some happiness of his own."

"Kier's been off groupies for a while." Dave gives me a look. "Yes, I did notice! Geez. I'm not that much of a narcissist!" I shake my head. "But it makes me wonder if he's wanting to settle down. He's the oldest of us."

"He's got something going on with him," Dave says. "I'm not sure what. But Gryff's been powwowing with him."

"Maybe he wants to join the SEALs," I suggest, totally joking. The look Dave gives me is priceless.

"Yeah — long-haired guitar virtuoso Kieran O'Connor... long-haired *Irish* guitar virtuoso Kieran O'Connor — is going to join the elite American military. At.... what... 35?"

"As of April or whatever — yeah," I confirm. "Man... Does that seem ancient to you?"

"To me?" He looks at me like I've said something ridiculous. "Nah — 35 is barely a blink of the eye. We've got a lot of years yet to live. All of us."

"Assuming none of us drown or anything," I say pointedly.

"Not a problem. I promise," he says. Again, this I believe. And that's a relief. With all this talk of family, I kind of want to get to know my brother a bit better. "You ready to do this? I mean, Piper and I are forever, like our ink. But we haven't even talked about making it legal."

"Dave, Callie's been my wife for nearly half my life. This is just getting us back on track, to where we should have been. I've never been happier or more relaxed or more ready to do anything. It's like rolling out of bed in the morning and straight into her arms."

He smiles at me.

"That's how forever should feel," he says.

"Yeah. It is."

# CHAPTER 55

## HOW LONG WILL I LOVE YOU

"Declan... Good to see you again," Lyric says as I open the door for her. She looks around, taking in the changes to the house since the last time she was in here, which had to have been soon after Nonna died.

"You, too," I tell her.

"You sure about that?" she asks, her smile full of mischief. "You can't say I didn't warn you."

"I would never claim you hadn't. Nor would I take it back. Ever. Yeah, things didn't exactly go smoothly, but it feels like we've come full circle, ready to move forward together this time."

"As it should," she says. "I'd say you two are very lucky, but this wasn't luck. It was fate."

"I know."

She gives me an appraising look.

"You've matured, Declan Carter," she says. "And your reputation..."

"Was well-earned. Past tense," I emphasize.

"Ah. Good. I mean, I'll renew your vows anytime you feel like it, provided I can find a sitter..."

"Who's with your...?"

"Kids. Plural. A boy and a girl." She reads me like a book, and it's Marina Matthews-level scary. "Their father passed a while ago. Suddenly."

"I'm sorry. I can't imagine..."

"No, you can't. Really," she says, sounding weary. "And I suspect you won't have to anytime soon." She gets a thoughtful expression on her face, almost like she's listening to some far-off sound. I don't ask. I won't ask. "And, to answer your question — Brighid is with them right now. She's teaching Aria macramé, and Tommy's watching his movie. So I have enough time to do a quick renewal, and then I'll invite her and Hunter to come out with us, as Callie suggested. It'll be nice to get out with the kids for a change. Now, where did you want to do this?"

"Out in the back yard, in the garden."

"Of course. It's perfect," she says. "Callie and I used to help her Nonna in the garden when we first met. I learned a lot of my herb-lore from Nonna. Mom was always more of a tie-dye-and-crystals type, a fluffy-bunny witch. Nonna... She fit the strega model, aptly enough."

"I have no idea what any of that means."

"You probably don't need to, aside from the herbs, probably. And you'll figure that out over time, just like Hunter is with Brighid. So... out to the garden?"

Once out in the garden, Lyric unpacks a few things from her bag — a big book with a fancy cover and binding, a small vial and some ribbons. She takes out a jar of what looks like salt but then looks around and puts it back again.

"Do you have the marriage license? I'd kind of like this one to be a little more concrete than the last one, even if I knew it would stick."

"Yeah. I stuck it in a drawer for safe-keeping. My brother just went to make a phone call before we got started, and he was going to grab it."

"Excellent. Callie should be here any minute. And then we can get started."

"Hey, Dec — is this all you needed? I grabbed a couple pens, just in case. Oh — hi."

"Lyric, this is my big brother, David Carter. Dave, this is Callie's friend Lyric. She's the one who did our wedding the first time, and she's going to renew our vows — legally, this time."

"Nice to meet you, Lyric," Dave says, shuffling pens and paper so he can shake her hand.

"Maybe she can do yours and Piper's wedding, like she's doing Brighid's and Hunt's," I suggest, wondering in the back of my head why Dave hasn't even talked about proposing to Piper.

Lyric takes his hand to shake it and blinks.

"Not necessary," she murmurs, seeming distracted.

Dave does a bit of a double-take.

Lyric shakes her head, as if to clear it.

"Nice to meet you, David."

"You, too," he says.

"OK," Lyric says, visibly getting down to business while I'm still wondering at her strange reaction to Dave.

"Are you all ready? Because I have a ravishing bride-to-be here who's eager to get married. Again!" Siobhan announces from the back door.

"I've been waiting for this for twelve years, Siobhan!" I call back to her.

"Siobhan? Siobhan's Callie's maid-of-honor?" Dave whispers to me, seeming a little off again.

What the heck is going on here? No one's reacting to anyone else like I'd expect today.

"Yeah. She kind of helped us get things sorted out again. Plus, you know, my tattoo."

"Yeah," Dave says slowly. "The tattoo." He runs his hand over his left shoulder. Where his own tattoo is. Did I mention the fact that I think we need a band meeting? Because there's some stuff going on here that I don't think we all are aware of.

Siobhan steps down into the yard, a mile of white-blonde hair and braids cascading behind her shoulders, bared in an off-the-shoulder top. Even with the designs peeking out from her top, she seems a lot less intimidating like this. Then I look down and realize she's wearing khaki cargo shorts, just like she was when she did my tattoo. Ink twines around her ankles, which I can actually see this time, because she's wearing flip-flops instead of combat boots. This bodes well — less likely she'll kick my ass today. But she's basically wearing a uniquely Siobhan and slightly feminine version of the same outfits Dave and I have on. And it's perfect.

Until she reaches the small group of us in the middle of the garden and Dave finally turns around to face her. She blinks, like she's seen a ghost. He looks stiff, like he's not comfortable with whatever this situation is.

"OK — what the flibbertigibbets is going on here?" I ask, no longer able to restrain my curiosity.

"Nothing," they both say at the same time.

Lyric looks at Siobhan and then at David and then back again, and then she closes her eyes, adopting that listening posture she had before. Her eyes open, and her mouth forms an O. She nods sharply.

"You," she says, pointing at Siobhan. "Stop it. It's fine."

"And you," she says, pointing at David. "Stop it. It's fine. Things are as they are supposed to be. And you're going to be seeing a lot more of each other in the future, so get comfortable with it."

"Would someone mind explaining to me what's going on?" I ask again, minus the Mary Poppins profanity.

"Nothing," they both say again.

"It's fine. Stop it," Lyric says, this time pointing at me.

O... K...

"Excuse me! Was anyone here planning on getting married today?"

That's Callie, calling out from the kitchen, the back door open just an inch or two.

"Yes, angel!" I call back. "I'm marrying you today! Again! And if I have to go drag two people in off the street as witnesses, I'll do that!"

I glare at both Dave and Siobhan. No one is messing this up. I mean — it was supposed to be quick, simple, relaxed. And instead, I'm dealing with an eruption of weird.

Fortunately, that seems to snap both of them out of their stiffness, and their attention turns to Callie, who is making her way down the steps into the yard, a vision in another white sundress, much like the one she wore twelve years ago, the straps a little wider, the skirt a little shorter... whoo-boy. The simple half-up hairdo she sported that day has been replaced with an elaborate set of braids gathered from around her face and trailing down among the loose waves of her rich brown hair as it settles around her shoulders. And instead of the small bouquet of white roses she carried at our first wedding, she's carrying a larger bouquet — the one I arranged for the florist to deliver to her at her apartment: creamy white roses edged in crimson, with three crimson roses arranged at the center, all tied together with red, white and green ribbon.

"Class act, Declan," Lyric says quietly, her eyes fixed on the bouquet. She lifts up the ribbons she'd pulled from her bag, showing the same color combination as the ones on Callie's bouquet, which I'd requested based on the ribbons Lyric had used in our first ceremony.

But I can't take my eyes off Callie. It's like a double exposure, the image of our past overlaid by a new vision of our present, our future — all of it uniting in one single moment as Callie arrives in front of me and reaches out her hand to me. After a moment of stunned silence, I grasp it, lifting it to my lips to kiss the back of her hand.

"You are... a vision. A true angel descended from the heavens. My wife. My muse," I tell her.

"And you're a romantic, Declan Carter. Once and future husband," she replies, smiling.

"You bring it out in me."

"Me, too."

"I'm not sure you need many more words than that," Lyric says, visibly touched. "But the ones you do need, I will give, and gladly, setting right what went awry and cementing what fate always meant for you two to have, together."

There's that word again.

Lyric holds her hand out to Callie, and Callie places in it more ribbons like the ones Lyric herself held earlier. She gestures to me to take Callie's hand, and I do. Lyric reaches out to dot something scented on both our foreheads, right between our eyes, and then she wraps the ribbons Callie gave her around our thumbs, draped over our joined hands. That's when I spot a small knot already tied in these ribbons.

"Are those...?"

"They are," Lyric confirms. "Never undone. Never severed. Just like the bond between you two. And now we'll reaffirm that bond, forge it anew, stronger than ever."

She looks at Callie. "Do you, Calliope Aoede Martin, take this man, Declan..." Lyric giggles, her mood suddenly lighter than it has been. "I don't think I even asked last time, since we didn't have paperwork to fill out."

"I don't think *I* ever asked. And I let you fill out everything on the license the other day," Callie says, sounding a little chagrined.

"You didn't have to ask," I tell her. "You already knew, on some level. Nonna knew. Somehow."

"It's not..." she says, disbelief etched on her face.

I nod.

"Declan Arthur Carter," I tell Lyric, but my eyes never leave Callie's, which glisten as she absorbs the revelation.

"Do you, Calliope Aoede Martin," Lyric begins again, "take this man, Declan Arthur Carter, to be your lawfully wedded husband, to shelter each other from the storms of life, to warm each other with the fires of passion, to inspire in each other growth and goodness, and to feed each other's souls?"

"I so very, very much do. Forever and always," Callie says, smiling at me with a love in her eyes that just takes my breath away.

Lyric wraps the ends of the new set of ribbons around our hands.

"Do you, Declan Arthur Carter, take this woman, Calliope Aoede Martin, to be your lawfully wedded wife, to shelter each other from the storms of life, to warm each other with the fires of passion, to inspire in each other growth and goodness, and to feed each other's souls?"

"I do. Today, yesterday, next year, a thousand years from now, I do."

Lyric wraps the other end of the ribbons around our hands. Then she reaches behind her and traces her hand through the water gurgling in the fountain before sprinkling Callie and I both with it. Both of us look at her, curious.

"You didn't realize this was a sacred fountain?" she asks, as if we're both a little oblivious. "The water's been blessed. I mean, it's got a nymph's name on it — daughter of the river god Achelous, sister to sirens. Of course it's blessed."

Callie and I look at each other, both of us visibly adding just one more thing to the ever-increasing stack of mysterious knowledge Nonna seems to have had but never shared.

"With your sworn promises confirmed before these witnesses, by the powers vested in me by the State of Delaware and whichever gods have wrought this most extraordinary union," she says, shaking her head, "I now pronounce you husband and wife."

She takes the two ends of the ribbon and ties them together loosely, pulling the knot tight.

"You may kiss," she says. "Not that you need my or anyone else's permission. Because you're now legally married adults," she says with a chuckle.

And I take that as my cue, using my free hand to pull Callie's face to mine and begin our lives together, for real... for—

"Forever," Callie murmurs against my lips.

My smile grows wide, and I marvel at this woman. My person. "Brain-sharing," I say.

We chuckle, our mouths still pressed together.

"How's it feel to be Mrs. Carter?" I ask her.

"Carter-Martin," she corrects.

"Oh. OK. I can handle that," I tell her. "Declan Carter-Martin. That works."

She opens her eyes and looks at me like I'm nuts. Which I am. About her.

"Are you serious?" she asks, dubious.

"A little."

"The label will pitch a fit."

"Probably. But that's kind of fun to watch, as I can tell you from experience."

"Declan…" Dave chides from behind me.

"Oops. Forgot you were there. Forgot anyone was there. Other than my beautiful officially official wife."

"Is it party time now?" Siobhan asks. "I wish I could reschedule this client, because Callie didn't have nearly enough tequila the other night, and if Declan's buying again, that's something I'd like to see…"

Callie and I chuckle, while Dave just looks lost, and Lyric groans.

"I am officially old, and a lightweight," she says. "But I hear there's a somewhat family-friendly private party tonight, with a halfway decent band…"

"Halfway? I'll have you know we are *very* decent," I tell her. "The band, that is. Me — all the way *in*decent!"

"I'll say," Siobhan says, smirking at me from behind Callie, who elbows her. "Ow! Watch it, woman! I've got piercings under there!"

We all look at Siobhan.

"Hey! *I'm* not the one who's naked and tied up on the internet!"

"Valid point," Callie says. "You sure you don't want to take that post down now?" she asks me. "It served its purpose. We're officially married."

"Wait… What?" That's both Siobhan and Dave.

"Here — everyone sign this, so I can file it. Then I'm going to go get the kids and get Brighid moving," Lyric says, providing a useful distraction.

Callie and I studiously avoid Siobhan and Dave's eyes while we slip our hands from both sets of ribbons and sign the license. And then I pull Callie against me, enjoying the sensuous feel of my wife's lips against mine. Wife. I've thought of her that way for so long, but now... We can finally tell everyone.

"Congratulations!" Lyric says, taking the signed paperwork she needs to file. "See you in a bit!"

# CHAPTER 56

## HOUSE OF LOVE

## Callie

"**D**eclan! We're supposed to be getting changed to go to the Pirate's Cove! Everyone's going to be waiting there for us! And they're going to be wanting answers!"

"And they're going to have to *bear* with us..." he says, grabbing me around my waist and nuzzling into my neck. "Get it? *Bear* with us?"

"Is your middle name really Arthur?" I ask, still skeptical. What are the chances? But then, it was Nonna, and I'm increasingly realizing that Nonna was an exceptional person, in or out of the kitchen.

"You want me to show you my driver's license?" he offers as I rub my hands along his arms. "I mean, you might want to make sure I'm of legal age for the kind of erotic activities you might have in mind for me, you seductress, you."

"If you weren't, we couldn't have gotten married today," I point out.

"Good point. Because we are definitely married now. I double-checked the paperwork before Lyric took it off to file."

I sigh, settling back into his arms.

"It finally feels like everything's the way it's supposed to be," I tell him. "Not just being married for real, but being here, in Nonna's house—"

"*Our* house," he reminds me.

"*Our* house," I agree, liking the sound of that, too. "And... there's something... I don't know..." I'm trying to put words to it.

"Fresh," he suggests.

"That's it! I should have known you'd know exactly what I was feeling..." I turn in his arms, holding his face between my hands and pressing a kiss to his lips.

"Like we've actually got a clean slate," he says.

"Yes! Full of promise. But where we also have this comfortable familiarity with each other."

"It doesn't hurt that we can finish each other's—"

"Sentences," we both say, though that wasn't exactly an unlikely guess.

"I love you so much, Mrs. Carter-Martin," he says, kissing me back. "I am the luckiest flibbertigibbeter on the planet."

"We're really stuck with that, aren't we?" I ask, chuckling.

"I think we might be," he says. "But you know what we're *not* stuck with?"

"What?"

"These clothes... We really do have to take them off if we're going to go put those sorry flibbertigibbeters out of their mystery misery." He slides the wide dress strap off my right shoulder and slides his fingers under the back of the strap on the left.

And he pulls back away from me, looking puzzled.

"Uh... Callie?"

"Yes," I reply with a smile.

"Are you wearing plastic wrap under your dress?"

"Not exactly. But yes," I tell him.

"What did you do?"

"Why don't you unwrap your wedding present and find out?" I tease, holding my hands out to the sides in offering.

His hand finds the zipper pull and slides it down, opening the back of the dress and baring my skin to his touch.

"No plastic back here," he says, sliding his hand down, cupping my ass, half exploring and half patently savoring the feel of me under his fingers.

"You're getting distracted," I tease him, just as he's teasing me with his fingertips. "Why don't I help you..."

I step back away from him and slip the dress off in one move, leaving me standing naked in front of him, except for a pair of lacy white panties, damp from wanting him, and a narrow swath of transparent plastic, my hands below it, barely covering my breasts.

"I am not *less* distracted right now, Callie. In fact, all of the blood has left my brain and rushed straight to my cock. I want inside my wife," he growls.

"Ah-ah-ah!" I warn him, moving back another step. "You haven't solved your own little mystery yet."

I drop my hands, letting him take in all of me that's not hidden behind a single scrap of fabric.

"Is that...?"

He closes the distance between us in an instant, cupping my left breast in his hand, running his thumb over my nipple. I shiver as my skin pebbles under his touch. Then he traces over the thin bit of clear plastic at the top of my breast.

"Siobhan did this? This morning?"

"Yeah. It didn't take nearly as long as yours, but it felt appropriate."

His fingertips trace the outline of the small grizzly bear Siobhan inked into my skin in a shade of blue the exact same color as Declan's eyes, leaving gaps of bare skin inside for the stars and connecting lines of the constellation of the Great Bear. It's a small bear, but that's not where the tattoo ends.

Declan follows the thin, wavering blue line that traces from the bear's back, up my chest and shoulder and then down again. He spins me slowly as the line disappears down the back of my shoulder, his fingers slipping across the surface of the clear plastic until they reach just below my waist and stretch wide along the space between my hip and spine.

"It's not exactly a portrait, but I figured it might capture enough of your essence to feel like you're with me — even when you're not, even when you're on the road," I tell him softly.

"My mic," he says, exhaled in a whisper.

"Siobhan and I found some photos online. I wanted to make sure it was the right one."

"SM-58. I've had that one since before we signed our first record deal," he says. "I had the old band logo — with just the comedy mask — engraved on it so none of the other bands we shared the stage with would walk off with it." His fingers touch the tiny design on the scaled-down image of his microphone, now etched permanently into my back. "You didn't have to do this," he says, spinning me back around to face him. "I got mine because you're my muse — no matter what happened with us." His thumbs run across my cheekbones, his fingers along my jaw.

"And I got this one because you've been a part of me since the first moment I laid eyes on you, Declan Carter—"

"Carter-Martin," he says, and I smile, even though I don't think he's entirely serious about that.

"I wanted to be reminded of that every time I look in the mirror — so that when I'm feeling unsure or reluctant to take a chance, to go on an adventure, to be myself and share what I'm feeling with the people around me, I'm reminded that you've built a life on taking chances, going on adventures and sharing your innermost feelings with people all around the world." I cup his jaw in my hand, marveling that after twelve years apart, he's really mine now, for good. On paper and in our souls. "I wanted to remind myself that you took me with you on those adventures, safe inside that little bear — so, in a way, I've already done all of those things that used to scare me. That don't scare me anymore, because I know you'll always be with me, even when you're far away, and you'll always keep me safe."

"What was the song, Callie?" Declan asks, knowing there's no way Siobhan would have done a tattoo this symbolic for me, for us, without enchanting it with a song.

"'Always Something There to Remind Me.'" I'm wondering if he remembers the importance of it. We never talked about it. Not once. No more than we discussed our middle names, which have turned out to be such an important link between us.

"The song I was singing that first moment we saw each other on the boardwalk. The day we met," he says, shaking his head, marveling. "It was a request. We were lucky all three of us knew it. I always remembered the bells in the beginning, even though we couldn't exactly replicate them right then... church bells..."

"Wedding bells," I remind him. "They're wedding bells."

"This was fate — you and me," he says, looking deep in my eyes, deep lake blue to the silver that matches the metal of our wedding rings. "Life tore us apart... and then fate brought us back together, at an engagement party for two friends at a bayside bar in the same little town where we first met."

"And where our friends are now waiting for us, wondering why it is that we asked them all to be there tonight."

"They'll have to wait and wonder for a while longer," he says. "First, I'm making love to my wife, my angel, my muse..." he adds, quickly shedding his soft shirt and showing off that astonishingly colorful work of art that's now a part of him.

"Just be careful…" I warn, reminded of how fresh my own is.

"Of the tattoo. I know," he says. "Like I could ever forget the Great Bear and my favorite mic engraved into your soft, sensuous skin, part of you, just like you're part of me."

"And I'm ready to have even more of you be part of me," I tell him, my fingers reaching for the button on his shorts, undoing it, sliding my hand down and taking the zipper with it. I cup that pertinent part, and he presses himself into my hand as soon as the shorts fall below his hips.

"Oh, that's definitely happening. Right after I finish unwrapping my wedding present," he says, sliding my panties down my thighs. "This gift is particularly delicious, if I recall correctly," he purrs in my ear. "In fact, it may just be my favorite flavor in the world. Did you know that?"

"Remind me," I tell him, wrapping my leg around his hip.

His hand sinks between my legs, teasing, tormenting, drawing even more moisture from me. A moment later, I'm on my back on the bed — our bed, in our house. And my husband has his hands between my thighs, pulling them gently apart. He licks his lips, then his fingers, sliding them slowly inside me. My head is thrown back, my eyes shut, enjoying the feeling of him playing inside me, like I'm the one instrument he was always born to bring to life.

I feel his hot breath as he sinks his head between my thighs, pressing a kiss atop my mound before sliding lower and sucking on my clit. My legs close around him, the feeling unbelievably intense. He flicks against it with his tongue before pressing my thighs back apart and against the mattress.

"I want to enjoy this meal with all my senses," he says. "Touch…" He slides his fingers down my slit. "Scent," he adds, pressing his nose against me and inhaling before exhaling with a satisfied sigh. "Sight," he says, looking up at me. "Taste," he adds, licking me from opening to clit. I moan loudly. "Yeah. That's the other one," he says, his smile set on high and his eyes to full smolder.

And then he falls on me, mouth open, exploring every curve, fold, petal and nub with his lips and tongue. I'm lost to the sensations, my fingers grasping the thick comforter as if it's the only thing keeping me from flying off into a weightless state where the only thing that exists is Declan's mouth on me, drawing on me, pulling straight from my core and then pressing himself inside, filling the ache he's simultaneously creating and soothing.

His lips surround my clit, and he sucks, hard. My legs spasm up, fighting his hold as he struggles to keep me in place. I grab hold of his head, cradling it and meshing my fingers into his hair. A flick of his tongue, and my legs jump again, but he keeps the suction going, driving me higher and higher until even my legs are a distant memory, the whole universe focused on that one spot as the tension within me spirals higher and higher, threatening to break... Break me in two, break like the dawn over the horizon... No — break like a crashing wave on the beach, which is what it finally does as he pushes me over into ecstasy and continues to lap and suck and flick until I'm a jangling mess of overstimulated nerves laid out boneless before him.

"Delicious," he says, licking his lips, cleaning the traces of my arousal off his face, his fingers. "Definitely my favorite. I could live on that," he says, catching my hazy gaze with his sharply intent one.

"Declan," I say, when I can finally form words again, "I want you. Now."

He skims his boxer-briefs off his hips in a moment and slides between my thighs, his mouth descending on mine, tasting of both of us now. And this might well be *my* favorite flavor, and I savor it, our mouths and lips and tongues feeding off each other as he fits himself in the one other place he's always belonged, other than my heart, and slides home.

"God," I say, unable to think of any other word to express how this feels, having my husband buried inside me like this. Any word for it would have to invoke the divine, because this is an exquisite miracle.

"Not quite," he says, "but close."

Ah, yes, my ever-cocky rockstar. Rockstar *husband*. Mine. No more groupies. All those hurled panties pointless in the face of what he feels for me. Autographed cleavages a remnant of the past, with my face permanently part of him — his angel, his wife, his muse.

He moves within me, peppering kisses along my neck and jaw, exploring me with his mouth while he rocks himself into me, propped on his muscular arms. His tongue traces the microphone cable where it crosses my shoulder. It's not the same as it will be once the protective bandage is removed, but, for now, the sensation carries with it an appreciation of this symbol of our intertwined lives. And I love him for it, just as I've loved every moment of love and caring he's ever given me.

It's our fingers that intertwine now as he pulls my right hand to the side, next to my head, and changes his angle, pressing deeper within me. I gasp, my eyes rolling up and then going wide as the feeling continues to build. His eyes are rapt, fixed on my face, his jaw set with determination.

"I'm going to make sure you come with me this time," he says, panting with the words and his exertion. "I'm so close... Holding back. Waiting for you. We're doing this together. Everything together from now on."

My heart soars. Maybe it will be literal, or maybe we'll remain tangled together in spirit, as we've always been and now both recognize. But this man is my husband, my family, my home, and nothing will ever come between us ever again. No misunderstandings or painful remnants of our past. Not time, space, a life on the road or a demanding career. Nothing.

"Come with me, angel... wife..."

I give myself over to his body's movements within mine, the feel of his strong hand grasping my own, and those deep blue eyes, boring into me and finding that place where our spirits connect, have always connected, and always will. And the universe explodes around us, our bodies and minds adrift in a sea of ecstasy, bound together in pleasure and love. No longer adrift, but tethered together, always anchored in that one intangible place that we both call home.

# CHAPTER 57

# HIGHER LOVE

## Declan
### *A half-hour later*

"What exactly are you two up to here?" Brighid asks the moment Callie and I arrive on the deck at the Pirate's Cove, her tone almost accusing. "You didn't need to rent the place out just to have a place to play your own songs, regardless of what David tried to tell us." Mostly, she sounds skeptical. Or suspicious. Or both. I guess that magical intuition of hers didn't give her a heads-up on what we've got planned.

"Yeah — I'd like to know why we closed down the restaurant for two days on basically no notice, even if everyone's still getting paid. And why I dragged my husband and baby out to a bar on a Wednesday night," Drew demands, focused on Callie, who's standing next to me, our fingers tangled together in what's become our natural posture.

It was like this when we were 16 in Nonna's restaurant kitchen, and it'll be like this when we're 90 and sitting in rocking chairs on the porch of the old-rockstars home. Well, our home, more likely, now that we have one. Together.

There are two people already here who have those answers, but Dave's standing silently, trying to hide a smile behind Piper's head as she hands me the wireless microphone I asked him to make sure was ready when we arrived, along with the regular band set-up on the stage. Lyric seems very well occupied at a table out of the way of most of the people here — my bandmates, Billy, Malcolm, Callie's friends, her employees, and some special guests of a sort.

It's not quite as many people as it had been the last time "Private Party" was on the marquee here, with a number of people beyond the band aware that Hunter was about to propose. But Callie and I are here for a slightly different, if related, purpose.

I pull Callie with me, up on the stage. She's not as reluctant as Brighid was when Hunter dragged her up here, but she's blushing with all the attention. Outside of her restaurant, or at least a culinary event, she's really not used to having the spotlight on her. It's my natural environment, though, and from now on, it's one we'll share. At least part of the time. We've got so many adventures ahead of us... A new home together, a second restaurant, an album, a tour... and some new side projects. Together.

"Hi, everyone!" I say into the mic. "I guess you're all wondering why we asked you to be here."

"No flibbertigibbeting kidding!" Rhys yells back at me.

Callie and I exchange a look, trying not to laugh, while Rhys gets curious looks from nearly everyone here.

"Well, we wanted you all to be here to share with us in celebrating the fact that we're back together," I tell them. "You want to explain this to them, angel?" I ask, offering her the mic. She takes it, if a little reluctantly.

"As a few of you know, Declan and I met when we were just 15, on the boardwalk here in Mystic Beach. We were instantly smitten with each other." She looks to me for confirmation, and I nod, but I think she knows her words mirror precisely what I would have said. "Two years later, circumstances intervened and pulled us apart. It's been a lot of water under the bridge," she adds, calling to mind the words I spoke to her in her kitchen weeks ago. "But Declan and I both realized when we saw each other again, for the first time in twelve years, that what we'd felt for each other had never gone away, and that fate seemed to have pulled us back together, despite all that had happened."

"So are you getting engaged? Because Bridge and I already did that, and you're not one for replicating someone else's performance," Hunter calls out to me from behind, his tone teasing. "Couldn't come up with something more original?"

Callie offers me the microphone, and I take it with an affectionate nod to her.

"Well, no. We did not bring you all here tonight to witness and celebrate our engagement. And, you're right, Hunter. I always prefer to do something original, even dramatic. So, first — an unveiling!"

I hand Callie back the mic and strip my T-shirt off over my head, then exchange it for the mic once more.

There's a wide range of responses from around us, from shock and surprise from all of my bandmates except Dave, to murmurs of appreciation from those who quickly recognize Callie's face as part of my personal take on the aMUSEd logo that all six of us now have tattooed on us in some form.

"Many of you will know that, until recently, my brother and I were the only two members of aMUSEd who did not have the band logo inked on us somewhere. And some of you will know that Dave got his own version of the aMUSEd muse tattooed on him earlier this summer, with the face of his beautiful girlfriend and our amazing sound engineer, Piper, at the center of the design."

Dave waves mildly from behind Piper, clearly not relishing being the center of attention, even briefly. But this needs to be said.

"Dave found his soulmate here in Mystic Beach, entirely unlooked-for. And I have never in my life been so envious of another human being," I admit. "As Callie just told you, she and I fell in love when we were just 15, right here in Mystic Beach, and it's been a long twelve years without her. So, when we got here to start working on our next album and all those old memories got stirred up for me, I was a pretty miserable S.O.B."

"And that's different from normal how?" Alex calls out, smirking at me.

"Ah! A very good point from our resident romantic busybody!" I reply. "What no one else knew, until Callie and I found ourselves face-to-face for the first time in more than a decade — at Hunter and Brighid's engagement party, of all places — was that I'd spent all those years pining for her, becoming that gargantuan dick—"

"Declan! There are children present!" Lyric calls from so far back that I can't even see her. Callie elbows me, frowning repressively.

"Sorry! I forgot!" I shrug. "Anyway, I was a pretty big... *appendage*," I rephrase.

"Yeah! We know! We all saw it. All over the feckin' internet!" Kieran calls out, to a round of laughter. "Cannot be unseen! No matter how much we all wish we'd never seen it in the first place!"

"Yeah, yeah... People normally pay to see that kind of beauty, in museums..."

"And adult theaters!" Alex retorts.

Lyric growls and throws her hands up, pulling a little girl up in her lap and putting her hands over the girl's ears. Oops.

"Get to the point, Declan! We're all waiting to know why we're actually here. Unless you taking your shirt off for everyone was the point of all this!" That's Raquel, and I smile down at her as I spot her amidst the group of culinary students standing around a table laden with food.

"The point is that I was a bitter, miserable man, wallowing in self-pity and self-punishment..."

"Is that what the cuffs were for?" Rhys asks not-so-quietly from behind me. Callie sputters in laughter.

"And," I continue, "I didn't always treat everyone around me nicely. So, the first reason we're here is for me to apologize to you all, and, indirectly, to everyone else I was ever less than kind or respectful to. I know I can't make up for it, but I'm hoping that explaining some of it, at least, will help you forgive me, if you can."

"Aww..." Alex intones. "He loves us! He really loves us!"

"Well, no. OK. Kind of. Sometimes," I admit. "But what I really want to say is that I love this woman, this angel of mine." I gesture to Callie. "And she, by some miracle, loves me. Still. Always has, just like I've always loved her, and always will." I pause to press a soft kiss to her lips, and she smiles at me, setting my heart to pounding like no sold-out crowd ever has. "And..."

She pulls the microphone out of my hand, shoving my shirt back at me.

"What Declan's trying to say, enjoying the spotlight of this stage perhaps a little too much, is that we're back together, we're in love, and we're *not* getting engaged." Looks of confusion from nearly everyone here.

"We got married! Again!" we say simultaneously into the microphone, brain-sharing as always.

OK — there we go. *That's* the response I expected when we decided to do this.

Jaws dropped, gasps, eyes bugged out, people turning to look to others for confirmation that they actually heard what they think they heard, then turning back to look at us, as if they'll see some neon sign light up over our heads, reading "Married. Really."

"Again?" Rhys asks loudly. "Why do people keep saying that and then not explaining!"

And with that, all I care about is my wonderful wife. Twelve years in the making. A miracle delivered to me by the whims of fate and the glorious generosity of a true angel. Even if she tried to kill me first.

"Happy wedding day, Mrs. Carter-Martin," I tell her, giving her a kiss.

"Happy wedding day, Mr. Carter-Martin," she replies. And at that moment, I'm pretty sure I'm actually going to change my name. She pulls me down to kiss her again, this time long and deep, and I get lost in her as the sounds of surprise and confusion shift into the hoots and hollers of celebration.

"Our wonderful friends, the culinary students at the local food bank, took over the kitchen at Castalia for the last two days and pulled out all the stops to help us celebrate with you tonight," I tell them all. "Make sure you tell them how much you appreciate their efforts! And my truly talented wife, Chef Callie, and I spent most of yesterday making a little—" she frowns at me "—not-so-little wedding cake to make sure you all know this is a legit wedding reception."

There's more murmuring and confusion as the culinary kids bring the cake out to place on the dessert table and people try to make sense of the fact that Callie and I made this together.

"He did most of the work, actually!" Callie tells them. And I did. She baked, humming all the while, and I oversaw the culinary students. Then, I decorated, her little melody embedding itself in my head, while she took over keeping the rest of the menu on track. And it all came out pretty well, if I say so myself. And, as happy as we've both been, chances are this food will only spread loving vibes among our friends. I wonder if someone will fall in love at first sight tonight, like we did fourteen years ago.

"My bandmates and I will be coming up here in a bit to entertain you all, too — assuming they're still willing to be seen on the same stage with me! And now, if you'll excuse me, I'm going to take my wife into the dressing room back there and bend her over the sofa!"

"Declan!"

Remind me to apologize to Lyric later. I know she's not a goddess, but I'm still not sure she can't hurl lightning bolts at my ass.

I pull a very willing Callie behind me, shutting and locking the dressing room door quite firmly.

"You really planning on bending me over this sofa, Declan?"

"Depends. Is that what you want me to do, angel?"

"If I was really an angel, I'd say no to that, Mr. Carter-Martin."

"Ah — but every angel needs a little devil inside her, Mrs. Carter-Martin."

"Or a lot of one..." she replies, that seductive smirk a mirror of my own.

"That, my dear wife, can be arranged."

# CHAPTER 58

## THANK YOU

## Declan
### *An hour later*

"OK. I'm not doing this again. Hunter and Brighid keep refusing to tell me what 'again' means! And they're not even married yet. And now you're saying you got married 'again.' It's going to make me crazy, Dec, Callie! Just tell me. Please!"

Well, the upside of this demand from Rhys is that I don't have the kind of supernatural circumstances to explain to him that Brighid and Hunter would. Circumstances I can't tell anyone about, because I'm pretty sure Brighid would indeed hex me, and between that and Lyric lightning bolts, I'm not taking any more chances with these witchy women who seem to congregate in this town now.

But then who am I to talk? I married the kitchen witch! Again.

I look at Callie, wordlessly asking for her permission to put Rhys out of his misery.

"Up to you, husband," she says, seeming content just to be able to call me that in front of other people. I know the feeling.

"Do you think he can be trusted not to share our secret with the entire planet, wife?" I ask.

"I won't tell anyone! I swear!" Rhys says.

"He did delete that photo he took of me, right when I asked him," I point out.

Callie and I exchange a look and nod at each other at the same moment.

"Declan and I got married when we were 17, Rhys," Callie tells him.

"But it wasn't legal, because we were too young and our parents wouldn't sign the papers to let us get married," I add.

"Is that why it took you twelve years to get married again?" he asks. "Did your parents keep you apart?"

"No," I admit. "That was me. Me making a big mistake that it took me way too long to fix."

"But we've got all of that fixed and put behind us now, Rhys," Callie says, reminding me that she doesn't want me feeling guilty anymore. The best kind of fresh start. "And we're married in every possible way now. Forever."

"Forever," I agree, kissing her on the side of her head.

"Again," Rhys says with a nod. "I like that. A happy ending. I'd like one of those someday," he says. "Congratulations. I'm really happy for both of you," he says, grabbing us both up in a single hug with those long drummer arms of his and lifting us up off the floor. He puts us down and gives us a beaming smile. "I won't tell anyone your secret." And, with that, he grabs up his drumsticks and sets up to tune his kit.

Rhys is the last of my bandmates to offer his congratulations. Alex spent way too long giving Callie a congratulatory hug. I'm pretty sure it was on purpose, because he was wearing this satisfied smirk as my hands fisted tighter and tighter, standing there, waiting for him to release her. Hunter had this knowing smile on his face, like he totally got why we'd jumped straight into getting married. He's getting close himself, and I suspect it's the trappings of the event and not the fact that he's getting married to his beloved Brighid — again — that's got him a little on edge. Kieran's eyes seemed a little sad, though his smile was full of affection for both of us. I was reminded of Dave's talk about Kier being burned out and dodging groupies. I suspect he's feeling at least a little like I was when Dave told everyone he and Piper were together and were expecting.

"You're killing me, Dec," Billy says, coming up behind me. "First that photo, and now this... Hunter off the market, and then Dave — though, thankfully, that's not a marriage yet, with everything on record — and now you. You remember that we came here talking about how much aMUSEd's appeal was enhanced by the fact you were all single? What are you guys doing to me?"

"You're the one who let them stick Hunt in a reality dating show," I remind him.

"And I'm going to end up on a reality show set in the ER," Billy says. "They'll be treating me for a coronary." He sighs, sounding really tired, and I start to wonder if we really need to keep an eye on his stress levels. Nah. He's fine. He thrives on stress. "Just do me a favor and keep this on the QT for a while, OK? Just so I can get out ahead of it. Are there any other surprises you want to tell me about while I've got you cornered?"

"If I tell you, Billy, it's not a surprise!" I reply brightly.

"Gah..." is all he says, deflating before my eyes.

"But I will warn you — I'm going to be taking a few weeks off here. Probably inside the month. Callie and I are going to take a trip."

"Honeymoon?" he asks.

"That, and some culinary traveling, get some ideas for our new restaurant."

"New restaurant? *Your* new restaurant?"

"Declan and I are partnering on a second restaurant here in Mystic Beach," Callie explains. "And we're going to start in Italy, maybe go to Paris, Marrakesh..."

"Copenhagen? I haven't been there in a while. And Tokyo."

"New Orleans," Callie says. "We have to stop in New Orleans on the way back."

"Sure. After a few days in the Caribbean? Granada? Barbados? Jamaica?"

"Ooh... I love Jamaican flavor profiles," she says.

"How long is this culinary honeymoon going to last?" Billy says, sounding resigned now.

"A month, maybe," Callie and I say together, making us both chuckle.

"Don't forget Hunter and Brighid's wedding!"

"We won't," Callie promises. "I owe her a lot. And Siobhan."

"Where *is* Siobhan?" I ask her. "I expected her to be here by now."

"She had that client. Couldn't be rescheduled," she says. "She said she'd try to make it later, but it was a big piece and the client came into town just to see her."

"That's OK. She was there when it counted today." Even if the vibe between Dave and her was really weird.

"And I need to thank Rory, too. I thought I saw her here earlier, with Lyric and the kids."

"The reporter?" Billy asks. "I promised her an interview with the band later. But I can reschedule it for another time if you all want to keep this separate. She promised to keep the personal stuff to a minimum, but it seemed like she was in on a lot of it already."

"She is," Callie says. "She's Lyric's best friend, former housemate, godmother to her son and daughter."

"Well, you all let me know when you're ready, and I'll bring her back to the dressing room for a sit-down."

"Will do."

Billy heads off, and I pull Callie into my arms, her back against my chest, my chin tucked in along her shoulder, just enjoying the feel of her skin against mine as we watch our friends celebrating our happiness and mingling with each other. Yeah. Together is word I'm getting very fond of.

On a whim, I pull my phone out, grabbing her left hand with mine, and snap a photo.

"What are you going to do with that?' she asks, looking at the close-up image of our wedding rings and our fingers laced together.

"Putting Billy on a reality TV show..." I tell her, pulling up my Instagram.

"Declan Carter."

Uh-oh.

I mean, it's a man's voice, so it's less of an uh-oh than it would be if it was Marina Matthews, but I didn't expect her to be here tonight. *This*, I expected, especially after I broke the news to Billy about our honeymoon plans.

"Malcolm! Glad you could make it!"

"Where else would I be, Declan? After all, it's not like I'm recording chart-topping band aMUSEd in the studio their label rented for the specific purpose of getting this album done."

"Sarcasm doesn't suit you, Malcolm," I reply.

"It's probably more suitable than the long string of profanity I'm trying not to deliver right now, amidst this happy news and with children present."

"I appreciate the discretion, Malcolm."

"And now Billy tells me that, after all of these delays, you're planning on taking off on a honeymoon? For a month?"

"In my defense, a honeymoon was originally *supposed* to be a month long," I tell him. "I'm keeping to tradition!"

"You don't give a rat's ass about tradition," Malcolm says, knowing me well enough to know that I don't follow anyone's rules unless I feel like it. Hence the Instagram post I hit Share on now, before anyone else notices.

"Nope," I tell Malcolm, being entirely honest about that particular character flaw. "But — I was nice enough to plan said honeymoon while Hunter and Brighid should be gone on theirs as well. So, you'll have very little down-time on the album where one of us is gone and the other is here."

"That would be a lot less discouraging if you all actually had an album's worth of songs written that we could start recording when you all get back. We're up to a sum total of six, between you, your brother, Hunter and Alex," he says. "If I don't get some songs from you guys really soon, I may have to consider letting Rhys have his six-minute drum solo, just to fill out the album!"

"Oh, god! Not that!" I say in mock horror. Though the horror is real. Rhys has been trying to get that marathon drum solo on an album since our first EP.

"I'm not that desperate yet, and I don't plan on getting there," Malcolm says. "So, let me tell you right now — if you don't come back from these honeymoons with half a dozen more songs written, I'm walking. You can find a new producer. I've got other projects I could be working on. And now I'm going to have to see if I can find another project to do on short notice while you're off gallivanting around the world! So, the least you can do is get some songs ready for when I get back."

"I can do that, Malcolm."

"You can? Half a dozen? Six? One more than five? One less than seven? You haven't written that many in the last two years total!"

Ah, skepticism from our producer. Why is this not surprising?

"I've been feeling very inspired, Malcolm." I hug Callie tightly, smiling down at her as she smiles back up at me.

"Yes, well... I hope you can put that inspiration into something tangible. Six somethings!"

"Not a problem, Malcolm. Don't you trust me?"

"Not as far as I could throw you, and that's been pretty tempting."

"Aww... Don't be such a pessimist, Mal." He hates it when I call him Mal. "I finished my sixth song of the summer yesterday."

Malcolm's trying really hard not to splutter. He's usually so even-tempered and professional. I'm enjoying ruffling his feathers a little. Maybe a little more than I should. Especially considering that Billy's about to lose it... oh, any minute now...

"I'll look forward to hearing them, Declan," Malcolm says, seeming a bit stymied and, reluctantly, pleased with me. Win! "Congratulations to you both," he says, giving us a nod and walking off.

"Well, Mrs. Carter-Martin," I say, pulling Callie around to face me and kissing her for about the hundredth time tonight. Not nearly enough. Never enough. "How would you like to have the chart-topping band aMUSEd perform for you at your wedding reception? I hear they're halfway decent."

"I heard they were *very* decent," she says mildly.

"That was the lead singer being very *in*decent," I correct her.

"Even better," she says. "I heard he's really hot. Naked photos on the internet and everything."

"Are you looking at naked photos of other men on the internet, wife? Before we've even gone on our honeymoon?"

"I would never! I mean, I don't even have an account on that TinderFace thing. I wouldn't know where to look for that kind of stuff. And I have eyes only for my husband. We promised each other forever, you know..." she says, putting her arms around my neck.

"I'd heard that. I guess you're stuck with the guy. Lucky devil, to be married to an angel like you."

"He's earned it. Turned over a new leaf, earned my trust, showed he's all-in. You know, that *forever* thing."

"Smart man, locking a girl like you in for eternity, putting a ring on it and everything."

"Two rings," she corrects, flashing her hand at me. "He gave them to a bear for safe-keeping."

"Again, a smart man. A romantic, even."

"He is. He even bought us a house, with a magical fountain in the garden."

"Then he might actually deserve you."

"He does. I'm looking forward to proving it to him," she says, her expression full of promises, decent and indecent.

"Do I really have to go on stage and sing for these people when I could be making love to my wife in our bedroom in our house?"

"We invited them. You promised them entertainment."

"Haven't I already provided them with sufficient entertainment, just by being me?"

"I'm not sure taking off your shirt and making jokes about the beauty and size of your penis qualifies as entertainment. Except for me, of course."

"I know my *real* audience," I tell her, smirking. "So I've got to do this, right?"

"Rhys is already sitting at his drum kit," she points out.

"Alright. But I'm performing for you, not them. And once I'm done with that, and Billy's little interview, I'm going to take you home, to our home, and then I'm going to give a totally different kind of performance for you. OK, Mrs. Carter-Martin?"

"I'll look forward to it all, Mr. Carter-Martin."

There's a strange noise from somewhere in the crowd. I smile.

"Declan!" Billy bellows, nearly matching my legendary vocal volume. "What's this post on Instagram? 'She said yes! Again!'? What happened to 'on the QT'! Now I've got a million fangirls to pacify!"

"I only have one fangirl that counts, Billy!" I call back to him. "Just tell them she's got me completely tied down now!" I add, smirking, mostly at Callie.

"Love you, wife," I tell her, kissing her softly, sweetly and slowly, right on that delectable mouth of hers.

"Love you, husband," she replies, unperturbed by Billy's concern over fangirls. Yeah. She's my person. And I'm hers.

I love being up on stage, really. But my most important job now is to make sure Callie's always smiling like this. I could live forever on the feeling that angelic smile gives me. Lucky for me, I've got exactly that long to enjoy it.

# EPILOGUE

## Rhys

"Hi there."

The boy looks at me out of the corner of his eye, but his gaze darts away before I can make eye contact. He reaches for my snare but pulls his fingers back at the last second, as if he's thought better of it.

"Tommy! There you are! Mommy's been looking for you!"

A tall blonde woman approaches from the side of the stage, snatching the boy up the moment he raises his arms toward her, even though he's really too big to be carried around.

"You have to stay with Mommy tonight, buddy. We're close to the water, so we have to follow the rules — like when we go to the beach. OK?"

She doesn't wait for him to respond, doesn't check his expression to see if he's even acknowledged her words. Which he hasn't. He's still staring at my snare.

"Sorry. We got distracted by his little sister, and he ran off. We try to keep an eye on him, but he can be sneaky when he sees something he likes." She nods at my kit.

"Here, bud — here's your contraption," she says, handing him a Lego... well, "contraption" is pretty much the word for it: bricks blended with gears, axles, elastic bands... It looks like fun, though. I should get myself some of those...

"No problem. I already loved drums when I was his age, so I know how that feels. I don't think you could have dragged me away."

She gives me an appraising look, then a gentle smile and a nod, before turning around and merging back into the small crowd on the deck, filled with friends of my bandmate Declan and his girlf— no, wife! They snuck off and got married today. Again. Go figure. All these years, I thought Declan was afraid of commitment, and it turned out he'd had a wife since even before I met him. I'm not sure how that works with all the girls he's been with since we got famous, but that's between him and Callie, and they seem really happy now. Declan's not even being much of a dick anymore. It's kind of weird, actually. Good weird, though.

It seems love is in the air here in Mystic Beach. We'd been performing here at this bar when Dave instantly fell head over heels for our sound engineer, Piper. And he's already managed to knock her up, with a little bass player on the way. Not soon enough to replace him on tour if he decides to stop going on the road with us, which would kind of suck. But then I guess if the kid was old enough to tour with us, they'd be old enough that Dave wouldn't be so reluctant to leave this place to go on tour. They seem to like this baby idea, though, so I'm happy for them.

Hunter and his fiancée, Brighid, got together earlier this summer, too, after years of saying they were just friends. They got engaged here in this very spot like a month ago.

If you'd asked me ten years ago who Brighid would end up marrying, I'd have said it was even odds whether it was Hunt or Mace Mason, who back then existed in a rockstar stratosphere we'd barely brushed our fingers against, even while standing on our tippytoes. And I'm 6-foot-4, so that's pretty high up there.

I saw Mace kiss Brighid once. Backstage at one of our shows, when we were opening for his band, Telltale Signs. They weren't making out or anything, but you don't usually kiss a girl on the top of her head when you just met her the night before — not unless there's something there. Something more than sex.

I don't think I've ever kissed a girl on the top of her head. I've had lots of girls in my bed, though. Just not *the one*. Even if I've been dreaming about her for months now.

She's blonde — not like the woman just now, with her golden-blonde waves, or Brighid, with her light blonde hair, but a more neutral shade, and almost straight — with what Mom always called "stormy sky" eyes, and more petite. Not little, like Piper, though. No, my dream-girl is the perfect height. How tall? No idea. But however tall she is, it's perfect, just like she is. The only thing wrong with her is I have no idea who she is.

I 've been waiting weeks to play this song in front of an audience. It's the one we usually open our shows with, and my adrenaline is already on an upswing. It doesn't matter that there's just a few dozen people in the audience — I'm already antsy, bouncing on the balls of my feet as I tap my sticks lightly on my legs.

Hunt captured it — that creative energy that licks through my veins like flame... like my blood is gasoline and the drumsticks ignite a spark that sets the world on fire the moment they hit my snare.

And then there's that moment when all six of us are in our spots on the stage — doesn't matter whether it's a little stage like this one at the Pirate's Cove (weird name, because I have yet to see a pirate here, and not even one parrot) or someplace like Madison Square Garden — Declan puts his hand on his mic, and Hunt straps on that green guitar his mom gave him, Dave drops his right hand down to rest his fingers on those thick bass strings, Alex finishes pushing all of the eight million buttons that make his keyboards sound right and Kieran pulls himself inside his shell, which then lights up the stage like the brightest spotlight we've ever had on us as he hits those first notes and the song blazes out and through all of us.

That's when it happens, when the sticks make that snapping sound I've loved since I was a kid no older than that one earlier tonight, regimenting the chaos of the world around me within the space between the beats. My feet match the heartbeat of the earth beneath them, which it seems sometimes like I'm the only one who can hear. Right now, it's got seven beats to it, but sometimes it's more, or less. That doesn't matter either — or, rather, it's all that matters.

The guys don't always get it when I tell them the song needs to be faster or slower to match that heartbeat. But we always find a place where they meet, like that lowest common denominator thing from math. School and I were not friends, especially before Mom got me put on meds that let me focus a little better. But math — I live in a world of math. Fractions of this, multiples of that, parts divided into even smaller parts, numbers running through my brain from the moment I get up until the moment I finally fall asleep, usually with my arms full of that wonderful soreness after a day of beating on my kit and my legs still tapping out the beat on the double pedals that aren't even beneath them anymore.

My brain is like a metronome. If you threw it into a tornado and let it keep time for the universe. I keep perfect time with every song. The guys rely on me for that, and that's like my mission in life, keeping the song on track, letting Dave know where to put his beats, guiding Dec and Hunt and Kier so they put their parts together in the right way to make each song work, cuing Alex's flourishes underneath and over the top of it all.

But when the song is the thing I'm focused on, all the chaos, all the distraction, all the excess energy... it just falls away, and I become the song. Dave's the spine, but I'm the feet that keep us moving, onward and forward, relentless and inevitable, until we reach that spot we stop, for just a moment, and then it starts all over again, on my count. And right now... now, I'm the song. Hunt wrote it, but it's part of me and I'm part of it now, floating through the air with the sound waves until my toes barely anchor me to the ground. It stretches me to my limits, until I feel like I encompass not just the song, but the universe — every star in the sky, every electron moving through the wires, every molecule of air, every ray of light, every dancer moving on the floor to the beat that I create.

But she's not moving. She's frozen there, watching... watching me. And I'm watching her. Can't take my eyes off her. Not now, not any more than I can in my dreams. She's too far away to see what color her eyes are, but that's OK. I know already. Those stormy-sky eyes I've seen nearly every night for months now. And I'm lost in them... My feet on auto-pilot, my arms flailing to reach toms and snare, high hat and cymbals, unguided, because the only thing I comprehend, the only language I speak right now is her.

And then, suddenly, like I've been shoved, I'm careening out into the space over the dance floor, peering down at her from above, where she stands next to the blonde woman from before — taller, broader, brown eyes lit up like amber in the sun as they move across the space between my dream girl and me... or rather my body, which I look back to see is, somehow, keeping the rhythm, the same as usual.

I look back down to find *her* looking up at me, with those storm-blue eyes, taking me in as if I wasn't some shapeless, translucent version of myself, like a cloud I might fall through on the way back to earth after jumping out of a perfectly good airplane, as Hunter always calls it. But she sees me. No — not just sees me, like she realizes I'm there, floating above her. She *sees* me. And I'm not sure anyone's ever done that before.

Too often they see giant red-haired Rhys, freakishly tall and with hair you wouldn't miss in a crowd, no matter how tall I was. Or Rhys the nutty inventor with his off-the-wall ideas that never amount to shit, except when things blow up, as they sometimes do. Or Rhys the rockstar, the crazy adrenaline-junkie who does backflips off his drum riser to drain excess energy before a show and can't pass up a climbing wall, because it's the only time, aside from when I'm one with the beat of a song, when my focus is absolute and my mind clear.

Except now. Now it's crystal clear, like a drop of rain falling from the sky, pure arctic ice, the tone of a bell or the fact that this woman... she *sees* me.

And then, suddenly, it's like a rubberband snaps. The blonde woman, the one from earlier, she touches her hand to my dream girl's arm, and she blinks, my girl, no longer seeing me flying above her, and suddenly I'm rocketed back into my head, peering out of the eyes in my skull and not the ones in my mind. And she's gone. Where'd she go? Did she leave? Did I dream her up when I was awake this time? Or did I just long so much for her to be real that my brain, high on beats, conjured her up out of thin air?

I feel a tap to the back of my head, and I expect to find Alex has somehow reached over from his spot behind his keyboards to snap me back into reality, but there's no one there. Alex stands amidst his "cockpit," looking at me curiously, like I've done something unexpected.

I'm not sure what that would be, because I'm still keeping the beat, and the only thing unexpected about me tonight is that I saw a girl with stormy-sky eyes look at me and truly *see* me. And now nothing's ever going to be the same.

*To be continued in Mad World...*

Thank you so much for reading Remind Me! I hope you enjoyed this latest book in the Mystic Beach Fantasy Rockstar Romance series. If you did, please take a moment to leave a rating or a brief review for the book on Amazon or Goodreads, or wherever you like to leave your reviews. Every positive review helps a reader like you find this book, and others in the series, which helps ensure that there will be more books in the series to come. I love my aMUSEd guys, and their ladies, and I've got much more of their story to tell. Your support is invaluable, and even a quick rating or review helps tremendously. Thank you!

If you want an extra taste of Remind Me, sign up for my newsletter, the Mystic Beacon, and you'll be able to download two subscriber-exclusive bonus scenes — one that answers the mystery of how that photo of Declan ended up as the wallpaper on Callie's phone and a second that takes place shortly after the end of Remind Me (see the aMUSEd series page on my website to get access to this bonus scene when it's released).

# Mad World

## Pre-order Now

Lyric's best friend is dating a legend. Literally. But when legendary aMUSEd drummer Rhys "The Madman" Madigan volunteers to help with a fundraiser at Lyric's school, hoping to win her heart, will the lingering presence of her late husband guide this single mom to a forever love, or will her new man's wild spirit put a permanent end to their love story, and possibly her career?

**Lyric**
*I had it all once. A man I loved, a child who needed me, another who needed me even more, a job that gave me purpose. And then my world was shattered. I've learned to live without him, to take care of two children like I'm the only parent they'll ever need, and to keep the light in their eyes. I've got a village to help me do it, but it's a never-ending, exhausting rollercoaster, haunted by memories of the husband I lost. The last thing I need to add to this ride is an adrenaline-junkie rockstar. But he won't take no for an answer. And I'm not sure I really want him to.*

**Rhys**
*I saw her across a crowded room. No — I saw her in my dreams first. But from the moment our eyes met in our waking lives, I knew she was the one. Yeah, her life is complicated, and I'm not a likely candidate for a father figure for her kids when my inner child ends up on the outside as often as not. But there's nothing complicated about how I feel about her, and there's no limit to what I'd do to make her life better, if only she — and her late husband — will let me.*

Mad World is a love-before-first-sight romance between a rockstar and a single parent, with an unexpected supernatural triangle twist, and a deep current of music and magic running throughout. It is the fifth book in the Mystic Beach Fantasy Rockstar Romance series. It can be read as a standalone, but it is part of an interconnected series and is best read in series order.

# WHAT'S NEXT

The next book in the aMUSEd series is Mad World, Rhys' story. Rhys is one of my favorite characters to write. He's my comic relief, my well-meaning wild-man, my unrepentant source of childlike wonder. And you'll get to know him firsthand when Mad World comes out in early 2023.

That'll be followed by a guitar solo that might just turn into a duet, as we get to Kieran's story later in 2023. Kieran's secrets are some of the ones I've held most closely since the series started, just like he has, but he may just find the perfect partner to bury bits of his past that he'd like to forget, as well as dig up the parts he'd like to bring back into the present.

Last (for now) will be our band-mom Alex's story, where we'll finally find out why our keyboard virtuoso is such a secondhand romantic and whether a shot at firsthand romance is finally in the cards for him.

If you want an extra taste of Remind Me, sign up for my newsletter, the Mystic Beacon, and you'll be able to download two subscriber-exclusive bonus scenes — one that answers the mystery of how that photo of Declan really ended up as the wallpaper on Callie's phone and a second that takes place shortly after the end of Remind Me (visit the aMUSEd series page on my website to get access to this scene when it's released).

As a subscriber, you'll also be able to download the series prequel novella, "Good Golly Miss Molly," Molly and Logan's story, and the pre-prequel short story "Here Comes the Sun," which tells the story of the day Brighid and Hunter first met, at age 6. There's also "Spooky," the Brighid and Hunter seasonal novelette that takes place a few months after their second novel, Dream Weaver.

Thanks so much for reading! I'm glad to have you along for this amazing ride!

# The aMUSEd Series Roadmap

- Here Comes the Sun (Mystic Beach Fantasy Rockstar Romance series No. 0.25) — Brighid & Hunter, sweet pre-romance pre-prequel short story (newsletter subscriber exclusive, February 2022, now available in the first Mystic Beach Fantasy Rockstar Romance collection, Dreams)

- Good Golly Miss Molly (Mystic Beach Fantasy Rockstar Romance series No. 0.50) — Molly & Logan, steamy series prequel novella (newsletter subscriber exclusive, March 2022, now available in the first Mystic Beach Fantasy Rockstar Romance collection, Dreams)

- Once Upon a Dream (Mystic Beach Fantasy Rockstar Romance series No. 1) — Brighid & Hunter, series opening act and part one of the Brighid & Hunter duo (May 13, 2022)

- Down to the Sea (Mystic Beach Fantasy Rockstar Romance series No. 1.5) — Brighid point-of-view interstitial novel (June 17, 2022) (spoiler warning for "Once" and those preferring to remain in the dark about some secrets)

- Dream Weaver (Mystic Beach Fantasy Rockstar Romance series No. 2) — Brighid & Hunter, part two of the Brighid & Hunter duo (July 14, 2022)

- Spooky (Mystic Beach Fantasy Rockstar Romance series No. 2.75) — Brighid & Hunter seasonal novelette, set after Dream Weaver (Oct. 15, 2022)

- Dreams — the first Mystic Beach Fantasy Rockstar Romance collection/box set (contains Books 1, 1.5 and 2, plus bonus material) (Oct. 31, 2022)

- Smoke on the Water (Mystic Beach Fantasy Rockstar Romance series No. 3) — David (Oct. 7, 2022)

- Remind Me (Mystic Beach Fantasy Rockstar Romance series No. 4) — Declan (Jan. 6, 2023)

- Centerfold (Mystic Beach Fantasy Rockstar Romance series No. 4.25) — Declan & Callie short story, set after Remind Me (Jan. 13. 2023)

- Mad World (Mystic Beach Fantasy Rockstar Romance series No. 5) — Rhys (2023)

- Drawn to the Rhythm (Mystic Beach Fantasy Rockstar Romance series No. 6) — Kieran (2023)

- Carry Fire (Mystic Beach Fantasy Rockstar Romance series No. 7) — Alex (Winter 2023-2024)
And much more to come...

# RETURN TO MYSTIC BEACH

**The Mystic Beach Fantasy Rockstar Romance series**

Once Upon a Dream (Brighid & Hunter duet, Part 1)

Down to the Sea (Brighid interstitial novel, 1.5)

Dream Weaver (Brighid & Hunter duet, Part 2)

Dreams (Mystic Beach Fantasy Rockstar Romances Collection I)

Smoke on the Water (David & Piper)
Remind Me (Declan & Callie)

Coming Soon

Mad World (Rhys)
Drawn to the Rhythm (Kieran)
Carry Fire (Alex)
and more to come...

Bonus Content
Included in the collection Dreams:

Good Golly Miss Molly (0.5)
(Molly & Logan, series prequel novella)

<u>Here Comes the Sun (0.25)</u>
(Hunter & Brighid sweet pre-prequel short story)

Newsletter subscriber exclusives:

<u>Spooky (2.75)</u>
(Hunter & Brighid seasonal bonus novelette)
Remind Me bonus scene "<u>Building a Mystery</u>"
Remind Me bonus short story "<u>Centerfold</u>"

***Visit AislinnArcher.com now to subscribe to the Mystic Beacon newsletter and get your FREE bonus content.*** *As a subscriber, you'll get early access to details on new releases, sales, exclusive content and more. You can unsubscribe at any time.*

**<u>The Mystic Beach Mysteries</u>**
(Aurora Carmichael contemporary/urban fantasy series)
<u>Coming Soon</u>
Safe Harbour

# PLAYLIST

Many books these days have their own playlists, especially rockstar romances, because what is a book about amazing musicians without amazing music to go with it? Some of these just fit. Others are at least a little ironic. You'll find this playlist informed by my own... eclectic... tastes in music. There are only a couple genres I don't listen to, and everything else runs the gamut from classic rock to world music to metal to folk and beyond. And maybe you'll even discover a new favorite in here.

## Remind Me playlist

Always Something There to Remind Me — Naked Eyes (One of my all-time favorite songs. The title was just a little too long to use as a book title, but this was the inspiration.)

I Will Find You — Clannad

Starlight — Muse (Once again, not the basis of the band name for aMUSEd, but a stellar band. And the song, yet again, just fit.)

Still Got the Blues (For You) — Gary Moore (I'll upload an amazing a live version of this one to my social media accounts, from my wonderful friends in Tranzfusion. Be sure to check it out!)

Food and Creative Love — Rusted Root

Kindred Spirit — Spiro Gyra

Crazy Little Thing Called Love — Queen

Lady Ice — Arcadia (This one's special for me, and one of the reasons I connected with Callie in a lot of ways. She's chosen to withdraw from the world — a self-imposed ice-queen with a heart of spicy lava, if only she felt like she had someone she could safely share it with. It's a journey to get her back to her passionate, vibrant self.)

What Do I Have to Do — Stabbing Westward

Nobody's Fault but Mine — Jimmy Page & Robert Plant

Ship of Fools — Robert Plant

Forever Young — Alphaville

Muskrat Love — America (Muskrat is a real-deal old-timey dish for some residents of the area of Delaware in which the series is set. I know of a butcher shop where you can buy them and at least one resident that serves them. Callie serving Declan one started with her thought that the first rockstar who showed up in her restaurant looked like someone who would cook in steel barrels and serve muskrat as an avant-garde chef. When it came time to torture Declan with food, it was an obvious choice.)

Fate — H.E.R. / Chaka Khan (These two songs are two sides of the same coin, which is fitting, considering how torn Callie is here.)

All In — Lifehouse

Love Potion, No. 9 — The Searchers

I Put a Spell On You — Creedence Clearwater Revival

Sweet Surrender — Sarah McLachlan

Girls on Film — Duran Duran

Bleed to Love Her — Fleetwood Mac (one of my favorite Fleetwood Mac songs)

Naked — The Goo Goo Dolls

I Want to Break Free — Queen (This was a total accident. I was looking for a song for an earlier chapter and this one popped up. In addition to being one of my favorite Queen songs, the moment I saw it, I knew this had to be the title for this chapter.)

Revenge — P!nk

I'll Be Waiting — Michael Franti & Spearhead (I love Michael Franti's positive, uplifting vibe. Even challenging situations in his songs have a positive outlook.)

Rolling in the Deep — Adele

Rose Garden — Stevie Nicks

Raisins — Barenaked Ladies (Callie gets her dislike of raisins from me. But I do love golden raisins. The onions — that's an Al thing. We routinely tease each other about our least-favorite foods. And they both made it into this book.)

Rumor Has It — Adele

Here Comes the Grump — Adam Ant

Higher Ground — Red Hot Chili Peppers

Between — Jerry Cantrell

Desperately Wanting — Better Than Ezra

Dice, Rice, Baby — I'm not going to subject you to the original, but the pun was too good to resist.

Love Like Bombs — The Turnback

Spoonman — Soundgarden

If I Were A Carpenter — Robert Plant (one of my favorite romantic songs)

Bigger Picture — The Waterboys

Here Comes the Rain Again — Eurythmics

She Talks to Angels — The Black Crowes

Heart and Soul — T'Pau

Only Thing Missing Was You — Michael Franti & Spearhead

Hanging By A Moment — Lifehouse (I love the acoustic version of this one.)

Angels — Robbie Williams (This entire album is amazing.)

Fresh Feeling — Eels (Another where I prefer the stripped-down live version, but this song is awesome either way.)

Policy of Truth — Depeche Mode (There are some great alternative mixes of this one out there. I'm partial to the Art of Noise mix.)

Stolen Car — Beth Orton

Rolling in the Deep — Adele

A View To A Kill — Duran Duran (I've got two spy-themed songs on this playlist, by members of two of my favorite bands.)

Twice As Hard — The Black Crowes

Tequila — The Champs

Tequila Sunrise — The Eagles

Theme from Mission Impossible — Adam Clayton & Larry Mullen (Declan's been sneaking around for a long time, even if he's done it less successfully than he thinks. I'm giving Gryff points for not calling him out on it, even when Declan thinks he put one over on him. If you're intrigued by this retired SEAL, be assured that we'll be seeing Gryffin more in future books, including one where he'll be a main character. I've even got a few chapters of that one written already.)

Headphones — Michael Franti & Spearhead (I love this notion of plugging oneself into their loved-one's heart, to really listen to them. We don't always do that, and it's both vitally important and incredibly connecting.)

Marry You — Doyle Bramhall II (My Arc Angels guys are back again for this one, if just one of their two lead singers/lead guitarists.)

Tattoos and Tequila — Jason Aldean (I admit it. I have two musical genres I'm not fond of: country and hard-core rap. But this song just fit.)

In the Clear — Foo Fighters (It was a total coincidence that I picked a Foo Fighters song for the book in which Declan has aMUSEd perform as the Flu Fighters. But never fear: more Grohl references are yet to come! And, Dave — if you're reading this, I apologize. But I've lost track of how many local Grohl sightings people have told me about. It had to go into the books!)

Hey, Brother — Avicii

How Long Will I Love You — The Waterboys (Another of my all-time favorite songs.)

House of Love — Robert Plant

Higher Love — Steve Winwood

Thank You — Led Zeppelin (This and How Long Will I Love You have very similar themes. While Declan and Callie may not be immortal, or even semi-immortal, but they promised each other forever, and I'm inclined to think they'll make that happen, even if it takes multiple lives.)

Drumming Song — Florence + the Machine (There's a primal, instinctive quality to this one that just fits Rhys. He's got some major surprises coming...)

# GLOSSARY & TRANSLATIONS

There's only one bit of Irish in this book. Kind of...

When Kieran responds to the question about why he has keys to unlock the locks on the cuffs, Declan says it sounds like Kieran says, "Kneeling on a rug, fuck-all." What Kieran actually said was, "Nílim ag rá focal," which is Irish for "I'm not saying a word."

And now you know.

# ACKNOWLEDGMENTS

I'm finishing this book up on Christmas Day 2022, and it's both a fitting reminder of how many people and things I have to be grateful for and a bittersweet moment of being back in my hometown longer than a few hours for the first time since we lost my dad to COVID-19 in January 2021. Indirectly, he's responsible for the fact that this series finally got written and published, and I know that he'd have loved seeing that happen. So, this one's dedicated to him.

I have a lot of people I need to thank for helping me get here, from the first friends who supported this endeavor from Day 1 through the new friends and loyal readers who've supported this continuing series into its fifth book.

My Mystic Beach rockstars: Jilleen Dolbeare and Sandy Ackers, who stepped up early to confirm I had written an actual book, and one that people would want to read, and then continued hand-holding as needed (and sometimes when it shouldn't have been) to get me through new-author anxiety so I could write the next one, and then the next one, and so on. And, in addition to Jill and Sandy, the other members of my urban-fantasy writing group, including Heather G. Harris and L.A. McBride, who were there to answer questions and offer support, even when they were incredibly busy with their own books and even though my first books have been cross-genre. Then there's Julia and Bene, who messaged me in the middle of reading these books to tell me how much they were enjoying them, and then stepped up to become part of my alpha and beta teams to ensure they were the best they could be for everyone who would read them afterward. Then there's Ce-Ce, who not only agreed to become part of my alpha and beta teams, but put her amazing editing skills to work for the series. And Chris sacrificed her usual slow, savoring reading this time to help with editing and seriously rocked it!

I owe deep thanks to Merissa and Jamie, who made room in their ARC reading lists for my books so that I could have professional reviews for each of the new releases, and to the other members of my ARC team, who've made sure their reviews were up so soon after these books were released to help other readers find them.

More recently, I've had incredible support from some of the most amazing authors in the rockstar romance and paranormal romance genres, again despite my series being cross-genre. Kaylene Winter, L.M. Dagleish, Paula Dombrowiak, Elizabeth Corva, Melissa Riddell and Connie Lafortune, you're the names I kept seeing on the bestsellers lists and said, "I want to be up there someday." And then you helped me make it happen! I'm still a small fish in this pond, but with your help, I feel like I'm growing and maybe making a place for myself there, too. And that's just incredible. Thank you so much! You have my lasting gratitude.

Hand in hand with these incredible authors, I have to thank the rockstar and paranormal fantasy romance groups and their owners/admins that have given me the chance to let readers know about my books. None of this happens without readers, and I owe deep thanks both to those readers (yes, that's you!) and the people who have helped them find my series.

Thanks once again to my co-workers who have ignored my endless rambling about release dates and rankings and marketing, etc., etc., etc., and have in some cases even bought a book. (I promise, I warned them all this was steamy stuff. I just hope none of them gave that warning too little weight.) And the same goes for my other non-writer friends who've been so tolerant of my focus on the series as I got these first few books finished and released. Your patience is appreciated.

I want to again thank all my friends who supported me in adding professional fiction writer to my professional journalist identity. From serving as early readers and editors to just plain encouraging me to keep at it — 12 years after an app glitch ate most of my notes for the first Aurora Carmichael/Mystic Beach novel — you made things a lot easier, and I appreciate it. I have to thank my family, both by blood and otherwise, for getting me where I am today, that I could start writing about these characters with whom I've fallen totally in love. Don't take some of my characters' dysfunctional relationships with their families as indicative of my own. All in all, I had a pretty normal childhood that gave me the leeway to do things I'm good at and enjoy, and I'm grateful for that.

My dear friend and soul-sister Melissa gets extra-special recognition here, too, for offering me a glimpse, a flicker of insight, that sparked so much in my mind's eye. And my new friend Chris, who found me through my books but who's become not only an incredible support for me as a writer but, along with Melissa, a constant reminder that I've got a community of like-minded folks around me, even though it sometimes seems like I'm the one oddball in a huge crowd (and, yes, she also helped edit this time).

I also have to acknowledge the late, great Dame Templar Patricia Kennealy Morrison, author of the Keltiad series of Celtic-influenced sci-fi/fantasy novels. I'm not sure we'd have this series without her. Patricia was a role model of mine from the first moment I picked up one of her novels, and the more I learned about her, the more I realized we had in common, from our love of Celtic lore and languages, our drive to tell tales based in that lore, our religious beliefs, Mensa membership, our trade as journalists, and music journalists specifically, and last, but hardly least, our soul-deep love of rock music. Patricia was also incredibly generous to me with her time and self, during not just one point in my life but two of them, and I forever will appreciate that. I miss knowing she's out there in the world, but I am so glad she's reunited with her love.

And last, but never least, thanks go to my best friend, Al, who was the first one who really said, "You're a very good writer, and what you've written is good." And he said that after having read the work, despite it not being at all his usual type of thing. He then defused the near-daily author freak-outs and tolerated my discussing fictional people like they were people he should know and remember. Al's a big part of the reason this series even exists, including giving me his insight as a working musician and tolerating me being the hanger-on at so many of his own gigs, as well as having brought me into work as a live sound engineer in my own right. Snippets of real-life have been pulled as inspiration for some of the elements of these stories, though the outcomes are different, and the names have been changed and the credit dispersed to protect the guilty and confuse the innocent. Al approved of me borrowing liberally from real life (he's married to a writer, so he knows how it works), but he gets the credit for the inspiration.

Once again, Chris Cornell's voice served as inspiration while I wrote this book (if you want to know what aMUSEd sounds like in my head, Temple of the Dog and Soundgarden are in the neighborhood), and I continue to lament that he's not still with us today, writing incredible music and letting us enjoy one of the greatest voices ever in rock. Then there are Freddie Mercury, Robert Plant and so many more. In my head, Declan stands a chance of reaching that top tier of legendary rock singers, but he's going to have to really work at it, because these guys truly are legends.

On the culinary front, I took inspiration from so many amazing chefs and cooks in writing this book, including many of the incredible chefs of Delaware's thriving real-life culinary coastal region. I'm not even the amateur chef that Alex is, but I am very much a foodie, and dining in some pretty amazing restaurants is one of my guilty pleasures and one of the best parts of living where I do. I can only hope that Callie's recipes pass muster and that my portrayal of life in a restaurant kitchen bears some resemblance to reality.

One of those inspiring real-life chefs, in particular, was chef Matt Haley of SoDel Concepts. I interviewed Matt when he was working on his first two restaurants in the Bethany Beach area, and he gave me hints about a life story that was inspiring even before I knew most of it. Matt had gotten into trouble with drugs and the law, and ended up in prison. When he got out, he'd gotten a break from a guy who hired him to work in a restaurant, and from there, Matt proceeded to pay it forward. He hired people who'd served time in prison, as he had, and worked to ensure disadvantaged youth got opportunities to work in restaurants where they got a hand up. He also put his focus on food insecurity — particularly among the elderly and children — and then extended that philanthropy overseas. So impressive was his humanitarian work that he was honored with the 2014 James Beard Foundation Humanitarian of the Year award. Tragically, just a few months later, while headed to Nepal for his humanitarian work, Matt was killed in a road accident. I know so many people whose lives were touched by Matt, in some pretty incredible ways, and I know we all lament his loss, along with celebrating his legacy. Along with more than a dozen restaurants, a big part of that legacy is SoDel Cares, the foundation set up in his memory, which carries on his incredible work in so many ways. A portion of my royalties from this book will be going to SoDel Cares, with an eye toward supporting the kinds of food bank and culinary training programs Matt always championed. They were the inspiration for Declan's path to redemption, which now puts him on track to more openly do something he loves, with the woman he's always loved, under the blessing of his label and with a focus on helping those in need.

I'll also add here my thanks to Herself, who has kept pushing me along on this journey, even when I was plagued by doubt and second-guessing us both. She knows I've appreciated it, but it feels important to publicly acknowledge Her role in this work coming to life.

# ABOUT THE AUTHOR

Aislinn Archer is an award-winning journalist, columnist and photographer, music and tech journalist, and editor, as well as a semi-retired live sound engineer.

She is in the process of writing two interconnected series spanning the urban fantasy and rockstar romance genres, set in her personal stomping grounds in Coastal Delaware. She is a member of Mensa and the Order of Bards, Ovates & Druids.

In her free time, Aislinn is an Irish language learner, persistent advanced-beginner guitar and bass guitar player, photographer, foodie, gadget guru, jewelrymaker and lampwork glass artist. She is a voracious reader of the urban fantasy, fantasy and rockstar romance genres, and dedicated music fan across many genres. Aislinn also loves attending concerts and spending time on the beach.

For release updates, freebies, sneak peeks and inside details, sign up at http://aislinnarcher.com/home/subscribe/ and follow Aislinn Archer on social media, at https://www.facebook.com/AislinnArcher; on Twitter

@AislinnArcher; and on Instagram and TikTok @aislinnarcher. Visit her website at AislinnArcher.com and MysticBeachRocks.com.

amazon.com/Aislinn-Archer/e/B09TQP3S3Q/

goodreads.com/author/show/22271645.Aislinn_Archer

bookbub.com/authors/aislinn-archer

facebook.com/AislinnArcher

instagram.com/AislinnArcher

tiktok.com/@aislinnarcher

twitter.com/aislinnarcher